OCT -- 2019

The
BAKESHOP *at*
PUMPKIN *and* SPICE

Center Point
Large Print

**This Large Print Book carries the
Seal of Approval of N.A.V.H.**

The BAKESHOP *at* PUMPKIN *and* SPICE

Donna Kauffman
Kate Angell
Allyson Charles

CENTER POINT LARGE PRINT
THORNDIKE, MAINE

This Center Point Large Print edition
is published in the year 2019 by arrangement with
Kensington Publishing Corp.

The text of this Large Print edition is unabridged.
In other aspects, this book may vary
from the original edition.
Printed in the United States of America
on permanent paper.
Set in 16-point Times New Roman type.

ISBN: 978-1-64358-367-9

The Library of Congress has cataloged this record
under Library of Congress Control Number:
2019945581

Contents

Sweet Magic

DONNA KAUFFMAN

Chapter 1

All Hallows' Eve was fast approaching, and Abriana Bellaluna O'Neill couldn't be happier about it. She and her grandmother were already hard at work at their family bakery, filling the display cases with delicious treats that celebrated their favorite magical, mystical holiday. What the townsfolk didn't know was that the Bellaluna women were a bit magical and mystical themselves. A visit to Bellaluna's Bakeshop, nestled in the little town of Moonbright, Maine, was guaranteed to cure any craving your sweet tooth might have. But if you happened to be the recipient of one of their special treats, they could satisfy the cravings of your heart as well.

Abriana—Bree to everyone except her grandma Sofia—loved this time of year. The harvest season was ending, the leaves on the trees were a rainbow of beautiful colors, swirling in the air like party confetti, celebrating the commencement of the holiday season. Temperatures had dipped, the sounds of logs being split echoed in the crisp morning air, and smoke wafted from chimney tops as fireplaces warmed the hearths in their

9

cozy, little village. Sweaters were pulled out of storage, gloves were fished out of coat closets, and Bree could feel the excitement begin to build as everyone's thoughts turned toward the celebrations to come.

Thanksgiving, then Christmas, New Year's, and finally, Valentine's Day kept things rolling along at the bakeshop, each holiday a festive, busy time for them, filled with traditions and joy. But for the residents of Moonbright, none was as festive and eagerly anticipated as the holiday that launched the season: Halloween.

There were parties, costume contests, and all of her friends and neighbors would outdo themselves decorating their yards for the wee ones who would be out on the trick-or-treating trail. The most anticipated part of the celebration, however, and what drew far-flung family members and tourists alike to their little coastal town, was Moonbright's grand Halloween parade. And, oh, how grand it was!

Every man, woman, and child—and a fair number of household pets to boot—dressed up in costumes that ranged from rudimentary, hand-made creations by the very youngest, to elaborate concoctions for some of the grown-ups that would have been right at home on a Hollywood movie set. Floats were made, and cars, firetrucks, along with a few tractors were decked out as well. The whole town got in on the fun.

The parade grew as it progressed, like a giant, costume-festooned conga line winding through the streets, as more and more people joined in. Music filled the air from the high school marching band, aided by those who brought along their instruments and played as they strolled. Impromptu sing-a-longs happened on every corner, and the shops that lined the main street through town stayed open until the wee hours, offering treats and specials to everyone who caravanned by.

Even though Bree spent most of the actual holiday inside the shop, baking, ringing up sales, and baking some more, she enjoyed looking out at the passing parade as she handed out treats. She loved the sense of community, of everyone she'd known her entire life coming together on one night to celebrate, sing, laugh, and have a good time. It was a no-pressure holiday. No gifts needed buying, no family ties needed testing. It was simply a night to play dress up, enjoy a few sweets, sing as loud as you liked, and dance until your feet gave out.

Bree spent all year planning her costume. Anticipating the holiday was as much fun as the event itself. She was always amazed at how fast the night flew by, and somehow, even though she'd been on her feet all day, the moment she and Sofia flipped the shop sign to CLOSED, Bree raced right out to join the happy throng. No matter how tired she was, the excitement, the music, the laughter always infused her with the energy to dance and sing long past the witching hour. The moment she recovered, she immediately set her sights on next year's event.

Even when the shop was filled to bursting and she was certain this would be the year when they wouldn't be able to keep up with the quickly depleting stock, she loved working side by side with her grandmother and her mom, too, when she and Bree's dad happened to be in town. That occurred less and less often now, in the years since their only child had become an adult. Bree was already missing them both as this season approached. They'd barely returned from a summer trip to the Netherlands before heading off on another "gallivant," as her grandmother called it. This time to the Galapagos Islands.

Bree missed her parents when they were gone—adulthood hadn't changed that—but Sofia had always sent her daughter and son-in-law off with her love and full support, and Bree did the same. She was happy her parents were out in the world, doing what they loved, and joined Sofia in cheering them on as they each continued to celebrate greater successes in their respective fields.

In turn, after Bree had finished culinary school and, at her parent's urging, agreed to a brief stint of formal pastry education in Italy, they'd respected their daughter's decision to return home and work by her grandmother's side, in the family bakeshop, happily content to remain in their small hometown.

Ultimately, as a family, they'd come to embrace that they were each doing what they were meant to do, and Bree held on to that. It had been her parents shared love of art that had brought them together in the first place, eventually leading to Bree's existence in this world. Photographer Patrick O'Neill, passing through town while on a magazine assignment, had spied Carolina Bellaluna's watercolors in the local gallery, which had led him to the bakeshop one fateful Halloween night. Well, fate might have had a little help from a certain Italian iced cookie. A Bellaluna Italian iced cookie.

Bree readily admitted to herself that her fascination with baking went hand in hand with her fascination regarding that other part of the Bellaluna family business. The magical part.

Bree worked hard, wanting Sofia to be proud to leave the bakeshop to her when the time came, knowing it would be in good, capable hands. Bree also knew that her *nonna* couldn't possibly be truly content with that plan until her only granddaughter came into her own, fully realizing that special skill all Bellaluna women were born with. That one, very particular skill was the only one Bree had yet to master, and the only one that really mattered.

In truth, she wasn't even close. And at twenty-nine, she was quite behind the curve compared to the Bellaluna women who had come before her.

"But no pressure," she murmured as she slid out the final trays carrying the results of her most recent attempt to achieve that particular goal.

Every year for as long as she could remember, part of the Halloween excitement for Bree had been waiting to see if there would be another Bellaluna match. Bellaluna magic worked on any given day of the year, but it seemed especially potent around this particular holiday. As the hallowed eve neared, Bree would spend her days wondering who it would be, what fortunate soul was about to cross paths with their one true love.

She tried not to be discouraged that she, herself, rarely got it right. But Sofia knew. Bree's mom would, too. Just as every Bellaluna woman who'd come before them would have known. Sofia and her mother had always explained that no spells were being cast, no enchantment bestowed. True love could not be made with magic.

However, from time to time, true love did require an extra little push. A sweet bit of magic could make certain orbits collide . . . so fate could then take its natural course.

Bree looked from the cooling racks on the worktable in front of her to the other tables that lined the kitchen in the back of the bakeshop, and scowled. The stainless-steel surfaces were filled with rack after rack of beautifully perfect, delicately iced cookies, each one representing a previous attempt. A previous failed attempt. Proof that she wasn't joining the Bellaluna magic circle this year, either. She picked up one of the finished treats. "How can something that looks so good taste so bad?" She examined it more closely. As if somehow the naked eye could see what her taste buds had already discovered. And deeply regretted.

The cookie appeared to be perfect in every way, something she could proudly display in the old-fashioned glass case that ran the length of the front of the shop. Perfectly brown around the edges, plump in the middle, with a dollop of their special Italian cream icing spread evenly on top. A delicate array of sprinkles added the perfect final touch. It looked like a little piece of bite-sized heaven.

Bree had followed her grandma Sofia's recipe down to the tiniest detail. The same recipe that Sofia had gotten from her mother, who'd gotten it from her mother, who'd gotten it from her own, and so on, for as far back as the Bellaluna family history had been recorded. But somehow, Bree had failed to perfect Bellaluna's secret trademark treat. What was not to love about butter, sugar, and Italian cream?

She set down the finished cookie and picked up a newly cooled one, taking her time to ice it with exacting precision, adding the sprinkles so they glinted in delectable, sparkling perfection as they caught the overhead light. Bree studied it critically. It looked perfect. But then, the others had, too.

"Focus," Bree murmured. She took a steadying breath, staring at the cookie as if she could infuse it with magic from sheer force of will. If determination could get her there, then surely, she was about to experience her long-awaited triumph. There simply wasn't any way this cookie could be anything other than perfectly delicious.

"Be the magic," she whispered before taking a determined, confident bite out of the soft, creamy cookie. She immediately grabbed a napkin and spit it right back out again. It tasted as if she'd used two cups of baking soda instead of cake flour. Disgusted, more with herself than the offending cookie, she tossed the napkin and its acrid contents in the trash, then glared at the remaining eleven on the most recently baked tray, as if they'd personally ganged up on her to dash her hopes and dreams. Again.

"Abriana *mimma*, I need you to cover the front for a few minutes," her grandmother Sofia called as she pushed through the swinging door that separated the public part of the shop from the extensive kitchen area in the back. "Ah, *cuore mia*," she said as she spied what her grand-daughter had been up to. Sofia's voice was still softly accented from a childhood spent in the sunflower fields of Tuscany.

Sofia was seventy-six, but had the timeless beauty of her namesake, Sophia Loren. Actually, Sofia Scicolone was the name the famed beauty had been born with. Bree's grandmother had been quite a stunner herself, and like her famous counterpart, her beauty had only deepened with age. Sofia's warmly hued skin still held a luminescent glow and remained remarkably free of creases and lines. Except for the ones that fanned out from the corners of her soft brown eyes when she smiled, which was often. She kept her hair the same rich brown she'd been born with, always styled in a pretty French twist, with carefully curled tendrils in front of each ear, accenting the cheekbones of her heart-shaped face. Her "vanity curls," as she called them.

She wore little makeup other than eyebrow pencil and a bit of lipstick. She didn't need any-thing more and never had. Her figure remained trim despite the fact that she never tired of sampling the treats the Bellaluna family had baked and sold for more than fifty years in Moon-bright, and another generation or two before that in the old country.

Bree could only wish she'd been as fortunate in the gene pool lottery. She'd taken more after her Irish father in coloring, her hair somewhere between auburn and brown that never managed to capture the luster of either shade, with hazel eyes that couldn't quite decide between being brown or gray, blue or green. Her pale skin was only remarkable for the bane of her existence, the freckles she'd never outgrown. They didn't just sprinkle across her nose in some cute, perky, delightful pattern. No, they'd splashed themselves with gay abandon on every part of Bree's body early on, and decided they were there to stay.

Along with her dad's fair coloring, Bree had gotten her mother's soft curves. Okay, maybe "soft" was just another way of saying slightly plump. It wasn't from oversampling the wares. Bree had been born soft, and no amount of three-mile-a-day running or brisk cross-country skiing had ever changed that. Nor had the salads. So many salads. But whether it was the running, all that lettuce, or a gift from the gene pool fairy, Bree did enjoy good health. Something she reminded herself to be grateful for every time she tried to find a blouse that would button over her ample bosom or jeans that would slide up her equally curvy backside.

"I've told you not to worry yourself with this, *mimma*." Sofia was a good six inches shorter than Bree's five foot eight, so she gave Bree a little squeeze around the waist. "You must have patience. Your time will come, *cuore mia*."

"Thirty is right there on the horizon," Bree reminded her grandmother with a wry smile. Bree hugged her back and pressed her cheek to the top of Sofia's perfectly coiffed head. "Now would be a good time." Then her gaze returned to the racks of cookies, and she sighed. "Shouldn't they at least taste good? They look perfect. And I tested each ingredient."

Sofia tipped up on the toes of the sensible brown pumps she'd worn every day of her adult life and kissed Bree on the cheek, then immediately wiped off the lipstick print left behind with the handkerchief she kept tucked in her apron pocket. "Looks can be deceiving," she told her granddaughter. "Bellaluna magic comes when it's time, and your time will come. You know you cannot help true love along until you've seen it for yourself."

"I've been in love," Bree said, though not with much confidence. This was well-trodden territory and she really wasn't up for the conversation again. "Maybe not the forever-and-ever kind," she grudgingly admitted, "but certainly enough to know it when I see it."

Sofia's responding smile was both gentle and wise. "When you've known it, *mimma*, you can't help but see it." She squeezed Bree's forearm. "It will happen when it's meant to happen. You cannot rush it, nor can you force it."

Bree nodded. This wasn't the first time she'd heard these words. Far from. She still felt like a failure, and as the years passed, it was hard not to feel a certain pressure to push, to reach. Okay, maybe to try and force. But what else could she do? It wasn't as if she could simply will herself to fall madly in love with the next guy who walked into the bakeshop.

Sofia untied her apron as she walked toward the back door of the shop. "I just have to run down to the pharmacy for a moment. I shouldn't be more than fifteen minutes. Twenty at the most."

"Is anything wrong?" Bree asked, concern wrinkling her brow as she was immediately pulled from her thoughts. Sofia might look and behave like a woman a good decade younger than her actual age, but time didn't sit still. Bree had long ago promised her mother she'd keep watch over the woman they both loved so deeply, each of them knowing Sofia would never be one to complain.

Sofia waved away Bree's concern. "I promised Janice Powell I'd help her pick out some lipstick and nail color for the cruise Hank surprised her with on their tenth anniversary last week." She slipped a tube of lipstick out of her purse and took a moment to refresh the pretty rose color using the tiny locket-style mirror that she'd clipped onto the cap.

"Nice gift," Bree said approvingly.

"Isn't it, though?" Sofia agreed. "He even dropped by and picked up a box of profiteroles to go with the tickets. Given this is where they first met, it was a lovely touch."

Bree nodded, knowing full well that the Powells were just one of the many couples who had fallen in love after meeting at Bellaluna's Bakeshop. Their bakery had quite a reputation for that, in fact, though no one suspected there might be something more than chance at play. Sofia took a certain proprietary joy in the ongoing happiness of the couples she'd helped to match, as Bree supposed she should. What a marvelous thing it must be, to play even a small part in sparking one of the most important, magical moments in a person's life. She carried her latest stack of bowls and spatulas to the big industrial sink, lost in her thoughts.

"Excuse me," came a deep voice from the doorway. "I hope I'm not intruding."

"I'll be right out," Bree said automatically without turning to look. She lowered the stack into the sink and set them down. "Sorry to keep you waiting," she added, a cheery note in her voice. She washed her hands, then looked at her grandmother as she straightened and dried them off with a fresh towel. "I've got it. Go on ahead. I'll clean up back here after you return. Tell Mrs. Powell I said hello."

But Sofia had already stepped past her granddaughter and was waving for the gentleman to join them in the back. "Come in, come in," Sofia said. "I'm so glad you could stop by."

Confused now, Bree turned as a tall man with a shock of dark curls stepped fully into the kitchen. His pale-green button-up and khaki trousers accentuated his lean, fit frame. With all those curls, though, it wasn't until he glanced at Bree that she noticed he wore glasses. Glasses that framed the softest blue eyes she'd ever seen. She'd never thought of blue as a warm color until that moment. In fact, she felt all kinds of warmth when a slow, quiet smile curved his lips. Which was odd. Wild curls, soft eyes, and a sweet smile weren't usually the kind of things that caught her attention where men were concerned. *Well, that's definitely not true any longer.*

"I know you told me to knock at the back door," he said, that deep voice something of a surprise when contrasted with his low-key demeanor and studious appearance. Well, except for those curls. And who knew rimless glasses could be kind of sexy?

Bree realized she was curling her fingers into the palm of her hand to curb the sudden desire to walk over and sink them into that riot of black silk. Maybe steam up those glasses a bit while she was at it. Which made no sense at all. She wasn't normally taken with wild manes any more than she was button-down shirts and professorial

22

spectacles. Maybe it was the contrast of all those things combined in one guy . . . with a voice that could seduce a nun. Or her, at least.

"I thought it might be best to introduce myself out front," he finished.

Bree looked from the man to her grandmother, brow lifting in question. What was Sofia up to now? Swallowing an inward groan, Bree silently prayed this was not her grandmother's latest setup for a date.

"Nonsense," Sofia told him. "We're all shop-keepers here. And cooks, too. Kitchen is home to us, and my guess it is to you as well." She gestured with one hand, her smile warm and sincere. "Welcome to our home." She turned to Bree, beaming with pride. "Meet my grand-daughter. Abriana Bellaluna O'Neill, my only grandchild and dearest love. *Cuore mia.*"

"*Nonna,*" Bree whispered, a bit abashed by the grandiose introduction, though it was pure Sofia, who unapologetically wore her heart on her sleeve.

Sofia merely smiled at Bree and said, "Abriana, this is Caleb Dimitriou. He's taking over his uncle's restaurant over on Vine while they are out of the country. You know George Castellanos, of course," she went on. "Caleb is his wife Alethea's nephew."

"Ah," Bree said, and looked back at Caleb, her welcoming smile also sincere, and perhaps more

23

than a little relieved. He was a temporary guest, so this wasn't a setup. "Welcome to Moonbright. It's a pleasure to meet you. I hope your aunt and uncle are okay and it's a pleasure trip?" She glanced at Sofia again with a questioning look. It was unusual in a town their size that she hadn't heard this news already.

"They're fine," Caleb responded. "Thank you for asking." His smile broadened just enough to add a bit of a twinkle to his eyes.

Bree felt herself all but leaning toward him, as if invited to join in whatever might be behind that sudden infusion of affectionate amusement. *Get a grip,* she silently schooled herself, wondering what on earth had gotten into her. The guy was talking about his aunt and uncle, for goodness sake. Not coming on to her. *Tell that to your parts that are ready, willing, and oh so very able if he suddenly decides to do just that.*

"It is," he replied. "A long-awaited one. Their honeymoon, actually." At her surprised look, he added, "They married young and didn't have the means then. As you probably know, my aunt and uncle never had children of their own, so work was pretty much their passion as well. They each love what they do for a living." His expression warmed. "Of course, Uncle George believes that working hard at something you love is its own reward. My aunt Alethea, however, feels that you should love your work, yes, but should be working toward the reward. Eventually she got George to agree that as soon as one or the other of them was able to retire, she'd finally get her honeymoon. George promised they'd go to Greece for an extended holiday. See family on both sides, explore, relax for once."

"Alethea retired last month," Sofia told Bree, "after more than thirty-five years as a nurse." She beamed at Caleb. "Long overdue, but something of a surprise, too. At least to her closest friends. She never mentioned she'd made the decision, just announced one day when we were playing cards that she'd already up and done it. I'm so glad George was able to live up to his end of their little bargain." She glanced at Bree, then back to Caleb. "And I'm so pleased you were able to come."

"It's really nice that you're able to do that for them," Bree said. "I'm sure they both appreciate it a great deal. So, you're here temporarily, then?" She'd included that last part for Sofia's benefit. She hadn't missed her grandmother's glance between them and didn't need her getting any ideas.

"Our family is a bit sprawling," Caleb replied. "We don't see each other as often as we'd like." His smile was back, with a flash of white teeth this time. "Which might be a good thing. We can be rather, uh, boisterous."

Even that brief flash made her heart flutter . . .

and a few other places as well. Bree told herself it was the love and respect that shone from his eyes when he spoke of his family. She identified strongly with that deep, familial bond. Surely that was the reason for this over-the-top reaction she was having to him. *Uh-huh.*

"I come from a long line of chefs," he went on, then looked to Sofia. "Cooks," he amended with a smile. "You are right about kitchens being our home. Not even our second home where some of us are concerned," he added, that twinkle flickering again. "My siblings and I spend more time at the restaurant than we do anywhere else. My sister actually lives above our restaurant. She converted what used to be unused storage space into a pretty decent apartment." He flashed a full-on grin then. "We've all been known to bunk up there from time to time."

"You've got feeding people in your blood," Sofia said, "so of course that is home for you." She nodded, as if that were that. And for Sofia and Bree, it was. Caleb, too, so it seemed.

Bree had just never really thought of it like that before. At the moment she was still busy being blindsided by the transformation to his handsome face when he grinned like that. She hadn't expected to see such strong hints of alpha hidden behind those rimless spectacles and sweet smile.

Caleb had also nodded in agreement with Sofia's proclamation, and Bree noticed his shoulders relaxed a bit, as did his stance, as if he'd found his people. She understood that, too. She could walk into any kitchen and feel at home. Finding someone who shared her feelings and connection to both family and food was new, though.

"We've got chefs and restaurant owners in pretty much every branch of our family tree," Caleb said. "Our crazy hours make traveling to see each other a challenge, but for something like this, you find a way."

"How long are George and Alethea planning to be gone?" Bree asked, telling herself she was staying on that topic just to make certain Sofia would see, unequivocally, that nothing could happen between them. *Mmm-hmm.*

"They've planned for a six-week stay," he replied.

"Wow," Bree said, having assumed it would be for a week or two at the most. "That sounds pretty wonderful." *And far, far too long to chance seeing you around town.* If she was reacting to this simple introduction like a woman starved for a little attention, she didn't want to contemplate how she'd handle repeated exposure.

"When you've waited as long as they have for a honeymoon, it seems about right," he said with sincere affection, his gaze then shifting exclusively to her.

"You're doing a really nice thing for them,"

Bree said, trying not to sound breathless. He might look professorial with that mane and those glasses, but that deep blue gaze didn't feel remotely . . . academic.

Sofia walked over to him. "George tells me you and your siblings have built up quite the place in Philadelphia. Coming all this way for such a long period couldn't have been easy to arrange." She took his hand and covered it with her own, giving him a pat. "You're good to your family," she said. "That's a lovely thing. They must be very proud of you."

Bree watched as a light flush crept into Caleb's cheeks, his expression a bit abashed. She wouldn't have thought a man blushing at a simple compliment would make her pulse thrum. Somehow, on Caleb Dimitriou, it was both a little endearing and a whole lot sexy.

"It wasn't a sacrifice," Caleb assured her. "There are four of us running Dimi's. My two older brothers, myself, and my baby sister, who, more often than not, is off on one of her learning expeditions. She's been in Africa for the past month or so. We're well used to handling things."

"Africa," Sofia said, not looking too surprised.

"She knows a little something about having a wanderer in the family," Bree explained. "My mom and dad are in the Galapagos Islands. My dad is taking pictures for his next book, and my mom is getting inspiration for her next series of watercolors."

Caleb's eyes widened at that. "That sounds pretty amazing. Is that her work I saw on the walls out in the shop? They're quite striking."

"It is," Bree answered proudly, pleased he'd noticed the watercolors on his walk-through. "And thank you, she'd be pleased to hear you say that. She has pieces in the local gallery here in town, as well as galleries in several major cities. In fact, it was her art that first caught my father's eye."

"Another Moonbright love story," Caleb said with a smile. At Bree's look of surprise, he said, "I've heard it's something of a tradition here. I can understand it. It's a picture postcard little town, and the ocean views are pretty spectacular." That twinkle returned to his eyes. "I can think of worse places to fall in love."

Bree's mouth suddenly went dry, and she had to swallow several times before she could continue. Who knew soft curls, a sweet smile, and cornflower blue eyes could be so lethal? "My, ah, my parents would certainly agree with you. My dad was here on a magazine assignment, actually, and saw her work at the local gallery. He tracked her to the bakeshop." Bree's smile returned naturally then and spread to a happy grin. "And the rest, as they say, is history. They've both gone on to achieve a lot in their fields." She flushed and let out a short laugh. "Sorry, I don't get to brag on them all that often. Everyone in town knows how amazing they are. We're all really proud of them."

"As you should be," Caleb said. "My parents are both gone now, so you're very fortunate."

"I'm so sorry," Bree said.

"It was a long time ago, but they were pretty wonderful, too. It's nice to hear someone brag on their folks. I think, too often, people are so focused on their own lives, they kind of forget or take for granted the treasure they have in family. It's great that the two of you get to work together." He caught her gaze again, and Bree swore she saw something flicker to life in his eyes when he looked at her now, as if he'd just made yet another kind of connection.

Oh, that's not good, she thought, most especially because it felt really good. *Stop talking.* They both needed to stop talking. Stop connecting. And still their gazes lingered. Yeah, maybe it was too late for that.

"My brother Matteo paints," Caleb said, somewhat suddenly, as if he, too, had lost his train of thought while looking into her eyes. "Which would surprise you if you met him," he added, his smile returning. "I'm in continual awe at what he can do with a brush, a set of kid's paints, and a cup of water." Caleb shifted his gaze to encompass them both, and Bree felt as if she'd been released from a physical embrace. His abashed smile returned. "I'm lucky if I can paint a wall without getting the stuff on everything."

Bree raised her hand. "I'm a lifetime member of that club." They both laughed at that, and she liked his deep rumble and the direct way he caught and held her gaze again. She was utterly confused by all the things he was so effortlessly riling up inside her, but that didn't stop her from staring right back.

"Do you have the wanderlust, Caleb?" Sofia wanted to know, looking between the two, her gaze openly considering now.

"*Nonna*," Bree said in a hushed tone. Sofia merely continued smiling at Caleb.

He responded easily. "Sometimes I've thought it would be nice to just hop on a plane or a boat and see some new part of the world. Cassi's been begging me for years. My sister, Cassandra," he added by way of explanation, then shook his head. "But for me? To be honest, I'm happiest in a kitchen."

"That's exactly me, only with my mom and dad," Bree heard herself say. "They've barely unpacked and they're already planning their next trip. I'm twenty-nine and I think I've finally gotten them to stop hoping I'll go along with them." *Stop flirting!*

"My sister would love them," Caleb said with a chuckle.

"We should introduce them," Bree said, sharing his laugh. "She might be the daughter they've always wanted. Me, I'm like you. Give me a kitchen, and I'm at home." She looked around the room. "This is right where I want to be."

"Yes," he agreed. His smile deepened, and that spark of love and affection was back in his eyes when he added, "Surrounded by my loud, wonderful, crazy, big family, laughing together, sometimes yelling at each other, feeding people, seeing them content. That's where I'm meant to be."

Exactly, Bree thought, and sighed. *So very exactly.*

Sofia beamed at Caleb. "I can't think of a better recipe for a good life." She looked at Bree. "And you are right, I've been blessed with a family who has a passion for my passion, so my life is full."

"We're not all that loud," Bree added with an affectionate smile of her own, "but we laugh often, and I like to think our customers feel that same kind of contentment." She nodded. "That's a good way to describe it. Contentment. That's what I want them to feel when they're here. Hopefully it stays with them when they're enjoying our pastries and cookies and cakes at home."

Sofia eyed the two again, then said, "Speaking

of our wonderful cakes and cookies, where are my manners?" She turned and picked up an iced cookie from one of the racks. "Here," she said, handing it to Caleb. "You'll see for yourself what a magician my granddaughter is with some butter and Italian cream."

"Wait, no!" Bree said, but it took her a beat too long to shift gears from losing herself in his gaze to preventing her grandmother from handing him what was absolutely the worst thing she'd ever created. He was already taking a bite. "They're really not good," she told him, grabbing a handful of napkins, mortified.

His eyes widened in disbelief as he chewed.

"Here," Bree said, all but thrusting the napkins at him. "I'm so sorry. She didn't know."

Rather than take the napkins, Caleb swallowed his bite and looked at the cookie in wonder. "Not good?" He studied the cookie much as she had just minutes before, but in awe rather than in frustration. He took another bite and closed his eyes. "I've never tasted anything like this." When he opened them again, his gaze went straight to Bree, wonder and appreciation clearly there for her to see. "What did you put in these? They're incredible."

Bree's mouth dropped open, then snapped shut again as a feeling of dread washed through her. She turned to her grandmother. "*Nonna*, you didn't," she said on a hushed whisper.

Her grandmother gave a slight shake of her head, a merry twinkle of delight shining from her eyes. Looking inordinately proud, she said, "No, *cuore mia*. You did."

Chapter 2

"Thanks, Cassi, I really appreciate your looking them over." Caleb pressed the phone between his ear and shoulder so he could shuffle the papers back into the folder he'd been compiling on top of George's cluttered desk. Housekeeping was definitely not his uncle's strong suit. *And apparently neither is bookkeeping.* "I'm sure I'm just missing something." Caleb wasn't sure of any such thing, but there was no point in going there until his sister looked things over. Aside from cooking, bookkeeping actually was a strong suit of his. Math and numbers came easily to him. Cassi was even better at it than he was.

"Doesn't he have someone who does his books? An accountant or something?" Cassi asked, and Caleb smiled as he could hear the rhythmic sounds of a knife repeatedly connecting with a cutting board coming through the phone while she spoke. There was also a clatter of background noise that could only mean she was in a kitchen somewhere. The Dimitrious were never far from food.

"He may for taxes and whatnot, but for the

day-to-day running of the restaurant, it looks like he handles all of that on his own." Caleb flipped open the notebook and shook his head as he looked at the heavily inked columns. "It's all in George's handwriting. Well, it's the same as all the notes and things he's got here, so I assume it's his handwriting. He doesn't have a secretary, or office help—I know that much."

"Handwriting? Like, he's still writing all this stuff down? In what, like a ledger?"

"Worse," Caleb said, his smile spreading to a grin as he flipped the book closed and looked at the cover. "You know those black and white composition books we used in school?"

"I've changed my mind," Cassi said with a laugh. "You're on your own."

"Would it help to persuade you if I tell you I discovered the most amazing bakeshop here? They make an Italian iced cookie that, honestly, I don't know what she put in it, but it was out of this world." He was actually underselling the cookie, but the vision that popped into his head as he spoke wasn't the delicately shaped and decorated pastry. It was the woman who'd crafted it.

In fact, he hadn't been able to get her out of his thoughts since they'd met. However, he wasn't here to meet someone, and he had no interest in starting up something short term. He might not be looking, per se, but if and when someone came into his life who completely turned his head around, it had to at least be someone who'd fit into the life he'd built back in Philly.

Abriana Bellaluna O'Neill had definitely turned his head. They had a lot in common, and not just the surface things. He'd seen that look of utter understanding in her eyes when they'd been talking about family and the bonds that tie people together. The kind of understanding he hadn't come across before. In fact, his family and his close ties to them, to the businesses they ran together, were largely the reason he was single. Unless you came from that world, it was hard to understand. And the women he'd met thus far definitely didn't understand.

Abriana—Bree, as she'd told him before he'd taken his leave of the shop yesterday—totally understood. Unfortunately, the reason why she understood was also yet another reason he had no business thinking about her nonstop, much less coming up with and discarding numerous reasons to drop by Bellaluna's again—both of which he'd been guilty of doing. It had only been the issues he'd uncovered here at the restaurant that had saved him from doing something he'd regret.

Now if he could just stop thinking about her. About the cupid's bow shape of her mouth, the lively way her lips curved and dipped as she smiled and laughed, which she did often. He'd felt a pull toward her he couldn't even describe, much less explain, and at the center of that pull was that mouth. And his seeming inability to stop thinking about what it would be like to feel that plump softness pressed against his own lips.

He was typically a low-key kind of guy, preferring to be in the background cooking, while one of his older brothers ran the front of house, seating their customers and handling all things social. And yet the moment he'd entered Bree's kitchen, he couldn't stop talking.

He was never like that. Not with people he didn't know, at any rate. But he couldn't seem to shut up. Every time Bree's eyebrows rose or furrowed, or the corner of her mouth curved either in smile or frown, then split wide in a grin . . . he kept talking, wanting more. Her laugh was as delicious as that sweet treat he'd experienced. Which was how he thought of food. Something to be experienced, with all the senses. Being around Bree felt exactly the same. Sight, scent, sound, touch, and taste. He'd wanted to satisfy his sensory needs so badly it was like a physical hunger, like he hadn't eaten in days.

The moment he'd left her kitchen, he'd started convincing himself that he was just tired from all the prep he'd gone through to leave Dimi's for six weeks, or distracted by the unknown that he was about to face in George's kitchen. That had to be it, because surely he was making more of his meeting with her and her grandmother than could possibly be true. Or real. That wasn't like him, either.

"Hello? Caleb? Have I lost connection?"

He snapped back to the conversation and the situation at hand. "No, no, I'm here. Sorry, juggling too many things, a lot to figure out." *And a lot you need to forget. Namely any further distractions with a certain bakery chef.* "Castellanos is a completely different setup from ours. Or from any of the family restaurants I've visited. He's not just old-school; he's prehistoric school."

Cassi laughed at that. "Well, given we can rarely get you out of our kitchen, you also don't have that much to go on," she teased. "I'm still surprised George asked for you. I thought you'd send Matteo up. You've never wanted to run a place. How many times has Matty bragged to Lander, when he's bitching and moaning about things, that he could run Dimi's with one arm tied behind his back?"

"Be thankful you were away at the time of deliberations," Caleb said dryly. "Matty was all about ignoring what George wanted and putting you here, thinking it might ground you a bit."

He'd expected her to laugh or toss out some pushback at their older brother. Instead, she paused, then said, "Yeah, well . . . about that."

Surprised, Caleb said, "About what? You okay?

Did something happen to you when you were in Botswana?"

"I was in Swaziland, but no, don't worry. Nothing happened. Not over there, anyway. You don't need to scan and send me any of George's book records. I, uh . . ." She trailed off, then laughed and simply said, "I'll look at them when I get there. Which will be in about two hours."

If it was possible to grin and frown at the same time, Caleb did. He adored his baby sister and always missed her terribly when she was gone, which was far too often these days. But he admired her for boldly going where she wanted to go, staking out her own path in the world and going after it. He just wished their older brothers were as supportive. "So, I'm guessing Lan or Matt got a hold of you anyway?"

"Unfortunately, cell phones work, even in remote southern Africa," she said dryly. "Apparently, I need to go much farther off the grid to gain my full independence from the Dimitriou tribe, but at this point, I'm not sure where that would be, exactly. Mars, maybe? And don't be mad, it's not that Lander doesn't think you can manage. It's—"

"Oh, I'm not mad at all," Caleb said on a laugh. "I'm also not too proud to admit I could use all the help I can get." He looked through the open door of George's office to the empty kitchen beyond. He knew the front of the restaurant was equally devoid of any people, staff or otherwise. He didn't need Cassi to help him run the place. But he'd take her very capable assistance in figuring out why George hadn't told anyone that his restaurant, as far as Caleb could tell, had one foot in the grave and the other one tottering close behind. He didn't mention that to Cassi. There would be plenty of time for talk when she got there.

Just as he hadn't said a word yet to his brothers. They were good, decent men, both of them, and Caleb admired and respected them every bit as much as he loved them, which was deeply. However, though Lander was only fifteen months older than Matteo, Matty was six years older than Caleb, and seven years older than Cassi. That didn't sound like a huge gap now that they were all adults, but his brothers had had the benefit and the challenge of having their very traditional father around for all of their formative years, and thus had a very different mind-set about how things should be done.

On top of that, the Dimitriou and Castellanos families were very close, and his brothers would think they were doing the right thing in rallying the troops to come and rescue one of their own. Caleb might eventually do that very thing. That's what his big, unwieldly, loving family did for each other, and they were wonderful at it.

However, since George hadn't already called

for help, and in fact hidden pretty much all of his problems from everyone, Caleb wasn't going to be the one to out his uncle until he understood fully what was going on. George was a proud man, as were most of the men in Caleb's family and not a few of the women besides.

Plus, there was the whole thing about George giving Aunt Alethea her much-deserved honeymoon. Caleb wasn't certain how George was financing that mission, either. The one person Caleb could trust to handle this exactly as he would was his sister. "I'm glad you're coming," he told her.

She must have heard a thread of his concern, because her tone changed, too. "Something else going on?"

"We'll talk when you get here," he said. "And where are you, by the way? I could have sworn I heard you dicing and chopping when you first answered my call."

"Oh, right. I was. I stopped for lunch at this amazing little deli I read about, or heard about, or . . . I don't remember where, but it was right on the way, kind of, so I decided to drop in. I got to talking to the owner about this new herb combination I learned while I was in Botswana and thought it would be amazing in the gourd soup. So, he invited me back, and I showed him." He could hear the triumphant sound in her voice when she added, "I was right. So now the Great

Baboo Deli & Tea House has a new soup—or an improved soup—on the menu. The Cassandra Callabaloo. Ha!"

"Deli and Tea House? That serves gourd soup? And I thought you said you were in Swaziland?"

"I was," she said. "After Botswana. And about Baboo's, I know, right? It's an amazing setup. But you're not distracting me, you know."

"We'll have plenty of time when you get here," he told her, not remotely surprised to hear his sister had found a way to have an adventure merely while driving from Pennsylvania to Maine.

"Good," she said easily, trusting him, as she always did. "So, in the meantime, tell me about the baker."

Caleb blinked. "What?"

"You were waxing rhapsodic about a cookie. I usually have to beg you to add something new to the dessert menu. Since when did you get a sweet tooth?"

"Since I bit into that cookie," Caleb replied. "And a traditional Greek dessert menu doesn't tend to run very deep."

"No, but that doesn't mean it has to be antiquated." She didn't let him reply. Their opposing thoughts on adding menu entries was a long-standing debate. "So, I ask again, who's the baker?"

She asked it in that way only younger sisters

can, all suggestive and filled with innuendo. If she were standing in front of him, he was certain she'd be fluttering her lashes at him as she asked. She was probably doing it anyway, and that made him smile.

"It's not about the baker," he told her. "It's about the cookie."

Cassi's laugh was delighted bordering on gleeful. "Ah, so then it's totally about the baker."

"When you try that cookie, you'll understand." That much was true. Cassi would go ape over the flavor profile, then immediately try to figure out what Bree had put into it. Caleb was more than a little curious himself. Not that they'd ever lift a recipe—that simply wasn't done. But learning new combinations of ingredients was always a catalyst for inspiration.

"Mmm-hmm," Cassi said knowingly. "I'll be right there."

"Cassi," Caleb said, a warning note in his voice. One he knew she would utterly ignore. Maybe having her there wasn't such a great idea after all. Caleb couldn't even get his own thoughts and reactions sorted where one Abriana Bellaluna O'Neill was concerned. He loved his baby sister to death, but he needed her perky, little nose ferreting out the problem with George's books. He did not need it poking into his personal life. Like their brothers, he and Cassi were also just fifteen months apart and from the moment she could look him in the eye, she'd always been able to read him like a book.

Cassi didn't just see too much where he was concerned, she saw everything. He'd relied on that more times than he cared to admit, especially when it came to gaining insight into the thought processes of the opposite sex. This time, though, sharing any part of it felt too . . . intimate. Private. Which was ridiculous, given the sum total of his interaction with Bree to date had been spilling his family's life story inside the first five minutes of saying hello, and biting into the most delectable combination of flour, sugar, and butter known to man. Or woman.

And wondering, imagining, pondering, day-dreaming, and night sweating to the point of distraction over what it would be like to taste the delectable baker as well.

"Well, well, well," Cassi said into the expanding silence. "Could it be true that my slave-to-the-kitchen, nose-to-the-cutting-board brother has finally had his head turned by something other than perfecting his dolmades and *keftedes*? I wouldn't miss this for the world."

"Cassi—" he started again.

"You're protesting too much," she told him, a wry note added to the unmitigated glee now. "Besides, you had me at Italian bakeshop."

A knock at the back door gave Caleb the out he needed to end the call. "I've got deliveries," he said, hoped. He'd placed four orders the night before from George's usual vendors and none of them had shown up this morning. He should have already been to the fish market and the grocers, but he'd been stuck waiting because the sous chef hadn't shown, either.

He'd tried to tamp down a feeling of dread. Surely George wouldn't have gone flying off to Greece and not bothered to mention that his business had fallen into such dire straits. "And thanks," he said. "For coming."

Her delight dimmed slightly. "Cay, what's really going on? Is it that bad?"

"Don't drive like a maniac. Enjoy the coastal view. I'll have your favorites for dinner when you get here," he told her. "Love you." Then he hung up. They really were far too good at reading each other.

He squeezed out from behind the small, wooden desk George had wedged into the office, along with overflowing bookshelves, ancient, beat-up metal file cabinets, and stacks upon stacks of everything that had accumulated since they'd filled up, too. Which, from the looks of it, had been sometime in the past decade. "Or more," he muttered. He knew he was here to oversee, keep the doors open, maybe cook a little, and nothing more, but one look at George's office had made Caleb's bookkeeper's brain hurt. He'd thought he'd do his uncle a favor and help organize the chaos. Now he was just hoping there was a reason to bother.

He skirted the stacks of notebooks, news-papers, and the third stuffed in-box, which was actually an old vegetable crate pulling double duty, and made it to the rear door just as he saw the shadow beyond the window blinds turning to leave.

He might have yanked the door open in his haste to not lose the one delivery it looked like he might get for the day, only to discover it wasn't a delivery at all. Or not the one he was expecting, anyway. It was the baker.

"Hi," Bree said, a bright smile on her pretty face. "Do you have a minute?" She lifted a square pink box tied with white string. "I brought breakfast treats." Her lips lifted at the corners and that perfectly bowed lower lip pursed, her tone dry when she continued. "Okay, so they're really just treats. But if you eat them before nine a.m. and there's coffee involved, then that constitutes a breakfast, right?"

He looked past her, at the empty rear lot tucked behind the restaurant, partly to check for a delivery truck. Mostly to stop looking at that perfectly bowed bottom lip. She looked over her shoulder, too, then back at him, confused.

"I'm sorry," he said. "I was expecting a delivery. Please, yes, come in."

"If now isn't a good time—"

He gave her a welcoming smile. "If what's inside that box is anything like the cookie I had yesterday, there will never be a bad time." *Stop flirting. You're not getting involved, remember? Your plate is overflowing. And now your sister's coming. Don't add anything more.*

Bree stepped inside and the scents of cinnamon, vanilla, and butter entered with her. He tried not to audibly inhale as he motioned for her to go on into the kitchen ahead of him, causing her to pass within inches of his already alert and exceedingly enthusiastic body. He turned his back to close the door, taking one last look at the lot behind the restaurant, mostly to buy him an extra moment to quell his physical reaction. *What are you, fourteen?* Actually, he'd had more game back then compared to this. When he turned back, Bree was glancing around the kitchen, no discernable expression on her face, but he suspected he knew what she was thinking.

"We don't open until dinner on Mondays," he said, by way of explaining the utter lack of activity in what should have been a bustling kitchen enterprise. In fact, they were the only two in the whole place at the moment. It wasn't just the sous chef who hadn't shown up today. "I'd invite you into George's office, but I can barely squeeze in there myself. Why don't we go out front." He started toward the swinging door at the far end of the kitchen, and the switches that would turn on the lights in the restaurant proper, but she stopped him.

"No, that's okay," she said. "Please don't go to the trouble. I only stopped by to check in and see if George, or you, had made any plans regarding the Halloween parade?"

He turned back to face her. "You have a Halloween parade?"

The hopeful look on her face dimmed. "Ah," she said, then gave him a rueful smile. "I think that answers my question."

He smiled with her. "George didn't mention it, I'm afraid." He could have left it at that. Should have. He had a lot to figure out and not much time to do it if Castellanos was indeed going to open for dinner. As it had every night for the past thirty-seven years. At least that's what his uncle had boasted during their brief phone call just before George and Alethea had boarded their plane for Greece. Instead, he heard himself say, "I assume George helped with the parade in some way?"

"He provides the Cadillac convertible we use to drive the Pumpkin Festival Queen in the parade." She grinned. "He usually drives it, too."

"You have a pumpkin festival?" he said, charmed by the idea.

Amusement filled her pretty hazel eyes. "With a queen and everything."

His eyebrows lifted. "Sounds quite . . . regal?"

"Oh," she said dryly, "you have no idea."

He chuckled. "I'd say I could imagine, but honestly, I don't think I could."

"Well, you will get that chance if you'll agree to sub for George and drive his car in the parade?" she asked, hopefully. She was fair and freckled, with hair that couldn't seem to decide if it was brown or red. She wore it as she had yesterday, pulled fully back from her face in a tidy bun at the nape of her neck. He had the most urgent desire to reach out and pull out the pins, or whatever held it in place, so he could see what her hair looked like framing her face. Maybe if her features were obscured, even a little bit, he wouldn't find himself so utterly enraptured by every little shift in her expression, every inflection in her voice.

Her laugh, he'd discovered the day before, was open and confident. Not lyrical or musical or any of those other delicate descriptions, but honest and unfiltered. He wanted to hear it again, wanted to hear her fully let loose.

"It's just a few hours, in the early afternoon of Halloween day," she said, seemingly oblivious to his ongoing inner struggle. "You'd be back here in plenty of time for the evening dinner rush if you're opening that night."

He commended her for keeping her gaze directed at him, without so much as a glance at their utterly silent surroundings. "I haven't been out to George's place as yet," he said by way of response. At her surprised look, he added, "Kind of like our place in Philly, the third floor upstairs here is actually a little apartment, held over from when George first bought the building. He basically lived up there while he was remodeling and getting the restaurant ready to launch. He's always kept it that way. Over the years since, he's let some of his kitchen and waitstaff use it when needed to get past a tough stretch or to set them up until they could earn enough to rent their own place."

"That's really nice of him," she said.

"He's a good guy," Caleb agreed. All the more reason he wanted to help George out of this mess. His uncle had helped countless others in his lifetime. It was the very least Caleb could do.

"I'm embarrassed to admit this," Bree said, "but I don't know your uncle all that well. He sounds a lot like my grandmother in that regard. She's a caretaker, too." She smiled. "In Sofia's case, they're usually four-legged and scruffy. They have a way of finding her, I swear. Fortunately, she also has a knack of finding the perfect homes for them." Her smile spread to a grin. "Otherwise we'd be the crazy cat and dog people."

"That sounds like my mother's youngest sister." His smile turned wry. "Only not the part about finding them new homes."

Bree laughed outright at that, and the sound was as engaging as he'd known it would be. "Possibly a good thing our families don't live near each other."

"Or not," he countered. "Sofia could help my aunt Daphne reduce her cat population."

"True," Bree agreed, laughing again. "It's funny. Moonbright is small compared to, well, pretty much any other town, and we do tend to stick our nose in each other's business as a matter of form. Sofia knows George and plays cards with Alethea from time to time. Maybe it's because we work similar hours, but I've never had the pleasure of really talking to either of them at any length. I'll have to change that," she added. "I can tell you from Sofia that your uncle is inordinately proud of his extended family and speaks of you all often." Her lips curved more deeply. "Deservedly so, I'm sure."

Caleb liked how her smile always reached her eyes. She came across as a sincere person who said what she meant. He liked that, too. "It apparently runs in the family," he said. At her questioning look, he said, "Going on about family. I don't typically regale perfect strangers with my family's entire life story, but I couldn't seem to shut up yesterday."

Bree laughed. "My grandmother has a way of getting even the most reticent person to spill, so don't beat yourself up. Besides, I didn't think you overshared at all. I was right in there with you, going on about my folks."

Caleb could have told her that as delightful and charming as her grandmother was, it hadn't been Sofia who had kept him sharing. And sharing. "I have a little understanding of what you mean about small towns. Philly is not small by any measure, but it's divided up into well-established neighborhoods that go back many generations, and they operate much like Moonbright. You know pretty much everybody's name, where they live, what they do, and most big news does travel fast. But go a block past the edge of my neighborhood? I couldn't tell you much of anything about anyone."

Bree laughed. "If we're being completely frank, I probably wouldn't know much about anyone if it weren't for Sofia filling me in on all the goings-on." Her gaze remained direct, but the most delightful flush colored her cheeks. "I might spend a little too much time in the kitchen."

He barked a laugh at that, nodding as he did. "My siblings would tell you that if it wasn't for them and my nosy neighbors telling me everything whenever they can waylay me coming and going from work, I wouldn't know anything at all." His grin returned. "Now, my kitchen staff and waitstaff? That's my village. I could tell you stories," he said in a dead-on impression of his grandfather, who had been born and raised in Greece.

"See, I don't even have that," Bree said. "Sofia loves working up front, taking care of the customers. She is absolutely a nurturer by nature. It's where she shines. I work up front, too, and I love our customers, love seeing them enjoy the things I've made, but given my druthers, I'm in the back. That's my domain and I get to rule my kingdom." She laughed. "Of course, the only one I'm ordering around is me, and I also get to do all the grunt work, but it's a trade-off I can live with." She raised a hand, as if she were taking an oath. "And full disclosure, when I'm not actively baking product to sell, I'm experimenting with new ideas. When I do go home, likely as not I have my nose stuck in a cookbook, or I'm online looking for new flavor inspirations, or in my own kitchen, trying them out. That is my social life in a nutshell. And I'm okay with that."

He raised his hand in the same fashion. "Guilty as charged." He grinned with her. "We probably shouldn't let your grandmother and my sister bend their heads together. Cassi is constantly trying to drag me out of the kitchen. And it's not like I don't hear everything anyway without ever leaving the back of the house." He lowered his hand and leaned closer. "Fair warning, my family are horrible gossips. Don't worry, it's just amongst themselves. Any secrets Cassi gets from Sofia will definitely make the rounds in our kitchens, but that's as far as it will go. The Dimitrious and Castellanos are their own village, but the village is sacrosanct."

"What happens at Dimi's stays at Dimi's?" she asked wryly.

He nodded and their gazes caught, and held for a beat, then another, and another after that. It felt like the most natural thing in the world right then to simply dip his head lower, slide his hand under that bun, cup the nape of her neck, and lift that delectably tempting mouth to his own. He had to actively keep his hands to himself. They were very clearly flirting, but it wasn't until that moment that he realized how close they'd gotten, as if inextricably drawn to each other while they'd been animatedly talking and gesturing. He wondered what she'd think if he closed the slim space that remained between them and took that slow, but bold move. It was entirely unlike him, and yet he had to curl his fingers inward to keep from going for it.

He couldn't recall ever being so easily and fully engaged in a conversation. Yesterday had been the same way. It was as if they'd known each other for ages. Only they hadn't. And given the way they were looking at each other, if he didn't nip this in the bud right now, he suspected they were going to know a great deal more about each other in a very short period of time. And not all of it with their clothes still on.

"I can respect that," she said, her open smile effortlessly drawing him in. She was utterly lacking in artifice, and what was so attractive about that was he suspected it was a deliberate choice on her part, not a by-product of naïveté. She was sharp and quick-witted. And she was attracted to him.

He might have been single for a long stretch, but he wasn't naïve, either. He wanted to assure her that the attraction was mutual, but he suspected she was as well aware of that fact as he was.

He should be making his excuses about George's car and hoping they could find their Pumpkin Festival Queen another carriage for the parade. Get back to the business he'd come here to do, which was so much more than he'd bargained for.

But when she finally broke eye contact, it was only so she could turn and loosen the string on the box of treats. Whatever excuses he might have come up with to end this little tête-à-tête before it went to a place they couldn't return from, died unspoken the moment the rich aroma of cinnamon and vanilla filled the air again, along with the scent of—"Anise?" His eyebrows lifted in surprise. "And is that . . . pears?" He automatically leaned over the open box, drawing in the sweet, fruity blend without even realizing he was doing it. It was the chef in him. Other people drew in air; he drew in scents.

She nodded. "Anise is traditional in some Italian baking, but I've been playing a bit with blending it with other flavors. Not everything we sell at Bellaluna's is traditional Italian, but the inspiration always comes from our roots." She lifted an oversized muffin with a crumbled topping baked into the top and peeled away the paper cup from the bottom. "Try it."

She handed it to him and his hand covered hers as he steered the muffin to his mouth. It wasn't as bold a move as stepping in and tipping her mouth to his, but it wasn't not a move, either. From the way her pupils flared, she was well aware of that, too. She didn't pull her hand away, and her gaze shifted from their cupped hands to his mouth as he took a bite. He'd meant to keep his gaze on her as he did, but his eyes closed the moment the blend of flavors and textures melted on his tongue and filled his senses. "My God," he mumbled as he swallowed the first bite, already thankful there would be more.

"You like?"

He opened his eyes then. She'd sounded, not surprised exactly, but inordinately pleased. He held her gaze directly. "I more than like."

Her gaze flickered down to his mouth— again—then quickly back up to his eyes. "You have a . . ." She reached up and touched a crumb at the corner of his mouth.

He should have quashed the urge, but he didn't, and felt no regrets for the decision, either, when he turned his head and captured the crumb on the top of her finger with his lips and heard her intake of breath.

He stopped short of pulling her fingertip fully into his mouth, choosing to close his eyes and kiss the tip of it instead. He smiled when he opened his eyes again, only to discover his glasses had fogged over. "So smooth," he said, shaking his head on a laugh.

"I don't know," she said, sounding a bit breathless as she laughed with him. "I thought you were doing pretty good there."

They were still holding the muffin between them when he slid his fogged glasses off so he could see her once more, albeit a little softer around the edges now.

"You have the prettiest eyes," she said on a sigh, then her own grew momentarily wide. "I said that right out loud, didn't I?"

He chuckled and nodded. "If it makes you feel less self-conscious, I've been fighting the urge to undo that bun since you stepped into my kitchen."

Her eyes widened again, but the continuing heat in them caused an immediate matching reaction throughout his entire body. The hand he still cupped trembled a little. "Yeah," she said, that breathless note still there, "I don't know if that helped all that much."

They both laughed, then continued to stand there, the poor muffin crumbling to the work surface below as their grip on it tightened a bit when his fingers squeezed hers. And yet, neither one of them moved to set it down.

Then Bree lifted her free hand and reached back behind her neck. It took a few tries with her clearly trembling fingers before she managed to pull two pins from her bun and let it uncoil. "So smooth," she said, the corners of her mouth lifting in a wry smile.

It was all he could do not to groan at the way it made those cupid's bow lips of hers pucker. Despite her fumbling, watching her take her hair down for him was somehow more erotic than any act other women had performed for him. Maybe it was the uncertainty he saw, even as she held his gaze with unwavering directness. It was the first hint of vulnerability he'd seen in her, and it brought a whole host of other feelings roaring to life inside him. She struck him as a woman who had no problem slaying her own dragons, thank you. He also wasn't the protective sort, or perhaps not the overprotective sort, at any rate. He liked capable women; his family was full of them. And yet, in that moment, he realized his instinct where Abriana was concerned would be to step in and do whatever was necessary if she so much as blinked in a moment of need.

"I don't know," he said, a rough note in his voice now. "I thought you were doing pretty good there."

She laughed then, and just like that, the flicker of vulnerability winked out and her confidence returned. Knowing that she had that side to her stayed with him, though. In a good way. Vulnerability wasn't the same as weakness, and feeling it from time to time generally gave a person greater empathy for others.

Lost in his thoughts, he reached out and loosened the unbound strands of her hair. It was longer than he'd expected, and he'd spread the tendrils across her shoulders before it occurred to him that maybe he should have asked first. She didn't stop him, though.

"Abriana—" he began.

"Bree," she managed, her voice a little huskier now, too.

He liked that. A lot. His fingers were still twined in her hair. "Abriana suits you so well, though."

"How could you know?"

He was operating totally on impulse now, not thinking, merely reacting. He drew the ends of one tendril up to brush across his lips. It wasn't the taste of her that he was literally aching for at the moment, but he needed to feel her on him like he needed his next breath. His reaction to her was completely out of proportion to anything that made sense given the short time they'd known each other. Yet, the truth was, he felt filled by it, invigorated rather than swamped, energized rather than overwhelmed. In fact, he couldn't recall a moment when he'd felt this good, and happy. As if all the elements he was made of had been switched on all at once. He was turned-on, both physically and mentally, and hungry for more.

It was like . . . all the indescribable things he'd felt when he'd bitten into that cookie was exactly how he felt right in that moment, just standing there breathing her in.

And try as he might to recall the myriad reasons why giving in to the utter temptation of Abriana Bellaluna O'Neill was a supremely bad idea, he couldn't do it. Nor did he care to try.

"Only my grandmother calls me that," she said, her voice barely above a whisper now.

He could feel the fine trembling in the fingers still pressed against his, saw the thrum of her pulse at the base of her throat when she swallowed against the dry rasp that edged her words.

"Would it bother you so much if I did, too?" he asked. He finally lowered what was left of the muffin to the table, then laced his fingers through hers. He kept their hands joined, down by his side, as he wound her hair around the finger that was still tangled in her silky tresses. He wound it once, then again, gently, until her head moved slowly toward his. He shifted that small bit forward, closing the last of the space between them as her chin tipped up so she could hold his gaze. "Abriana?"

She nodded, as if unable to do more. Her throat worked and her gaze dropped to his mouth. It was as plain an invitation as he had ever received, and all that he needed.

"There's one thing I definitely don't know about you yet," he said, his own voice even deeper now, almost a gravelly whisper, as he slowly lowered his head. He wanted her so badly, yet he also wanted to draw the moment out, savor every scent, every touch, every taste.

"What is that?" she asked, the words almost but not quite causing her lips to brush his. Her words were a bit slurred, as if she were a little inebriated by the palpable, all but tangible tension steeped in the air around them.

"How you taste." Then he took that perfect bottom lip of hers between his . . . and found out.

Chapter 3

What on God's green earth was she doing? She'd come over to make sure the parade car situation was resolved as a favor to the coordinator. Not to jump Caleb Dimitriou right in his uncle's kitchen.

Oh, come on. You all but fell over yourself offering to help when you heard it involved talking to Caleb. With your flirty little muffins and come-hither talk of pumpkin queens and family bonds. This is exactly what you were hoping for.

Okay, that last part wasn't true. Not entirely. She'd had no idea she'd end up being pulled up against his hard chest and kissed breathless by a man who absolutely knew what to do with his mouth. And hers.

Then there was the way he said her name, with that hint of a Greek accent when she was used to hearing it with a hint of Italian. He'd had her at *Abriana.*

He slid his palm from the nape of her neck, cupping her cheek so he could take the kiss deeper, all the while his other hand was still entwined with hers, dangling so innocently beside their hips. She was experiencing intimate sweetness with him on the one side, while at the same time being utterly seduced by his clever, confident, total ownership of her mouth on the other. The combination of the two took down every wall she might have erected. Had she been trying to do so. Which she wasn't.

Instead, she was quivering, quite literally, in response to all the places he was touching her, both directly and indirectly. It was as if she'd never felt or experienced what it was like to have a man's hands on her, or his mouth. She wasn't inexperienced, and yet nothing had ever prepared her for how he was making her feel. It was exhilarating and not a little thrilling. It should be a bit terrifying, feeling so much, wanting so much, in such short order with someone she'd just met. She couldn't explain it, though, even to herself, but her instinctive gut feeling, at the core of this sensual maelstrom swirling around them, was of being . . . well, content. Of being right where she was supposed to be.

She was with Caleb, and he'd take care with her, just as she would with him. Which, she thought, contained not a shred of logic, given they were five seconds away from tearing each other's clothes off. Without so much as a tiny sliver of expectation that this could lead to anything other than a brief, if very energized, fling. That was the opposite of taking care of one another.

So, what did she do? She sighed in bliss and let herself sink in. She kissed him back, opting to revel in the utter perfection of this moment, of him. Exult in how he tasted, like sugar, sweet pears, anise, and Caleb, how he handled her, confidently, respectfully, hungrily, all at the same time. There was no chance rational thought would gain so much as a toehold of leverage, nor did she want it to. That would mean ending this. Why would she want to do that?

It was a measure of just how good it felt being wrapped up in him that she could manage to so deeply bury the other reason she'd come to talk with him. The real reason she'd jumped at the chance to see him again.

From the moment he'd left the bakeshop with Sofia, after finishing the iced cookie and praising it again, and then again, Bree hadn't been able to stop thinking about him. At all. Nor had she been able to stop the almost overwhelming urge she'd felt to be near him again, talk to him again, find out more about him, just . . . be with him. Not even sexually, or just sexually, but all of it. She wanted to feel that sense of connection, of discovery and revelation . . . of, yes, contentment that she'd felt from the moment he'd started talking yesterday.

Most importantly, she wanted to know—needed to know—if it was a real connection . . . or one that existed only because of magic. Bellaluna magic. *Her* magic, if Sofia was to be believed. When it came to magic, Bree had no base of experience. She'd observed it, but she'd never wielded it. And she'd certainly never been tangled up on the receiving end of it. Or, more to the point, tangled up with someone who'd been on the receiving end of it. Was that all this was?

His lips left hers as he trailed kisses along the edge of her jaw, then caught her earlobe between his teeth. She let out a soft moan and tipped her head to the side, allowing him to kiss the curve of her neck as he slid his hand around her waist and gently tugged her up against him. Her body leapt in response to that contact, all of her soft parts aligning so perfectly with all of his hard ones. His so very, very hard ones.

To think she'd initially thought him the pro-fessorial type. That glimpse of the more alpha side of him hadn't been a false flag. Far from.

She willfully ignored the questions she needed to be asking, should have asked before ever coming over here in the first place. Instead, she slid her free hand over his shoulder, loving the lean, defined muscle she felt there, then did what she'd wanted to do, much as he'd said he had, since first laying eyes on him. She sank her fingers into those dark, glossy curls. They felt as glorious as they looked, and his soft groan as she raked his scalp lightly with the tips of her fingers made her thighs quiver. She wanted to see what other sounds she could elicit from him, whether she could make him feel as wanton as he was making her feel. And they were just kissing.

Her head was swimming, and not just from Caleb's touch. It took Bree a moment to realize he wasn't nuzzling her neck any longer. She opened her eyes to find him looking into hers. She had no idea what she'd thought she'd see in his or hoped to see.

What she found was . . . acceptance. Of this moment, of what they'd just done, of her, of whatever else he hoped would come next, she wasn't sure. But he wasn't sorry. And neither was she. It was that quiet confidence, even more than his exquisite kisses, that shook her, even as it calmed her. Maybe it was okay if they'd been given a little boost by her magic. Because standing there, with his arm around her, their fingers entwined, looking into those beautiful eyes of his, felt so good. So . . . right.

He pushed a tendril of hair behind her ear and gently squeezed the hand he still held. So very alpha and sweet and tender, all at the same time. Everything she'd ever wanted, without ever knowing it even existed.

Was it fair to him to let this continue without saying anything? And what, exactly, would she say? *You're only feeling this way because I spiked your cookie with some good, old-fashioned Bellaluna magic?*

And if it was magic, then why was she feeling it, too? She'd been just as swept away as he was and she hadn't eaten a magic cookie. *So many questions.* How was it she'd come this far in her adult life and never asked them all already? *Because until this moment, you wouldn't have known what to ask.*

"Caleb," she began, at the same moment he said, "Abriana." And she sighed, just a little, because she was pretty sure she'd never get tired of hearing him call her by her full name.

He nodded for her to speak first. "I didn't come over here for—I mean, I wasn't expecting . . ." She trailed off, then shook her head and let out a short laugh. "Okay, that's not entirely true." She met his gaze again. "I've been thinking about you since we met, which was just yesterday, hard as that is to believe. I don't typically—in fact, I've never once . . ." She let that trail off, too, but found herself smiling when he smiled and nodded, essentially saying "me too."

She believed him, which might have been naïve of her, given his very capable seduction. Yet, she didn't think those sweet and sexy cornflower blue eyes could be lying to her. His gaze was much too sincere, and she wanted nothing more than to lean forward, tip up on her toes, and feel those lips pressed to hers again.

"The, uh, parade question was actually real," she made herself say, trying to stay on topic. She dipped her chin then and felt a bit of warmth flood her cheeks, which was ridiculous given what they'd just been doing. *Now you're self-conscious?* "I didn't have to bring the muffins, though. That . . . might have been a bit more calculating. Not for this," she hurried to add, looking up at him again. "More as a way to maybe stretch the conversation a bit."

"I'm a big fan of stretching our conversations whenever possible. Muffins not required," he added, then grinned, "but greatly appreciated."

She wanted to confide in him, about the iced cookie, tell him he might be all worked up because of a bit more than a sugar rush, get his take on that, then discuss what they should do next, taking her confession into consideration. Oddly, it felt funny *not* talking to him about it. Not for all the ethical or moral reasons, which she'd most definitely have to address before doing this again, if they were ever to do this again. She wanted to confide in him because it just seemed like the kind of thing they'd always done, would always do. Talk things out, help each other brainstorm and problem-solve, have each other's back.

None of that made any sense. They'd kissed. Wildly and deliciously, yes, and she was pretty sure they'd have an even more memorable time if they decided to get naked and try it again. But none of that was relationship building. It was carnal expectation building, which wasn't at all the same thing.

"You're temporary," she blurted out, thinking maybe that was for the best. Cut straight to the chase, to the actual reality of the situation, and just walk away and not look back at the fantasy-land stuff they'd just been doing. Magic cookie problem solved, and all issues related to it. They'd had a nice little interlude, gotten that whole insta-attraction thing dealt with, and now they could move on. *Total lie. That's not any part of what you really want.*

Okay, okay. So what if she wanted him even more now than she had before? What good would it do her to take what he was offering? She'd only want more, then more. Wouldn't it be better to simply avoid, at all costs, so much as looking at him, much less talking to him, because she didn't need to know he was any more perfect for her than she already did. Yes, she'd have to survive the next six weeks, aching to the point of pain for the want of his hands on her again, preferably all of her this time. But then he'd go back to Philly, and she'd have to get over it. Move on.

Fine plan, her increasingly annoying little voice pointed out, *except you're forgetting that part where your Bellaluna magic finally came into being for him. Never before. No one else. Just him. Specifically him. What happens if you let him go, and . . . that's that? No more magic, ever again?*

She told herself maybe that was for the best, too. Wouldn't it be better to settle for something almost as good, and know it was true and real and not connected in any way to magic?

He brought her out of her merry-go-round of thoughts by tipping her chin up with his finger when she would have otherwise ducked his gaze. *Why would you ever settle for almost as good,* she thought, getting lost all over again in his eyes, *when you could have this?*

"I'm a big believer in fate," he told her quietly, as if reading her thoughts. And maybe he could. That would explain a lot. A smile played around his lips, lips she knew so intimately now. "My whole family is, always has been."

"Meaning . . . ?" she asked, hoping beyond hope he had some solution that would allow her to stay right where she was.

"I was the last person George should have chosen to come up here," he told her. "I'm not a management type. I'm a chef. Food is my focus, always has been." He lifted a tendril of her hair again; this time he brushed the tips over her lips, causing a ripple of awareness to zip right down her spine and pool in that place she was trying so desperately to ignore. "Yet here I am. And here I meet you."

"But you'll eventually go back to Philadelphia,"

she said, just as quietly. "Back to your home, your work, your family. For me, all of those things are here. This town is my place, my family is my heart, the bakeshop is my home, just like your neighborhood in Philly, your family, your kitchen in Dimi's is yours."

His smile spread slowly and she tried to take on the confidence he projected, so wishing she felt it for herself.

"All of that is true," he said. "We trust in fate, but we can't see into the future or know how things will eventually work out. You and I have only just met, and the connection feels so strong. Maybe that should seem strange, but it doesn't to me. It makes perfect sense to me. You make perfect sense to me. You understand things about me most people simply would not get. I'm usually the one in the background, letting others do the talking, happy to observe. Happier still not to be there at all and be off cooking somewhere. Yesterday? I couldn't shut up. I felt like not only could I tell you everything, anything, but that I had to, so you'd know it was happening, too." His grin was disarming and wholly endearing. "Maybe right now, too, with the chatty part. But if I don't take this chance . . ." He shook his head. "That's, like, not even an option. I have to take this chance."

Instead of being overwhelmed at everything he was laying at her feet, or being alarmed that someone could feel things with such intensity for her in so short a time . . . she listened to his words, looked in those eyes, and felt her heart wobble. Because he made sense to her, too. She couldn't let him lay that revelation at her feet and not be honest in return. "You aren't the only one feeling that way," she said softly.

She felt the relief in him. "I'm not discounting what you said, about your life being here and mine being in Philly. This is not how I envisioned finding someone."

"I know," she said. "Me either." She let out a little sigh, wishing for clarity, for some miracle solution. But there wasn't one. "My behavior just now notwithstanding, I'm not wired to handle short term . . . anything." She lifted a shoulder. "I know myself—I would get attached." *Am already getting attached.* "And I can't give pieces of myself away like that, not for nothing." She looked up into his eyes. "I can't predict the future, either, but I think we both know this feels like it could be a whole lot more than nothing." She slid her hand from his hair and pressed her palm to his chest, forestalling whatever he'd been about to say. "So, jumping in when it could be everything, knowing from the outset that it can't be anything, at least not anything long term, doesn't seem like a good idea. For either of us."

His shoulders let down a bit, and she watched as he searched her eyes, as if looking for a different answer. Finally, he nodded, agreeing with her, when what she wanted him to do was talk her out of it, tell her they could find a way. Rather than letting her go, and stepping back, he surprised her by cupping her cheek in his palm again, sliding his fingers into her hair, and lifting her mouth to his. This kiss was slow, gentle, and far more intimate than anything they'd shared thus far. It felt so much like a promise, rather than a goodbye, that she felt tears gather at the corners of her eyes. Maybe he was going to talk her out of it after all, by making her feel everything, so she would be willing to risk anything. Including her heart.

"Caleb," she whispered against his lips, as he ended the kiss, feeling wrenched and doubting everything she'd just said. "Maybe we—"

"Should take a step back," he finished for her. "You're right." He lifted his head, and for the first time his expression was entirely unreadable.

That alone felt like a kick to the gut. His openness and genuine frankness were such a big part of who he seemed to be.

He let his hand slide from her cheek and stepped back, then slid his hand from hers as well. She went from being warm and content, all tucked up against him, *right where she was supposed to be,* to feeling cold and set adrift. That shook her, too.

They were doing the right thing. She'd look back on this years from now and shake her head at the conversation they'd had, and wonder what in the world she thought she'd been doing, spouting all that stuff about life and how they could be everything, with a man she'd known less than twenty-four hours.

If this intensity and all-at-onceness was what Bellaluna magic brought with it, she'd be far better off going back to the time when she had no idea how to wield it, happy to leave that part to the grown-ups like her mother and grandmother. She turned away and smoothed the shirt she wore, then picked up the pins from the table and made quick work of putting her bun back together, albeit far less smoothly than she normally wore it. He didn't say anything, but she could feel him watching her. She didn't know what to say, either. It didn't feel awkward. It just felt . . . sad. *And wrong. Listen to your heart. Stop leading with your head.*

"Can I keep the muffins?" he asked, a half smile briefly lifting up a corner of his mouth. "If you don't mind." The smile didn't reach his eyes, but they no longer were unreadable. Now they just looked . . . bereft.

She nodded, thinking maybe unreadable was better after all. She took another step back, toward the corner of the table, thankful her knees didn't wobble out from under her, then put the worktable between them as she moved closer to the back door. She paused there. *You still have time to fix this. Stop this.* Only she didn't see how. If there was a solution, she'd have shared it with him, or he would have with her. "I'm, um, I'm sure we can find someone to drive. In the parade. So don't worry about that."

He looked as though he was about to say something to the contrary, but then apparently thought better of it, and nodded. "If I can find the keys, they're welcome to still use the car."

"Thanks," she said, feeling ridiculous now. So polite. So nice. Like they hadn't almost ripped their clothes off and taken each other right there on the table. And the floor. Up against the nearest wall. And then maybe in a booth out front. Or three.

She let out a shaky breath. *You're really going to need to stop thinking about that. About him. Anytime now.*

"Just, uh, give the mayor a call. He'll put you in touch with the right people. I appreciate it. I know the town appreciates it, too."

"Not a problem." He sounded so distant now, despite being perfectly polite. She'd brought that on herself, so she could hardly blame him.

With one hand on the doorknob, she looked back at him, and they stood there for another long moment, gazes locked. *Tell me to stay. That I'm wrong, that we'll figure this out.* He didn't. She didn't, either. She wrangled the doorknob behind her and finally pulled the door open, but just an inch. It was old and a little warped. She started to say that if he needed anything, she'd be happy to help. Just as she'd do for anyone. But that wasn't a good idea, either. Instead, she nodded and turned to leave.

"Goodbye, Abriana Bellaluna O'Neill."

Her breath caught in her throat and she glanced back, even as she schooled herself not to. He'd said it quietly, softly. She saw he'd mustered up a smile and everything. It was the first time it didn't warm his eyes, though it was hard to tell as he'd slid his glasses back on now.

"Goodbye, Caleb," she said, opening the old door the rest of the way with a decisive little tug, thankful for the rush of cool morning air that swept in. The perfect temperature for the cold, harsh reality that awaited her once she stepped outside of Castellanos for good. Once outside, she turned to pull the door closed behind her, careful not to look at him this time, then paused and rested her forehead on the frame, just for a moment after hearing it click shut. As if that brief moment would be long enough for her to recenter what felt like her entire world.

It was only because she'd paused like that that she heard his voice when he said, "I didn't use to have any regrets. Now, I think I do."

Chapter 4

"Earth to Caleb?" Cassi waved her hand in front of her brother's face, drawing him from his thoughts. Again. "Where is your head, *adelfouli*?" she asked, her teasing smile crinkling the corners of her matching blue eyes. "We're never going to get through this if you can't focus."

She gestured to the biggest steel table in the Castellanos kitchen, presently strewn with a variety of papers, thickly stuffed folders, multitudinous receipts, and a big stack of those marbled black and white notebooks. And that was just what they'd managed to narrow things down to after spending the previous two days tearing through the most immediate piles on George's desk.

Caleb shook his head, his expression abashed. "Sorry, I'm just distracted by what we're going to tell the family." That much was true; it just wasn't the entire truth. The look on his sister's face told him she knew it as well. "It's already clear that Castellanos isn't operating." He propped his elbows on the table and felt the tightness in his chest grow heavier as he looked around the empty kitchen.

"Well, it was operating a week ago," she said. "And from what I can tell, it looks like it's still been operating in the black, or should be given the receipts. But he's not paying his vendors fully, or his staff." She set the sheaf of papers she held back down on the table and raked a hand through her dark curls. "That's just not the George we know and love. He wouldn't do that. I say we figure this out before we say anything." She shrugged. "Maybe we can work out where things went so terribly wrong and turn this thing around, get the doors open again. No one needs to know about the road bumps. That's for George to tell them, if he chooses to." Her smile turned wry. "Of course, he's going to owe the two of us a very big conversation, but beyond that?" She lifted a shoulder, as if this was all something they could handle.

Caleb's brief laugh was humorless. "When did you become the eternal optimist?"

"Since I've gone out and seen a lot of this big world. When you see how much people are capable of doing with so very, very little, it makes this situation look like a cakewalk." She propped her elbows on the table, rested her chin on her curled hands, and fluttered her eyelashes, much as he'd imagined her doing several days ago. "Speaking of cake, when do I get to meet the baker? Someone promised me a trip to cookie heaven."

Caleb smiled at that. Cassi was nothing if not determined. "Bellaluna's is just a block or so away. Corner of Pumpkin and Spice. You can head over there anytime. Sofia would love to meet you."

"Sofia? Is that your baker's name? Pretty. And have I mentioned how much I love the street names here? Honestly, it's like the most adorable little coastal town, ever. It looks like some idealized picture postcard of the Maine seashore, only it's real. And with pumpkins! Have you seen the pumpkin patch at the edge of town? I don't know what they're feeding those things, but as soon as we sort things out here, I intend to find out. They're the size of small cars."

Caleb just let his sister bounce from topic to topic. It was oddly calming, as if things were normal, when they absolutely were not normal. And he wasn't only thinking of the utter debacle that his first management position had turned into.

"Tell me more about Miss Sofia," Cassi said, circling back. Some would listen to her scatter-shot conversational style and assume she was equally scattered. Nothing could be further from the truth. She merely had the ability to conduct multiple layers of conversation at the same time, without ever dropping a thread.

"Sofia is Sofia Bellaluna, current owner of the bakery," Caleb said, a tired but very real smile curving his lips as he thought of the delightful older woman. "If I were a few decades older, I would definitely be considering my pursuit." His smile grew and it felt good. "I'd be flattered to think of her as my anything. She's a remarkable woman." Maybe it was because this was the closest he'd allowed himself to get to speaking about Abriana, but it felt like some part of the unrest constantly stirring inside of him settled, just letting the Bellalunas into his thoughts at all.

"She's the baker?" Cassi looked sincerely surprised. It wasn't often she got things wrong.

Of course, she hadn't gotten it wrong this time, either. Caleb debated what to say. It wasn't that he didn't want to talk about Abriana. In fact, he was dying to talk about her. He wished he was sitting there right now telling his sister all about this amazing woman he'd met, instantly connected with, and planned to do everything in his power to keep in his life. The only thing stopping him from talking about it, putting that plan into motion, was the hard-to-get-around fact that Abriana had been right. Leaving Philly, the family restaurant, not to mention the extended Dimitriou and Castellanos clan was unfathomable to him.

To do what? He looked around the room. Try to reestablish his uncle's restaurant? The restaurant that still belonged to said uncle, who would be returning to it, at some point? Managing Dimi's or starting his own place wasn't a job Caleb had ever aspired to in the first place. Lander was the born manager in the family, and Matteo would very probably take over one of their uncle's restaurants, also in Philly, when he retired in the not-so-distant future. Caleb was a cook, the natural-born chef of the family, and that's where he quite happily planned to stay.

The touch of Cassi's hand on his arm startled him. She'd come all the way around to his side of the table and he hadn't even noticed. She squeezed his arm, then tugged one of his curls, a habit she'd started somewhere around the time she'd taken her first step.

"What's wrong?" she asked him quietly and kindly. "Beyond this mess," she added. "I thought you were just worried about George, about being handed this family disaster-in-the-making. But this restlessness is more than that. I've never seen you like this."

Caleb dipped his chin for a moment, then shook his head. He needed to talk to someone, and there was no better listener than his baby sister. He covered the hand she'd laid on his forearm and squeezed. "I'm sorry. I am. I ask you to help me figure a way out of this mess, then can't stay focused on it myself."

She pulled up a stool and sat next to him,

shifting so she faced him. "I've been teasing you about the baker, but . . . this is about her, isn't it? What's the situation? Didn't you two just meet? How could there be a problem already?" She offered him a teasing smile. "Maybe that's a cue to run and run fast."

He let out a short laugh, shook his head. "The problem isn't that we have issues when we're together. The issue is that we can't be together in the first place."

"Is she seeing someone?"

"No, it's not that. She's a lot like me."

"Ah, married to her kitchen, is she?"

Caleb nudged Cassi's knee with his, but his smile was abashed. "Maybe."

He let out a sigh and rubbed a hand over his face. "She's genuine and open, no artifice and no bull, and expects the same. She's fast and sharp and has a laugh you want more of. She's easy to talk to and pays attention. She listens, and she shares, even when it makes her a little uncomfortable. She's not the type to shrink back, but she makes me want to step in and find a way to help." He turned to his sister. "She's like me, Cass. Like us. She is dedicated to her kitchen, to feeding people, to her family. She doesn't accept mediocrity, in her work, or—"

"In her choice of companionship?" Cassi filled in, her smile one of love and affection and not a little surprise at his heartfelt tribute. "Well, she couldn't possibly hope for any better person than you, then. And if she turned your head, got you to think of something other than whatever recipe you're working on, she really must be something, too."

"That's just it, Cassi." He looked directly at her and just put it out there. "I think she could be everything."

Cassi's dark eyebrows lifted and her eyes widened. "Well. Whoa." She took a moment to process his statement, then shook her head. "I . . . never thought I'd hear you say that." She slid off the stool and kissed him on the cheek. "But I'm so glad I did. So, is it that she's not feeling what you're feeling?" She slid back on her stool, her feet dangling well above the floor. She was the opposite of her tall and, in the case of both Lander and Matty, burly brothers. "Because, and I'm not trying to tamp down your enthusiasm, I'm sure she's as wonderful as you say she is, but for a person you just met, that was a pretty major tribute speech you gave right there. Maybe you need to dial it back a little. Maybe you're scaring her off."

Caleb looked at her in disbelief. "This is not Matty you're talking to, king of the broken hearts. Or Lander, the white knight who never met a damsel in distress he didn't want to sweep up and save. We're talking about me. Guy with nose stuck in cookbook who usually doesn't notice a woman unless he actually trips over her, and that would probably be because he misplaced his glasses."

"Again," they both said at the same time, and laughed.

"All true. And yet, big tribute speech," she repeated. "Just saying. Might be construed as too much, too soon by the fairer sex."

"It's not just me, Cass. I'm not in it—wasn't in it—alone. Like I said, she's direct and up front."

"So, she told you she felt the same way? Actual words?"

Caleb chuckled at that. "Actual words."

"Hmm." Cassi folded her arms and crossed her legs as she studied him. "How are both of you so certain? I mean, how do you know so much about her? You just met her the day before I got here." She grinned and wiggled her eyebrows. "Just what did she put in that cookie, anyway?"

"Wait until you taste one. I should have saved one of the muffins she brought by before you got here, but we sort of mangled one of them, and then I was trying to figure out what else she put into them, and suddenly there weren't any left."

"How did you two mangle a muffin?" Cassi lifted a hand. "Maybe I don't want to know." Then her eyes grew wide. "Caleb Vasilios Dimitriou, you did not."

"Did not what?" he asked, totally confused.

She made a swirling motion with her hand.

"You know what. You might be guy-with-nose-in-cookbook, but you're still a guy. Please tell me you did not pull a Matty and end up in bed the first time you were alone with her for more than five minutes."

"Stop. This unbridled respect you have for me is just too much," he said dryly. "When have I ever given the impression that I—"

"When have you ever waxed rhapsodic over a woman?" she countered. "So, just how much knowledge do you have of her, and by knowledge, I mean—"

"I know what you mean. And we did not pull a Matty," he said, then ducked his chin. "But we might possibly have wanted to."

"Ah-*ha!*" Cassi crowed. Then reached out and swatted his arm, and not gently. "Also, how dare you? You're the one who gives me reason to believe that good guys do exist. Don't go ruining that for me."

"I am a very good guy," he told her. "I also don't kiss and tell," he said, rubbing his arm. "Not even to you. But, so we're clear, there's nothing to tell except for the kissing."

"Well," she said, mollified. "Good." She swept her gaze over the chaos of paper strewn across the table. "Because this is the only table big enough to hold all this stuff, and I don't need to be sitting here thinking that you—"

"All right, all right," Caleb said. "No worktables were impugned or otherwise used in an unsafe or unsanitary fashion. Satisfied?"

But Cassi's thoughts had clearly already raced on ahead. "I should meet her. Talk to her. Girl-to-girl. Woman-to-woman." She wiggled her eyebrows at him. "Sister-to-future sister-in-law."

"Now, hold on," Caleb said, feeling the first stirrings of alarm. "I told you all this because I trust you. There will be no independent acts of matchmakery."

"Ha," she told him. "I think you underestimate me. Remember when you were pining over Jessica Bastallanos but too chicken to ask her out? Who got you that date to the winter dance of your sophomore year?" She pointed to herself. "I believe that would be me."

"She dumped me for Braden Stackhouse right in the middle of the final dance," he reminded her.

"Let's not quibble about the details. I can hardly be held responsible for your poor judgment in picking her in the first place, or for her being a ridiculous, two-timing bi—"

"Water under the bridge," Caleb cut in.

"I was going to say bimbo," she replied primly.

"Right," he said with a chuckle. "And thanks for the offer." His voice gentled then. "I mean it. This is . . . I need to figure out what I want to do about it, or if I want to. Her life is here. Mine is in Philly. That is our issue, and she's not willing to risk getting involved in the short term when there's no foreseeable way to get to a long term. I respect that. I have to. Because I agree with her."

"Ah," Cassi said, softly this time. "Ouch. I'm sorry, Cay. That sucks."

"Indeed. But Abriana was right to nip it in the bud before someone got hurt. Or both someones."

Cassi eyed her brother, her expression contemplative. "I think you're right to step back," she said. "It's hard not to go after what you want, but if there's just no compromise to be had, that means one of you would have to give up all of what you love, so the other person can have what he or she loves. And that's not good for either of you. So . . . yeah."

Perversely, that wasn't at all what he wanted to hear.

He'd shifted his gaze back to the table, but when she didn't say anything else, he looked back to find her holding him in steady regard.

"She really is all that, huh?" Cassi asked.

He didn't have to nod, certain his sister could read everything there was to see right there on his face.

"And she was swept away, too?" She didn't let him reply. Her smile was sincere, and full of love when she said, "Of course she was."

His mouth curved briefly at one corner; then he looked away, wishing now that he'd never brought this up.

Cassi sighed a little herself. "I'm sorry, *adelfouli*. You deserve all the love." She looked back at the table, then sat up straighter and squared her shoulders. Cassi might be able to read him like a book, but the one advantage of that was she always knew when it was time to shift the subject. "So," she said, "who is going to call Uncle George and drag this story out of him? You? Or me?"

It was pushing midnight when Caleb finally began climbing the stairs to the little third-floor apartment. Cassi had opted to stay out at George and Alethea's house, thinking maybe she could find more clues there to what was going on. They'd agreed to hold off on contacting George or anyone else until they dug through everything. With Castellanos closed for business, they had plenty of time on their hands.

They had been able to get a timeline of sorts established, at least from the restaurant side, as to when the money coming in had stopped aligning with the money going out. But they had no idea where it had gone, or for what purpose. Caleb and Cassi were both struggling to understand why George had chosen to handle things as he had, why he'd asked Caleb to come. He could have just locked the doors, gone off to Greece, and no one would have been the wiser.

Except that probably wasn't true, either. Their

families were too closely connected. Everyone knew George and Alethea were going to Greece. In any other family, George could have just said he was having his staff take care of things during his absence, but that wasn't how things were done in their family. When someone had to temporarily step down, either because of travel, or illness, or a new baby, whatever the case, someone from the family stepped in. There was never a time when a Dimitriou or Castellanos wasn't at least overseeing things for any property they owned. Not due to a lack of trust in their employees—most of them were like family, too—but because it was their responsibility to look after their own, no one else's.

None of that explained why George had taken off as he had, leaving the place to Caleb's care, knowing full well what his nephew would be walking into. Whether it was pride, or fear, or just plain stubbornness that had caused George to handle things as he had, Caleb couldn't be sure, but until he and Cass figured out more of the story, George's secret was safe with them.

The first thing Caleb had done was try to contact the staff, many of whom had worked for George for most of Caleb's lifetime. Whether it was out of loyalty, or from frustration, or they simply had no interest in being part of whatever was going on, Caleb didn't know. He hadn't been able to get a single one of them to return his calls. He'd debated just showing up on a doorstep or two, and that was still an option, but there was still too much he didn't know. Before he involved anyone outside the family, even long-term employees, he needed to be armed with more information. That not one of those employees had reached out to anyone in the family to sound the alarm said a lot, too, and none of it good. They were protecting their current or former boss, even though he hadn't been able to pay them full wages for the work they'd done. *But what are they protecting him from?*

In the meantime, Castellanos remained dark for yet another night. Caleb shouldn't feel personally responsible for that. It had nothing to do with him. Yet, while he was in charge, he carried the mantle of the family name. He was responsible for keeping that name in good standing. He also had no idea where things stood between George and Alethea and their neighbors, fellow business owners, friends, and other folks in the town. Caleb had been overwhelmed just trying to get the paperwork sorted and stacked, so as yet, his only contact had been with Abriana and Sofia. Sofia was the only one who knew his aunt and uncle well, and she hadn't given him any reason to believe George was held in anything but the highest esteem, and she'd spoken quite fondly of Alethea.

Even so, surely in a town this size, it wasn't

lost on everyone that the place hadn't opened in at least three days. Cassi said folks probably thought it had to do with George taking his first vacation in all the years he'd been running the place. Caleb thought that if the staff wasn't getting fully paid and had already hightailed it out of there, surely there had to be some gossip floating around.

He let himself into the apartment and turned on the light over the small stove. Vestiges of a headache had been hovering for most of the day, so he didn't turn on any of the other lamps. The place was small by any measure. The main room held a galley kitchen and small table that seated four on one side and a cozy living room on the other. A faded old couch and a single easy chair were arranged around a small coffee table, all three of which fronted a small brick fireplace. A stand holding an ancient television set had been positioned so that it could be seen from either the easy chair or the kitchen table. There were two doors on the far wall. One led to the bathroom, and the other to the single bedroom in the back of the place. It wasn't much bigger than the living room and held just the basics. Double bed, nightstands, and a wardrobe in the corner that doubled as both dresser and closet.

Caleb wondered how his aunt and uncle had lived in such cramped quarters together when they first got married, but then he thought about what it would be like to be tucked up here with Abriana, and decided maybe it wouldn't be so bad after all.

He took his glasses off and shrugged out of the fleece pullover he'd put on earlier when he and Cassi had decided to keep the thermostat set as low as possible. George was behind on the electric bill, too. Caleb rubbed the bridge of his nose, wanting nothing more than to crawl into bed and not have to deal with things until morning. He took the time to stack logs in the narrow fireplace and get that started. The apartment was an icebox at the moment, but small enough that the fireplace warmed the place up quickly. He remained crouched in front of the open grate until the kindling caught and the underside of the logs began to glow. He slid one more log on the stack for good measure, then stood, arching his back as he did for a long stretch.

Maybe tonight he'd sleep, instead of tossing and turning, worrying about George. *And wishing you weren't going to bed alone.* He was tired enough that he didn't fight off thoughts of Abriana as he'd been doing since she'd slipped out the back door two days ago. Talking to Cassi about her earlier had both helped and . . . not.

He'd needed to say all the things that had been rolling around inside his head on repeat play, and hearing himself talk about her had brought him some clarity. That clarity being that he was an idiot for not even trying to figure out how they could have . . . something. Anything.

"Everything," he muttered. But one life-changing crisis at a time.

He sank down in the worn, leather easy chair that fronted the fireplace so he could take his shoes off. Once done, he let the fire warm him some more. Propping his elbows on his knees, he lowered his forehead to his hands and raked his fingers through his hair. Now that they'd established a timeline, tomorrow would hopefully bring some answers regarding the restaurant. Cassi was going to look for George's bank statements out at the house. Initially that had felt like a gross violation of their uncle's privacy, but as the hours had crept by, and they'd slogged through mound after mound of paperwork, trying to figure out what had gone wrong, and how to get the place up and running again, respect and concern had turned to annoyance and frustration.

There was also the question of how much Alethea knew. Was bringing Caleb up here also a show for his wife, so she wouldn't suspect anything was wrong? And how on earth could George whisk her off on a honeymoon leaving such a catastrophe behind? Hopefully the bank statements or other records at their house would help to answer a lot of those questions.

If that didn't happen, Caleb had already told Cassi he was sorely tempted to just turn off the lights, lock up the place, and head back to Philly, leaving George to clean up his own mess upon his return. At first, that hadn't felt like the right thing to do. Family helped family. Now, Caleb wasn't so sure. He didn't have a magic wand, nor a deep bank account. Even if Cassi found the statements, or bills of some kind, and they did figure out where all the money went, then what?

Maybe George had thought Caleb would go back home once he realized what had happened. "Maybe that's what I should do. This is George's business, literally and figuratively." Yes, they were family, but did that give Caleb the right to do what he was doing now? Dig when he hadn't been asked to dig? He'd been asked to come run the place, not uncover the great mystery of what George had done with all his money.

Caleb leaned back in the chair and let his head tip back. He closed his eyes and groaned. "Why are you doing this, Uncle George?" *What do you want from me? Am I supposed to fix this? Save Castellanos? Turn around? Go home?*

The latter was starting to look like maybe it was the right thing after all. Maybe all George had wanted was to set things up so they looked kosher, then once he was overseas, the shit could hit the fan and he wouldn't have to face it. At least not until he got back. Maybe he assumed Caleb would call in the troops and have things all fixed by the time he got back.

Maybe the best thing to do was send George a message saying that Castellanos was locked up tight and safe, and he was going to return to Philly. If George wanted things handled some other way, then he was going to have to come out and ask. Caleb would promise his uncle discretion.

A light knock at the back door startled Caleb's eyes open. A glance at the clock on the mantel showed he must have dozed off. It was after one in the morning. Who would come around at one in the morning? *Cassi.*

Had she already gone digging and found something? It wouldn't surprise Caleb in the least. "Who else would it be?" he said under his breath as he eased out of the chair and stood up again. Couldn't she have just called him or texted? It wasn't like they were going to be doing anything about whatever it was she'd found until morning, anyway. A good night's sleep was the most important thing for both of them at the moment.

He got up and walked through the kitchen to the door that led to the exterior set of stairs. The light on the small third-story landing had come on automatically, but the blinds were drawn. He fumbled with the lock on the knob and the deadbolt. "Hold on," he told his sister, "I can't get this darn—" Then the dead bolt finally slid open. "Why didn't you just call?" he said as he opened the door. "What we need right now is . . ." He trailed off, having gone completely still the moment he saw who was on his doorstep. He spent a moment wondering if he was still asleep and just dreaming this. If he was, he didn't want to wake up. "Abriana?"

She was bundled up in a thick coat, stretchy black leggings, and big, furry boots. Her arms were crossed in front of her, her hands tucked underneath her elbows, hugging her sides. Her hair was down and flowed in waves around her face and shoulders. Her eyes looked both dark and luminous in the porchlight, her skin even more luminous with the dark, starry sky as a backdrop. "I—can't explain this," she said. "I know it's crazy. Showing up like this. And this might sound even crazier, because you look just fine, though I've clearly woken you up and I'm very sorry for that, too. But the light was on and—"

"That's okay," he said, wide-awake now.

"I just needed to know if . . . are you okay?" She searched his face, concern clear on her own, maybe a little confusion as well, as if she couldn't actually believe she was doing this.

It had been a couple of long, stressful days, filled with so many emotions, most of them pertaining to his family, his uncle in particular. Underlying all of that, however, was a feeling he couldn't shake, that he was making the biggest mistake of his life by letting her just walk away.

Only right now, she was standing right in front of him, shivering, worried about him. And he'd never been so happy to see anyone in his life.

"I am now," he said, meaning every word. He opened his arms, and without hesitation she walked right into them.

Chapter 5

Bree buried her face in his shoulder, still shivering, still at an utter loss to explain, even to herself, what in the world she was doing. But at that moment, she couldn't care. She was exactly where she wanted to be. *Where I'm supposed to be. Finally.*

She couldn't shake that thought, any more than she could shake the very real and urgent concern she'd felt when she'd sat up in her bed less than an hour ago. She'd tried to make herself believe it had been something she'd been dreaming about and just couldn't recall, certain the feeling would recede now that she was awake. Only it hadn't. She'd felt like a crazy person when she'd finally gotten out of bed and gotten dressed, having made a deal with herself that she'd walk the two blocks over from her place to the restaurant and just look it over, make sure it was still standing, nothing was on fire or . . . whatever. Then surely the feeling of urgency would go away, and she could go back home to her nice warm bed, and no one would ever know she'd momentarily gone all looney tunes.

And the restaurant was fine. Caleb's car was parked out back, as it had been when she'd come to the back door the other morning. Everything was fine. She could go back home. But, despite the late hour, the light was still on in the upstairs apartment. Just a little light, maybe the flickering glow of a fireplace. Did that mean he was still awake? Same as her? If so, okay then, the restaurant was fine; he was fine. She was good to go.

She'd even turned around to head home, but that sense of urgency just got stronger with every step she took. It was the strangest thing, and so she'd looked back. She walked back around to the rear of the building, spied the exterior stairs, and thought she'd just go up, peer in, make sure he wasn't sprawled on the floor unconscious or something. Which was a completely insane thing to even consider—she knew that. But she just couldn't shake the feeling that he was in trouble . . . or something was in trouble. She'd never felt anything like it before.

So, she'd climbed the stairs, thinking it would serve her right if someone called the police, thinking she was a prowler, because . . . she kind of was. Then the blinds were closed and she couldn't lean far enough over the railing to look in the small kitchen window. Maybe she'd just tap on the door, really quietly, so if he was asleep, it wouldn't wake him.

Only he wasn't asleep, or he wasn't now, at

any rate, and suddenly the door was open and he was standing right there. Right in front of her. Where she could reach out and touch him, be in immediate contact with him. Again. The urgency had died in that instant. In its place had come a longing so deep, so swift, so all-consuming that when he'd opened his arms to her, she'd all but fallen into them.

She felt his arms tighten around her, and she slid her arms around his waist and held on just as tightly. And oh, this felt so good. So, very, very good. *Home.* Contentment welled inside her, replacing the fear, the longing, the urgent sense that things weren't as they were supposed to be, and she needed to fix them. Right away.

Now she had. She was where she was supposed to be. *Finally.* The word echoed again through her mind, through all of her, to be honest.

The knowledge that nothing else had changed, that she was now back to where she'd started, was pushed aside. No, shoved aside.

The chill night air rustled around them, and they finally let go long enough so she could move fully inside the small apartment and close the kitchen door behind her. He was undoing the buttons on the front of her coat before she could decide whether she was going to be staying long enough for that to be an issue. He was okay. The urgency was gone. She could go home now, back to bed.

He helped her off with her coat and turned her right back into his arms. And who was she kidding? She wasn't going anywhere. She wasn't sure whose lips met whose first. This time it wasn't a slow, seductive kiss, one of exploration, or discovery. This kiss was pure, unadulterated need, and his matched hers, touch for touch, taste for taste.

A whole new kind of urgency filled her. She sank her fingers into all those curls and held him right there, so he could take her mouth, and take it again, then let her in as she took his right back.

His hands cupped her shoulders, then slid down her torso, framing her hips, and pulling her in snugly against his own. She moaned at the contact, or maybe that was him. His fingers flexed into her hips and she thought she felt him tremble. Or . . . maybe that was her. He slid his hands under the hem of her sweater, and the warmth of his skin on hers made her shudder with pleasure. That moan had definitely been hers.

She began unbuttoning his shirt as he nudged her chin to the side and kissed along her jaw. He nipped her earlobe, then worked his way down the curve of her neck, much as he had in his uncle's kitchen . . . and at the same time, nothing at all like in his uncle's kitchen. She worked faster at the buttons, and he lifted his head long enough to slide her sweater up and over her head. He peeled off his shirt, and she helped him pull up the white T-shirt he wore underneath.

Then they were back in each other's arms an instant later, and she reveled in the feel of his bare, warm skin against hers. His hands were every bit as confident as his kisses, as he slid one arm around her waist to pull her in, while sliding his other hand under the thick fall of her hair so he could cup the nape of her neck and tilt her face back up to his. He slanted his mouth across hers and she opened to him, wanting him inside of her however she could get him.

She raked her fingertips down his back, the resulting growl at the base of his throat thrilling her. Thrill went to shock, and back to thrill, as he lifted her to her toes, then off her feet, urging her to wrap her legs around him. No one had ever done that, and if she'd had the chance, she'd have told him not to try. A dainty feather she was not. But he hadn't given her that option, and she would be grateful for the rest of her days. She felt wanton and female and maybe not dainty, but quite literally swept off her feet. It was exhilarating, and new, as were all the emotions he was roiling up inside of her.

One thought shoved its way to the front of the line: This was Caleb. This was not some mindless mating of tongues with someone looking to assuage a mutual need. This mattered.

He'd been carrying her to what she assumed was the bedroom, knocking over a lamp and clearing a side table full of books as they crossed the small, cramped space. At the exact same moment that thought entered her mind, he paused beside the bed. Then, rather than lower them both to it, his body on top of hers, he instead turned and sat on the edge of the mattress, keeping her wrapped around him, now sitting on his lap, her now-bare feet crossed and resting on the bed behind him.

She held on to his shoulders as he framed her face with both of his hands and looked into her eyes. "Abriana . . . I—"

"Want to wait," she finished for him.

He nodded but didn't say anything else. His eyes, so dark blue, all filled with want and need a moment ago, now held all of that but with an apology and a flicker of hope as well. She understood.

"This is important," he added, still searching her eyes. "To me. And I don't . . . I don't want this first time to be—"

"Mindless," she said, then nodded. "This matters." She smiled then. "That's what I was thinking right at the exact same moment you stopped." At any other time she would have wondered whether their connection was purely organic . . . or helped along by Bellaluna magic. But he was smiling now, too, and she decided that whatever it was linking them together didn't really matter.

"I want you," he said.

She didn't need more proof of that, she'd felt it, all of it, from the rigid length of him pressing into her, to the urgency in his touch, and, most of all, the honest, open look right there on his handsome face, for all to see.

"But I want more than this, Abriana," he told her. "I want to know you, spend time with you, let all the other parts of us catch up to this part that seems to have figured things out already." His smile turned sweet then, and impossibly tender. "I want to do this right."

"Yes," she said, unbearably touched. "I want that, too."

"I know nothing else has changed," he said.

"I know," she said, not wanting to think about that, knowing they had to think about that. "Well," she said, striving for a lighter tone, "who knows, maybe we'll figure out this is just pent-up lust." She smiled. "A case of two people spending way too much time in their respective kitchens and the moment they find each other, boom, things happen."

"Boom?" he said with a chuckle.

"It felt like a boom," she replied matter-of-factly, and they both grinned.

"Maybe you're right," he said, still smiling. "It would explain a lot. The thing is," he went on, more serious now, "I haven't been able to shake the feeling I've had since you walked out of the kitchen the other day."

"Regret?" she said, and smiled when he looked surprised. "Me too."

"I don't have any new answers."

She nodded, and they sat like that for a while, him toying with the ends of her hair, her toying with his curls, each deep in their own thoughts, but content because they were together, wrapped up in each other. "Maybe we have to work at this first, get to where we know enough to make informed choices," she said at length. When he shifted his gaze to hers, she said, "It's something my mother said to me when I was debating on whether or not to go to Italy to study for a year after I graduated from culinary school. All I wanted was to come back here, back home, and bring everything I'd learned with me. At the same time, I didn't want to miss the chance to discover things I could only learn over there. Mom made the point that if I got over there and, after giving it an honest go, it wasn't where I wanted to be, I could always pack up and come home. But that I couldn't really make the choice between there, or here, until I knew something of both places."

"So you went," he said, and she nodded.

"I knew it wouldn't be permanent, that I wanted to come back home. That didn't change. But as I settled in there, I discovered the experiences

I was having would shape all that was to come when I returned, and that it was the right time, maybe the only time, I'd get the chance to do it. I kind of surprised myself. Once I decided to stay for the full program, I dove all the way in. I loved my time there. I was able to explore my family's homeland, learn about my heritage. It really was a special time."

"It's hard to predict what you'll be willing to do until you're invested enough to know," he said.

"Exactly." She grinned. "Of course, my mom and dad tried to use my enthusiasm for Italy to get me to continue my international education, maybe apply for additional courses in Belgium and France. But the moment I had that degree in my hands, I was on a plane back to Maine. Being in Italy helped to really clarify what I wanted for my future." She lifted a shoulder. "And that was to build my life here. I'm not like my parents, with that unending curiosity to go and see everything there is to see. I'm more like Sofia, wanting that grounded feeling of hearth and home, and working to carve out my place in my community, make the people in it happier."

Caleb leaned back and pulled them both to the center of the bed. He propped up some pillows and leaned back against them, and she curled up next to him, her head on his shoulder, arm across his waist. The intimacy felt normal; they fitted together well, as if they had lain like this often.

"I didn't go to Greece for a proper education," he told her, "but I have been there to see family and, like you, learn more about my heritage." His grin matched hers. "I did a lot of cooking while I was there, but nothing formal."

"You probably learned just as much, if not more, from your family's recipes, especially in the old country."

He nodded. "I think so. Like you, I knew I was coming back home, so I was always thinking of that as I tried new things, learned new techniques or recipes. How I could work them to fit in with our menu at home. My stays there were a week here and a week there, not months or a year. But spending time in Greece has definitely fueled me. It feeds my soul, I guess you could say."

"You've never been tempted to pack up and move there? I've heard it's breathtakingly beautiful."

"It is," he said. "Any photos you've seen can't do it justice. But to answer your question . . . no. It's exactly what it's supposed to be to me. A time out of time, a place to go be inspired, so I can come back, like you, and share that with the people who mean the most to me."

"How did your aunt and uncle end up in Maine? From what you said, and what Sofia has told me, it sounds like both of their families are in and around Philadelphia. Are the two families also geographically close in Greece? How did they first meet?"

She could feel his smile against her hair as his cheek was resting on the top of her head. "How much has Sofia told you?"

Now it was her turn to smile. "I might have asked a few questions about the Castellanoses. And the Dimitrious."

"Was that before or after you dropped by with a box full of muffin porn."

She spluttered a laugh at his term, but given where it had led them, she couldn't exactly refute it. "Before," she said. Her thoughts shifted to the cookie he'd tried, but she really didn't want to go there. Not now. Not yet.

She'd initially planned to talk to Sofia, maybe even her mother, about the Bellaluna magic, about how, specifically, it worked. Of course, she'd pestered them with dozens of questions about it growing up, but they'd always put her off with a loving smile and a promise that she'd understand when she came into her own. Now that time had come, and she still had questions. Maybe more than she'd had before.

But once she'd left Castellanos the other day, she'd put off expanding that part of her education. How could Caleb be "the one"? Their lives were so fully committed to different places, and not simply to a job or career, but to family. If she'd started asking questions, especially with

Sofia knowing full well it had been Caleb who'd tasted her first magical cookie, she'd never hear the end of it. She'd decided she'd wait until Caleb was safely gone; then they'd talk. So she'd be ready. Next time.

Only that hadn't felt at all right, either. In fact, it had felt dead wrong. Then she'd woken up in the middle of the night with that sick ball of dread in her gut. She'd often heard how members of a family had a sixth sense when one of their own was in trouble. But that didn't explain Caleb. He wasn't one of her own. *Isn't he, though?*

"So, are you trying to tell me that you want me for my mad skills with sugar and butter?" She'd meant it as a tease, but somehow it had come out sounding a lot more serious.

He rolled her to her back, surprising a little squeal out of her, then a soft moan when she felt his weight on top of her. *Finally.*

"You had me with that first smile." He leaned down and kissed a spot on her cheek, then another, then another. Then a kiss to her forehead, and one to the tip of her nose. "And these are pretty beguiling, too."

"Beguiling? My . . . freckles?"

"What can I say," he murmured, as he made his way across her cheek and down the other side of her neck. "I'm a connect-the-dots enthusiast."

That got another choke of laughter out of her,

and she heard and felt him chuckling, too, as he continued his path.

She squirmed beneath him, trying not to push her hips up against him. Failing. "I thought we were going to do this the right way," she managed on a gasp as he slid her bra strap over her shoulder.

"This feels pretty right," he said, his voice even deeper now, with a hint of a rasp to it. However, he reluctantly slid the strap up and lifted his weight off her, eventually settling them back into their previous positions.

She was still trying to get her body to calm the heck right back down, and her line of vision, with her head tucked against his bare chest, gave her plenty of proof that he was having to do the same thing.

She felt him press another kiss to the top of her head, and decided she liked those kisses, liked that he punctuated their conversation that way.

"I just wanted you to know, it's not about the muffins, or the cookie," he said. "This is about you." There was reverence in his voice when he added, "They're just a really, *really* nice bonus."

She gently knuckled him in the ribs, making him wince and laugh at the same time. "I suppose I should be careful teasing you. You haven't cooked for me yet."

He pulled her closer, settled them more deeply

into the pillows. "We can take care of that tomorrow."

"I'd like that." She lifted her head and looked up at him. "A lot."

She leaned her head on his shoulder again. "So, tell me how your aunt and uncle ended up in Maine. Are there other Castellanoses or Dimitrious up here?" Her mouth curved. "Somehow we got sidetracked. Again."

He kicked up the folded blanket at the foot of the bed and spread it over the two of them. She settled back against his side, his arm wrapped around her.

"It was for Alethea," he said. "She was just out of nursing school and George was working in his parents' restaurant. His younger brother and one of his cousins run it now. He and his folks didn't necessarily see eye-to-eye on how to run the business." Amused, he added, "He was young and full of ideas and thought he knew everything. Right at that time, through one of her school connections, Alethea got a really good job offer up here in Maine. They were young newlyweds and ready for some adventure. So, they came up here, fell in love with the town. George found this old building, rundown and abandoned. An eyesore, basically. As I understand it, he made some kind of deal with the bank that owned it and the two made this space into a little apartment so they didn't have the added expense

114

of renting one. She worked any shift she could get and he put the sweat equity into getting the building renovated. It took them a good couple of years to see it done, but then Castellanos finally opened—"

"And it's been something of a landmark in Moonbright ever since," she finished for him. "They're still close to their families, though, right? Your family and George's?"

"Other than the folks back in Greece, they are the only ones not in Philadelphia, but yes. There is no ill will, if that's what you mean. That they ended up not having children sort of made it easier for them. I think the families would have had a harder time if they'd started a whole branch up here and they couldn't all regularly get together. George and Alethea come down from time to time, but all in all, we don't see them all that much, nor they us." He nudged her so she looked up at him. "It's not like we have a rule that you can't cross state lines. We're all free to go and do whatever we want. We'd have family support, no one would want to see us fail, or be unhappy. My parents are gone, so in that regard, my siblings and I have more of a sense of freedom." He smiled. "My sister has definitely taken advantage of that. We don't stay close to each other because we think we have to, but—"

"Because you want to," she said softly. "I know what you mean. I wish, often, that my mom and dad were more like Sofia and me. I would love to have them around all the time."

"I know some of the younger relatives, my cousins' children, will likely not follow in the family footsteps. They're already scattering off to colleges here and there and . . . so times are changing." He trailed off then, and she could feel the restless tension seep back into his body.

"And now George and your aunt are in Greece on a much-deserved, much-delayed honeymoon," she said, quietly though. She tipped her head up and rested her chin on the hand she'd pressed against his chest. "But all is not right in Castellanos-ville, is it?" she asked gently. "Sofia said there's been some talk about the restaurant being closed all week. Nothing bad," Bree hastened to add. "I think folks assume it's because they went on this dream trip. But—"

"But why bring his nephew up if he's going to keep the place closed," Caleb finished for her.

"You don't have to talk about it," she said. "I just thought you'd want to know."

"No, it's okay. Actually, and this will sound weird, I guess, but I've wanted to talk to you about it. My sister, Cassandra, is here, and she's great at—"

Bree lifted her head straight up. "Your sister is here? In Moonbright?" She immediately looked toward the open door to the tiny living room.

He chuckled. "She's staying out at George and Alethea's."

Bree let out a long breath and let her head drop back to his chest, laughing at herself. "Yeah, I guess you wouldn't have carried me off to bed with your sister sleeping on the couch. Sorry. I just—"

He shifted so he could lean down and catch her mouth with his. The kiss started out gentle, sweet, but quickly turned into more. He lifted his head. "I'd like to think I wouldn't have," he told her. A slow smile curved his lips. "But until we get done doing this the right way, I make no promises."

She laughed at that and gave him a fast kiss. "Me either," she said, wiggling her eyebrows. "So, why would I think it's weird you wanted to talk to me about it?"

"It's not because it involves you, or your grandmother, in any way. It was more like . . . I have this situation that I'm trying to figure out, I'm not sure how I want to handle it, and so the natural thing to do is go talk to Abriana about it. I wanted to run it past you, get your take. Like I would if . . ." He trailed off.

She decided she wasn't ever going to get tired of hearing him call her by her full name. Just the way he said it. "If we were together," she finished for him, realizing they did that for each other a lot. That didn't surprise her.

It was the very fact that they were so solidly on the same wavelength that she was lying where she was at the moment. Half dressed in an old, decidedly unsexy white bra and fleece leggings, with him shirtless and still in his belted khakis.

"So, talk to me now," she said quietly. "I don't know if I can help, but I'll do what I can." She laid her head back down, thinking it might be easier to talk about what was troubling him if he could just speak into the dimly lit room without having to look at her, or anything specific. The tiny lamp on the bedside table had been on when he'd carried her in. It cast a small pool of golden-yellow light that didn't reach much farther than the bed, creating a sense of intimacy, of privacy.

He pressed another kiss on her head and rubbed his hand down her arm, pulling her more snugly against him. He was silent for a few moments; then he said, "We didn't know—my brothers, my sister, or me—that George's restaurant was going to be closed when I got here. I came up expecting to take over the reins for six weeks or so, mostly just so he'd have a family member overseeing operations. That's kind of how we do things.

"I thought it was odd that the place was deserted when I got here, locked up tight, but thought maybe I'd misunderstood George and he'd closed for a few days between his leaving and my arriving. I started placing orders online with his list of vendors on Sunday so we could hit the ground running Monday. Only no one showed up Monday morning, no deliveries, either. I waited before going to the fish market and grocer until the sous chef and at least one of the line crew arrived, but no one showed."

"Except me," she said, understanding now why he'd been a bit distracted when she first got there. "I wondered the same thing," she admitted. "If maybe your uncle had closed for a day or two."

"I started looking through his order folders, then his books, thinking maybe I missed something."

"You talked to him directly before coming, right?"

"Briefly. George spoke first to my oldest brother, Lander, about setting it up. I talked to George directly while on the drive up here. He and Aunt Alethea were already at the airport. He just told me where to find things, who to call first, where he'd left the keys to the place and to his house. I . . . honestly, I didn't think anything sounded unusual, even looking back on it. He was a bit flustered, but I could hear an announcement for their flight in the background, and I wrote it off to being excited about the trip, maybe nervous about flying. He hasn't in a very long time, or so he told me."

"So, what is going on? Have you figured it out? Spoken to any of his employees? Or to him?

Did your brother fill you in on anything else he might have said? Maybe it's just a big misunderstanding."

"I reached out to the employees when no one showed up Monday. I haven't heard back from any of them, which sounds odd, I know, but I think they're protecting him, or covering for him—I don't know. I could push it, but I want to know more first."

"It sounds like there's something going on besides George just closing the place and not telling you."

He paused then, and she could feel and hear his sigh.

"It's okay, Caleb," she told him. "Truly. Anything you tell me will stay between us. I won't mention it to Sofia. But please don't feel you need to—"

"No, it might help to get your perspective. Cassi knows the whole story, but we're both very close to the situation. So, we see things through a filter of family and long-standing traditions. It's hard to be objective. You also understand the world of food, different from a place with a big staff, I know, but the dedication it takes to run a place and keep it going is much the same."

Bree listened as he told her about the money in and the money out not adding up, that they'd discovered George was behind in some of his utilities at the restaurant, and worse, he hadn't been able to pay all of his staff. Caleb and Cassi hadn't been able to find any big business expense to explain the lack of funds, or why he'd have gone about handling things as he had.

"Do you think it was this big trip to Greece?"

"I don't know. From what we gather, they're staying with family for the most part, same as I've done in the past. That's also tradition. Our relatives there would be insulted if we didn't. I'm sure there will be some sightseeing and so on, but this would not be an outrageously expensive trip. It's likely he'll never pay for a single meal there, either. Cassi is going to look to see what she can find while she's out at the house, bank records or whatever might shed some light."

"This might sound obvious, but why don't you just call him?"

Caleb sighed. "That's the tricky part. George did this for a reason. I'm guessing it's pride based, but he didn't tell anyone. And we're not sure what Alethea knows. I can't imagine she'd have let him whisk her off to Greece for more than a month if she knew the business was failing. Well, it's not failing, it seems to be quite healthy, but something is failing."

"Maybe you send him a text or e-mail or something, tell him to pick a time he can make a private call. Clearly he has to know the moment you got here you'd realize things weren't on the up-and-up."

"He's not a big technology guy. He doesn't do texting. Alethea handles all the phone interaction. I'm not sure who would see an e-mail first, either."

Bree sighed. "You're right. It is complicated. What about your brothers? What do they say?"

"They're great men, both of them, but a bit older than us, and a lot more old-school. They'd want to rally the troops and get the whole extended family on board. And trust me, there's nothing the Castellanoses and Dimitrious love more than some family drama or excitement. Any excuse to cook way too much moussaka and baklava, and gather around to solve everyone else's problems." He smiled. "Don't get me wrong. I have the most wonderfully big-hearted family ever, and they would literally give their home to someone in need, but they are a lot all at once, and they never forget. Anything. George could have put the word out himself and they'd have dropped everything and come running."

"But he didn't," Bree said, pondering everything Caleb had told her. "He just asked for you, didn't he?"

Surprised, Caleb said, "How did you—"

She lifted her head and smiled at him. "Because you're meant to be here." It was all suddenly starting to make sense to her. All the things Sofia and her mother had told her over the years when she would beg them to explain how the Bellaluna magic worked. Their magic was gentle, giving fate a little nudge, so destiny would have a chance to fulfill itself. Caleb had been called to Moonbright, put right in her path. He'd come into the shop right when she'd been trying to make her magical cookies. Because they were for him. He'd felt regret the moment she'd walked out of his kitchen. She'd woken up tonight, knowing he needed her.

Fate was all but screaming at them to get on with it already and make their destiny happen. The cookie might have made a lingering impression on him, but he'd told her he'd already been interested before then. He'd kissed her freckles, for goodness' sake. She smiled at that, too.

"So, what will you do when you figure out where the money went?" she asked him.

"Actually, that's exactly what I was thinking about when I came upstairs tonight. Cassi and I had gotten so fixated on figuring out what was going on, as if solving that mystery would solve everything else, that we sort of lost sight of the bigger picture."

"Which is?"

"We don't know what George wants," he said. "I don't know if he thought I'd go digging through his personal stuff. Maybe he chose me because, unlike my older brothers, I've never shown the least bit of interest in running a place of my own. I want to cook. Owners and managers don't get to do that. I like taking care of my kitchen staff, but I don't want to be responsible for staffing, or hiring or firing, or—"

"Preaching to the choir," she said with a soft laugh. "We don't have staff, or operate in the chaos that you do, but while I absolutely do want to own Bellaluna's one day and am thrilled that it's my birthright, I'd be even more thrilled if my mom felt the same way and wanted to actually run the place so I could just bake."

"So, what will you do when it passes to you?"

"Oh, I'll run it. Maybe with age will come wisdom," she joked. "Or the will to manage. Or maybe my mama will stop globe-trotting at some point and be content to pick up where Sofia leaves off. She's great with people, too. Or I'll hire management help. I can't run it completely alone anyway. Whatever happens, Bellaluna's stays in the family. It means I get to be right where I want to be." She rested her head back on his chest. "It's like you said earlier. It's hard to predict what you'll be willing to do until you're invested enough to find out. I'm invested enough now to know I'll do whatever it takes."

He made a sound of agreement but didn't say anything. She felt him toying with her hair, and the little frissons of pleasure it sent trickling down her spine were so lovely, she closed her eyes and enjoyed the sensations.

After a few moments' thought, she said, "So,

you think maybe George believed you'd just turn around and go home?" She tried to hide the panic that possibility provoked.

"Good question," he said, then covered a yawn with his fist. "Cassi wants us to go talk to the older, long-term employees, see if we can get an idea what was really going on. I'm not sure I want to involve anyone else or signal to anyone that we're poking around." He settled down farther in the pillows and pulled the blanket up a little higher. "However we proceed, we will keep whatever we find to ourselves."

"And to me," she said, feeling drowsy now, too.

He leaned down and kissed the top of her head again. "And you."

"I won't tell," she said on a yawn of her own. "Not even Sofia."

"I know," he said, and snuggled her closer. "So, enough Greek drama. Tell me about Italy."

So, she did. And somewhere in the middle of her tales of sleepily told culinary school mishaps and meeting some of her relatives, they drifted off, and stayed that way, right up until Cassandra walked in on them the next morning.

Chapter 6

Here, Bree." Cassi passed her a stack of bank statements. "These are from last year."

Bree leaned forward from her cross-legged position on the floor of George Castellanos's living room and took the stack. "Do you think the problem would go back that far? We're almost at the end of this year."

Cassi lifted a shoulder. "I don't know. The books at the restaurant show the overhead so far this year had the typical fluctuation. Some expenses went up, but not enough to really impact the profit margin, much less wipe it out." She flipped through the stack of current statements in her hands. "But he's not depositing it. Well, not all of it. He's got a new mortgage on the house that he took out just this spring. My aunt and uncle owned it outright before that. But it wasn't for a lot of money. Less than fifty thousand dollars. And he's making payments on that on time."

Caleb was seated on the couch. He turned one of the composition notebooks around. "This one is for this quarter. There have been layoffs, but

George is still turning over the same number of tables every night, so the employees he kept were working more. He didn't start cutting back on their hours until just last month." Caleb set the book down. "From the two Cassi spoke to this morning before giving us our wake-up call, they didn't seem mad at George, but they didn't want to talk about it."

Caleb noticed Bree's cheeks flush a little at his comment about the wake-up call, but Cassi spoke first. "Don't go making her feel self-conscious there, *adelfouli*. I've already profusely apologized. If it were Matty, I'd have knocked first. I just never expected . . ." She trailed off and looked at Bree. "We're good, right?" Bree laughed and nodded, and Cassi added, "Besides, you should take that as a good sign. He's not a hound dog like our other brother. I mean, you were both still half dressed." She turned to Caleb. "Maybe you should talk to Matty. Your skill set might need a little boost."

Bree shocked both brother and sister by saying, "Oh, I don't think that will be necessary."

Caleb choked on a short laugh and felt his own cheeks heat. "Okay, okay. My love life—our love life—is officially off-limits for discussion."

Cassi hooted with laughter. "Have you met our family?" She turned to Bree. "You might want to bide your time, build up your Dimitriou defenses a little, before letting him bring you to Philly.

Maybe we should send Matty and Lander up here first, you know, as a warm-up." She turned to Caleb. "And Aunt Daphne."

"The one with the cats?" Bree asked.

Cassi sent a surprised look from Bree to her brother and back to Bree. "Oh, so you're already hearing the stories. Well, wait till you get to hear the stories about this one."

Caleb shot his sister a brilliant smile. "I'm rethinking the seating for Thanksgiving this year. How do you feel about taking that spot between cousin Eudora and Uncle Santos?"

Cassi turned an equally blinding smile to Bree. "I love Maine. Could you recommend a good real-estate agent to me? And do you happen to have room at your table this Thanksgiving? I make an amazing baklava."

Without missing a beat, Bree said, "There will always be a chair for you. Sadly, we'll have only the one, so I guess Caleb will have to take your seat in Philly." Both women turned to him as if on cue with sad, pouty faces. "Poor Caleb."

He shook his head. "I never should have let the two of you meet."

"I don't recall there being any 'letting' about it," Cassi said, then turned to Bree. "He might not be a hound dog, but he is still a Greek. And a man." She patted Bree's knee. "We'll talk later. Also, I would love a tour of your kitchen. I've heard wonderful things, like you have an anise

129

pear muffin?" She grinned. "So much to talk about."

Caleb just groaned and turned back to his notebooks. "As I was saying before I lost complete control of my life, it sounds like George's employees were really loyal to him."

She nodded. "They both said they wanted to stay as long as they could. They could see that the restaurant was still doing good business. They were more worried about George than anything." She shook her head. "But they're loyal to him, they won't speak ill of him. I think they'd come back if they could. He's a beloved man, from everything I can tell. And I still believe he wouldn't stiff his own staff unless it was something . . . I don't even know. What would it have to be? What could be more important to him than that? To make him risk his good name, his wife's good name?"

"Do you think it could be something like gambling debts?" Bree offered, then immediately lifted her hand when both siblings turned to her, surprise on their faces. "I'm not casting aspersions. I just know that might be the kind of thing where you get in over your head with very few options to get back out again. It can be like an addiction, right? I was just trying to think what kinds of payments wouldn't go out from the bank or show as being paid by a check or credit card. The missing money isn't stashed in a savings

130

account, and we can't find any evidence of some other account he might have opened."

"I can't imagine George getting into trouble like that," Caleb said.

"Well, if he got himself in deep enough, maybe there were threats made." Bree shrugged, then gave them a rueful smile. "I watch too much crime-of-the-week TV, but that is a real thing, right? Bookies? Or whatever? Assuming the money isn't going into an account somewhere, then maybe it's being paid to someone, most likely in cash since we can't find any paper trail. That's the only thing I can think of that might result in having to make regular, large, off-book cash payments."

"No offense taken," Caleb said, feeling a bit shaken by the possibility. "It's a logical con-clusion. Just . . . I find it really hard to believe of George. He's never even been a sports fan. From what I can tell by the time clock cards—which he was old-fashioned enough to use, even for himself—he was pretty much always at work, or here with Alethea. He didn't even play golf, or cards, or whatever," Caleb added. "Alethea had more regular hours, but George was always at the restaurant. No regular time off or any other kinds of expenditures that would indicate he took off for the track or to some other kind of thing, like a casino. If there is even anything like that around here."

"I think you can do that kind of thing online now," Bree offered.

Cassi brightened at that suggestion. "Maybe that is a clue, though." She glanced up at Caleb. "Maybe we should look at George's computer. I know he's so old-school he even does all his banking in person, but there is an old desktop model in the office. I saw it when I went looking for files. We can look at the search history or list of sites he's visited. That might tell us a lot."

"Considering he still gets paper statements for everything and doesn't even have a debit card, I'm not sure how much we'll learn," Caleb said, "but it's definitely an overlooked resource." He turned to Bree. "Thank you," he said sincerely. "That's the kind of outside perspective I was talking about."

Cassi got up and stretched. "Okay, I'll go see if I can boot up the old thing. He's so technology averse, I never thought about it. Silly, really. Thanks, Bree."

Bree nodded and Cassi fluttered her fingers at the two of them. "Please feel free to get all googly-eyed and mushy-faced while I'm gone. I've sworn off all that for at least a year, so I could do without the reminder of what I'm missing." She smiled sweetly at them both, then did a little boogie as she strolled out of the room.

"Why have you sworn off romance?" Caleb

called out after her, suddenly concerned. "Did something happen?"

"You're wasting smoochy time," she called back. "And don't worry," she added dryly, "I'll be sure to make a lot of noise before I come into the room this time."

Caleb chuckled and turned to find Bree had both hands covering her face.

"She's just teasing," he said. "Though I guess I should warn you, that will never end."

"I consider myself warned," Bree said, letting her hands fall back to her lap. She was smiling. "I like her. A lot. She's so different from you and yet you're really great together. I don't have siblings, and I've always wondered how I'd have felt about it." She grinned. "I liked being an only. But it might have been cool to have a big brother." She tapped her chin and her expression turned to one of consideration. "As long as he didn't try to take over the kitchen."

"I have two brothers I'll be more than happy to loan out," he said. "Though no promises on that last part." Caleb stood and stretched his arms over his head, then raked his hands through his hair. He was going to go cross-eyed if he had to stare at statements and handwritten ledgers for even another minute. He offered her his hand. "Let's go see if there's something we can scrounge up for lunch." He rubbed his flat stomach with his other hand. "I'm starved."

"You fed us this morning like you were cooking for an army of ten," she said, looking surprised. "I won't need to eat for a week."

He grinned. "More for me, then. I knew we made a good pair."

She laughed and took his hand. He pulled her to her feet and conveniently right into his arms. He smiled down into her face, thinking that the world around them might be confusion and chaos, but at that particular moment, he was right where he wanted to be.

"So," Bree said, giving his admittedly smug expression a considering look of her own, "this brother of yours, Matteo? He sounds interesting."

Caleb bent his head down and kissed her. Gently at first, then with a little more heat, and that was just the first part.

"Matty who?" she said faintly, when he finally lifted his head.

Caleb grinned, liking the pink flush on her cheeks, already hungry to feel those bow-tie lips on his again. "Looks like my moves are getting smoother," he told her, then wiggled his eyebrows. "My glasses didn't fog this time."

She surprised him by moving in closer. "Then I must not be doing my part right." She pulled his head down and kissed him, and took her sweet time about it, too. They both laughed when they finally opened their eyes and there was a distinct mist on his lenses.

He slid them off to clean them and she held his hand down by their side, smiling into his eyes. "Ah, I see your plan now," he said.

"Guilty," she said. "I can't help it, I like looking at them. I always wanted an actual eye color," she told him. "Yours are so beautiful."

He leaned in and dropped a short kiss on her mouth. "I rather like the magic of yours."

She blinked at that, looking startled. "What did you say?"

He faltered for a moment, but couldn't see how there was any offense in his observation. "Just that I never know what color yours will be. They're kind of grayish blue with a little brown when you're laughing or smiling." He tipped her chin up and very slowly, very deliberately, took her mouth in a deep, scorching kiss. When he lifted his head, his smile was slow. "And more of a grayish green when you're aroused. Magical."

She smiled, but something else flickered in her expression, and he couldn't tell if it was a bad thing, but it wasn't clearly a good thing, either.

"What did I say?" he asked quietly. "I meant it as a compliment."

"I know," she said. "And I like it. I do." She smiled then, and it was sincere. "I've never had cool eyes before. I'll take it."

She was avoiding something, though, and it really gave him pause. The one thing about Abriana that drew him in so fully and had moved things forward between them so swiftly was her absolute openness. She was right up front, no games, no guessing what she was really thinking. Whatever subject came up, whatever they talked about, there was some connection. Oftentimes it was their like-mindedness, and where they differed, there was sincere interest to know more.

When two people were being so transparent, there was no time wasted. He always knew where they both stood, and to his utter delight, that was most often right where they were just now. Deep in each other's personal space, laughing, talking, wanting.

Maybe he was hoping for too much, wanting immediate, full access. He tried to think of a single thing he wouldn't be willing to tell her, or discuss with her, but nothing came to mind. He truly was an open book. And he'd thought the same of her. So it was a tiny bit disconcerting to discover there was at least one part of herself she was holding back.

If he needed a cold dousing of reality to slow down this fantasy relationship train, this might be the thing to do it. Trust was important to him. Imperative. But did that mean he had the right to expect her to be willing to reveal all to him? Or was the real meaning of trust that he believed if it was something he needed to know, she'd tell him, but otherwise he should respect her silence?

"I'm sorry," she said, and he realized that his thoughts must have shown on his face.

"There's nothing to apologize for. Just because I want to know everything about you doesn't mean I have the right to expect you to tell me everything. I respect your privacy. It's your business."

She ducked her chin, took a moment, then looked back at him. "Thank you," she said. "I want to talk about it. I want to tell you everything." A smile teased the corner of her mouth. "Bore you to tears, make you wish you'd never asked."

Her admitting there was indeed something she was keeping from him jarred him. He'd been hoping he was just being hyperaware. "Somehow I doubt that," he said, and reached up to tuck a strand of hair behind her ear. He waited for her to assure him that it wasn't anything he needed to worry about, or didn't pertain to them, but she didn't say anything more. Then another thought occurred to him. "Are you?" he asked.

"Am I what?"

"Having doubts?"

"About . . . this? Us?" She laughed. "Of course I am. Like a dozen of them every other minute. It's kind of terrifying, actually, when I let myself think about it."

That was the kind of thing that should have given him pause. Instead, her immediately laying out her truth without even pausing to think about how it might sound actually had him relaxing a bit. That was the Abriana Bellaluna O'Neill he was falling in love with.

"Good," he said, and might have actually sighed a little in relief.

"Good?" Now her eyebrows climbed. "Are you having second thoughts?"

"No, no," he assured her. "I meant good that you're—that we're—being realistic about this. It is a whole lot, all at once."

"It is," she said. "But if we only have six weeks, then . . ."

Now he frowned. "Wait—"

She reached up and pushed at the curls that fell over his forehead, her smile reassuring. "Six weeks to get invested enough to know what we'll be willing to do to keep it. Wise words from some guy I met in my kitchen."

He bent down and kissed her, thinking he already had his answer. For as long as she'd have him, he wanted a life that had Abriana right in the middle of it. What that meant he'd have to do, he wasn't sure. "Well, if we spend enough time together, the solutions might eventually present themselves. We just need to know enough to make the right choice. Something I learned from this baker who once tried to seduce me with sugar and Italian cream."

She ducked her chin, but he didn't miss the

return of that flicker. Then she was looking up at him again and her smile was sincere, her gaze open and directly on his as she slid her arms around his waist. "Is it working?"

Whatever he might have said to that was lost when Cassi spoke from the door to the living room. "I haven't found proof, but I think I know where the money is going."

Caleb and Bree's expressions simultaneously went slack at Cassi's solemn tone. Caleb turned to find his normally buoyant sister looking very small, and far too young, as she stood in the doorway, a clutch of printouts in her hand.

"What is it?" Caleb asked, and both he and Bree immediately crossed the room to her.

Cassi entered haltingly and sank down on the edge of the couch. Bree sat beside her and Caleb crouched down in front her. "*Athelfi*," he said, "tell us?"

She looked up and her pretty blue eyes swam with tears. "It's Aunt Alethea," she said. "They're not in Greece for a belated honeymoon." She lifted the sheaf of papers. "Or maybe they started there, for Alethea, so she could have her long-awaited trip first."

"First?" Caleb covered his sister's hand and felt the trembling there. "Cassi," he said, his voice gentle but urgent.

"I think they're actually in Switzerland." Her voice hitched as her breath caught in her throat.

"All that money . . . George used it to pay for her to get experimental treatment. She has a rare blood disorder, Cay." Tears spilled down her cheeks. "A rare, high-mortality-rate blood disorder."

Chapter 7

A h, *mimma*, come here." Sofia had taken one look at her and pulled Bree into a hug the moment she stepped into the kitchen at Bellaluna's. Even with the height difference, it felt so good and comforting. "Sit, sit," she said, and pulled a fresh hankie from her apron pocket. "I'll make tea and you can tell me what has gone wrong."

Bree knew better than to say no, or that she was fine. The truth was, she wasn't fine, and a cup of hot tea couldn't hurt. She pulled a stool over to one of the worktables, sat, and rested her head on her folded arms while Sofia started up the kettle she always kept simmering and went into the office to get her box of special blend tea. It wasn't magical, but it might as well have been.

Bree lifted her head when Sofia slid the delicate china cup in front of her. "Thank you, *Nonna*."

Sofia pulled up a stool and perched next to Bree, her own steaming teacup close at hand. "So, this morning you asked for some time to spend with Caleb and his sister, Cassandra. You sounded so happy. What has happened?"

141

"I'm still happy," Bree said. Caleb had given his blessing to Bree's sharing the information with her grandmother. He understood better than pretty much anyone how important it was to have family support during challenging times. It was why he'd welcomed Cassi's surprise arrival in Maine.

Even though this wasn't happening to someone in Bree's family, it was happening to someone her grandmother called friend. Caleb had believed that Sofia could be trusted to handle the news with utmost discretion. Bree had debated not telling her, because she didn't want to make her grandmother sad. But she also wanted to talk to her *nonna* about Caleb, and about those iced Italian cookies. It just seemed best to handle things as was the Bellaluna way, directly and honestly.

Bree took Sofia's hand, and in that instant, the concern that had colored Sofia's brown eyes took on a more worried look. "I have some difficult news," Bree said.

Sofia turned over the hand Bree had covered, then laid her other hand on top and squeezed Bree's palm between them. "Give your burden to me, *mimma*," she said. "A burden shared is a burden lightened."

"It's about Alethea Castellanos. And about George, and the restaurant." Bree held Sofia's gaze. "You must keep this between us."

"Of course," Sofia said easily. "Come now. Ease yourself."

Bree told her the whole story, leaving out only the part about her spending the night in Caleb's bed and being found there by his sister. Not that Sofia wouldn't have understood, she was a progressive and pragmatic thinker on such things, but this was about the Castellanoses, not about her and Caleb. Not yet, anyway. She would get there, too, eventually.

She told Sofia about George taking money from the restaurant profits to help pay for Alethea's treatment, how the new mortgage had been for that, too, but they'd underestimated how much it would take and hadn't asked for enough. Then the disease began progressing faster than anticipated, and George panicked and did the only thing he knew to do.

"We would have helped them," Sofia said. "His family would have, too."

"Alethea didn't want them to know," Bree told her. "She didn't want anyone to know. She just wanted to live out her days with her husband in peace. That's why she retired sooner than she'd originally planned. But George, the man who doesn't even operate his cell phone, wasn't ready to accept that fate for his wife. So he started doing research, and he found the treatment facility overseas. The process is new, and largely untested, which is why it's not available here. At

George's urging, she's agreed to be part of the test group."

"I can understand this," Sofia said, nodding. "Troubling times make for tough decisions. I just feel sad they had to contend with that extra burden."

Bree nodded. "George wanted to keep his promise to his wife, take her back to Greece. She has medication that keeps her fairly steady. She sleeps more and needs occasional transfusions, but they timed the trip to work around that. They didn't stay long in Greece, just two days, but she did get to see her family. Then they flew to Switzerland and entered her into the treatment center. The relatives in Greece thought the two had simply gone on to do some sightseeing, sail to some of the Greek Islands, enjoy their long-delayed honeymoon."

"So, Caleb has spoken to George and Alethea directly, then," Sofia asked. "It's all been sorted out."

"Yes," Bree said. "Caleb and his sister called them right after I left. Caleb said I could stay, but I felt like that conversation should be private, and I also knew I'd imposed on you enough today. They didn't talk long. Caleb called me when I went home to take a shower and change for work. I think the only thing we're still not sure about is why he asked that it be Caleb who came, but—"

"Because he would be the one to handle it the

way George wanted it handled," Sofia said. Then a brief smile touched her lips. "And because it was his destiny to meet you."

Bree smiled at her grandmother but said nothing. She had plenty of questions regarding all of that, but this needed to be talked about first.

"Did they have word, on the treatment? Or is it too soon?" Sofia asked.

"Too soon," Bree said. "No word at all on that yet, except Alethea is there and is in the program." Before Sofia could ask, Bree added, "They don't know what the best prognosis is. George didn't offer specifics. He's being strong for his wife, but Caleb said he's barely holding it together, that he's never heard his uncle sound so shattered. So, I feel like this is a last-ditch effort. The information Cassi found on the subject didn't really elaborate, other than to say that in the previous studies, the treatment had been shown to significantly slow down the progression of the disease. So that, at least, seems like a good sign."

Sofia nodded. "Alethea is strong, and she has much to fight for. She will do as well as is possible, this I know. And George will be there for her."

Bree smiled briefly, thinking she didn't want to imagine what would happen to George if he lost his wife. Caleb had been so worried about whether or not to dig into his uncle's affairs, about his pride, but George was well beyond caring about any of that now. "You'll be a good cheerleader for Alethea when she gets back."

Sofia's expression brightened. "That's the spirit," she said, then squeezed Bree's hands again. "Now, no more solemn faces. We must send only positive thoughts to her, and to George." She slid her hands from Bree's and picked up her tea, nodding to Bree to do the same.

Bree had just taken a sip when Sofia said, "Now, when it comes to your young man, your true love, don't let your magic confuse you, *cuore mia*."

Bree might have choked, just a little. She pressed a napkin to her mouth, but before she could recover and say anything, Sofia continued.

"I blame myself for not being more forthright as you've become an adult. You're not the dreamer that your mother was, or the hopeless romantic I was." She smiled then, a bit wistfully. "You're the pragmatic one. You expect to mix ingredients together and get a certain outcome based on their elemental properties, and that allows you to dream up combinations I'd never imagine."

"You're so much more creative than I am, though," Bree protested. "I always feel like a mad scientist whose lab just happens to be a kitchen. Your recipes are like works of art; mine are far more prosaic."

"We come at baking from different angles, you

and I, and your mother has her own way as well. But your results are no less of a success than mine. I am continually inspired by you, *tesoro mia*."

Bree flushed with pleasure at that sincere compliment. She liked being her grandmother's treasure. The feeling was reciprocated, tenfold. "Thank you, *Nonna*. From you that means everything."

Sofia nodded, pleased, then said, "I mention this, because while your methods stand you in good stead in the kitchen, I feared your using the same practical, sensible approach to life might keep you from ever willingly giving your heart."

Bree opened her mouth to protest, then closed it again. Unsurprisingly, her grandmother had a point.

Sofia took another savoring sip; then the curve of her lips deepened. "Then I watched you come alive the moment dear Caleb stepped through those doors, and I knew my worries were for naught." She lifted a slender shoulder. "You simply hadn't met him yet." She set her cup down and placed her hand on Bree's arm, her delighted expression turning a bit more serious. "But perhaps I did not prepare you as well as I should have. Even looking at your destiny and seeing all the potential that is there, you're still applying logic and reason." She lifted her carefully penciled brows. "And I suspect you're a little worried that your dear Caleb is enchanted, that his feelings for you aren't founded in reality." She squeezed Bree's arm. "Nothing could be further from the truth. He was as captivated as you were. In fact, your fate didn't even need that little nudge." Her soft eyes twinkled with affection. "But it was lovely seeing you come into your own."

Bree had already come to these conclusions herself, but every time Caleb mentioned anything to do with magic, she realized that she still had her doubts. "So . . . he's not still 'affected' by that cookie?" Bree asked, using air quotes.

"My darling *mimma*, he was 'affected,' as you say, the moment he laid eyes on you."

Bree laughed at her grandmother's mimicking of the air quotes, though the laugh was also partly in relief. Maybe a lot in relief. She'd known the truth, had seen it with her own eyes, felt it in her heart, but hearing it from someone who shared this strange new gift she'd just discovered for herself was more needed than even she had realized.

"Was he similarly affected by those muffins? There was no magic, then," Sofia pointed out.

Bree nodded, thinking it all sounded so obvious when her grandmother explained it. But there were still a few unanswered mysteries. "You have no idea how happy I am to talk about this with you." She sipped the last of her tea and set her cup aside. "There is one other thing, though. Well, there will likely be many other things, but there is one thing I'm curious about now."

"If I can help you to understand, I will," Sofia said.

Bree told Sofia about taking the muffins to Caleb, and how their meeting had ended up with them deciding that because their lives were grounded in two separate places, they wouldn't pursue the attraction they felt. She left out the soul-searing kiss part, but wouldn't have been surprised if Sofia somehow knew about that, too. In fact, *knowing things* was the reason she'd shared the story. "So, Caleb and I made a decision not to pursue things. And we didn't. I went my way; he went his. We didn't see each other, not even by chance, or talk to each other. No phone calls, no texts. At that point I had no idea what was happening at the restaurant, though I did think it odd the morning I was there that it was utterly quiet, with no one in the kitchen but Caleb. Still, I honestly didn't give that another thought." She smiled. "I had a harder time not thinking about Caleb, but my decision hadn't wavered. Then, very suddenly, I woke up in the middle of the night last night, feeling this overwhelming sense of urgency."

Sofia didn't look particularly surprised or concerned by this, and Bree wasn't sure if that should reassure her or not. She'd been kind of hoping that maybe her premonition had nothing to do with Bellaluna magic and was just one of those sixth sense things.

She explained the rest of the story to Sofia, up to her knocking on the door to the third-floor apartment. "The moment I saw him, the urgency vanished." She snapped her fingers. "Just like that."

"Are you asking if that feeling, demanding you go to him, is also part of your magic?"

Bree nodded, and waited.

Sofia nodded also and was serious when she spoke. "When we give our little assist to those couples whom fate sends our way, neither of them has any awareness of that magical little push. With you, however, as it was with me and your mother, it's a bit different."

"Did Mom and Dad need that nudge? I know they met here."

"Your mother was very much a dreamer and had no qualms about tying herself to your father's wandering star. His fortunes shifted right about the time you came along, with his first book being published, allowing them to settle in to a life here that was, at least for a time, more grounded. And now, they are off again together, as they are meant to be."

"So, no cookie for them?" Bree asked with a smile.

Sofia leaned closer and whispered, "I might

have hedged my bets." She placed a fingertip along the side of her nose. "That stays here in this kitchen."

Bree was still grinning ear to ear as she nodded, delighted by the story and the shared secret. "And you and *Nonno*?"

"My mother did not offer him the cookie, no," Sofia said. "I was smitten from the moment I laid eyes on him." She let out a little laugh then and shook her head, her cheeks taking on a delightful hint of pink. "Perhaps I have a bit of a practical side, too, though."

Bree's eyes widened. "You hedged your own bets?"

She lifted a slim shoulder. "I didn't think it would hurt matters. I wasn't sure he was as smitten as I was. I wanted to make sure he stuck around long enough to figure out that he was."

Bree laughed. "And? Did he need that extra nudge?"

"I think we'd have found our way, but I have no regrets about ensuring we had the time we needed. I loved your grandfather with every breath I took. I'd have done more than offer him a bite of Bellaluna magic if I thought it would make him mine."

Bree sighed, delighted, her heart squeezing with memories of her beloved *nonno*, who had always looked at his wife with adoration, as if he was continually discovering new reasons to love her. "So, did you always know things about him? Like if he was in distress, or needed you? Or with mom when she was a baby? Or even now?"

"We all have a sense when someone we love needs us," Sofia said. "To me, love is like a gossamer thread that binds us all to each other, and we feel a tug on it if one of us is faltering."

"But Caleb wasn't—I mean, he's not my— we're just starting out."

"I think you know the answer to that," was all Sofia said with a knowing smile. "You may not be ready to claim it as yet, and that's to be expected. You are in the early days, which are a delight of brand-new discovery. That will continue, throughout your life. Don't rush them, *tesoro mia*. Follow your path—it will always lead you to the next thing. You must savor where you are and not be in a hurry."

Bree nodded again and let her grandmother's wisdom sink in. She didn't want to rush her time with Caleb. She was in no hurry to get to the day he would need to leave, or the decisions that they would have to make when that day finally arrived. "What was my sense of urgency about, though?" she asked, thinking back to how she'd felt that night. "He wasn't in danger, he wasn't ill or hurt."

"He wasn't the one in danger, *mimma*," Sofia told her softly. "You were. Or perhaps you both were. In danger of losing each other for good.

You said he'd just come to the conclusion that maybe he'd be better off leaving Castellanos closed up and head back to Philadelphia. That's why the urgency didn't leave until you'd actually gone up to see him."

Bree smiled as the final pieces fell into place. "Giving fate another little nudge."

Sofia nodded and slid off her stool, carrying both of their cups to the sink. She paused beside Bree to press a kiss to her cheek. "You will feel things more strongly, *mimma*," she said, so softly that the words just reached Bree's ear. "Sense things. See things that others will miss. This gift will stand you in good stead." She shifted back enough to make direct eye contact. "You'll learn how to manage it, and you'll be able to look after those who matter to you just a little bit better. Yes?"

Bree nodded, taking in a steadying breath and releasing it, but with a tentative smile on her face. "Ready, set, here I go."

Sofia nodded, looking satisfied. She pressed another kiss to Bree's cheek, then took their tea cups to the sink.

Bree tried to sort through all the dozens of thoughts and feelings that were filtering through her. It was a lot to take in. "Do I tell him?" she asked. She thought about her father, and her grandfather, who hadn't passed until she was a teenager. They'd never spoken directly about the magic, and her mother and grandmother never spoke directly to them about it, but Bree felt they'd always known. They had to know, didn't they? She couldn't imagine keeping something that was such a special part of who she was, of her heritage, a secret from Caleb much longer. It already felt wrong, not telling him. She just didn't know how without his thinking she was crazy.

Sofia turned then. "You won't have to find the words. Just be yourself and be open to things, and to him. He'll come to know. It will just be one more special thing about you for him to love."

Bree nodded, relieved, but left wondering if she'd start reading minds herself now, because she was becoming more convinced that Sofia had a much broader range of magic than she'd shared with her only granddaughter. "Yet," Bree whispered, then smiled to herself.

Feeling more optimistic than she had since she'd made the decision to stay with Caleb last night, she stood and went to get her apron. Taking the morning off to be with Caleb and Cassi had put her far behind in baking stock for the day and prepping for tomorrow. She and Sofia fell into their rhythms naturally and easily, each one lost in her own thoughts.

Bree didn't want to think about how she would be able to pursue a future with Caleb, what choices she would be willing to make, but it was impossible not to start considering what their choices might be, and what each of them might be willing to do in order to be together. And that led her to another question, possibly the most important one of all.

"*Nonna*," she said, when Sofia bustled into the back an hour later.

Sofia arranged the cupcakes Bree had just finished on the two-tiered glass stand she'd carried into the kitchen. "What is it, *bella*?"

"What would you have done if I'd turned out more like mom? If I'd wanted to wander the globe with them rather than stay in one place, stay here and bake? What would have become of Bellaluna's?"

Sofia took the question in stride; in fact, it seemed as if she'd been waiting for it. She finished arranging the cupcakes just so before looking at her granddaughter. "I don't know," she said, simply. "I don't worry about such things." She smiled. "Given time, *mimma*, and an open mind, solutions always present themselves. That is when you make your decisions." With that, she lifted the display and headed back out front, where Bree could hear the shop was doing a brisk business.

Bree nodded, not sure if she felt better for Sofia's reassurances or more concerned. For her part, whatever else happened, when it was decision-making time, Bree knew that the bakeshop's future had to remain secure. *But what if my decision ends up being heading to Philadelphia? What solution will there be for Bellaluna's then, Nonna?*

Chapter 8

It was ridiculous to be nervous now. Yes, it was finally time. He and Abriana were going to have their night. The whole night. Together. He was excited to spend time with her, away from their respective jobs and families, just the two of them. *So why are your palms sweating?*

Perhaps it was the other thing he planned to do. Before leaving with Bree, Caleb had made arrangements to see her grandmother first. Alone. Sofia had made it quite clear over the past month that she was very pleased with where things were headed between him and her only grandchild. But it was one thing for Bree's *nonna* to be happy that her granddaughter was dating. Quite another for her to entertain a young man who was planning to declare his intentions.

Caleb worried that Sofia would think it was too soon, but things had never moved slowly for him and Abriana, and with all that had happened since he'd decided to stay on in Moonbright for the full six weeks to help get Castellanos back up and running again, that pace had only accelerated.

Right after they'd found out the news about his

aunt, Caleb and Cassi had officially called in the troops. Their mission was to get Castellanos back open for business and help George get back on his financial feet. There were other debts he and Cassi hadn't found, so it was going to take some doing to get the restaurant back in the black. In the weeks since then, Caleb and Abriana had spent as much time together as possible, but they had rarely, if ever, been alone.

Added to that were all the preparations under way for the town's big annual Halloween festivities. The holiday brought with it a substantial increase in customer traffic, which affected both the bakeshop and the restaurant in a positive way for business, but made spending personal time together all but impossible. There was a steady influx of tourists in town for the fall colors, the pumpkin picking, and eventually the grand parade. That meant that Bree and her grandmother were every bit as tied to overseeing the bakeshop as he was to commandeering the new crew at Castellanos, most of whom he was related to and who weren't exactly used to taking orders from him.

They were lucky to carve out time for a quick lunch at Castellanos, or a kiss over the counter at Bellaluna's. They'd talked, with increasing frequency as time went on, about finally having their big night together, but Caleb had two cousins bunking in with him now in the tiny apartment over the restaurant, and, frankly, by the time they ended their respective days of chaos, they were fighting yawns more than they were fighting to keep their hands off each other.

Today, however, that was going to change. He suspected this evening, when they were no longer surrounded by multitudinous, if unintentional chaperones, they would quite gleefully put up no fight at all to keep their hands off each other. He was nervous about that, too. Not about the actual act, but . . . okay, maybe that, too. The long delay had just amped up their expectations. Or, at least that was what he worried might be the case.

He wanted this to be their *moment*. For her mostly, but for him, too. He'd begun wishing he hadn't stopped things that first night. There would never be a time between them that wasn't special, he knew that now, but because they had taken that extra time, planned or not, they knew each other far better now. How could the wait not raise expectations?

Phone conversations every morning, every night, often running well into the wee hours, a running day-to-day text conversation, and a few steamy kisses behind her business or his whenever they could sneak them in, might seem like a scattershot way to get to know someone, but though they had little time together, that continual stream of calls and texts had kept them connected off and on all day, every day.

Bree knew what was happening in his life as it happened, and vice versa. If either of them saw something, thought something, wanted to know something, or just plain flirt a little, or a lot, they shared it in a quick text. Bigger conversations were reserved for their morning and nighttime phone calls, when they often used video chat so they could see each other while talking, laughing that they needed to do that despite being just a few blocks apart. Hopefully that was going to change after today. Modern technology was wonderful. "But it doesn't replace the real thing," he murmured, as he climbed out of his car and straightened his jacket.

And the one very real thing he knew, after all this time, was that Abriana was the woman he wanted to take to bed, not just tonight, but every night for the rest of his life.

Which meant talking to Sofia.

Caleb looked at the back of Bellaluna's, thinking about how much his life had changed since he'd first seen the place. Smiling, thinking that sometimes change was pretty damn good, he took the short flight of steps up to the back door of the shop. The same door Sofia had asked him to use when he'd called her after getting to town, to let her know that Alethea had suggested he check in with her when he first arrived, to say hello. He hadn't used the back door then, thinking it seemed like a private, family entrance.

But he did now, and thought that had turned out as it should have, too.

"Come in, come in," Sofia said when she opened the door to him.

He took her hand and gave the back a quick kiss, then leaned in when she pointed to her cheek, and kissed that, too. It had become a little routine with them that he'd started as a joke. He'd swept up her hand and kissed it one day, thanking her with great gallantry for holding down the fort so Abriana could share a quick, surprise picnic lunch at the pumpkin patch with him. Sofia had just been so sweetly charmed by the gesture, he'd made a habit of it ever since.

"We'll talk in my office," she said. "The girls are handling the front, so we have a little time."

Caleb knew "the girls" were the high school girls who worked as part-time seasonal help. The kitchen was otherwise empty at the moment, save for the racks and racks of baked goods he knew Abriana had come in early to bake so they could have this extended time off alone together.

Sofia's office was a lovely mix of old-world antiques and feminine touches, which perfectly suited its owner. There were two comfortably padded chairs upholstered in lively floral prints facing a delicately scrolled teak desk. They both sat in the padded sitting chairs, leaving the chair behind her desk empty. This was far more up close and personal than Caleb had imagined, but he supposed it was also only right. He took a moment to gather his thoughts. He'd had a whole speech prepared. Not a single word of which he could remember now that Sofia was right there, with a patient, expectant smile on her face.

"With Bree's father away for the immediate future, I wanted to talk to you," he began, then had to pause to clear his throat. *Get it together, man. This is everything right here.* "Bree thinks so much of you," he went on. "And in the time I've had the pleasure of knowing you, I can see why." He smiled. "I wish my *nonna* was still alive. I have a feeling you two would have been marvelous friends."

She took his hand in hers. It was warm and soft and went a long way toward relaxing him.

"What a delightful thing to say," she told him. "And yes, I am certain of it." She squeezed his hand. "It is rather dashing and shows you to be a man of character that you chose to sit here with me today." She smiled. "Your *nonna* would be proud." She kept his hand between hers as she spoke. "I like to think I'm a fairly modern woman, but I confess there are some traditions I still find admirable, and this is one of them." She nodded to him and said, "Proceed."

Then added a wink.

He smiled at that and gathered himself. "Mrs. Bellaluna," he began. "You have helped to raise a remarkable woman." He met her gaze directly and said, "One I've come to love more than I thought was possible." She nodded, looking pleased, and he tried to take that as one small victory. "I know it hasn't been the longest of courtships," he went on. "I've never been one to leap or to rush into things, but our path hasn't really been a typical one from the start. I wish I could explain the depth of the connection we've found, but you've watched us together on many occasions now, and I'm hoping what I can't put into words is something you've been able to witness with your own eyes." He paused, but when she didn't say anything, he faltered slightly. "I don't want to rush us into marriage, and I won't. We won't." He found a smile then, knowing she had to be feeling the slight trembling of his hands. "It may or may not be a long engagement—I honestly don't know how long we'll be able to wait. But I do know that we will have to make some big decisions in the next few weeks, and I want Abriana to know that I'm committed to making us work, that I'm serious about wanting her in my life." He covered Sofia's hands now and gently squeezed. "I'm hoping for, and I'd be honored to receive, your blessing when I ask your granddaughter to marry me."

He held her gaze as steadily as she held his, thinking he might actually be sweating a little now, too, when she didn't speak right away. She didn't withdraw her hands, so he waited, respecting the time she seemed to need to formulate whatever it was she wanted to say.

She glanced down for a moment, and then another, and he thought he saw her shoulders tremble, just the tiniest bit. He was further shocked to see the sheen of tears in her eyes when she lifted her gaze back to his. He honestly hadn't known what her response would be to his request. He knew she approved of him, but she might not approve of the time frame.

"Sofia," he said, concerned now, "if I've—"

She lifted one hand and waved him silent, then slid a hankie from her sleeve and dabbed at the corners of her eyes. "One thing I've wanted, the only thing I've wanted, is for my girls to be happy. I've hoped they would lead a good life, do something that fulfills them, and have someone by their side to share it all with. My daughter has found that for herself, much as I did, and I have felt truly blessed on both counts." She paused again and took a moment. "Abriana is a headstrong girl, with her own ideas about things, and a heart the size of the moon. I didn't know what would be in store for her. The world is very different now. And yet, here she is, happily tied to this place, to this town, to me, and to her heritage, which means so very much to me, and all of which are things I know you understand all too well."

"Yes, I do." He realized she was afraid he was

going to take her granddaughter away from her. "Sofia—"

She gave a slight shake of her head, and he fell silent. "Even before my daughter fell in love, I knew she had the spirit of a wanderer. And she found a man who would give her the world. It's not that I'm afraid of losing Abriana," she said, surprising him by all but reading his thoughts. "I know that couldn't happen no matter what choices she makes in life, any more than I've lost a daughter. I have not. I have gained a wonderful son-in-law who loves my daughter as fully as is possible. What mother could want for more?" She dabbed at her eyes then and looked directly at him again. "These tears are joyful ones, because now I know I've had the good blessing to live long enough to see the two people who mean the most to me find the happiness that I once had." She took his hand. "You will make your choices, the two of you, and whatever they may be, you will have my support and my blessing. Love her, care for her, be loved by her, and you will live a life richer than you can ever imagine."

She held his hand when he would have taken hers, his own eyes a bit blurry now. "Put each other first," she told him. "At the end, that is what you will value most. It isn't always easy, but find a path that brings you both fulfilment, then take it. Those who truly love you will always champion your choice and support you both."

"We will," he said. He stood then and gently lifted her hand as he helped her to her feet. "I couldn't ask for a better start for us," he added, then leaned down and hugged her, kissing her cheek. "Thank you," he said quietly. "I already felt like the luckiest man in the world when your granddaughter smiled at me for the first time. Now I feel twice blessed." He kissed her cheek again and straightened.

Sofia took out her hankie again and made a little shooing motion with it. "I have a bit of repair work to do here before I can go out front," she said, dabbing at her eyes. "And I believe you have a proposal to make."

Caleb grinned then, feeling almost shaky with relief. He took Sofia's free hand in both of his and pressed a kiss to the back of it. "I won't let you down," he said, then let himself out the back door and climbed the stairs to the second floor, so he could claim his bride.

Chapter 9

W here are you taking me?" Bree asked on a laugh, holding up the scarf he'd loosely tied around her head, over her eyes, so it wouldn't slip back off. She let him lead her around the car by the elbow.

"Almost there."

She'd had the scarf over her eyes since they'd left Bellaluna's. They hadn't driven far, but they'd been in his car long enough that she wasn't sure if they were still in Moonbright or not. She could hear waves in the distance and taste the tang of salt in the air, so they were still near the shore. The cry of the gulls flying overhead pierced the sky and she could feel the sun on her face, though it did little to cut the chill of ever-present breeze.

"I wanted our first time together to be memorable," he said, "and maybe a little symbolic." He helped her up one step, then stopped their forward progress and shifted behind her, pulling her back against him, into his arms. He drew the scarf off and she gasped, then looked back at him.

"That's . . . adorable," she said, then turned back to the small bungalow. She wasn't sure what she'd expected, but, well, she still didn't know what she expected.

The house wasn't very big, but the tidy clapboard siding was a freshly painted white, and the shaker roof shingles looked new as well. There was a stone pathway leading to the front door, with a row of little night-lights on either side. Neatly trimmed shrubbery lined the front and sides of the house, kept in order by the white scallop brick trim fronting the beds. The mailbox was a cheerful red, which matched the front door. Neat black shutters with wrought-iron clasps framed the door and the windows, finishing off the look.

She turned back to Caleb. "Is this a bed-and-breakfast?" She didn't see a sign.

"Well, it does have a bed, and I am planning on making you breakfast," he said with a grin. "Does that count?"

She laughed, still confused, and said, "Sure."

"Come on, I want to show you inside." He took her hand and they walked up the path to the front door. He took a key from his jacket pocket and unlocked the door and the deadbolt, then swung the door open and gestured for her to enter first.

He has a key? Totally flummoxed now, Bree decided to just go with it and stepped into the tiny foyer. And felt utter bemusement all over again. *So, not a bed-and-breakfast. At least not at the moment.* The interior of the place had also been freshly painted, the hardwood floors gleamed, and the sun shone brightly through sparkling clean windows. The layout was interesting, with open rooms and cool little niches, the door to the kitchen that she could see down the hall was an archway, and there was a fat, wood-burning stove in the far corner of the main room, presently chugging away. All of which was very charming. But save for that and a sign propped up facing the coat closet door, the whole house was completely empty.

She turned back to Caleb, then stilled and turned back to glance again at the sign. A real-estate sign. She swung her gaze back to him, eyes wide. "Did you—you didn't buy—"

He shook his head and she didn't know whether to sigh in relief or disappointment.

"I rented it," he said, and lifted his eyebrows and his shoulders, as if he was just as surprised by that as she was. "I haven't done anything with it, obviously, except in here, and upstairs." He took her hand and led her still-stunned self down the short hallway to the kitchen, where she got another little surprise. A small kitchen table with an inlaid tile top and two matching wooden chairs were perched by the bay window that looked over a rambling and spacious backyard. It was the view beyond that had earned the gasp. She could see the ocean. "Oh, Caleb," she said, "what a beautiful view."

He stepped around her and opened the fridge, which was fully stocked. "I just got the basics as far as cutlery and dishware, some cooking supplies, but we'll eat well."

She still wasn't processing all of this yet. "You're cooking me dinner? Here?"

"And breakfast," he said, wiggling his eyebrows.

She smiled. "That takes care of one of the Bs," she said. "But while I can well imagine, given how long we've waited, that the tile table and maybe that countertop could see some recreational use that they weren't exactly intended for"—she turned to face him, her smile wry now—"I draw the line at our first time being on a hardwood floor. That potbelly stove will only go so far to making things cozy."

"I promise, no hardwood floors will be used for sleeping surfaces." The corner of his mouth curved. "However, I retain the right for other usages as we are so inspired." She laughed at that and Caleb walked up to her and pulled her into his arms. Their banter was fairly typical of the way they'd been teasing each other for weeks, so neither of them was shocked by it. A little turned-on, maybe, if the slight fog on his glasses meant anything.

She slid them off and set them on the counter, then tipped up on her toes to kiss him.

"Are you hungry?" he asked, catching her mouth again, then again.

"For dinner?" She smiled, then shook her head.

"Then allow me to show you the rest of our accommodations." He led her up the hardwood stairs to the second level. The two front rooms were small, with dormer windows and slanted ceilings. A bathroom was at the far end of the hall. He opened the double doors on the other side of the hall and swung them wide.

"Oh . . . my," Bree breathed, and walked into the room as if drawn inside. The master bedroom took up the full back half of the second floor. She saw a door that led to the master bath and another that looked like it led to a large, walk-in closet. There was indeed a bed, a big, wide one, with a thick white duvet on top, and an array of pillows, also in white linen cases. There was a braided rug covering part of the rich, golden oak flooring, but none of those things were what had drawn her in. The back wall of the room was a series of sliding doors that led to a deep, covered deck. And at this level, there was an unobstructed view of the Atlantic.

She walked out onto the deck and simply stood there and took it in. "Wow."

Caleb joined her. "Yeah, this was pretty much when I handed the real-estate agent the check."

"Boom," Bree said.

"It felt like a boom," he agreed, and they both laughed.

She turned back to the view. "I don't think I'd ever get tired of looking at this."

Caleb took her hand and brought her around to face him. "That's exactly what I thought the moment I saw it." He reached up and touched her cheek, caught the strands of hair that the breeze had lifted into a dance, and tucked them behind her ear. "That's exactly how I felt when I first saw you."

Her heart, which had long since tilted and fallen headlong at his feet, dipped and swooned again. He did that to her often. She would never get tired of it, either. "And here I thought it was the cookie that was your love at first sight." She'd been more open about such things after her talk with Sofia that day, weeks back. She didn't freeze up when he mentioned magic anymore, and he hadn't asked her again to tell him what had been bothering her back then, either.

She suspected he would realize there was possibly a bit more to her than met the eye soon enough. She knew him well enough now to know he'd be charmed by it, most likely, and definitely curious. She could live with that. What she couldn't live without was him.

"Not the cookie," he said, looking into her eyes. "That was most definitely you."

Her heart was caught then and held. The words had been there, on the tip of her tongue, dozens of times, but she hadn't said them. Neither had he. Until now. "That's pretty convenient," she said, searching his eyes, loving what she saw there. "Because that's the exact same thing I've been thinking about you."

His smile was slow, and sexy, and filled with so many promises. All of which she knew he would keep. She wanted to make him some of her own.

"Speaking of thinking," she told him, "I was hoping to talk to you tonight. About Philadelphia." Given the whole house rental, she wasn't sure where they were headed at the moment, but she wanted him to know her thoughts anyway.

His eyebrows lifted at that. "You were?"

She nodded. "I've been talking with Cassi, about Thanksgiving."

Caleb's eyes went from surprised to worried. "Honey, that is a lovely, wonderful gesture, but it's like making your very first football game the Super Bowl. I was thinking we'd ease in a bit—"

"I've been meeting new members of your family for weeks at Castellanos. How many more could there be?" At the look on his face, her mouth went a little slack. "That many, huh?"

"Maybe I should tell you my plan. About this place," he said. "And us."

"That's sounding like it might be the better deal at the moment," she said with a laugh. "Although

173

I do want to go to Philadelphia," she added. "I even sat down with Sofia and started to work on a business plan that would let us possibly hire part-time help on a regular, ongoing basis, and a baker—who I would personally train—so I could spend stretches of time with you there. I haven't figured out a full-time solution, and . . . I don't know how I feel about that yet." She smiled brightly. "But I'm thinking that Philadelphia can be my new Italy. Only in stages." She'd planned to lay this all out over dinner, before they went to bed together, but when had anything they'd done gone according to plan? "I figure, like Italy, I have to go there and experience it, live it, before I can make any long-term decisions. I know I want to keep Bellaluna's in the family, so that's tricky, but . . . I want to figure it out. For you. For us." Her smile turned hopeful and more than a little nervous. "I hope that's a good start?"

"That is . . . wonderful," he said. "And if I didn't already know that I love you, that . . ." He trailed off and shook his head, looking more than a little stunned by her news. "Thank you," he said, and drew her to him for a long, impossibly tender kiss. When he lifted his head, he said, "I've been thinking, too. And I might have an even better start for us in mind."

And with that, he bent on one knee and knelt before her.

Bree's hands flew to her mouth. She'd hoped,

one day, for this very moment. "Caleb," she whispered, stunned. She hadn't expected it to be today.

He drew a small box from his jacket pocket. "I don't know where this crazy path we've started will take us, and it's quite possible I want to get this ring on your finger before you meet my family and run for the hills," he added, a crooked smile on his handsome, beloved face. "No matter what plans we make, life will throw curveballs. The biggest one I've had yet brought me to this little town, and to you. I could never have seen that coming, and now I can't imagine my life if it hadn't. I love you, Abriana Bellaluna O'Neill. More than I thought I could love anyone, or anything. And all the rest, my family, my home, my work, wouldn't be the same now if I couldn't share it with you."

"Oh," she said, and felt tears gather at the corner of her eyes. "Caleb," she whispered.

He stood then and took her hands in both of his, placing the small box on her palms, then curling his hands around hers, holding them both tight. He held her gaze, and said, "I've been making plans, too. This town is growing on me." He smiled then. "And heck, half my family is up here now, so it's like a home away from home already."

She let out a short laugh at that, even as she felt her legs start to tremble.

175

"George will be taking care of Alethea at home for a very extended time, and her prognosis, while really hopeful, is still a long way from being certain. So various members of the Dimitriou and Castellanos brood will be coming and going from here for as long as it takes. We'll be doing what we can to keep that Moonbright landmark open for business and make sure George keeps his livelihood, and his good name." His smile spread to a grin. "I've kind of enjoyed getting to boss my family around a bit, but we've got it planned out now so that we can all help George, but still each tackle the jobs we're trained to do. Which means I'll be back in the kitchen." He sighed. "And I can't tell you how happy that makes me." He gestured to the house. "I'm also done bunking with my cousins. I was going to ask you to come look with me and tell you all of this, but then this place popped up and I swung by and well . . ." He gestured to the view. "So, I signed a lease before someone else did, but if you—"

Bree just shook her head. "I love it. It's perfect." She thought her heart couldn't swell any further. She'd been wrong. "That is such a lovely thing you all are doing for your family, for George and Alethea," she said, and pulled her hands free so she could wrap her arms around him and hug him tight. When she let go, she lifted the ring box between them, then looked him in the eyes. "Caleb Vasilios Dimitriou," she began, then wiggled her eyebrows when his lifted in surprise at her use of his middle name, "you are my lovely thing. You are the reason I am smiling when I wake up, and when I go to sleep, and countless, countless times all through every one of my days." She looked up into his eyes. "I would follow you anywhere. When this is all said and done with George and Alethea, we will figure out our next adventure, make those decisions then."

"There's one decision I'd like to ask you to make right now," he said, then opened the box. "With my grandmother's ring, a woman who would have loved you every bit as much as I do, Abriana O'Neill, will you be my wife?"

She was already nodding. "Easiest decision I'll ever make," she said on a watery laugh.

He slid the ring on her shaking finger—his weren't all that steady, either—then picked her up, despite her protestations, and carried her in to the bed.

This time he didn't pause, and they didn't suddenly decide to wait, or talk into the wee hours of the night instead. They did take their time, reveling in each touch, every new discovery, undressing each other slowly, gasping with delight and laughing together, too. Then he was rolling her to her back, and she felt the glorious weight of his body on top of hers. Their gazes locked on one another, and he pushed deep inside her for the first time. *There you are,* she thought. *Finally.*

We're home.

Epilogue

Bree adjusted her Betty Boop costume and checked her bright red lipstick in the mirror, then tugged her wig to make sure it was on securely before stepping out of Sofia's office and into the kitchen.

Caleb had taken one look at her costume and her painted lips and almost hadn't let her leave the bungalow. She'd almost let him get away with it. But he had a Cadillac he needed to drive so he could chauffer a very surprising Pumpkin Festival Queen in for the annual parade, and Bree had some very special Italian iced cookies to bake.

Bree had planned a completely different costume for the festivities this year, but she'd come to realize that Caleb had a thing for the shape of her mouth, so she'd decided to tease him a little bit. She was sure they'd both be very happy with her decision later that night.

She made one last tug on the snug fit of her skirt, then started toward the door to the front of the shop. She and Sofia had decided that this year they were going to do all their baking for the shop beforehand, and when they ran out, they ran out. The CLOSED sign would get turned, and they'd both be free to enjoy the rest of the festivities. That meant Bree would be working the front counter the whole evening, and she was kind of looking forward to it this year. Because it was her tray of iced Italian cookies that was presently tucked under the display case in their special drawer.

She'd barely made it behind the counter to ring up her first sale, when a towering, broad-shouldered gentleman walked in, dressed in a Clark Kent suit, complete with hat and horned rim glasses. He looked around, as if searching for someone, but without any luck. Clearly disappointed, he waited a minute, checked his watch, then turned to leave. Bree happened to glance toward the back of the shop at that moment and noticed a woman with dark shoulder-length hair had just stepped out of the ladies' room. *No way,* Bree thought. *It can't be that easy.* The brunette was dressed as Wonder Woman.

Bree saw the woman catch sight of the man as he turned to leave. She opened her mouth, as if she might call out for him, but then changed her mind. Bree hadn't missed the way she'd looked at him, though. *I know that look.* Without even having to think about it, she grabbed her tray of cookies and slid out from behind the counter, stopping Clark Kent before he could walk out the door.

"I've been working on a new recipe," she told him, gently placing her hand on his arm. "Won't you try one? On the house."

He looked as if he were going to politely decline, but Bree picked up one from the tray and offered it to him. "Honest opinion," she asked, and took hold of his arm when he accepted the cookie, easing him around in the guise of keeping him from blocking the doorway.

"Sure," he said, sounding distracted. "Happy to." He didn't seem at all happy to, but he did the polite thing and sank his teeth into the soft cookie . . . at the same exact moment he made direct eye contact with Wonder Woman.

He finished his bite, then polished off the rest. And all the while the pair only had eyes for each other. Without looking at Bree, he said, "Keeper," then walked directly to Wonder Woman.

Bree couldn't see Clark's face, or hear what he said, but Wonder Woman's tentative expression immediately split into a blinding smile. Bree wanted to go pull up a chair at their table and get a front-row seat to what was about to unfold. *Her first match!*

The shop was bustling, though, and she had customers waiting. She took another second to just stand there with a pleased expression on her face as Clark and his superhero clasped hands on top of the table.

Nodding in satisfaction, and not a little thrilled,

Bree turned, tray in hand, only to find Caleb standing in the doorway leading from the kitchen to the shop front. Her eyes widened appreciatively. She wasn't the only one who'd made a last-minute costume change, it seemed. He'd mentioned something about going as the Lone Ranger, but instead, she was looking at a fully rigged-out pirate. *Johnny Depp, eat your heart out.*

She walked immediately to him and went up on tiptoe to kiss him on the cheek.

"If you put those lips on any part of me, my lovely," he said, in seductively deep, but absolutely terrible Greek-pirate accent, "I won't be responsible for me actions."

"Promise?" she asked, batting her eyelashes and pursing her lips.

His eyes flared and for a second she wasn't too sure he wasn't going to push her up against the nearest wall. And she wasn't too sure she might not let him. Then his gaze dipped to the tray she held in her hand and he did a double take. "Are those . . . ?"

She nodded but lifted the tray away. "Special order," she told him, and turned to put them back in the drawer under the display case.

From where he stood, Caleb could see where she'd put them. He glanced at her, then at Clark and Wonder Woman, who'd just risen from their table and were heading to the door, hand in hand, then at where she'd stowed the cookies, then finally back at her. Clearly, he'd been in the doorway long enough to have watched her little maneuver with Clark and the cookie. She smiled brightly at him but said nothing. *He'd figure it out over time.*

The rest of the afternoon and evening flew by. She had run outside for a moment to watch Caleb drive his uncle's Cadillac in the parade; afterward, he'd gone back to the restaurant to help out. The bakery had stayed packed, and the contents of the display case had swiftly sold out. By seven o'clock, Bree was texting her pirate to swing by and pick her up. She was just tidying up the last of it when Caleb came in through the front door. "It's quite the party out there."

"Let's join them," she said, thinking this was already the best Halloween yet, and the night was still young. And when the dancing and singing were over, she got to go home with a pirate. *No complaints this year.*

"Any of those cookies left?" he asked, as he flipped the sign and locked the door.

He didn't have to explain which ones he was talking about. In fact, all of the remaining cookies were still on their tray in the secret drawer. Bree had only given out the one, and she was okay with that. But she wasn't thinking Caleb needed any more nudges. "I've got a different recipe I want you to try," she said, walking right up to him.

"Oh?" he said, immediately interested.

"Flavored lipstick," she said, sliding her hand suggestively along his sword and nipping at his ear.

The cookies were forgotten.

They ended up missing the dancing and the singing. And it was, in fact, the best All Hallows' Eve ever. She couldn't wait to find out how they'd top it next year. No magic required. *Har har har.*

Anginetti
(Italian Lemon Cookies)

COOKIES

1 cup butter (2 sticks), softened to room
 temperature
½ cup confectioners' (powdered) sugar
¼ cup white granulated sugar
1½ tablespoons lemon zest
3 to 4 tablespoons fresh lemon juice
2½ cups flour
½ teaspoon baking powder
¼ teaspoon salt

Preheat oven 375 degrees Fahrenheit.

Cream together the butter and confectioners' sugar until smooth.

Stir the white granulated sugar together with the lemon zest and lemon juice.

Add sugar/zest mixture to the creamed butter/ confectioners' sugar and use hand or stand mixer to blend until smooth.

In small bowl, whisk flour, baking powder, and salt.

Gradually add the flour mixture to the butter mixture, blending till smooth after each addition.

Refrigerate dough for a minimum of one hour or until firm. (Overnight is okay.)

Take tablespoon-size scoops of dough and roll into balls.

Line two cookie sheets with parchment paper.

Place cookie balls approximately two inches apart on the lined cookie sheet.

Bake 10 to 12 minutes. Cookie bottoms should be lightly brown.

Let cool completely on racks. Makes approximately four dozen cookies.

ICING
3 tablespoons whole milk (2% okay)
2½ teaspoons lemon extract
1 box confectioners' sugar
Red and green nonpareils

Add milk and lemon extract to sugar and blend until smooth.

When cookies are completely cool, use metal spatula to frost the cookies.

Add a sprinkle of nonpareils on top of the frosting.

Love Spells Disaster

ALLYSON CHARLES

Chapter 1

Cassandra Hie tugged at the purple jersey knit, which in theory covered her breasts, praying the fabric would hold out until it had served its purpose. She sucked in a breath, pulling her stomach in tight, but the dress didn't magically grow into full coverage. Shoulders sagging, she exhaled like a stuck balloon. The bodice of the dress slid down another inch.

Casually, or as casually as a woman standing in line at a bakery wearing a skimpy cocktail dress could, she crossed her arm over her chest, gripping her opposite shoulder. She still felt exposed. Everyone else in Bellaluna's Bakeshop wore jeans, woolen skirts, knee-high boots. Solid fall fashion choices for the denizens of Moonbright, Maine. She was the only idiot making a pastry run in stilettos.

She sighed. She was going to kill Franca.

"I know, right?" the man in front of her said. "I just want to sink my teeth into one of them so badly."

Cassie pressed her forearm tighter against her breasts and leaned backward. "Excuse me?"

So, she might have let Franca talk her into this provocative getup and her girls were on display. That was still no excuse for such—

"I think I want a cannoli today." He pointed at the display case. "But the caramel ricotta cheesecake smells incredible. I can never decide."

Cassie's cheeks heated. "Oh. Right. The food." She tugged at her bodice, but the reality was it didn't matter. At Bellaluna's, she could have been standing in line naked and everyone's attention would still be on the pastries. They were just that good. The feeling that every eye was trained on her in her borrowed dress and ridiculous high heels was only in her mind.

The cash register dinged, and the man in front of her stepped up to the old-fashioned glass display.

The older woman behind the register gave him a smile as sweet and warm as a freshly baked batch of cinnamon rolls. "Ralphie! Back for more?"

"You know I can't get enough, Sofia." He dropped to a squat to peer at all the goodies in the case.

Sofia pulled a tray of delectable-looking cream puffs from behind the counter. "I know what you'll like. How about a nice profiterole? It's sure to bring a little bit of joy to your day."

Ralphie popped up and rolled onto his toes. "Perfect. I'll take four."

He moved aside to pay, and Cassie stepped forward, examining her options. Her mouth watered. She wanted one of everything, but this mission wasn't about her stomach. It was what would appeal to Samuel the most.

Sofia handed Ralphie his change and turned to Cassie. The woman had to be pushing seventy, but only the faintest of lines crinkled the edges of her pretty brown eyes. Her figure was as trim as an athlete's, and her hair a rich sable. Sugar must truly be a great preservative.

The older woman brushed her hands down her apron. "And what can I get for you, *cara*?"

Cass chewed on her bottom lip. "Well, my friend reminded me of that saying that the way to a man's heart is through his stomach." And with boobs. She tugged at the bodice again. Really, why did she listen to Franca? "What do you think, are cannolis the most tempting of treats?"

"Our cannoli are sure to tempt anyone." Sofia tilted her head. "Have I seen you in here before with the lucky man? He's about six-two, with dark hair?"

"No, I haven't been here with him." Had never gone anywhere with him, actually. Samuel was very strict about fraternizing with his employees. A quality Cassie could admire. She never had to worry about working late alone with him, never had any apprehension about an inappropriate touch in the snug copy room. He was the perfect gentleman. "And the man in question has blond hair."

"But I thought . . ." Sofia stared into the corner of her busy bakery, her eyes clouding.

"I've been here before," Cassie said with a smile. "Many times." She tugged at the hem of her dress. Too many times. When she'd first moved to Moonbright nine months ago, she probably would have fit into Franca's clothing. "You didn't imagine me."

"No, of course, I've noticed you before. But—" Sophia snapped her mouth shut. Smoothing her hands down her apron, she gave a small shake of her head. "No matter. So, tell me about this fellow of yours. How do you know he's the one?"

Cassie looked at the line of people behind her. "I'm sure anything will be fine. Everything here is delicious."

"Nonsense." Sophia waved a finger to a girl assembling pink boxes in the back corner, and pointed at the other customers. The girl skipped to the counter and helped the next woman in line. Sophia turned back to Cassie. "Now, how am I supposed to give you the perfect treat if I don't know anything about this man?"

Cassie pursed her lips. The woman really took the idea of food being the way to a man's heart seriously. Maybe she was a believer in food chemistry, that different ingredients would have different chemical effects on people.

The idea was a little off the wall, but shouldn't surprise Cassie. Ever since moving to this town, she'd met nothing but interesting people. Take her coworker Franca, for example. Even though she was a staunch Roman Catholic, the woman had more spells and tonics that she wanted Cassie to try than a Wiccan. Her advice to dress sexy and seduce Samuel with sweets was positively tame compared with some of her other suggestions.

Cassie mentally shrugged. She'd moved to Moonbright because of its quirky charm. She might as well roll with it. "Well, first of all, he's brilliant. An absolute genius with numbers. He's kind, handsome, and very stable."

Sophia arched one dark-lined eyebrow. "Stable?"

Cassie flushed. Okay, that wasn't the most romantic of qualities, but it was an important one. After the roller-coaster ride of deadbeats she'd experienced in her former life, stable sounded heavenly. "I've been waiting for him to notice me for a long time," she said quietly. "I'm ready for real love."

Sofia studied her for a moment, then glanced into the corner again, at an empty table by the window. She tapped her finger against her pink lips before nodding, once. "Yes, I believe you are." Turning, she pulled a tray of succulent-looking cookies out from behind the counter. The edge of each cookie was lightly browned, and colorful sprinkles dotted the icing dolloped on top. Sophia placed two on a doily in a small box and tied it up with string. "Here you are, *cara*. A gift. For true love."

Cassie took the box with one hand and slid her purse off her opposite shoulder. "No, I couldn't accept them for free. Not after all the time you've spent talking with me. How much?"

Sofia waved her wallet away. "Nonsense. Just promise me that if love does find you, you'll accept it, in any of its forms."

Cassie tilted her head. "O-kaay. Of course." She slid her purse back on her shoulder. "Well . . . thanks. I appreciate it."

Sofia gave her a farewell waggle of her fingers and turned to the next customer.

Clutching the box to her stomach, Cassie hurried out the door and across the street. Samuel Bunker Insurance was only five doors down, but that was five doors too many in four-inch heels. By the time she pushed through the entrance to the insurance agency, the balls of her feet were aching and the muscles around her ankles had locked in place.

The bell above the door rang with her entrance, and Franca looked up from her desk. She and Franca shared the open front reception area, and Samuel's office, the copy room, and the restroom were crowded into the back.

Franca lifted her head and sniffed. "Mmm, I

can smell the lard and sugar from here. What did you get?"

Cassie hobbled to her desk and set her purse and the box down. "Some Italian cookies." Cocking a hip against the edge of the desk, she toed off one pump and flexed her foot. "I don't know about this getup, Franca. I don't think it's work appropriate, and you know how Samuel likes everything professional."

Franca scowled. "I've worn that dress to work lots of times. What are you saying?"

Cassie pointed to her boobs. "Yes, well, it doesn't look the same on me as it does on you, does it?" Franca was two inches shorter than Cassie's five-seven, and far smaller across the bust. "I want Samuel to notice me as a woman, but not necessarily as this kind of woman."

Franca stood and circled her desk. She stood in front of Cassie and ran her hands up and down Cassie's arms. "I know this is a big change for you. You're used to being as fully covered as a nun in her habit, but trust me. You look beautiful. And not slutty at all." She chewed the left side of her lower lip into her mouth. "Maybe the tiniest bit slutty, but in a good way."

Cassie's jaw dropped. "I don't dress like a nun. I just think there's a time and a place for everything." Dress sexy for dates, conservative for work, and scary for Halloween. Easy rules to live by.

"Franca?" Samuel ambled into the reception area, his head down, focused on a sheaf of papers in his hand. "Did you get the estimate from head-quarters?"

Cassie shoved her foot back in her shoe and tugged at her bodice.

Franca slapped her hands away. "Not yet, boss. I'll let you know when it comes in."

"Okay." He looked up and paused when he saw Cassie. "Oh—hi, Cassie. I didn't know you were in yet today. How did the dentist appointment go?"

"Fine." The back of her neck burned. The dentist appointment had been her first lie to Samuel, but what else was she to say? She couldn't very well tell him she was going to be late to work because she needed time to primp that morning in order to seduce him.

Franca elbowed her in the ribs as she walked past, circling back behind her desk.

Right. She had the cookies. She had the boobs. Time to start that seduction. Cassie pushed her shoulders back and prayed she wouldn't spill out of the dress. Well, here went nothing. "Samuel, I stopped at Bellaluna's Bakeshop on my way back." She untied the string and opened the box. Sauntering toward her boss with as much hip action as she dared, she held the box up, right in front of her cleavage. "Would you like to nibble on something?"

His gaze flicked straight to the pastries in the box, then back to her face, bypassing all her interesting bits. "No, thanks. I started a new keto diet yesterday." He patted his flat stomach. "Have to get in shape for that half-marathon next month." He turned and strolled back to his office, his face again buried in his paperwork.

Cassie blinked, fighting the tears behind her eyelids. She tossed the box of cookies back on her desk. "Well, now we know. Even showcasing all my assets, Samuel has zero interest."

Franca let out a low whistle. "That boy has the control of a monk. And not the fun kind that makes beer and likes to drink. Why do you want him again?"

Cassie stomped around her desk and slumped into her chair. "You know why." They had discussed her feelings enough that even Cassie had started getting tired of hearing her own voice. "And just because he isn't interested in me isn't a character flaw on his part. It's just . . ." She gripped the edge of her desk and turned her face away. She wouldn't cry at work. She. Would. Not.

"Hey," Franca said, her voice soft. "Of course, it's not a flaw. He's a good person; you're a good person. I'm just wondering, even if you got what you wanted and turned that boy's head, would it be worth it? I'm thinking there wouldn't be much heat brewing in that cauldron, if you know what I mean."

"You don't know that." Cassie dug her hand into the bakery box and pulled out a cookie. The beautiful, sprinkle-dusted concoction that wasn't allowed in Samuel's disciplined, hard-bodied lifestyle. She shoved it into her mouth whole. "Besides, heat isn't everything," she mumbled around her mouthful.

Her past relationships had heat, at least in the beginning. She'd dated men who had a magnetic pull but couldn't offer anything of substance. And her mother . . . Well, she didn't even want to go there. It had taken Cassie too long to realize that relationships weren't about using her heart, or parts farther south. They required the use of her head. Companionship with a man she could respect. Security. Those were the things that mattered.

Franca wrinkled her nose and pushed her glasses back up when they began to slip. "What was that? I couldn't hear you around the cookie."

"I said," she began, and swallowed her mouthful. Her throat clogged, and Cassie coughed. Or tried to. No air escaped out of her windpipe.

Cassie blinked. And tried coughing again.

Franca held up a hand. "You said . . ."

Adrenaline flooded Cassie's veins. She pounded her desk with one hand and pointed at her throat with the other. White dots flickered in her vision.

"Oh, crap!" Franca bolted around her desk, her hip slamming into the corner. She ran behind Cassie's chair, yanking Cassie to her feet.

Cassie's fingernails clawed across the desk as Franca wrapped her arms around her middle.

Her friend heaved her backward, but the cookie remained lodged. Franca squeezed her again, her hands plumping up Cassie's breasts like a human push-up bra.

Cassie slapped at her hands, shoving them down lower. Dear Lord, she was going to die. Die, because she'd talked with her mouth full and her friend didn't know how to do the Heimlich. Her vision started to narrow, collapsing in on itself like a house of cards. Ears ringing, Cassie felt a tear roll down her cheek.

Franca released her, probably realizing the futility of her actions. This was the end of the road for her. She was going to die in a skimpy dress and hooker heels. She hoped Franca would make sure all her parts were decently covered before anyone saw her body.

Her knees gave out just as a strong set of arms wrapped around her waist, holding her upright. A fist jerked against her abdomen. Once.

Her chin dropped to her chest, her lungs screaming.

Twice.

Her hands went numb, her mind going dark.

One last jerk, and a wet glob of mashed-up

cookie flew from her mouth, splattering on the carpet.

Cassie wheezed, sucking in a fresh draught of sweet, blessed air. Her greedy lungs sucked in more than they could hold and she coughed, uncontrollably. Planting her palms on the desk, she waited for her body to calm.

"Thanks," she croaked. She straightened, her legs feeling like half-set jelly. "I really owe you one, Franca."

"It wasn't me, hon." Admiration dripped from Franca's voice, and Cassie wobbled around.

Six-foot-something of tall, dark, and handsome stood before her. Her savior had wavy chestnut hair about two weeks past a cut and dark green eyes that examined her with concern. A worn, long-sleeve T-shirt stretched across a firm chest, and a light scattering of sawdust was sprinkled across wide shoulders. She looked down past a pair of jeans that hugged him just right to the toes of his mud-caked work boots.

A slow smile stretched across his face, one edge of his lips curling higher than the other. "I guess it's me you owe."

Chapter 2

Most of the woman's beautiful auburn hair had spilled around her shoulders, although one chunk was still firmly held in the clip at the back of her head. Her heart-shaped face was slowly turning from a deep beet red to a lovely pink flush. Big brown eyes blinked up at him, their color a perfect match to the caramel that enveloped the apples he'd passed in the candy shop two doors down. And that body . . .

No, best not to think about the curves bursting from that clingy dress. Not when the woman had just had a near-death experience. That wasn't cool. Not. At. All.

"Are you okay?" Ducking his head, he peered into those doe eyes, relief slipping through him when he saw them focus with intelligence.

She nodded and cleared her throat. "Yes . . ." Pressing a hand to her chest, she breathed deep and blew it out slowly. "Yes, thank you. That was . . ." She shrugged. "Thank you again, Mr. . . . ?"

"Chip Gneiss." He held out his hand and tried not to look too obvious as he sniffed the air around her. The woman smelled delicious. Was that her perfume? "I have an appointment with Sam to get some life insurance. This was quite an introduction to the office."

She slipped her hand in his and squeezed. "I'm Cassandra Hie, Cassie, the office manager, and this is my coworker, Franca. And you've made the right choice coming to Mr. Bunker for your insurance needs. As you can see, not only will you get top-notch insurance coverage, but all policies also come with a floor show."

Chip chuckled. A sense of humor after a near-death experience? That was a rare quality.

Her gaze zeroed in on his mouth, dropped to his chest. She bit her bottom lip as she scanned him to his boots and back before she gave a small tug on her hand.

Chip let it slip from his. The skin of his palm tingled as her fingertips dragged free.

The other woman, Franca, hurried to her friend and rubbed her shoulder. "Are you sure you're all right, Cassie? Jeez, that was scary as hell. I don't understand it." She shook her head. "I did the same thing he did, but it wasn't working for me."

Cassie cocked an eyebrow. "You were giving me a breast exam. Whatever facility trained you in the Heimlich should be shut down."

"I learned from Moonbright's very own fire department." Franca planted her hands on her hips. "It was part of their CPR course."

"And I'm sure you were listening with bated breath to every instruction instead of ogling the hunky firefighters?" Cassie plucked a tissue from the box at the corner of her desk and strode to the half-chewed glob of whatever had clogged her throat. She scooped it up while her friend protested.

Chip's stomach gave a low rumble. Hooking one finger over the edge of the bakery box on Cassie's desk, he slid it toward him as the women bickered. Mmm. Office cookies. And there was one left. Cocking a hip on the oak surface, he watched the two women argue. Somehow the disagreement had spun from CPR and firefighters to a borrowed and missing library card to . . . cats? They reminded him a bit of his sisters, except for the fact he was having decidedly unsisterly feelings toward the redhead.

He slid his gaze to her waving hands. No ring. Was she seeing anyone? Cassie had given him the up-and-down earlier. That usually meant there was at least some interest.

He bit into the cookie, and the explosion of sugary goodness on his tongue almost made him moan. This office really was great. Tasty snacks. A woman he couldn't tear his eyes from. He should have thought about life insurance a long time ago if this was what he had to expect from visits to Bunker Insurance. He licked a bit of powdered sugar from the corner of his mouth before popping the rest of the cookie inside.

"And really, if Jinx or I ever have a heart attack, please don't attempt CPR," Cassie said to Franca. "If you confused my breasts with my stomach during the Heimlich, I don't even want to know where you think a mammal's heart is."

Franca opened her mouth, but Cassie interrupted. "Why don't you call Samuel to let him know his client is here, and I'll show him back." She turned. "If you'll just foll—"

Her mouth fell open and her eyes flared wide. She hurried to the desk, if rapid, mincing steps on wobbling heels could be considered hurrying. She stopped so close to him that he could smell her tantalizing scent again. It was similar to the cookie, but not quite.

She grabbed the empty pastry box and shook it in his face. "Did you eat this cookie?"

Outrage vibrated from her body. Her cheeks turned pink again, but with her pinched mouth and eyes shooting arrows at him, this time the flush didn't look so delightful.

He eased off the desk and took a step back. "Cookie? Uh, nope."

She advanced and whipped her hand up toward his face.

Chip flinched, but she only wiped her thumb along his lower lip. His belly pulled tight at the intimate contact, and he just barely stopped himself from darting his tongue out to taste her.

She held up her digit dusted with white power. "That cookie wasn't meant for you."

"Sorry?" Jeez, what was the big deal? It was just a cookie. And you'd think after he'd saved her life, she wouldn't begrudge a man a snack.

He licked his lip. It *had* been one of the tastiest cookies he'd ever eaten. It must have come from Bellaluna's, the best bakery in town. Chip could understand why someone would get proprietary about those pastries. He'd been known to give the side-eye to anyone who got too close to his almond croissant.

Franca plopped into her chair and pulled herself in behind the desk. "And the person that cookie was intended for didn't want it. Remember? Maybe you should give your cookies away to a more appreciative audience."

"How does he know he doesn't like my cookies if he's never tried one?" Cassie stalked to the garbage can next to Franca's desk and chucked the box inside. "Some people just need the right motivation. The right incentive. That cookie was an incentive so he would come to love my . . . other cookies."

Chip rubbed the back of his neck. What language were these two speaking? Screwball with a heavy dialect of subtext? Why couldn't women just be straightforward, tell it like it was, like guys?

Cassie tugged at the bottom hem of her dress,

drawing his attention to her acres of exposed leg. Okay, so there were clear compensations for women not acting like men. A little confusion now and then was the price to pay for enjoying feminine society.

Besides, as his mom would point out, he *had* been rude eating the cookie without asking. And Cassie was probably still freaked out over nearly choking to death. She was allowed to be a little high-strung.

"Hey, I'm sorry." He dipped his chin and gave her his best smile, the one that had worked on everyone from the nuns at grade school to irate homeowners when an order didn't come in on time. "I didn't realize it was a special cookie. But I don't want you going hungry on my account. How about dinner tonight? My treat."

Cassie drew her shoulders back. She shifted her weight, and the swishing of her nylons rubbing together tickled his eardrum. "Um, that's nice of you, but not necessary." She started to tuck a strand of hair behind her ear, fingered a large clump, and frowned. Raising her arms, she scraped her wavy mane back into a knot and reclipped it. "And I'm sorry about making such a fuss over the cookie. Don't worry about it." She flinched and drew her arm behind her back to swat at something.

"I know it's not necessary." Chip hooked his thumbs in his front pockets and widened his stance. "Dates never are. They're supposed to be fun. Come out with me tonight," he urged. "I promise I'll show you a good time."

Cassie's body jerked, and she jumped away from Franca's desk, glaring at her friend.

Franca gave her a narrow-eyed smile and lowered a pair of scissors she was holding by the blades to the desk.

"Thanks again," Cassie said between tight lips. She was addressing Chip, but her eyes never left her friend. "But I'm not interested. Franca, have you called Mr. Bunker yet?"

Chip's stomach clenched. Well, that couldn't have been clearer. He must have misread the situation. It didn't happen often, but it wasn't the first time he'd been shot down. Which didn't explain why this rejection dug under his skin more than usual.

Cassie stalked to her desk, shifting the air between them.

The scent of sugar and some unknown spice teased his nose again and his feet turned to follow her, like a puppy after its master.

"Chip!" Sam Bunker strode into the reception area, arm outstretched. "It's great to see you again."

Chip shook the insurance agent's hand. "Yeah, you too."

An awkward silence descended, with Cassie avoiding everyone's eyes and Chip's own gaze dragged unwillingly to her time and again. He shifted on his boots.

A line creased Sam's forehead. "Anything wrong?"

"Well, Cassie almost killed herself on a cookie," Franca drawled.

"Oh, my God." Sam turned to Cassie. "Are you okay?"

"Fine." She waved a hand in the air, dismissive. "Thanks to Mr. . . ." She dipped her chin. "I'm sorry, I forgot your name."

"Call me Chip."

A wince rocketed across her face so fast Chip must have imagined it.

"Yes, well, Chip gave me the Heimlich. He saved my life."

Sam whistled. "Well, he is a handy man to have around." He knocked Chip with his elbow, laughing.

Cassie's eyebrows drew together.

Chip shrugged. "It's a joke," he explained. "Because I'm a handyman by trade."

"Ah." She gave him that quick up-and-down again. "Well, I was very lucky you were around."

Sam gestured down the hall. "Shall we head back to my office?"

With a nod to Franca and a small smile, unreturned, to Cassie, he ambled after Sam and settled into the guest chair in front of the desk.

"So," Sam said, dropping into his chair and folding his hands above his desk, "did you look over the policy options I sent to you? Do you have any questions?"

"No, as we discussed over the phone, I like the first policy you showed me." Chip crossed his legs at the ankles. "I'm ready to sign."

Sam turned to his computer and typed something on the keyboard, his fingers flying. "All right, then. And is Judith Gneiss still your beneficiary?"

"Yes, my mother." Chip scooted to the edge of the chair and rested his forearms on his thighs. "With this new project I'm starting, I'll be going into some debt. If something happens to me, I want her to be able to pay it off." He lifted one shoulder and smiled. "And maybe a world cruise for her, too."

Sam arched an eyebrow. "Yes, I'm sure she'd want to go out partying after her son passes."

"You don't know my mom." His mom was great. But she did like to throw it down every once in a while. Of course, Chip didn't think his mom would ever get a chance to cash in the policy. He was careful, but this new project was a big step for him and he wanted every *i* dotted and every *t* crossed. If all went as planned, the profit he made from this flip would fund the next one and so on until he built himself quite a business. He could be like that other guy named Chip in

Texas, creating a little real-estate empire up here in Maine.

Sam hit a button on his keyboard and the printer behind him came to life. He swung his chair around, picked up two pages, and turned back. "Okay, if you'll just sign here. I'll have Franca e-mail you a copy of your policy. And if you have any questions, feel free to call me."

Chip took the pages and scanned them to make sure they matched the sample he'd looked through before. Samuel Bunker Insurance had to be doing a gangbuster business if all his clients were in and out of the office this fast. The man was nothing if not efficient. Chip clicked the end of the pen Sam handed him and scrawled his signature at the bottom of page two.

There. One more task finished. Ever since he'd decided to flip his first house, his to-do list had grown exponentially. Get his funding in place, nail down the remodeling he needed to do, order the supplies, get the permits . . . so many damn permits. It felt nice to finally scratch something off his list for once.

He pushed the papers across the desk and stood. "Thanks for squeezing me in today. My work schedule appreciates it."

"Anytime." They shook hands, and Sam started to circle his desk.

Chip waved him down. "I can see myself out."

And maybe he'd get another chance to charm Cassie into going out with him. One last shot. What could he say? He was a glutton for punishment.

He stepped out of Sam's office and strolled toward the front.

"I said no." Cassie's hushed voice slid down the hall. Whatever the conversation topic was this time, it sounded serious. Chip hesitated in the shadows, not wanting to interrupt.

"But this one's into you," Franca said. "You wouldn't even need any of my *nonna*'s spells to help you."

"I can't believe I'm saying this," Cassie muttered, "but I think I want to try some of your *nonna*'s spells. Nothing else is working. Why not turn to the dark side?"

"Hey, my *nonna* isn't dark. She likes to help people."

"So help me." Cassie sighed, and a shiver whispered down Chip's spine at the sound. He leaned forward, his body feeling a tug at her distress. "I promise I won't make fun of you or your *nonna*'s ideas anymore," she said.

"But what about the hottie who actually wants you?"

Yeah. Chip was assuming he was the hottie, and he thanked the hours of manual labor he'd done for giving him some muscle. What about him? And what the hell was a nonnaspell? And was there actually some idiot out there who wasn't interested in Cassie?

"Franca, come on." Chair wheels squeaked, and Chip could imagine Cassie pushing herself away from her desk. Perhaps standing and stretching her arms overhead, giving that dress a challenge to hold everything in. He grinned.

"Once you've set your sights on filet mignon," she continued, "you can't then lower them to ground beef. Besides, I want a man who can count higher than two by four."

Chip's shoulders hardened into blocks, and he straightened from his slouch against the wall. Well, his mom was right. Eavesdroppers never heard anything good about themselves. Couldn't count higher than two by four? Because he was a handyman who worked with lumber all day? Cute. His stomach churned. Good thing he'd heard her now. Saved him from the humiliation of getting rejected again. Or worse. Having her give in to a pity date, thereby sentencing him to spending an evening with this stuck-up witch.

He ground his teeth together. He'd never mis-read someone so badly.

He stalked into the reception area and a lick of satisfaction lashed him when Cassie looked up, her eyes going wide, her gaze darting from him to the hall and back.

"Yeah, I heard." He breezed past her. "Don't worry. This piece of ground chuck won't be bothering you again." He pulled open the door and had just enough self-control to keep from slamming it on his way out.

That was the thanks you got for saving a woman's life: snide insults and unapologetic conceit.

Well, his insurance policy was bought and paid for. He wouldn't need to come back to the office of Sam Bunker Insurance.

He never had to see Ms. Hie and Mighty again.

Chapter 3

Cassie teetered on the step stool, braced her hip against the wall, and heaved the plastic tub from its spot on the high shelf above the washing machine. The hard rubber edge smacked into her collarbone, and she stumbled from the second step, dropping to the floor with a shriek.

Heart pounding, she blew out a breath and rolled her shoulders, waiting for a bolt of pain to assault her. None came.

She was almost disappointed. She deserved a broken bone or sprained ankle after her behavior yesterday, and having a physical ache to worry over would have seemed a reprieve from living with her self-reproach.

The hurt in Chip's eyes when he'd walked out of the office dug a hole into her gut. Her and her stupid mouth. She'd tried to be funny, to make Franca laugh while still impressing upon her friend that she wasn't ever going to change her mind about Samuel.

That had worked well. She snorted. Not.

Cassie lugged the bin to the living room and dropped it next to the others. Jinx looked up from her spot on the back of the sofa and lashed her black tail back and forth, annoyed at the disturbance.

"Thanks for coming to see if I was okay," Cassie said to her cat.

Jinx sniffed and tucked her head back into the chenille blanket.

Cassie twisted her lips in a rueful smile. Aside from the occasional snuggle, Jinx wasn't the nurturing and caring type of pet. She was more the I'll-feast-on-your-dead-body-in-victory kind of cat. Which was fine. Cassie respected her fierce attitude, and in return Jinx tolerated Cassie's sarcasm. A perfect partnership.

If only it were that easy with people.

She dropped her forehead in her palm. Less than twenty-four hours ago she'd insulted a man who'd just saved her life. She didn't know how many flowers she was going to have to send him in apology, but it had better be impressive. Maybe a couple of those cookie bouquets.

At least Franca had agreed to help her win Samuel. After consulting with her mother on the phone, she'd written a list of her grandmother's spells for Cassie to try.

Spells. Cassie couldn't believe she'd come to this. She wasn't necessarily a disbeliever. Her aunt Hildy had, as Cassie's mom used to say, "the witchy-way." But Cassie was of a more practical bent. If she couldn't see or touch something, she tended not to give it much credence. Still, she was down to her last trick. It was time to either go big or go home. Come Monday, Samuel wouldn't know what hit him. She had the whole weekend to decide which spell to use first.

Which left her with plenty of time to prepare for her favorite holiday. She dropped to a squat and peeled the lid off the bin she'd brought out. This was the last batch of Halloween decorations in her house, and the pouncing spider just had to be in it. Orange lights, black lights, another fog machine . . . Aha! She tugged the box free and held it up in triumph. One battery-operated, pouncing spider with glowing red eyes. Perfect.

A knock sounded at the door. Cassie stood and shuffled through her entry, trying to cut with her thumb nail the tape she'd used to secure the box last year. "Just a minute, Jack," she called out. She hissed in a breath. Damn it. Cardboard cut. Ten times worse than a paper cut. Cradling the box to her chest in one arm, she sucked on her thumb and pulled the door open.

A man's back greeted her. He turned. "Ms. Hey—you!"

The box slipped, and Cassie juggled it before wrangling it tight to her body. Her stomach twisted like she'd eaten three-day-old guacamole. She swallowed, gaping at one Chip Gneiss standing on her doorstep as if he were her latest package from the Halloween superstore. A squinty-eyed, growling package in a blue flannel shirt that under normal circumstances she would refuse delivery on. But if he looked as angry as a bear who'd just had his honeypot stolen, he had a right to it.

She met his glittering emerald eyes and swallowed. "You're not my usual handyman, Jack."

"And you're not a"—he looked down at his phone—"Ms. Heyer." He crossed his arms over his chest and glared.

"No." She shifted the box to her hip. "When I first called to hire someone from the Handyman Network, the guy on the phone got my name wrong. I've never corrected it."

"Perfect. Yet another reason I regret joining that association. I prefer dealing with my own clients, people I can vet." Nostrils flaring, he glanced over his shoulder to the large pickup truck parked at the curb.

"Wait." She shot her hand out and grabbed his arm. Her box fell, hit the doorframe, and rolled onto the porch. She ignored it. "Whatever reason you're here instead of Jack, I'm glad of it." Well, glad might not be the right word. Facing someone you'd acted like an ass to was never easy. But it was necessary. "I need to apologize for yesterday. I can't even imagine how horrible I sounded to you, and there was no excuse for what I said."

"You're just sorry I overheard." A muscle ticked next to his left eye. Those eyes had been soft yesterday, looking friendly and open when he'd asked her out. Today was a different story, and an ache spread through her chest at the change.

"I'm sorry for both, that I said it, that you had to hear it, that I became that person, even for a moment." She bit the inside of her cheek. "I'm usually not like that. But sometimes Sam— someone makes me crazy and I act like a bitchy teenager. Please." She squeezed his arm, trying to ignore the flex of the muscle under the soft flannel. She wasn't attracted to big muscles. Not anymore. "I'll understand if you don't want to do this job, but please accept my apology."

She waited, not breathing.

The muscles beneath her fingers loosened, and Chip gave a terse nod. Really more of a head bob, but Cassie would take it.

She clapped her hands together. "Great!"

Chip bent over and picked up her box. He eyeballed the picture of the spider on the side before handing it over to her. "Jack broke his ankle this morning. The service asked if I could take the job instead."

"And?" She hugged the box. "Will you take the job?"

He blew out his cheeks and looked at the sky. Finally, he nodded. "Yeah, the work order was a little skimpy on details, though. What do you need done?"

"Great," she repeated. They stared at each other

for an awkward moment before Cassie remembered her manners. "Please, come in and we'll discuss it." She led him down the hall into her kitchen and set the box on the counter. Opening her freezer, she pulled out an ice cube tray. "Do you want any coffee?" she called over her shoulder.

"Sure."

After turning the oven on and pulling a cookie sheet out from a cabinet, she retrieved her mug from the sink, got a fresh one, and poured them each a cup from her half-full coffeepot. "Cream? Sugar?"

"No, thanks."

She placed the mug in front of him, then picked up her ice cube tray. She flipped it over onto the baking sheet and spread the wedges of dough about evenly.

"Uh, you keep cookie dough frozen in ice cube trays?" He tapped his thumb on the rim of his mug.

"Yes, for emergencies." She slid the tray into the oven and shut the door.

"Cookie emergencies?"

Leaning back against the counter, Cassie picked up her own mug, holding it between both hands, enjoying the warmth. She gave him a small smile. "More the I-need-work-done-pronto-but-have-insulted-the-handyman kind of emergency."

The skin around his eyes crinkled. "Well, since

I'll be the beneficiary, I applaud your creativity." He took a sip of coffee. "So, tell me about the job."

"I'm having a haunted house on my driveway and I need help building it. Along with the frame for the walls, I'll need a pulley system installed, and maybe a pergola built in front of the garage."

"A haunted house?" He cocked his hip onto a stool behind her kitchen island and wrinkled his nose.

"Don't tell me you're one of those people who doesn't like Halloween." She pinned him with a look. "Because our working relationship would have to come to an end right here."

One corner of his mouth curled up. "I live in Moonbright, Maine, where Halloween is the biggest event of the year. Of course, I like the holiday."

"Have you lived here your whole life?" She took a sip of coffee, winced, and reached for her sugar bowl.

Chip nodded.

"Lucky." Her spoon clinked around the rim of her mug. "I'm from Massachusetts, but I heard about the parade the town has every Halloween and came up to see it last year. I bought this house three months later."

"Because of Halloween?" He raised his eyebrows.

"Well, I found a good job here, too." But mainly it had been the fact that Moonbright was basically Halloweentown. These were her peeps, right down to the competitive bobbing for apples and impromptu pumpkin races. She rolled onto her toes. "But I can't wait for this Halloween. I've been designing this haunted house ever since I moved in."

Chip pulled a small notepad from his back pocket. He laid it on the island and uncapped a pen. "There's not that much space on your driveway. How big is this thing going to be?"

"Are you kidding? This driveway is twice the size of my old one." She leaned across the island and dragged his notepad in front of her. She held out her hand, palm up, and he dropped the pen on it. Turning to a fresh page, she sketched out a rough plan. "It's all about utilizing the space you have. The haunted house will be more of a maze really. When you wind the corridors tight and keep sharp corners, you have a lot of room for monsters to jump out at unsuspecting victims." Flipping the pad around to face him, she shoved it in his direction.

His lips twitched. "Why don't we go outside and you show me what you're thinking." He rose from the stool and downed his coffee.

"Okay, but it's all right there." Putting the mugs in the sink, Cassie circled the island and stopped in front of him. The scent of cut wood and musk drifted off Chip, and Cassie's breath quickened.

"Darling, I don't know what that chicken-scratch is supposed to represent, but it isn't a plan of any sort that I recognize." The endearment rolled off his tongue, as sweet as honey. Something about it made her knees go the littlest bit weak.

Which was something she couldn't have, so she focused on the insult to her sketching skills instead. "Jack never has a problem understanding my diagrams," she said, and sniffed.

Chip threw his head back and laughed, the relaxed, happy expression on his face doing nothing to help her knees. Her fingers itched to stroke the dimple that appeared in his right cheek when he smiled.

Stupid fingers. They should know better. A cute face and a laid-back attitude had never brought her anything but trouble.

At least his forgiveness seemed genuine. No one could laugh that hard and still be mad. Chip tucked the notebook back into his pocket. "Whatever you say."

She led him to her front door and pulled it open. She looked back and frowned when she saw Chip frozen by the kitchen entrance. "What's wrong?"

"Nothing." He rubbed the back of his neck, looking sheepish. "I didn't know you had a cat. It startled me when it ran into the kitchen. Crossing my path," he muttered.

"Don't worry about Jinx. If you leave her alone, she'll leave you alone."

He tilted his head to the side. "You have a black cat and you named her Jinx."

Cassie shrugged. "What can I say? I like to tempt fate. Now, should we go outside?" Not waiting for an answer, she stepped onto her porch. Even though the sun was bright, the air held a chill.

She wrapped her arms around her middle and headed for her driveway, heard Chip's footsteps falling behind her.

That lie had slipped easily past her lips. She used to tempt fate. Act impulsively. Follow the first man who made her stomach flip. But she'd learned her lesson. Broken the pattern.

Chip stepped next to her and pulled out a measuring tape. He offered her one end and, when she took it, walked across the driveway to measure the distance. He scribbled in his notebook, then sauntered back to her, his long legs eating the distance in a couple of steps.

Cassie looked away from his thighs. Nope. Nada. Nuh-uh. Chip seemed like a nice man. Sweet even. But not for her. She'd decided on Samuel, made a list of all the reasons why he was perfect for her, and she was sticking to it.

She focused on the work, pointing out what

she wanted installed and where. When they were done, he whistled, long and low. "This is going to be some setup. Are you charging for admission?"

"No." Cassie squeezed her hands together, visualizing the screaming, the excitement. A grin crossed her face. "But some of the local high school kids are going to help me run it. You know, be the monster that grabs you and such. There will be a donation jar and any money we get will go to their football team."

Chip glanced at her from the side of his eye. "How long have you been doing these?"

"This will be my eighth." And her best. She only wished . . .

"How did you get so into Halloween?" he asked. "I mean, this town is Halloween-crazy, but having your own personal haunted house is taking it to another level."

"My grandfather." Cassie's throat went thick, and she swallowed past the pain. "After his stroke he came to live with us. He was the biggest Halloween fanatic you'll ever find. He loved decorating the house, trying to scare the trick-or-treaters. I think it made him feel useful after his capabilities diminished, that he was contributing something to make people happy." Her heart squeezed. "Every other day he thought he was a burden on us."

"Is he still . . ."

She cleared her throat. "No, he passed six years ago."

He laid his hand on her arm and squeezed. Heat passed from his palm through her shirt and warmed her whole body through. "I'm sorry."

"Thanks." Her shoulders curled and she wrapped her arms around her middle. "I know this year's mansion is going to be my best yet. I just wish he could have seen it."

Chip offered a deep sigh. He lifted his hand and slid his arm around her shoulders, going in for a side hug.

Cassie went stiff. Before she could decide if a hug from a purely platonic male who just happened to smell as delicious as a cedar wood fire was something she wanted, he stepped away, his arm falling to his side.

"Well." He ran his hand up the back of his head, mussing his hair. "I guess I should start adding up the supplies I'll need. Let's go back to your kitchen and I'll come up with an estimate."

"Sure." Cassie slapped her palm to her forehead. "Oh, crap, the cookies!" Spinning, she sprinted for the porch and raced through the door. The house smelled of sugar and chocolate. She pulled open the oven door and sighed in relief. Perfectly browned around the edges.

Finding an oven mitt, she pulled out the tray as Chip took his stool. Without waiting for them to cool, she plated five cookies and placed them on the island. "Get 'em while they're hot."

"Thanks." Chip picked one up and juggled it on his fingers before blowing on it.

"More coffee? Milk?"

He stared at her a moment before a slow smile stretched across his face.

Her breath caught. Samuel's smile was just as sexy, she reminded herself. Maybe.

"What's so funny?" she asked.

"You." He opened his mouth and brought the cookie to his tongue. She followed each movement as he took a bite, chewed languidly, and swallowed. "Yesterday you were pissed when I ate your cookie, now you're plying me with them. You really do feel guilty."

Cassie didn't know how she should respond to that, so she decided to ignore the comment. "So," she said briskly, "what do you think it's going to run me?"

He flipped open his notebook and made a list. A column of numbers trailed along the right-hand side, growing larger and larger. After totaling it, he spun it around to show her the figure. "For labor and supplies."

"Okay." That was doable. "When can you get started?"

"Tomorrow morning."

"And you can get it done four days before Halloween? I want it to run for three nights."

He drew his eyebrows together. "It's not going to be open on Halloween?"

"I can't compete with the parade and festivities downtown," she told him. "And I wouldn't want to. I'm going to be there myself."

"Fair enough." He cocked his head. "Are you going in costume? Maybe a sexy witch?"

"No."

"Sexy nurse?"

"Sexy nothing." She crossed her arms. Really, she hated that trend of sexing up a holiday that should be for children, of all ages.

He held his hands up, palms out, and chuckled. "Okay, I guess I'll have to wait and see."

"Do you think you'll be able to set up the pulley system? I want it for the exit of the maze. When people finally escape and think it's over, then bam! The bats swoop around their heads and attack."

His lips twitched. "The pulley system shouldn't be a problem. It will be like the cameras at football games, but on a much smaller scale." He broke open another cookie, trails of melted chocolate stretching from both ends. "Do you bake a lot?"

She raised an eyebrow. "Don't worry, I'll keep you well satisfied while you're working here."

His shoulders tensed.

That hadn't come out the way she'd meant it to. Her cheeks flared with heat. "I mean—"

"I know." He shifted his weight on the stool. "But I wasn't asking about my snacking times. I was just wondering if your house always smells like this. That could explain it," he muttered to himself.

"Explain what?"

He locked his gaze on her, the color of his eyes darkening to a forest after a rain. "You. You smell like the most delicious cookie I've never had. Sweet with a little bit of spice. Absolutely mouthwatering."

Her heartbeat pounded in her ears. He sounded like a starved man ordering a juicy steak. Never had a man looked at her with such appreciation, and her skin tingled in response.

She frowned. Just because her body was finally getting some male attention didn't mean it had to fire up its rockets and prepare to launch. Samuel's attention might take longer to get, but it would be worth the wait. He was the man she wanted.

"No." She clenched her fist. She wasn't going down this road again. She was finally making smart choices for her life. She wouldn't become her moth— She grabbed a sponge from the sink and scoured the counter, cutting off that train of thought.

A frown line appeared between his eyebrows. "No, what?"

"Uh, no, I'm not always baking," she covered. She tossed the sponge back down. Damn it, was this going to get weird again? Him asking her out around every corner of the haunted mansion?

She tossed him a bright smile. "But it's nice to know baking cookies is a scent that men appreciate. Instead of bringing my man a box of cookies, next time I'll just dab some vanilla extract behind my ears."

A muscle tensed in Chip's jaw. "Right. The man who hasn't shown any interest in you. I almost forgot about him."

"That's not true. He just likes to take things slowly." It was completely true. But she wasn't giving up hope. Samuel was her perfect match. She only had to make him see that.

"Uh-huh." Chip turned the cookie plate in a circle with his finger. "So, tell me about this guy. The one who's slow to interest yet good enough for you to wait around for. He's someone who can count higher than eight, I'm guessing."

Eight? She opened her mouth to ask, and then it hit her. Two by four. Two times four. She grimaced. His forgiveness unfortunately hadn't come along with forgetting. "Yes, he's extremely smart."

"Good looking?"

Cassie pursed her lips. Samuel was all long lines and toned muscles. Elegant manners and fine features. Nothing like Chip's blunt good looks. Both had their place. She flicked a glance at Chip. One just happened to be sexier than the other. But sexy wasn't what counted in a relationship.

She nodded firmly. "Very, but that's not why I like him. He's even-tempered, stable, secure."

Chip huffed. "That sounds like a good time."

Cassie grabbed her opposite elbow, holding herself stiffly. "He's lots of fun." Probably. Samuel had to have more hobbies than working out and running actuarial numbers. He just wouldn't show them off at work. Besides, she didn't need a laugh-a-minute guy. Sitting side by side, reading books by the fire, smart conversations over a glass of wine, that was all she wanted.

"Are you sure your crush is available? Or straight?"

"I don't have a crush." She grabbed the tray of remaining cookies and placed it on the counter. She shoved her spatula under the edge of one and dropped it on a kitchen towel spread over the counter. "I'm not a fifteen-year-old girl." She stabbed another cookie, breaking it in two. She tossed both pieces onto the towel. "Just because I happen to be attracted to men different from you, I don't see what right you have to judge."

He reached his arm around her, and she sucked in her breath. She hadn't heard him leave his seat, but the heat from his body surrounded her own. Chip took the spatula from her hand. "You're killing the cookies." He scooped the remaining cookies off the tray to cool. "And I'm not judging." He tilted his head. "Okay, maybe a little bit. But no more than you keep judging me. I just think it's stupid to pine for something you're not getting and ignore what's right in front of you."

"Oh, so now I'm the one who's stupid?" She dumped the empty tray in the sink and fisted her hands on her hips. "Listen, Chip, I'm hiring you for your labor. Why don't we just focus on our business relationship? Will that work for you?"

"Works fine." He plucked up three more cookies and cradled them in one hand. "I'll keep my thoughts to myself and just work on taking care of your haunted house."

He strolled toward the front door, the denim of his jeans pulling snug across his rear end as he moved.

Cassie followed him into the hall, happy he was leaving but not wanting to see him go.

He pulled the door open and paused, glancing over his shoulder. "Just have to wonder how long you're going to wait to let someone take care of you."

Chapter 4

Franca, no, I don't think you should come over." Cassie raised her voice to be heard above the hammering. "This spell requires me to get into a meditative state. I can't do that if you're here."

"Why are you yelling at me?" her friend asked. "I only want to help."

"I'm not yelling at you," Cassie yelled. "And I know you want to help."

Thump, thump, thump.

She scowled at the ceiling of her living room. What the heck was that man doing up there? How many nails did it take to attach a strand of wire to the roof?

"Could have fooled me," Franca said.

"I'm yelling because of all the noise here. Chip is pounding holes in the roof." Poor Jinx. When the percussion had started, she'd hightailed it upstairs to burrow under the pillow on Cassie's bed.

"Oh," Franca said. "Well, that won't help your meditation during the knot spell, either. Better try another one today."

Cassie looked at the items spread around her on her yoga mat. A twelve-inch length of silk string. Red, of course. An incense burner. And a bottle of Oshun Oil to anoint her forehead. She liked this spell. All she had to do was concentrate on Samuel, visualize their future, and tie a knot in the string. Easy peasy.

"No, I want to do this one." She crossed her legs to sit in lotus and closed her eyes. Resting her hands palms up on her knees, she took a deep breath. Another. Her muscles eased and—

Thump, thump, thumpity-thump, thump.

"Son of a beehive!" Cassie rolled to her feet. "Let me call you back," she told Franca.

"Wait. Promise me you'll try that last one we talked about." Something crunched over the line.

"Are you eating?" Cassie asked. Her own stomach rumbled.

Franca ignored her. "The mirror spell is supposed to show you who your true love is. I'm not convinced Sam is the one for you. So tonight, at midnight, do this spell. As a favor to me."

There was no way Cassie would be awake at midnight, much less aware enough to walk backward down her staircase looking over her shoulder using a mirror. But her friend was like a terrier with a bone. "I'll think about it." As spells went, that one was one of Nonna's weirder and less useful ones. She *knew* who her true love was. What she needed was the spell to make Samuel take his head out of his butt and figure it out as well.

The pounding rose from headache inducing to eardrum bursting. "I'll call you back," she said to her friend, not knowing if Franca heard her or not. Tossing her phone on the couch, she shoved her feet into the flip-flops by the door and slapped outside.

The sun burned her eyes when she looked up, and she quickly shielded her gaze. The dark figure of a man kneeling with one knee raised was limned by the bright light. "What on earth are you doing up there? Trying out to be the next John Bonham?"

Chip pulled a nail from between his lips. "Who?"

"John Bonham. The drummer for Led Zeppelin."

He shrugged. "I was always more of a Black Sabbath fan."

Cassie's jaw dropped. "Okay, that's it. Off my roof. I can't have a Sabbath fan working for me."

He grinned, and a stupid part of her melted.

"When I was up here setting up the bat deployment system, I noticed you had some shingles that were about worn through. Two more nails and I'll be done replacing them." He raised his hammer and pounded the last few home. "There." He stood. "You shouldn't have any leaks this winter."

Her eyes tracked his surefooted steps to the ladder propped against the roof. His tool belt was slung low around his narrow hips. When he grabbed the top of the ladder and turned, the grip of the hammer smacked across his tight behind.

Cassie shook her head clear and hurried forward to hold the ladder. No way was she jealous of a hammer.

Chip's boots and thighs clambered down into view, and Cassie averted her gaze before her stupid endocrine system got any other ideas. That's all this feeling was. Hormones, plain and simple. And there were plenty of other men who got her engines going. There was nothing special about that.

She just couldn't remember any of the other men when Chip was near.

"Thanks." Chip stood inches from her. If she scooted forward the littlest bit, the tips of her breasts would brush against his chest. He inhaled deeply, and his eyes sank to half-mast.

His bedroom eyes, she imagined.

No. She stepped back. No imagining anything. Samuel was the man for her and it was wrong to think about other men like that. A form of emotional cheating, even. And she wasn't a cheater. Not even on hypothetical future partners.

"No problem." She shifted her weight from one leg to the other. "Thanks for fixing my roof. I appreciate it."

Chip collapsed the extension ladder and swung it up onto one shoulder. "Anytime."

"So . . ." She took another step back, refusing to look at his bunched biceps or the way his cotton shirt clung to his pecs. "You want to see what I got in the mail today?" Without waiting for his answer, she hurried across the porch and into her entry. She pulled the furry contraption from its shipping box and returned to Chip, who was leaning the ladder against the porch.

He tilted his head one way, then the other. "What is it?"

"A new hairy spider!" She set it on a low table by the door and rubbed her hands together. Not only did she love her new purchase, guaranteed to make at least one person scream, but this was more familiar footing with Chip. Talking about the haunted house. Creepy decorations. As long as she kept them focused on the project, everything would be fine.

She pulled one furry leg from its bent position around the two-foot body, stretching it out long. Two more down and it definitely looked more spider-like than the big ball of black fuzz it had been shipped as.

Chip picked up a plastic box that was attached to the spider with wire. "A battery pack? What's it do?"

She flipped the spider onto its back. "The batteries will get tucked up in here," she said, showing the sleeve in the belly of the beast. "It powers the spider to scuttle forward and backward." She combed her fingers through the long hair on one of its legs. "The eyes glow a creepy red. Can you imagine seeing this thing coming at you through the fog?"

"How much did it cost?" Chip asked.

"As long as it makes one person shriek, it will be worth it."

Chip arched an eyebrow. "You're a little weird—you know that?"

"Thanks." She patted the monster on the head.

Chip leaned into her house and picked up the empty box, examining it. "I think I'm going to have to get one of these for my mom. I'll keep my eye out when I go shopping for her later."

"Shopping for her? Is it her birthday?"

"Nah." Chip leaned the box against the wall. He slid his hands into his pockets. "She had cancer a couple years back. Went through three nasty rounds of chemo. She's cancer-free now, but I still like to grocery shop for her, cook her up a couple of meals for the week. That kind of thing."

She blinked. "That's . . . really nice."

"You thought I wouldn't be nice to my mom?"

"No!" She paced to the porch railing and leaned against it. "I meant it's nice that you and your mom are close like that." It shouldn't have surprised her. Most people had good relationships with their parents. She was the oddball out.

Chip dipped his head. "You and your mom aren't?"

"She's passed now." Cassie scraped at a bit of loose paint, focusing on her fingers. "But even before, no. She was . . . let's just say we're very different people. But she did bring my grandpa to live with us after his stroke, and for that I'll always be thankful."

He covered her fidgeting hand with his own.

Cassie hadn't even heard him move. She stared down at his big hand, brown from the sun. Calloused. Comforting.

He squeezed. "I'm sorry. My mom is my rock. I'm sorry you didn't get that."

Eyes burning, she shrugged and slid her hand out from under his. "It's not a big deal."

"Cassie—"

"Well, you're not here to listen to me mope." She forced a smile. "Did you come to any conclusions about whether we need a pergola? Or will just a simple frame do for our purposes?" Her chest tightened. *Please, let it drop.* She looked up, into eyes that had turned moss-soft again. They invited her to spill all her secrets, promising they wouldn't judge.

She couldn't do it. Not without breaking down, and she wasn't going to turn into a bawling mess on her front porch with Chip Gneiss.

Luckily, he took pity. "*We* don't have to build the pergola." One edge of his lip curled upward. "I think if I plant posts there, there, and there," he said, pointing at spots next to her driveway, "we'll be able to create the same effect without the added cost. Unless you want the pergola as an improvement to your house. I know some people grow vines across them and use them as virtual carports. But time is also an issue. I'd have to bring in another guy if we want the pergola up in time for the haunted house."

"Nope, if the posts work, that's all I care about." She pushed thoughts of her mom from her mind and let the excitement of Halloween cheer her up. She stared at her driveway, imagining the twists and turns of the maze. At one corner, she'd have a high school student appear to have his head slip from his neck. That trick was always a big screamer. But it needed the right lighting. If Chip's simpler structure would hold the lights, then it was all good with her.

She bounced from one foot to the other. It was going to be fabulous.

Chip raised his eyebrows and shook his head. "Weird."

Cassie lifted one shoulder. "I told you. Halloween is my jam. And speaking of jam, are you hungry? I can make us some sandwiches."

"Sounds great." He hopped off the porch and plucked up the ladder. "I'm going to hang the other end of the wire to that maple in the corner of your yard."

"Okay. I'll let you know when lunch is ready." Picking up the spider, she held it to her stomach and stepped into the house.

"Oh, Cassie?"

She paused on the threshold, glancing over her shoulder. Her body tensed. He wasn't going to bring it up again, was he?

"I don't suppose you have any more cookies, do you?"

She grinned, relieved. "There might be a couple left in the cookie jar. They'll be dessert." She hurried to the kitchen, placing the spider on the island. She pulled sandwich makings from the refrigerator, whistling the melody to "Dead Man's Party" as she prepared a meal for her and Chip.

As long as things stayed lighthearted and platonic, she really enjoyed Chip's company. Who knew? This could be the start of a beautiful friendship. Even though he wasn't the man for her, Chip would be a great catch for some lucky woman. She ran through the names of the single ladies she knew.

Susan was a free spirit and would appreciate that Chip wasn't afraid to get his hands dirty, but she wouldn't get his sense of humor.

Juanita was a sweetheart and had a thing for a man in a tool belt. But she liked to go out dancing every weekend, and Cassie pictured Chip as more the relaxing-in-front-of-a-fire kind of guy.

Alina, now she would be perfect for Chip. Down-to-earth and funny, she'd find him charming, which Cassie had to admit he was. In his own way. They could go to the occasional metal concert together, and she would keep him knee-deep in her famous chocolate chip cookies.

Cassie's stomach twisted. She set the mayonnaise knife down and stared at her spider. They would be good together. She should try to set that up.

And the hollow ache in her chest told her she never would.

"What the hell?" She tossed the knife in the sink and wiped her hands on her pants. This wasn't happening. Six months ago, she'd decided that Samuel was the man for her. Educated and refined. Someone who'd be a good companion, who'd provide security for their golden years. That was what she wanted. She'd spent the past couple months trying to get his attention, and she wasn't going to waste all that effort on a handyman who looked sexy in a worn pair of jeans.

She stalked to her living room and picked up her phone to call Franca. Tossed it back down. She knew what Franca would say.

Cassie eyed the staircase up to her second floor. Nonna's spell was silly. And unnecessary. She tapped her toe. Oh, screw it. Tonight, at midnight, she'd get confirmation that Samuel was the man for her. She eyed the stairs again. How difficult was it to walk backward down the steps, looking into a mirror, in the dark? A test run might be in order.

Taking the steps two at a time, her flip-flops slapping at the wood, she bustled into her bathroom and picked up the tabletop swivel mirror on her counter. She grimaced and flipped the mirror from the horrifyingly magnified side that made her pores appear the size of moon craters to the normal reflection. Time for a facial. After she confirmed her true love.

She stopped by her bed to pet Jinx. "I'm sure you'll love Samuel, too. He's got a nice house we'll move into after we marry."

Jinx rolled away from her, stalked to another spot on the bed, out of Cassie's reach, and curled back up.

"Okay, I'll suggest he move in here." Jeesh. So judgmental. She left her bedroom and walked to the top of the staircase. Turning, she gripped the handrail and tilted the mirror to reflect over her shoulder. She lowered her foot, searching for the next step with her toe.

Okay, this was doable. The dark of midnight shouldn't be an issue. And she didn't feel like a dumbass doing it, at all. Not. At. All. She made it down four more steps, and the back of her flip-flop caught and bent under her heel.

Wobbling, she dropped the mirror but caught it before it hit the floor. She gripped the bannister tighter and shook her foot until the rubber sole flipped right-side out. No shoes tonight, she told herself as she stretched her foot for the next step down.

She raised the mirror back into position and looked into it. And screamed.

A large, distorted face stared back at her.

Her foot missed the next step. Her fingernails clawed at the bannister. She toppled backward.

Anticipating the crack of her head against the stairs, she winced, rounding in on herself.

Firm arms circled her waist, stopping her fall.

"Whoa! Are you okay?"

Cassie peeled one eyelid open, then the other, and stared up into Chip's face. She was alive! And a complete idiot. She reached for his tool belt to pull herself up, missed, and flushed even hotter at what she accidentally grabbed.

A muscle ticked in Chip's jaw. "Cassie?" He hauled her upright, his arms banding around her waist and holding her flush to his body. "Are you okay?" he asked again.

"Great." Her body tingled. Her pulse raced. She pressed closer, loving how soft his Henley felt, like he'd washed the shirt a thousand times.

His brows drew together. "Great?"

"Uh, fine. I mean fine." She forced her hands to stop petting his shoulders. It was hard. After another near-death experience, her body felt entitled to a little recompense. "Thanks." She gave him a weak smile. "Good catch."

He settled his hands at her hips and moved from the first step to the ground floor. He looked her up and down. "Well, there's no blood, so I guess you're good. But what were you doing?"

"Nothing." She dragged her hands from him and ran them through her hair, making sure nothing was sticking up. She searched for the mirror and spied it on the living room rug, thankfully unbroken. She didn't know what kind of magic juju she would have needed to counteract seven years of bad luck.

"Were you walking down the stairs backward?"

"No, that would be weird."

He dipped his chin and raised an eyebrow. "Babe."

Okay. She and weird went together like pumpkin and spice, but no way was she admitting to walking down a staircase backward to see the face of her true love.

Her heart stalled. His face. She'd seen his face. Grotesquely distorted because of the magnification. But it had been Chip's face.

He gripped her shoulder. "You've gone pale. Are you sure you're okay?"

She bobbed her head. "Yep." She needed to stop nodding. He was looking at her like he was about to throw her in his truck and take her to the hospital. But it couldn't be true. It wasn't supposed to be Chip's face.

Her body grew warm. *Would it really be that bad?* She looked him up and down, wondering what he'd look like in a suit. Or at least business casual. He'd probably clean up well. "Thanks again, Charles," she said, trying out his full name. A perfectly respectable name. One people could depend on.

Chip twisted his lips. "That might be the name on my birth certificate, but I'm only a Chip." The look in his eyes told her she'd been caught out. Embarrassment burned in her gut. He wasn't a house to be gentrified. Chip knew who he was, and a part of her respected the hell out of that.

But that proved he wasn't the man for her. No matter what the stupid mirror had shown. She stalked over to it and plucked it off the floor.

Her breath caught. It wasn't midnight. Seeing Chip's reflection had meant nothing.

Her stomach rolled. That was a good thing. She should be relieved.

Her brain knew it was for the best. So why wasn't her heart getting the message?

Chapter 5

Chip sneezed at the cloying vanilla scent of the wax stuck in his nose. That one wasn't even close. He gazed around the candle and potpourri shop and sighed. It wasn't in here. Nothing came close to that delectable scent that emanated from Cassie's skin.

The Monday morning rush, if there was such a thing in Moonbright, had ended an hour ago, and Chip was the only customer in Scentabulous. The woman behind the counter had offered to help him when he'd first come in, and now shot him increasingly annoyed glances with every candle or bundle of leafy crap he smelled. Like he was manhandling her merchandise. Which, okay, he kind of was, but he couldn't get that scent out of his head. Couldn't get Cassie out of his head. Which made no sense. Sure, she was smart, funny, gorgeous, and generous with her cookies, but she took every chance to tell him she wasn't interested. Chip wasn't normally the kind of guy who pursued a woman. Too much work when there were plenty of other fish in the sea.

What was it about Cassie?

He nodded goodbye to the clerk and escaped from the store. That had been an idiotic detour. If he'd found her scent, what would he have done? Lit the Cassie candle each night, wishing she were in his bed with him instead of just her smell? He snorted and flipped his sunglasses from his head to the bridge of his nose.

Striding down the sidewalk, Chip made a mental list of what he needed to get done that day. Picking up his lumber delivery was number one. His house had finally closed, and he should at least start the demo he had planned. Even though he wouldn't have much time for it. Cassie's job had a deadline, so most of his day would be spent there. He'd be working long nights, heading over to his flip house after he put in his time with her haunted one.

All solid reasons to get his butt into gear.

But he couldn't get the scent of her, the feel of her as she'd tumbled into his arms, out of his head.

He walked past his truck parked at the curb and made his way to Bellaluna's instead. That cookie, the one that had gotten him into trouble, had been very close to Cassie's scent. Besides, he was hungry. A cookie and a cup of joe would hit the spot.

He pushed through the door, causing a small bell to tinkle overhead. The smell of everything delicious in the world seduced Chip's nose. Only one customer was in line in front of him, and Sofia was handing her a cake box.

She turned her smile on Chip. "Hello, young man. It's been a couple of days since I've seen you in here. You want your usual?"

His mouth watered at just the thought of the flaky almond croissant he normally ordered. Maybe he'd get the croissant and the cookie.

Rubbing his stomach, he scanned the display case. "I had a cookie a couple of days ago that was in one of your boxes. About so big, with a bit of cream and sprinkles on top?" He held his hand up, thumb and index finger spread.

Sofia tilted her head. "I'm sorry, *caro*. If you don't see it in the case, we don't have it today."

His stomach chose that moment to grumble. "Okay, then, my usual."

He pulled out his wallet, paid, and took his plate and mug. Only two tables were occupied, and Chip sat at his usual spot by the window. He pulled out his phone to check the news and bit into breakfast heaven.

The bell above the door tinkled, and something much more entertaining than his phone walked into the bakery.

Cassie didn't see him as she beelined to the counter. She held a hushed conversation with Sofia before her shoulders sagged. She nodded, and Sofia reached across the counter to pat her hand. She handed Cassie a mug of coffee.

Cassie turned and took a step toward the nearest table.

Chip raised a hand, catching her attention.

Her eyes widened and a smile streaked across her face when she saw him, making Chip's pulse race. No way was that the look of someone who just wanted to be friends.

Just as quickly, her excitement disappeared and the look she shot him was purely professional. "Hi, Chip. How are you doing today?"

Standing, he pulled out a chair. "Good. I'm planning on heading over to your place after lunch."

She sank down and reached for a packet of sugar. "If you need to get inside for any reason—to use the bathroom, get a cookie—there's a spare key under the back doormat."

Chip frowned. "That's not a very secure system."

"This is Moonbright." She doctored her coffee and took a sip. "The chances of my locking myself out far outweigh the chances of a burglar checking my back mat."

Sofia bustled over, a small white plate in her hand. A chocolate-dipped cannoli sat in the middle on a white doily. She set the pastry in front of Cassie. "I know you were asking about that sugar-free, gluten-free nonsense, but I thought you could use this instead. You have a lovely figure. You don't need to diet."

Cassie's cheeks turned an adorable pink. "Thanks."

Sofia nodded and strolled back behind the counter as Cassie took a bite.

Chip narrowed his eyes. "You came to Bellaluna's looking for health food?" He eyed Cassie's form. And Sofia was right. Lucky for him, Cassie wasn't stick-thin like those models he saw on magazine covers nowadays. Nothing needed changing on her body.

"It wasn't for me." Cassie brushed a bit of cream from her bottom lip.

"More cookies for the mystery man?"

She raised one shoulder. An auburn curl broke loose from her bun and drifted down to brush against her collarbone.

Irritation curdled in his stomach, and he pushed his almond croissant away. "Sam's the guy who doesn't appreciate your cookies." Son of a—Chip inhaled sharply. Cassie was right. If that was her sort of man, there wasn't much chance she'd be interested in him. Chip liked Sam well enough, but the dude was like a robot, with no passion for anything except keeping fit. A robot in a suit. Didn't get his hands dirty, and was probably ten times smarter than Chip.

"How did you know?"

"He told me last week he was cutting carbs."

She leaned forward, resting her elbows on the table. "You and Sam socialize?"

He crossed his arms over his chest and bit back an angry retort. Like that would have been unheard of, he and Sam hanging out and having a beer together.

He twisted his lips. Okay, yeah, that probably would never happen. "He jogs on Spinney trail and that's where I walk my dog. It's how we met."

"You have a dog?" Her eyes went as liquid as melted chocolate. "What kind?"

"A retriever/Lab mix. His name is Max."

She sighed. "And Samuel wanted to pet Max and that's how you met."

Chip snorted. "You don't know much about this guy you're stuck on. When we talk on the trail, Sam ignores Max. He doesn't like dogs."

She scrunched her face up. "What are you talking about? Everyone likes dogs."

"Not Sam." He and Sam had met when the guy had gotten in Chip's face about some dog shit he'd stepped in. When Chip had pointed out the bag full of crap he carried—he cleaned up after his dog, thank you very much—Sam had been decent enough to apologize.

But he still didn't like Max.

"What do you see in the guy?" Chip leaned back in his chair. "His only sense of humor seems to be corny one-liners. The guy's so tightly wound he could single-handedly turn a piece of coal into a diamond. And I can't imagine he'd appreciate your Halloween craziness."

She turned her mug in her hands, staring into its depths as though trying to read her future. "Have you ever looked at someone and just known? One glance, and you could see your future written out as clearly as a novel?"

He stopped short of rolling his eyes. Love at first sight. Such a chick thing to believe in.

She raised her gaze from her coffee and locked it with his. She looked a little sad, a bit vulnerable, and sexy as hell, a weird combination, but it worked on her. His chest squeezed, as if he'd been hit with a load of bricks. Unbidden, the word *yes* slipped from his mouth.

Her cheeks went pink again and she dropped her eyes to the table.

"Go out with me." He didn't say it like a question. He didn't want to give her the chance to say no.

She buried her face in her mug and took a large sip. When she put the coffee down, she sighed. "No, I can't."

"Bull. You absolutely can, and you should." He raked a hand through his hair. "You'd realize that if you'd wise up and forgot about Sam. He's not right for you."

She waved her index finger between the two of them. "No, *we're* not right for each other."

"Because I work with a hammer instead of a computer?" A low burn of anger spread from his gut up behind his breastbone. "You don't want a pair of calloused hands marking your skin?"

A fine shiver went through Cassie's body, but her face remained set. She stared over his left shoulder. "We just aren't suited. It has nothing to do with the man you are."

"Like hell." He stood and tossed some bills down for the busboy. "You don't think I'm good enough because of my job. That's the only thing stopping this." Shit, he should show her his balance sheet. He wasn't doing so badly. He worked hard, saved his money, and was now investing in real estate. But no way was he going to grovel for her attention. Try to buy her affection.

She grabbed his arm, her grip like an iron vise.

"Have you ever been poor?" she asked. "Not college-kid-eating-ramen poor, but the power's-been-out-for-a-week-because-your-mom's-latest-loser-boyfriend-took-all-the-money-when-he-left kind of poor. The haven't-eaten-anything-but-gum-in-three-days kind of poor, and that's only because gum was the only thing an eight-year-old was brave enough to steal from the corner market." Her fingertips dug past his shirt and got right into his skin.

He swallowed, a sharp pain lancing the back of his throat. "No." Jesus. God. She wore a nice silk blouse and cute shoes, and he'd assumed that the way she presented herself now was the way she'd always been.

"I deserve better than that life," she whispered.

His heart flopped like a dying fish. He squatted next to her and cupped her cheek. "Babe."

She leaned into his touch for the briefest of moments before drawing back. She blew out a long, slow breath and as he watched, rebuilt her walls. Her spine hardened to steel; her gaze became shuttered.

And that right there was why he wasn't giving up. She was such a complex mix of grit and need, and he felt right down to his bones that his purpose was to satisfy each and every one of those needs.

His muscles tightened, as though preparing for battle. But this was a long game, and he knew when not to push.

He leaned over and pressed his lips to her temple. "You do deserve better." Better than settling for the safe bet. Better than trading love and passion for security. "You deserve it all."

Chapter 6

Cassie turned her car down her street, her hands gripping the steering wheel. She'd thought about taking the coward's way out—going out for dinner after work and getting back home after Chip had left. After her stupid mouth had gotten away from her that morning, the idea had been tempting. But then what about tomorrow? Or the next day? Eventually she'd have to face the man if she wanted her haunted house finished.

She smacked her head on the back of her seat rest. She'd admitted something to Chip she hadn't even told Franca. She didn't want to face the pity that was sure to be in his eyes.

Maybe he'd had a traumatic brain injury in the meantime and forgotten. A girl could only hope.

She slowed as she approached her house. Her dark house. "Huh." All her pep talks about facing Chip and it hadn't even mattered. He wasn't here. And by the looks of her driveway, he hadn't put in an appearance all day.

She parked at the curb and got out, slamming her door shut. Just when she was beginning to think he was different. Stalking to her house, she pulled out her phone to check for messages. Nothing.

It was her own fault. She'd waited too long to start work on her haunted house. She knew how flaky handymen could be. She just hadn't wanted her driveway taken over for a week ahead of time.

She pushed into her house, flipped on her lights, and stalked to the living room. Jinx lay in a straight line across the sofa's arm rest, and Cassie flopped down beside her. "I hope your day was better than mine," she said, and stroked Jinx's back.

The cat batted her hand away, as if the show of affection was interrupting her nap, and hopped off the couch.

"That fancy kibble you get can always be downgraded." Cassie glared at the cat's retreating form. "To generic brands!"

She kicked her feet up on the ottoman and slouched farther into the sofa. Fine. Samuel didn't love her, Jinx didn't love her, Chip—

Nope. Cutting off that thought right there.

And speak of the devil . . .

The low rumble of Chip's truck approached, headlights flashing through her front windows.

She pushed to her feet and tugged on the hem of her jacket. Sure, he showed up now when, in the next thirty seconds, it was going to be too dark to work. Well, she'd tell him just where he could stick whatever excuse he had.

She marched out and confronted him on the driveway as he climbed out of his truck. His hair was damp, as if he'd just come from a shower, and instead of his usual jeans or chinos, he wore gray sweatpants slung low on his hips.

He opened his mouth, but she held up her hand to stop him. "Whatever you have to say, I don't want to hear it. All I want to know is if you'll still be able to get my haunted house finished in time."

"Yes." He took a step forward. "But, listen, I had an emergency—"

"A gym emergency?" She snorted and shot another glance at the incriminating sweatpants. "You just had to get those last couple of sets in?"

A ball of golden fur hurtled from the open truck door and leapt at Cassie, knocking her back a step. The dog grinned up at her, his whole butt wagging right along with his tail, and Cassie couldn't help but melt.

"Hello there, cutie." She scratched behind his ears. He licked her wrist, then jumped down to explore her yard. "Don't tell me that sweet dog is yours."

"Hey, I can do sweet."

Cassie rolled her eyes and stalked back to her house. "You will be here tomorrow, I hope?"

Chip caught up to her and matched her stride.

"Yes, I'll be here tomorrow. And I would have been here today except—"

"Except you're a flake." She stopped on her porch and gave him her sweetest smile. "Don't worry about it. You probably can't even help it. You're a handyman. And that's why handymen are on my professions-not-to-date list."

He crossed his arms, his pecs flexing. "You have a do-not-date list?"

"Of course." She ticked them off on her fingers. "Musicians, actors, fitness trainers, *handymen,* and bartenders. All flakes. I've theorized that people who work gig-type jobs can't handle steady work because they are undependable people."

"Thought about this a lot, have you?" He took a step closer.

Jinx peeked out the front door, saw the dog on her turf, and tore between Chip and Cassie to find a spot in the bushes to plot.

Chip grimaced and stepped back.

"Yes." Cassie planted her hands on her hips. "I've dated the wrong men for years. So, when I moved here, I decided to get smart. Wrote down a list of all the qualities I want in a man and those I don't. The do-not-date list was a side product of that." It was also a best hits of the losers her mom had dated. Musicians had been her mom's main weakness, but there had been the odd bartender or handyman thrown in there, too.

She turned and marched for her door.

Chip's hand on her arm stopped her from going through. "The house I'm working on had a sewer pipe explode. Even calling in friends and favors, it took five hours to fix. I couldn't just leave it."

She studied his damp hair again. That could explain the shower. But she couldn't let all her indignation slip away. "You could have called. Heck, even a text would have worked."

"I was elbow-deep in waste." His nostrils flared. "I wasn't going to pull out my phone."

"And one of your friends couldn't have contacted me?" She shook off his hand. Her breath hitched. "Look, I get that I'm a minor job for you, but my haunted house is important to me. If you don't have the time for it, for me, please let me know now."

Her hand trembled, and she clenched it. It shouldn't matter that he'd turned out to be another unreliable male. She'd been expecting it.

"I'll get it done." He moved into her space, close enough for her to smell the cedar and citrus scents of his soap. "Cassie, I won't let you down."

She lifted her chin. "I guess we're just going to have to see about that." And with a haughty toss of her head, she stomped inside and slammed the door. A fine exit if she ever saw one.

Jinx yowled from the porch.

261

Slouching, Cassie tugged the door open a crack to let her cat inside. She ignored the tilt to Chip's lips and pressed the door closed for a much less dramatic farewell.

Chapter 7

Now, this is a spell I can get behind." Cassie rubbed a dab of the melted soy wax into the back of her hand. The patch of skin turned silky-smooth.

Franca sighed over the speaker on her phone. "You're using it as lotion again, aren't you?"

Cassie snapped her hands behind her back. "No."

A tongue lapped at her fingers, and Cassie turned. "Wax isn't good for you, silly." She scratched behind Max's head and received a tongue to the mouth. She made a face. That was one advantage to cats: They never slipped you the tongue. Chuckling, she straightened and padded to her cookie jar. She picked out one of the newly baked dog treats and fed him one. "That's your food. Jinx!" she called. She shook a bag of cat treats. "I have a snack for you, too!"

No cat appeared. Still sulking, then. Jinx hadn't appreciated Max's appearance in her house and had stalked off, bristling tail held high.

Cassie sighed.

"How many treats have you given that dog?"

Franca asked. "He's going to burst soon, and that won't be pretty."

"Oh, let me have fun with him." She'd always wanted a dog but had never felt the time was right. Besides, any bursting would probably happen on Chip's watch. His excuse last night had sounded reasonable, but that's all it had been. An excuse.

Max plopped his butt in front of her and tilted his head from side to side. Cassie slumped her shoulders. "You're right. It was a legit excuse."

"Uh, are you talking to me or the dog?" Franca asked.

"The dog." She gave Max one last scratch, then turned back to her twelve-quart stockpot full of melted wax.

Chip had arrived at her house early that morning. Cassie had taken the day off, offering to lend him a second pair of hands to make up for yesterday's lost time. Based on the muscle throbbing in Chip's jaw, he hadn't appreciated her helpfulness. So, she'd decided to refocus on her plan. She'd given Chip a tight smile, stolen his dog, and moved on to the next spell on her list to turn Samuel's head.

The whine of Chip's skill saw cut through her thoughts of Samuel. Cassie tossed a frown in the direction of her driveway. With all the noise that man made, it was hard to keep her boss in her head at all.

She dumped some crushed rose blossoms into the pot and beat the wax into submission with her heavy wooden spoon.

After this Halloween, she needed to make sure her path didn't cross Chip's. He was bad for her plan. Bad for her heart.

"Are you ready for the incantation yet?"

Cassie started, and peered into the pot. "Yep, the new batch of wax is ready. I have my baker's twine cut into wicks and weighted. But I think I've got it now. You don't need to stick around to read the spell with me." Hearing Franca's low voice chanting over the phone, joining in the spell with Cassie, just made her feel like an even bigger ass than she would on her own. It was one thing to stand alone in her kitchen and feel like an idiot. It was quite another to have a witness, even if it was only over a phone line.

Max leaned into her thigh and gazed up at her adoringly.

She rubbed his head. "You don't count." She had no qualms acting like an idiot in front of such a sweet, nonjudgmental creature.

"What?" Franca asked.

"Nothing."

Franca sniffed. "Well, let's get on with it. I helped with the other batch. Let's finish it off. Besides, the spells have more power when more people join in."

"Okay." Cassie glanced over her shoulder,

waited for the next whine of the saw. She held her hands over the pot, feeling warmth leech into her palms. "Let's start."

"We call upon Aphrodite, Parvati, and Isis," they intoned in unison. "Hear the sound of my heart. Heed my call."

Cassie blew out her cheeks and picked up a wick. She folded the middle of the wick over her finger, then paused. "Wait. You were saying 'hear the sound' of *your* heart, not mine. Is that going to mess this up?"

"Huh," Franca said around a mouthful of her lunch. "We probably should have thought of that before."

Cassie stared at her tainted magic wax and shrugged. It couldn't make the situation any worse. She dipped both ends of the wick into the wax, waited five seconds, then dipped the ends into a pot of cold water. She repeated the steps, watching as two tapers took shape.

"This takes an annoyingly long time."

"What are you complaining about?" A bag crinkled. "I'm the one stuck here at work. Not everyone has saved up vacation time."

Dip, dip. "Then don't go on vacation."

Franca huffed.

Cassie's stomach rumbled. "You're always eating when we're on the phone. What is it this time?" Cassie pondered what was in her fridge. She didn't think she had many lunch makings.

Maybe she and Max would go get some takeout.

"Pizza Pringles." Franca munched on another chip.

"Sounds disgusting." Cassie hung the candles over a string she'd wound around two cabinet knobs and moved a paper towel underneath to catch any drips.

"Delicious," Franca mumbled.

Cassie doubted that. But pizza didn't sound half bad for lunch. She'd have to ask Chip what kind he liked. Which meant facing him. Talking to him again.

"Did you put your thumbprint on the wax?"

Darn it. Cassie lifted a taper and pressed her thumb against the base. She repeated on the other candle, grateful the wax was still soft enough to take the imprint. "Done."

"Done with what?" a male voice asked from the entrance to the kitchen.

Cassie spun, pressing her palm to her chest. "Jesus, Mary, and Joseph! You startled me."

"Sorry," Chip said, not looking sorry at all. A streak of dirt crossed the right knee of his jeans. He'd unbuttoned his flannel shirt, a red one today, and his white undershirt clung to his chest in damp patches. He'd rolled the sleeves of the flannel up to reveal corded forearms dusted with dark hair.

Cassie ignored the flutter in her stomach. "Why are you smiling?"

"I like the idea that I can scare the scare queen." Chip prowled to the refrigerator and pulled out a bottle of water. He bent over and gave Max a good chest rub.

Cassie grumbled. She didn't like that idea at all. She also wasn't happy that she had a tendency to look like a fool in front of the man. First, choking, then falling down stairs, then almost crying on his shoulder in Bellaluna's. She scraped the toe of her sneaker along a small crack in her porcelain tile. She'd been so angry at him last night, she'd forgotten to feel embarrassed about the bakery incident. "Uh, I was hoping to talk to you about what I said at Bellaluna's."

Chip leaned a hip against the counter. "What about it?" he said quietly.

She ran her hand along the ledge of her sink. Her feet drew her a step closer to him. Stupid feet.

"I was hoping you'd forget the conversation happened."

"Why?"

She shrugged and stared at his chin. It was too hard to look into his eyes. Something in them made her feel stripped bare. "I don't talk about my childhood. Not with anyone."

His chin moved closer, came to hover right in front of her.

Chip cupped her cheek and tilted her head back until she had no choice but to look at him. "You told me, and it's something I won't forget. I

268

consider it a privilege that I'm the only one who knows that secret." His thumb brushed across the corner of her mouth. "I want to know all your secrets."

Cassie's body tingled. Stupid body. She took a deep breath and squared her shoulders. Self-control. She had it somewhere. She just had to dig deep. Stepping back, she turned to her row of dangling candles. She knocked a dry one with her finger, setting it to swinging. "Well, thanks for your discretion."

She heard fabric shift. "Cassie—"

"How's it going outside?" She pulled a set of tapers down and lined them up on her counter. "Do you need a second pair of hands for anything?"

He reached around her shoulder, his body curving around hers, and picked up the candles. "No, I've got it."

Cassie sidestepped away from his heat.

He sniffed the candles. "These smell good. I don't think I've ever met a woman who made her own candles."

"It's a new hobby." She snatched the candles from his hand. Chip rubbing his testosterone all over her candles for Samuel couldn't bode well, magically speaking.

"I'm surprised you didn't dye them orange and black."

She cocked her head. That wasn't a bad idea.

There was no reason all of her candles had to be imbued with a love spell. Maybe tomorrow she'd make up a muggle batch for Halloween.

"These are for the office. For Samuel." She needed to drive that point home. Chip was good at making her forget her plan. The reminder was as much for herself as for him.

His lips pressed into a white slash. "I see." He unscrewed his bottle of water and tossed back a swallow. "You think waving sweet-smelling candles in front of him is going to change anything? If he's such a dumbass that he hasn't scooped you up yet, I don't think candles are going to do the trick." He glared at the tapers, as if they'd personally insulted him.

She gave him back his glare and then some. "They're just a small gift that will hopefully brighten his day." And when the candle burned down past her thumbprint, light up his heart.

Jeez, that sounded stupid. Even Aunt Hildy would have mocked her attempt at a love spell. Blushing, she stepped to the stove and turned off the heat. When she faced Chip again, he was still looking as grumpy as a man who'd just had his house egged by trick-or-treaters. But now his scowl was focused on the half-eaten cookie in his hand.

The cookies she had made for Max.

She tried to smother her laugh, and it escaped as a snort.

"What the hell's funny?" He swallowed his bite.

Max planted his butt in front of Chip and whined softly.

Chip rubbed the dog's head and lifted the rest of the treat to his mouth.

She shook her head. "Don't eat that."

He grimaced. "Honestly, it's not your best work, but it's good enough."

"It's also a dog biscuit." She stepped to the cookie jar, reached inside, and tossed one in the air. Max leapt onto two legs and caught it. "I baked them for Max this morning."

"Oh." He swept his tongue around his mouth and laid the treat on the island.

"Look, I have a few things to finish up here and then I'm going to make a lunch run. Pizza okay?" she asked.

Chip swigged the rest of his water. "Yeah, I'll finish up what I'm working on." He walked out and all the energy in the house seemed to go with him.

Cassie's shoulders curved, her chest hollowing out.

"Well, hell's bells." Franca's voice bellowed from the counter, making Cassie jump. "Seriously, what are you doing"—*crunch, crunch*—"wasting Nonna's juju on Sam when there's enough sexual tension"—*crunch, crunch*—"between you and Chiperoo to start a bonfire?"

271

"Jeez, I forgot you were on the line." Cassie chewed on her lip and tried to remember if she'd said anything incriminating. "And you shouldn't talk with your mouth full."

"Do you know"—*crunch, crunch, crunch*—"how hard it was to have a canister of Pizza Pringles in front of me and not eat?" She chugged down some liquid. "I didn't want to make any chewing sounds and spoil your moment."

"There was no moment. And if there had been, you should have hung up."

Max placed his front paws on the island and licked up Chip's half-eaten cookie.

Cassie frowned. "That's the last snack for you."

"Uh, I've got half a can left."

"Not you, Franca." Cassie wiped down the counter to clean the dog drool. "I've gotta go. I'll talk to you later."

"Wait. About this childhood secret of yours . . ."

Cassie dropped her chin to her chest. "It's nothing." She shook her head. "Really, just me bitching about some tough times. Old news."

"Not to me." Franca paused. "You know I will get it out of you."

Cassie couldn't help but grin. Her friend would. She was as tenacious as a pit bull. And maybe opening up to her wouldn't be so bad. It was probably time. But not today. "I'll talk to you later. Thanks, Franca." She disconnected. Putting

272

down her phone, she picked up the pot of warm wax. How to dispose of it?

"I forgot—"

"Gah!" Cassie spun. The pot slipped against her stomach, the heated metal burning her through her shirt. She held it away, moved to settle it back on the counter, missed, and dropped the whole damn mess.

Wax splashed across her tile floor, oozing out in every direction.

"Damn!"

"Are you okay?" Chip asked. He circled the island.

"Yeah, I just need to clean it up." She reached for a roll of paper towels. The heel of her shoe slid in the wax. Desperately, she windmilled her arms, trying to regain her balance.

And failing.

She went down, a wave of wax squelching out beneath her butt.

"Cassie!" Chip darted toward her.

She held up her hands. "No, watch—"

His boot hit wax and skidded sideways. He crashed onto his stomach, his breath escaping him in a wheeze.

"Out for the mess," she finished.

Chip did a push-up and sat back on his knees. "You're all right?"

"Fine. You?"

He ran a hand down his shirt, sloughing off

some wax. "Just peachy. At least I'll smell good."

She pressed her lips together. He was coated, from his thighs to his chest. He looked like he'd been slimed. "It's also good for your skin. Your hands will look ten years younger."

He ignored that and planted one palm on the counter and the other on the island. He pulled himself to his feet. Glancing over her shoulder, he said, "Max, don't lick that."

The dog slinked away from the wax pool and lay down in front of the refrigerator.

Cassie took Chip's hand and let him haul her up. "If you give me your shirt and pants, I can throw them in the wash." Her foot slid, nudging into his boot, and Chip wrapped an arm behind her, drawing her snug to his body.

"It usually takes a little more effort from a woman to get my pants off." His eyes twinkled with mischief.

"Uh, that was a poor choice in words." Her breasts brushed his shirt, her breathing going choppy. An image of a pants-less Chip skirted around the edges of her mind. She leaned back over his arm, wanting to make space between them, and only managed to press her belly and parts farther south tighter to his body. She tried to inject snark into her voice, but her words came out breathy instead. "And I highly doubt that."

She should step back. Clean up the wax before it hardened. She didn't move. All the parts of their bodies seemed to fit together, like a puzzle.

Remember the plan. Remember. The. Plan. Samuel is the man. . . . Her heart stalled. She couldn't say it anymore. Couldn't even think it. She didn't want Samuel to be the man meant for her.

Chip lowered his head, his lips inches away.

Screw the plan.

She rolled up onto her toes and closed the distance between them.

The kiss started out sweet, tentative even. The poor man was probably frozen in shock at her action after all the pushing away she'd done.

He recovered quickly. His lips went soft beneath hers. His kiss tender.

She wrapped her arms around his back, feeling a buzz from her lips straight down to her toes. This couldn't have been what her mom felt, not with any of her boyfriends. Cassie had seen how they'd treated her. None of them had held her mom like she was the best gift in the world. Kissed her like she was the very oxygen he needed to breathe.

She opened for him, and he slid his tongue inside her mouth, tasting every part of her. With a whimper, she pressed closer, wanting to crawl right inside his body.

He gripped her butt and lifted.

Wrapping her legs around his waist, she slanted her head and took the kiss deeper. It turned desperate, devouring, and was taking them some-place she wasn't sure she was ready for. Especially not in her kitchen while they were both covered in wax.

The wax.

She yanked her head back. "Oh, crap. Put me down."

It took him a moment to blink the dazed look out of his eyes. "What? Are there cookies burning?"

She wiggled, and he released her hips. She slid down his body, thought about ignoring the wax problem and picking up where they'd left off, but got a grip on herself. "Not everything's about cookies." The wax on the floor had hardened, and Cassie strode across it to pull a clean dishrag from a drawer. She wet it in the sink, then turned on Chip. "We need to get this wax off your skin."

She attacked his arm, scrubbing until his skin was pink.

"What's wrong with the wax?" he asked. "I thought you said it was good for my skin."

"Weeell . . ." The tips of her ears burned. "The wax itself is fine. But what I added to it might not be great for you." Would a love spell for another man affect Chip? Getting the wax all over him couldn't be good. Although the magic was supposed to happen when the candle burned down, so maybe they were safe. She'd have to call Franca to ask.

He grabbed the towel and started scrubbing her exposed neckline. "What the hell's in it?"

She stopped his hand. Jeez, he was scraping her skin off like a power sander. "Nothing that would hurt me."

He paused. "Explain."

Her heart beat unnaturally loudly. This was it. Not only had Chip ruined her for Samuel, but now when he found out how strange she was, he was going to drop her, too. She squeezed her eyes shut. "Iputalovespellonthecandles. For Sam." She screwed open one eye and prepared for his reaction.

Chip drew his eyebrows together. "Did I hear the words *love spell* in there?"

She jerked her head up and down. "Franca knows some old-school love spells, and I thought, well, since the usual methods weren't working on Samuel . . ."

"That you'd try the unusual." His voice was even, not giving her any hint of what was going on in his head.

She gulped down a breath. "You think I'm crazy."

His lips twitched.

Cassie narrowed her eyes. "Chip?"

He burst out laughing. That dimple in his right cheek made an appearance, but its adorableness didn't stop her ire from rising when he threw his head back and roared.

"It's not funny." She crossed her arms over her chest. "Magic is a serious business."

He laughed harder, clutching his ribs. Max trotted over to check on his person and nosed Chip's thigh, whining.

It wasn't that funny. She stomped to the utensil drawer for a butter knife. Yes, she might have had her doubts about Franca's spells, but it darn sure wasn't Chip's place to judge.

Chip wiped his eyes, his laughter tapering off. "Don't be like that." He glanced at her hand. "What's with the knife?"

"To scrape the wax off the floor." Although a little jab to his midsection was awfully tempting. "Obviously."

"Babe, with you nothing's obvious. You might have got the knife out to prick your finger for another spell for all I know."

Slapping the blade of the knife against her palm, the very dull blade that could barely cut through butter, much less her finger, thank you very much, she gritted her teeth. "Magic isn't a joke," she spit out. "And don't act like you're so immune to the supernatural. Do you walk under your ladder?"

He hooked his thumbs in his belt loops. "Well, come on, that's just common sense."

"Mm-hmm." She poked the air with the knife. "And do you, or do you not, avoid crossing my cat's path? My black cat?"

He rubbed the back of his neck. "Well . . ." He shrugged. "Maybe I am a little weird, too. That's why we're perfect for each other." The smile that slid across his face was devilish and did funny things to her stomach.

She rolled the knife between her fingers. "You don't think the juju wax on your skin was the reason why you kissed me, do you? The love magic didn't rev your engines, so to speak?"

He dropped his head level with hers. "I don't know much, but I do know that it wasn't your mumbo jumbo that made me kiss you. I've been wanting to kiss you ever since you started breathing again in my arms. No magic required."

"Well, okay." They stared at each other. She tossed the knife on the island. "I don't know where to go from here. I still have misgivings."

"You're scared."

She opened her mouth to object, and he placed his finger over her lips. "When it comes to relationships, we all get scared. But I have to warn you, I'm a determined man."

Her lungs froze. Her grandfather used to say it would take a determined man to capture her heart. After seeing his daughter's disastrous relationships, he'd wanted a hardworking, moral man for Cassie. He would have loved Chip. The only question was: Could she?

"Since I know how much Halloween means to you, I've got to get back to work." He leaned down and kissed the side of her mouth. He strode out of her kitchen, leaving her a messed-up bundle of mixed emotions.

Her plan was gone and buried. Once Chip's lips had met hers, she'd known she could never settle for Samuel. Her boss had been the safe bet. If it didn't work out, she wouldn't have been crushed. She wouldn't have been invested. But with a man like Chip . . .

There was nothing safe about him. If she let him, he could have the power to destroy her.

And give her everything.

Was such an all-encompassing love worth the risk?

Chapter 8

Chip adjusted the coffee-stained gauze around his neck and set his shoulders. He knocked on Cassie's front door and waited.

And waited.

And waited some more.

For a woman who was so all-fired up about the opening of her haunted house that night, she sure wasn't pouncing at the prospect of potential victims.

He checked his watch and blew out a breath. He was early. The high school boys hadn't even arrived yet. But damn it, he was the one all-fired up.

She wouldn't talk about the kiss when he'd left last night, and that was a conversation that needed to happen. She hadn't wanted to talk about much at all. Cassie had just told him the haunted house looked great, then scuttled inside her home, tossing a "Good night" over her shoulder.

He knocked again.

Well, there'd be no more avoiding the issue.

The door swung open and a pair of glowing

red eyes peered ghoulishly out at him from the face of a skeleton bride. The eerie figure tipped its bony head. "Chip?" She stepped out onto the porch and scanned him from head to toe. "You're a mummy."

He held his arms out. "I didn't think my Captain America costume would scare anyone."

"But . . ." Cassie turned her head to look at the finished structure on her driveway. Black sheets were hung between painted PVC frames. Orange spiders, light projections from a hidden device, seemed to crawl over the makeshift walls. In the burgeoning dusk, he could just make out the wires crisscrossing overhead and the bats dangling from them. "What are you doing here?"

"You didn't think I'd build your haunted house and not see it in action, did you?" Jinx padded out onto the porch and meowed up at him. Chip bent down and picked her up, with barely a shiver tracking down his spine. "I was hoping to get to scare some kids with you."

The black paint around her mouth stretched into a gruesome smile. "You want to scare children with me?"

Chip tilted his head. She really did look ghastly. The black and white face paint stretched down her neck and chest, disappearing behind her ragged wedding dress before peeking out again at her hands. Her hair was a sickly purple gray that looked so stiff he'd probably lose his fingers if he tried to run them through it.

Why, then, did his heartbeat race and his palms tingle? "I wouldn't want to spend my night with anyone else."

Cassie pressed her creepy hand against her heart. He couldn't read her painted face, but Chip suspected he might have just hit a home run. And it was about damn time.

Jinx pawed his arm, and Chip stroked his hand down her back.

"No Max?"

Jinx scrabbled against his grip and Chip let her down by Cassie's feet. "Max doesn't do scary. If a kid started screaming, he'd probably try to launch a rescue operation."

"Well," she said with her skeleton smile, "no one's perfect. Come on in."

Chip wiped his boots on the doormat and followed her inside. He paused in her entry. Lifting his face, he sniffed the air. Sugar . . . butter . . . and . . .

"What is that smell?" He hurried after her, heat unfurling in his belly. Whatever was baking in her kitchen was the scent he couldn't get out of his head. Her scent.

"My grandma's Annie cookies." She stopped at the threshold to the kitchen and glanced back at him. Could a skeleton look flirty? "I'm icing the last batch. And you"—she flicked a glance up and down his body—"should definitely try one."

He trotted after her, his mouth watering. He didn't know if it was from the aroma of the cookies or the soft sway of her hips under that dress.

She picked up an icing bag and bent over a tray. The stained and torn gown she wore didn't cling to her curves, and her makeup certainly wasn't intended to attract. She shouldn't have looked sexy frosting—he examined the gingerbread men–shaped cookies and grinned—bandages for her mummy cookies, but damn it, she did.

A crunchy-looking strand of hair drifted down to her chin. She puckered her lips and blew it off her face.

Something shifted, fluttered in his chest.

But was she his?

Thinking about how to raise the subject, he picked up one of the warm cookies and took a bite. He moaned. "What is this?"

"I told you." She finished, adding eyes peeking out from the bandages on her cookie and moving to another. "Annie cookies. Or more precisely, anise cookies. The name got butchered some-where along the way."

He took another bite and let the flavors explode on his tongue. "It's sweet and spicy and tart all at the same time. Your grandmother was a genius."

Cassie arched a white-painted eyebrow. "I don't think she invented anise cookies. But yeah, I like the mix of the licorice flavoring with a sugar cookie. She used to make them for Christmas, but I think they're better for Halloween. Anise just seems like a darker, more complex spice, something suited for goblins and ghouls rather than a jolly Santa Claus." She reached up and wiped a bit of icing from his lip, then blushed. She ducked her head back to her cookie. "The icing has a bit of lemon juice in it. I think the citrus gives the anise a nice punch."

Chip rubbed his mouth, his flesh still humming from her touch. Cassie was the one who packed a punch. She was just like her grandmother's cookies: a mix of sweet and heat, spice and tart. Every part of her he found appealing, knowing it all added up to this complex woman.

"Can I help with something?" He grabbed another cookie. "Besides the taste testing," he added before biting off the mummy's head.

"You can grab me that platter behind the toaster oven and start plating the cookies that are dry."

Chip rose and retrieved the purple platter. A folded piece of red construction paper toppled onto the counter. He picked it up. It must have been tucked behind the plate. He turned to hand it to Cassie when his gaze snagged on the words written in bold black print.

His body went rigid.

"Do you have the plate—" Cassie sucked in a sharp breath. She reached for the cardstock, but

Chip lifted his hand. "It's not what you think," she said.

"What were you supposed to do with this one?" The back of his throat felt raw. The romantic poem written under Sam's name could only have been another attempt at magic. He'd really thought that he had a chance. That she'd given up on the idea of her and Sam. "Stick it under his pillow?"

She swallowed, her throat rolling. "Burn it and bury the ashes. But—"

"Am I ever going to have a shot?" He ground his back teeth. "I can fight a lot of battles, but I'm having a hard time fighting against a screwed-up fantasy. It's like fighting against a ghost."

She snatched the card from his hand and crumpled it. "I made this stupid card days ago and never got around to throwing it out. It means nothing. I . . . I've changed my mind. Sam isn't the man for me."

Chip clenched his hands. He wanted to believe her. But she wasn't the only one taking a leap of faith.

She stepped up to him and placed her hands on his hips. "I thought a man had to have a steady, nine-to-five job in order to be a steady person. I didn't want to turn into my mom, busting her butt not only to take care of me, but to take care of her latest boyfriend who couldn't fend for himself and usually ended up stealing her money.

But I was only trading her mistakes for my own. And I was about to make the biggest one of all by letting you get away."

Chip gripped her shoulders. "I'm not one of those guys. I'm a safe bet. I need you to know that."

"I do." She rolled up on her toes and brushed butterfly-soft kisses over his cheeks, his jaw, the corner of his mouth.

Heat pooled low, but this was important. He ignored the urge to press her up against the fridge and have his way with her. "Cass, I'm serious. I know you think handymen are as undependable as musicians, actors, and any other flake profession you think of—"

"I don't. Not anymore." She ducked her head to press her lips to the underside of his jaw.

"But I'm not just a handyman. I have plans. I'm—"

She pressed her finger against his mouth. "I don't care if you're Bill Gates or the pizza delivery man. The profession doesn't make the man. You're kind and funny and too independent to ever take advantage of a woman."

He arched an eyebrow. "Babe, I've been trying to take advantage of you from the moment we met."

"Is that so?" She ran her hands around to his back and leaned into him. "Well, now that you have me, whatever are you going to do?"

His mind raced with possibilities. The kitchen island was good and sturdy, but at this point in their relationship that seemed a bit presumptuous, even for him. Besides, she must have spent hours on her costume and makeup. If he did everything he wanted, all that hard work wouldn't survive.

So, he said the only thing that came to mind. The only thing he knew to be true. "I'm going to keep you."

She gave him the most beautiful, grotesque smile a skeleton bride could. The red contacts she wore couldn't hide the glistening of her eyes, or the joy brimming within.

She arched her neck and parted her lips, and all thoughts of saving her makeup flew out the window.

The buzz of a doorbell cut through the moment like a skill saw.

He dropped his forehead to hers. "Saved by the bell."

She leaned back. "What?"

"Your paint job. It was about to get very, very messed up."

The doorbell rang again.

Cassie sighed and stepped out of his arms. "That must be the high school kids. Rain check?"

"You can count on it." He knew that rain check would pay dividends. A future of mussed-up hair and ruined makeup. Laughing by her side, and holding her close when the times weren't so funny. Years of making kids scream in terror, and always having a front-row seat to her unique brand of weird. Heat radiated through his chest at the thought.

He raised his arm in an after-you gesture. "It's time to get this scare show on the road."

His stomach fluttered.

He didn't want to wait one moment longer.

Epilogue

Cassie shivered, and Chip wrapped his blue and red arms around her, pulling her back against his front. She snuggled into his heat.

The air was crisp, the perfect temperature for the Halloween parade. People crowded the sidewalks, everyone chattering excitedly as they waited for the parade to start. Jack-o'-lanterns lined the street, and the storefronts on Pumpkin Lane were packed with shoppers and trick-or-treaters.

Jinx batted at a stray Tootsie Roll.

Leaning down, Cassie scooped up the candy and put it in one of her pockets to throw away later. "That's not a treat for you." She adjusted the dirndl on her cat, then pulled a bag of treats from a lumpy pocket in her skirt. "This one's for you."

Max trotted over to investigate, his lederhosen twisting at his tail.

Cassie fed him a treat from another bag and tugged the costume back into place.

Chip shook his head. "You know, when I

suggested you dress as a witch for Halloween, this wasn't what I had in mind."

Cassie gave Max one last pat on the head. "You wanted a witch. You got the witch who tried to eat Hansel and Gretel." She fingered her grimy cloak and grinned. Their costumes had turned out pretty darn good, if she said so herself, especially for a rush job.

Max nudged her hand, and she slipped him another biscuit.

Chip sighed. "You really are like that witch, fattening my dog up with sweets."

"I don't know what you're complaining about." She pulled out another bag. "I have something sweet for you, too." She held up an Annie cookie. "Besides, Halloween is supposed to be creepy, not sexy."

He took the cookie with one hand and waved his other in front of his body. "And you asked me to wear this because . . . ?"

She fought her smile. The double standard wasn't fair, but when he'd mentioned a Captain America costume, she knew she had to see him in it. Was it her fault he filled it out so well it made every red-blooded woman come to attention and want to salute?

She patted the star on his chest. "Because ever since I met you I've nearly choked to death, I've fallen down a flight of stairs, and almost cracked my head open in a freak wax accident. The odds are higher than average that some other calamity will befall me today." She batted her eyes at him. "I thought I might need a hero to rescue me."

He tapped the fake wart on her nose. "Rescuing you might be a full-time job."

"Think you're up for it?" she challenged.

"I think," he said, and turned her until she was leaning back against him again, "that I'm the only man for the job."

Cassie's throat went thick. She thought that, too. It had taken her some time to realize it, but now she knew she wouldn't trust any other man to have her back.

Cheers erupted as the local high school marching band kicked off the parade. A blue Caddie rolled behind them, the Pumpkin Festival Queen sitting on the edge of the backseat, waving like a member of the royal family.

Cassie burst out laughing. Instead of one of the young beauty pageant winners, an octogenarian had captured the title that year. It was another one of those wonderful twists that life liked to toss into the mix every now and again. Like the twist of fate that had taken the cookies she'd bought for one man and used them to throw her into the arms of another.

She rested her hand over Chip's gloved one at her belly.

And she wouldn't have had it any other way.

Annie Cookies

COOKIES
2 cups sugar
½ cup lard
¾ cup milk
2 eggs
8 drops (or 2 tsp) anise oil
½ teaspoon salt
1 teaspoon baking powder
7 to 8 cups flour

Preheat oven to 450 degrees Fahrenheit.

In a large bowl, beat together sugar and lard. Add milk, eggs, anise oil, salt, and baking powder. Mix well.

Add flour, one cup at a time, until the dough is stiff. Roll out and cut into your favorite shapes.

Bake for 10 to 12 minutes, until lightly browned.

ICING (optional)
2 cups powdered sugar
1 tablespoon milk
1 tablespoon fresh lemon juice
¼ tsp vanilla extract
Food coloring with your favorite Halloween colors (optional)

Combine all ingredients. Stir in food coloring if desired.

Annie cookies taste better as they age and are delicious dunked in coffee. Enjoy!

Sweet on You

KATE ANGELL

To all the readers who find the
Halloween magic in Moonbright, Maine!

Dr. Angela Butts, my veterinarian.
This novella is for you and your love
of Halloween!

Chapter 1

W"e're breaking up. It's not *me,* it's *you.* Sorry."

"Me?" Lara Shaw choked on her almond cupcake with salted caramel buttercream frosting. She snatched a napkin from the vintage metal dispenser on the white café tabletop and wiped crumbs from her mouth and frosting from her chin. Swallowing proved difficult. She crushed the napkin in her fist. Gripped it tightly.

She eyed her boyfriend, or rather *ex-boyfriend,* from across the table. They had dated for six months. She'd been happy and felt secure. Until that moment. Her stomach now sank. Knotted. Keeping her voice low, she asked, "Why? What's happened?"

"Janice Stanley-Stark happened," Glen Meyers said.

Lara blinked. Confused. "Janice? I don't understand."

Glen was slow to explain. He stuffed half a powdered sugar cruller in his mouth. The big bite puffed powdered sugar onto his short red beard. At any other time she would have handed him a napkin. Been considerate and caring. Not so today. Not after his bombshell. The bakeshop was packed, and his public announcement had embarrassed her. She left him sugar-faced. Not a good look on him. Messy and sticky.

He seemed to feel no compulsion to whisper. His words carried from the glassed pastry display case to the front door. "Look at Janice and look at you," he said, comparing them. "She's slender, gorgeous. You're big, ordinary."

Big? His assessment was cruel. She was curvy and carried a few extra pounds. *Ordinary?* She had dark blond hair and hazel eyes. A natural complexion. Cosmetic free. She was comfortable with her looks. Even if Glen found her average.

Janice, on the other hand, created a stir wherever she went. She drew male attention. Men looked at her, and she looked back. Guys tripped over their tongues to talk to her. She was as glossy as a photo in a fashion magazine. A male fantasy. She used her beauty to tempt and to entice. To turn guys on. To disrupt couples' relationships.

While men wanted to date Janice, women kept their distance. Her personality put them off. The lady was a shark attack. Pushy, pretentious, and used to getting her own way. She'd grown up with one goal in mind: to marry well, not necessarily for love, but for money and social standing.

She'd left Moonbright the day she'd graduated from high school, moving to Bangor. Only to return years later when her grandmother's health failed and the older woman was unable to live alone.

Janice's own parents lived on the west coast. They'd refused to return to Maine and the frigid winters. But her grandmother rejected the move to California. No sand or surf for her. Maine was her home state. She was staying.

So Janice came home. What initially appeared a loving, selfless gesture eventually proved to have an ulterior motive. The older woman was well-off, and Janice led a cushy lifestyle. She was far from hands-on in attending to her grandma. Instead, she'd hired round-the-clock nursing care and a daytime companion. That left Janice a lot of free time. To meddle in other people's lives. Husband hunting was her sport. She was good at it.

Glen gobbled down the remainder of his cruller. A fresh dusting of sugar settled on his beard. "I've always wanted to date Janice," he stated. "She's finally agreed to go out with me."

The moment seemed surreal. Lara felt chilled. Numb. She drew the outer ribbed green cardigan on her sweater set over her matching turtleneck pullover and curled her shoulders protectively. "You asked Janice out while we were still dating?" she forced out.

"We were never exclusive."

His words were confusing. Disappointing. Not

what she wanted to hear. "I care for you, Glen. We've gotten along well."

"Not well enough." He downplayed their relationship. "You're boring. Our dates were dull. Same old. I'm into Janice now."

"She's interested in you, too?" Seemed hard to believe.

"I'm a catch."

Not quite the catch of Janice's previous Bangor husbands. Twice divorced, she'd parted ways with both an orthopedist and an oral surgeon. Glen's family owned the local lumberyard. They were solid, community-minded New Englanders. He was an only child. Janice was calculating. Perhaps she saw him as a third husband. Marriage, divorce, alimony seemed a game to her.

Lara sighed. He had blindsided her. She'd yet to fully wrap her head around their breakup. "I can't believe we're over."

"Over and done."

"Glen . . ."

"Don't beg," he hissed between his teeth.

Their exchange drew attention. Moonbright was a small town. People seated at nearby tables quieted and openly eavesdropped on their conversation. Her personal business quickly became public knowledge. Men raised their eyebrows, showed concern. Women pursed their lips, commiserated with her. Their sympathy touched her.

Lara drew deeper into herself. She wished she was invisible.

Glen pushed back his chair, stood. "Got to go. I'm meeting Janice later for lunch. See you around."

He shoved in his chair with enough force to jar the table. The edge jabbed her in the middle. He left Lara and her half-eaten almond cupcake alone at the table. "A cupcake is happiness with frosting on top," her mother used to say. Not so today. Sadness squeezed her heart.

She attempted a small bite of the moist cupcake, now dry in her mouth and difficult to swallow. She felt sick to her stomach. She took a sip of her hazelnut latte. The flavored coffee was still warm. A reminder that she'd only been in the bakeshop a short time. Fifteen minutes seemed like hours.

Her body felt heavy, unresponsive; her feet lead weights. She didn't have the energy to get up and go. Customers clustered before the display case, their eyes wide and their mouths watering, as they chose their pastry selections. One pastry was never enough. Most of them walked out of the store with a large bakery box. Tables were in high demand. A few regulars glanced her way, anticipating her departure. She would leave soon enough, once she finished her latte and pulled herself together.

"Morning, Lara," her apartment manager

greeted as he stopped by her table. Jay Ingram held a small pastry box in one hand and two coffees in a cardboard cup container in the other.

She eyed the box and managed a smile. "Macaroons?" she guessed. His wife was pregnant and had a constant craving for the French cookies.

He nodded. "There are so many flavors. Yesterday Holly requested strawberry cheesecake, today lavender coconut. No telling about tomorrow." His smile slipped slightly, and he grew serious. "Glad I caught you."

Caught you sounded ominous. Rather unsettling. "I'm not late on the rent," she was quick to say. She had another week before it was due. Along with a three-day grace period.

"You're a good tenant," he told her. "Unfortunately with a baby on the way, life got a whole lot more expensive. I need to raise the rent. To make ends meet."

More bad news. Glen had dumped her, and now a hike in her rent. "How much higher?" she hated to ask. Her apartment in the two-story brick building was small, a one-bedroom, located three blocks from the business district. She didn't have a traditional lease. She rented month by month. She didn't own a car. There was no need. She could walk to work. Easily. Even in winter. However twenty-five extra dollars would stretch her thin. She couldn't go much more than that.

"Sixty bucks," Jay said. "I have to look out for my family."

Her face fell. Pressure built in her chest. "I can't swing that amount."

"I'd hate to see you go. You've been a quiet, considerate renter. Try and find a way to stay," he encouraged.

"How long before I'd have to move?" Apartment hunting would be a nightmare.

"Two weeks."

Two weeks would put her on the street by Halloween. She lived paycheck to paycheck. Most rentals wanted a first, last, and security deposit. Which she did not have. "I'll let you know shortly," she promised.

He patted her on the shoulder. "I'll wait to hear from you, then. The sooner the better." He and his box of macaroons took off.

Lara dropped the napkin she'd been clutching. Her sweaty palm left the paper as wilted and shredded as her life. She had a lot to think about. She presently worked a thirty-hour week at Keepsake Antiques. She loved her job. The past was more appealing than her present. She'd recently asked her boss for more hours, even though business was slow. He'd hinted that her employment was only secure through the Christmas holidays. He couldn't guarantee her a job after the first of the year.

She faced a triple ego blow. Harsh setbacks and

let-downs. This wasn't her day. She wanted to go back to bed and sleep the day away. However tomorrow might not be much better.

The crowd had thinned, and she stared out the wide front window. Sunshine winked, casting a false warmth. Temperatures played in the forties. There was no sign of snow in the long-range forecast. A blessing. Snowplows wouldn't have to clear Pumpkin Lane for the October parade. Parents wouldn't have to shovel sidewalks. Children wouldn't have to fit their costumes over their snowsuits. There'd be no red noses or chattering teeth.

The entire town would turn out for *Pumpkins, Scarecrows, and Costumes, oh my!* Moonbright's Halloween-themed parade and all the attendant festivities. The town laid claim to the largest pumpkin patch in the state of Maine. Located on the outskirts of the village, the acreage produced palm-sized to 400-pound pumpkins. Designated paths wound through the fields like a maze. Locals and tourists alike bought pumpkins to carve, then display. Both grinning and grumpy-faced jack-o'-lanterns would line the parade route. The procession was family-friendly fun and a sight to behold.

Lara drew a deep breath. She still felt weak in the knees but slightly more composed. She mentally counted twenty steps to the front door. She had a clear path. For the moment. She could leave without speaking to anyone or reliving her embarrassment.

She took a last sip of her latte, now cold, and collected her dignity along with her uneaten cupcake. She was focused on the door when it suddenly swung wide and a rush of customers entered. She recognized the courthouse crowd. Mayor Jack Hanson and several of his staff took their daily coffee breaks at Bellaluna's. He treated his employees well. They spoke highly of him. He was a generous man, honest and approachable.

He was also young, elected to office at thirty-five. Moonbright born and bred, Jack understood the strengths and positive aspects of a small town. He valued his heritage. No other candidate had come close to his political platform. He'd appealed to both the youthful and older voter. Stability mattered to his supporters. He wasn't out to make major changes or shake up the community and economy. What worked now would work in the future. He'd given his word.

He was impressive, Lara thought. Handsome and intelligent. It was casual Friday at the courthouse. Personnel had dressed down. Sweatshirts and jeans. Jack sported a University of Maine Black Bears zippered hoodie and Levi's. She watched as he greeted his constituents. He called each one by name, shook hands, and smiled. Nothing cheesy. He was sincere. People gravitated to him. His staffers had ordered and taken seats by the time he reached the counter. The majority of the chairs were occupied. All but the empty one at Lara's table. Jack spent several minutes speaking with Sofia Bellaluna, the amazing baker who owned and ran the shop with her granddaughter.

Lara studied the mayor. She and Jack knew each other in passing. He'd been two years older than her in school. A hockey jock. The play on the rink was always fast-paced and physical. Back then, she and half the girls at Moonbright High had a crush on him. She had sat in the stands at the outdoor ice rink and watched every one of his games. All red and runny-nosed in the freezing cold, even with her hooded down parka, Joan of Artic boots, and thermal gloves. She'd been one of few fans to last the entire game. She'd worried about her butt freezing to the bleachers.

To him, however, she was no more than a face in the crowd. There'd been far prettier faces cheering him on. He'd had his fair share of dates, but no serious relationships. It was rumored over the years that two women had asked him to marry them. No ring on his finger. Apparently he'd declined and was still single.

"Mind if I join you, Lara?"

She startled. She'd been lost in the past and hadn't noticed Jack approach. He curved one big hand over the back of the empty chair and politely remained standing, awaiting her reply.

"I was just leaving."

"No need to leave on my account."

"It's not you, it's me. I wouldn't be very good company."

"Let me be the judge of that."

He sat before she could rise. He scooted his chair over to her like an old friend. He surprised her with a fresh cup of coffee and a small china plate of Italian cookies. A considerate gesture. She stared at the treats. The delicate cake-like cookies were glazed with icing and topped with colorful candy sprinkles. Sparkling sprinkles. They looked delicious. Almost too pretty to eat.

Lara thought back on her earlier arrival. "I don't remember seeing them in the display case," she said. They would've been her first choice.

"Sofia offered them as a special treat," Jack told her. "She noted you looked sad, and hoped the cookies would cheer you up."

How thoughtful of Sofia. "It's been a rough morning." She wondered if the bakeshop gossip had reached the street, then jaywalked to the courthouse.

"How so?" he asked, seemingly unaware.

"You haven't already heard?"

He shook his head. "I don't listen to gossip."

Good to know. The grapevine account would be long and detailed. Embellished. She gave him the condensed version. "I was dumped by my boyfriend, had my rent raised, and my future employment is in jeopardy."

He gave a low whistle. "That's a lot to handle before noon."

She silently agreed. Life weighed heavily on her shoulders. He sipped his black coffee while she selected a pumpkin spice creamer from a decorative ceramic bowl. She added one to her cup. The scent rose on the steam. Pumpkin and fall.

Jack soon picked up a cookie, took a bite. One corner of his mouth tipped when he said, "Best ever."

She watched him eat. This man with the dark hair and eyes and strong bone structure. A hockey scar marred his forehead, but it didn't detract from his looks. If anything, it made him appear more rugged. Edgy. She'd been at the high school game that cost him forty stitches. An unforgettable memory.

Two rival teams had faced off that November afternoon. The score was tied one-one in the third period. Sixty seconds remained when the high-pressure offense crashed the net. Center and team captain, Jack had skated full steam into the goalie's space, maneuvering the puck with skilled precision. Only to be cross-checked by a defenseman. A dangerous, illegal, penalized move. The hit was so hard that Jack crashed to the ice. He lost his helmet and hit his head on the goalie cage, yet the ace stick handler had miraculously scored the goal. A fierce effort and an astonishing win.

Cheers had risen, then quickly died. Fear compressed the crowd. Jack lay facedown on the ice. Bleeding and unmoving. Emergency medical personnel placed him on a stretcher and transferred him by ambulance to Memorial Hospital. Classmates kept vigil in the waiting room and hallway. He'd remained two days for observation. A brain scan cleared him of head injury. His blurry vision sharpened. Three weeks, and he was back on the ice, as formidable as ever.

"You're staring at my Frankenstein scar."

Her cheeks heated. There was no getting around her stare. She'd hurt for him. Soul-deep. His scar was a stark reminder of his commitment to the game. His leadership had taken the team to a state championship. One of Moonbright's proudest moments.

"No more neck bolts," he said tongue in cheek.

He had a sense of humor. Jack had worn a neck brace for a short time. Thick Velcro, no bolts. "I was remembering the game that led to your stitches," she said honestly. "Hearts stopped in the stands that night you were injured."

"Did yours?"

"Are you asking if I was at the game?"

"I'm aware you were there."

"How would you know?" She'd sat on the top

311

bleacher, where she was slapped by a northerly wind. She'd layered her clothing and wrapped herself in a blanket. She'd been a pile of Sherpa and wool with two eyes peering out. Hardly recognizable.

"Trust me, athletes know who supports them. Which fans are loyal, which are fair weather." He ate a second Italian cookie, then nudged the plate toward her. The rim brushed her thumb. "You'd better have one before I eat all four."

She made her selection and enjoyed the sweet treat. Then ate a second cookie. Both melted in her mouth. The rainbow sprinkles tasted of hopes and dreams and sugary goodness. She dusted the crumbs off her fingers, followed with a sip of her pumpkin spice–laced coffee.

Moments of silence passed, and her mood slowly shifted. For the better. Her breathing eased. The knot in her stomach loosened. She no longer felt sad or defeated. A dose of the mayor had done wonders. She managed a small smile. "Thank you for the coffee and cookies."

"Thank Sofia, too," he said. "She chose the Italian cookies for us."

Lara shifted on her chair. She glanced over her shoulder and caught the bakery owner's eye. Lara kissed her fingertips in appreciation. Sofia winked at her as she filled the display case with mini custard cream puffs and chocolate ganache éclairs.

Jack's wristwatch gave a soft beep. "My pro-
grammed alarm," he told her. "Coffee break's
over. I allow twenty minutes. It's time to return
to the courthouse. My office is suddenly overseeing the Halloween festivities and it's a bit of
a madhouse." He scratched his head. "Not sure
how that happened, but it happened. The door
now revolves with people offering ideas and
suggestions. Committee members have taken
over my conference room. My staff is inundated
with extra work. All administrative duties and
town development are temporarily on hold."

He finished off his coffee, noted, "We have a
parade policy: Those who want to participate will
participate. No one gets left out. It's about fitting
them all in, and keeping everyone happy."

Lara understood. The small-town parade was
inclusive. Parents pushed strollers with their
costumed babies and toddlers took baby steps
along the route. The parade stretched for six
blocks, but often lasted several hours. It moved
slowly.

"It's a huge job," she agreed. "You have your
hands full."

The mayor rested his elbows on the table,
leaned toward her. He lowered his voice and
drafted his thoughts aloud. He had numerous
concerns. Lara became his sounding board. "The
biggest issue at the moment is who gets to lead
the parade? Should it be the Halloween-themed

floats or those floats advertising local businesses? The hay rides? Edward Daniels of Daniels Excavating wants to decorate and drive a compact tractor. Then there's the individual masqueraders, pumpkin jugglers, garage musicians, high school band. The costumed pets."

Lara always enjoyed the dogs, occasional cat, and the kindergarten classroom rabbit dressed for Halloween. She recalled a bichon frise outfitted as a ballerina in a pink tutu and ballet slippers on her paws. A Great Dane turned out as Superman, his cape flapping on the breeze. A tiger cat wore a lion's mane. A guinea pig was a bumblebee. The animals always received the loudest cheers and applause. They were Lara's favorite part of the parade.

"Then there's Parker Price," he confided. "He has an enormous Mickey Mouse pumpkin-faced helium balloon. He's assured me it's not as large as a Macy's Day Parade character, but would still need handlers. Five to be exact. A possible closure to the parade. I'm not certain such a balloon could float safely along the main route. They'd have to navigate a corner."

She sympathized. "You have lots of decisions to make."

"That I do." His brow creased. "Sorry, I got carried away. I didn't mean to unload on you." He paused. His gaze warmed. "You're a good listener."

"The parade interests me." But then so did the mayor, Lara realized. She'd enjoyed talking with him. He cared about the parade and would work hard to satisfy the participants. She wrapped up with, "Have a nice rest of the day." He had a lot to accomplish.

"You too. Hopefully yours will improve."

"I'm hoping so," she said on a sigh. "Job hunting is at the top of my list." Full-time, well-paying employment would save her apartment.

Jack slowly rose and stared down at her. His expression shifted from courteous to contemplative. He lowered his voice and said, "Should you have time later, stop by the courthouse and let me know if you've found a job."

She appreciated his concern. "I can do that."

She pushed off her chair and stood, too. Just as a renewed surge of customers entered the bakeshop. Moonbright had a sweet tooth. Lara was accidentally bumped, and she fell against Jack. The mayor steadied her. His hand on her shoulder was supportive and strong. The warmth of his palm penetrated her sweater. He guided her to the front door. His staff awaited him outside on the sidewalk. On the corner of Pumpkin Lane and Spice Street. Lara recognized four of the five. The women were middle-aged, long-time residents, and loyal employees at the courthouse. Nods and smiles were exchanged.

The fifth was pretty and younger, someone

315

Lara had yet to meet. For casual Friday she wore a white T-shirt with a Halloween question and answer scripted in bright orange. The joke made Lara smile.

Where does Dracula water-ski?
On Lake Erie.

Jack noticed her interest in the shirt. "Lara, Paula," he introduced the two women. "Paula attends the University of New England in Biddeford. A political science major."

"I'm taking off the fall semester," Paula explained. "Tuition is steep, and I need to earn money for the winter session."

She was ambitious, Lara thought.

"Paula's a full-time file clerk," Jack added. "She splits her hours between clerk of the court and my office."

"The day goes fast," said Paula. "I'm always busy. Never bored. We're presently swamped with parade strategizing."

"We'd better get going," Jack nudged. "I have a meeting with the city council in fifteen minutes. Later, Lara?"

She nodded. They parted ways. She stared after them. Jack looked back over his shoulder. Their glances met, and her body heated. One corner of his mouth tipped up. She gave him a small smile.

Lara watched the courthouse crew until they

reached the end of the block, then crossed to the administrative building. Constructed in gray brick, the 1889 town landmark had aged gracefully. The two-story structure had weathered the harsh northern winters. The clock tower created a solid sense of place and presence. With the addition of an electronic carillon, the enormous Seth Thomas clock rang on the hour. Everyone knew the time.

She stood quietly, deep in thought, and mentally debated where to begin her job search. There were no big chain department stores in Moonbright. Not even ones nearby. The majority of businesses were small and family owned. There was a slight chance that Amelia Rose at Rose Cottage might have an opening. The bed-and-breakfast hosted the largest and best Halloween party in town. It started at five and went to the witching hour. Both locals and guests at the inn showed up in costume. It was an incredible night. The B and B was at full occupancy year-round. There was seldom a vacancy. At Halloween, the waiting list filled a notebook.

Deciding that Rose Cottage was worth a try, she squared her shoulders and buttoned her outer cardigan. Then headed north on Pumpkin Lane, passing the redbrick storefronts. The summer awnings would soon be detached in preparation for the severe winter ahead. The sidewalk soon narrowed. A strong breeze pushed fall toward winter. It shook some of the leaves from the trees. The branches weren't yet bare. But close to it. Those leaves remaining were dark orange and crinkled brown. She inhaled the faint wafting smoke from across the street, as a homeowner burned a pile of the fallen leaves.

The cottage soon welcomed her. Lara had attended the Halloween party the previous year. Ghostly and creepy would take over the inn before long. Both inside and out. Hellhounds and headstones would haunt the yard. An enormous black inflatable spider would spin a web on the roof.

Spooky sneaked inside as well. There'd be life-size skeletons and scarecrows propped against the walls. Bouquets of black roses. A haunted grandfather clock. On the hour, the hands spun wildly. Mechanized cackling witches would fly on broomsticks across the ceiling. Banshees wailed. A ghoulish buffet, scary music, and empty creaking rocking chair all set the mood.

Lara hoped to attend the party again this year. As it was a gathering of singles, couples, and families, she didn't mind going alone. Most importantly, she would need to locate a costume. Charade was the local costume shop and offered every outfit imaginable. She'd previously attended as Wilma Flintstone. This year, perhaps the Queen of Hearts, currently showcased in the store window. It was sexy and daring.

She'd stood before the window and admired the red velvet corset constructed with boning and support like old-fashioned royal dresses. A short gold brocade skirt worn over a black gauze petticoat added a sassy modern twist. It sported a black lace train, an elaborate choker with a faux gem heart pendant, and a heart motif, all topped off by a red velvet crown edged in gold.

The Queen costume took her outside of herself and into Wonderland. An escape from reality. But the costume was expensive. It would be a major splurge should it come in her size. The one in the window fit a petite mannequin. Lara had curves. She hoped the costume would stretch. Just a little.

Her thoughts walked her along the cobblestone path that led to the front porch of Rose Cottage. She took the wide, wooden steps to the front door. It swung open before she could knock. She faced the proprietress, Amelia Rose, a lovely older lady who was rumored to possess a psychic sense. The years accumulated but never seemed to touch her. She appeared youthful, ageless, and was always welcoming. Lara felt an affinity with her.

She admired Amelia now. Her long, braided hair was the same soft gray as her eyes. Attired in a black velvet blazer, ivory lace blouse, and a cranberry gauze skirt, she had her own unique style. Elaborate crystal earrings hung at her ears.

The thin gold chains on her three-tiered necklace sparkled with rhinestones and mirrored discs. Hammered gold rings circled each finger and thumb. *Gypsy-charming,* Lara thought.

Amelia was first to speak. She smiled warmly. "I saw you coming up the pathway. Please come in." She ushered Lara inside.

The cottage was spectacular. The décor merged past and present, and brought out the best in both. An Oriental rug done in a plum, navy, and cream geometric pattern pulled the richness of the antique furniture together. A turn-of-the-century collection of satin and velvet upholstered chairs blended with brocade sofas.

Amelia studied her closely. "Can I offer you something to drink? Decaf coffee or green tea?" she asked.

Lara hesitated, but declined. "I recently had coffee, a cupcake, and cookies at the bakeshop."

"A nice way to start your morning. I often purchase an assortment of Sofia's scones for my guests. Delicious additions to our daily brunch."

"Have you ever had her Italian iced cookies with sprinkles?"

Amelia was thoughtful. "No, can't say that I have. But they sound delicious. Magic tasting." She motioned toward the glassed-in sunroom. "Come sit. Let's visit. I sense you have something on your mind." She was intuitive.

Sunshine gleamed on the green wicker furniture, potted plants, and a bookcase stocked with novels, decks of cards, and family board games. Amelia chose a fanback chair and Lara relaxed on a rocker with a red rose needlepoint cushion.

She set the rocking chair in motion and got right to the point. "I hate to impose, but I'm looking for work. I'm capable, dependable, and need full-time employment."

Amelia clasped her hands on her lap and gently asked, "You're leaving Keepsake Antiques?"

"Not willingly," Lara admitted. "Business is slow now, and will only slow down further during the winter."

Amelia was sympathetic. "I'm sorry to hear that." She leaned toward Lara and lightly touched her on the arm. "I'm not prying, but I sense there's more, dear."

Lara hadn't planned to go into detail about being dumped by her boyfriend and possibly losing her apartment. A lump rose in her throat when she relived her morning. She finished with, "I'm resourceful and will work through it. You're my initial stop." Her first hope of employment.

Amelia squeezed her elbow, drew back. "I wish I could help you, but I have nothing to offer at this time. I have two employees who've been with me for twenty years. They are loyal and reliable, and I've no reason to believe they won't be here another twenty."

Lara nodded. "I understand. I appreciate your time."

"You might check with my goddaughter Grace at Charade," Amelia suggested. "She has an established clientele that extends beyond Halloween."

"I'll stop by. Thanks."

Amelia walked her to the door and gave her a reassuring hug. "You'll find work," she said confidently. "Right place, right time, right offer."

Lara left Rose Cottage and headed south on Pumpkin Lane, back in the direction from which she'd come. Defeat edged her mind. But those thoughts were soon followed by the recollection of Jack Hanson, and the coffee and cookies they'd shared. He'd been encouraging. Positive. Her mood improved. Greatly.

Several blocks later, she entered Charade, a costume shop for all reasons and seasons. The store held wall-to-wall racks of hanging costumes and shelved accessories. A world of make-believe surrounded her. Several customers were trying on outfits, then admiring themselves in three-way mirrors outside the dressing rooms. Lara stood on tiptoe and located Grace Alden behind the checkout counter. The brunette promoted Halloween by wearing a spandex printed glow-in-the-dark skeleton catsuit. Petite and slender, she had the body for it.

Lara maneuvered around a cowboy, ballerina,

and steampunk sky-pirate to reach the store owner. She stood quietly, patiently waiting for Grace to ring up a sale.

Once the sale was complete, Grace turned to her. "Hello, Lara, what can I do for you? Are you here to try on a costume?"

"No costume at the moment," Lara explained. "I'm"—she drew a breath—"seeking employment."

"I see," from Grace. She leaned a hip against the counter, crossed her arms over her chest, thoughtful. "The store is pretty well-staffed. Although I could add a part-time evening sales clerk from now until Halloween."

Part-time wouldn't pay her bills. She passed on Grace's kind offer. "Thank you, but I need full-time work." Especially if she wanted to buy the Queen of Hearts costume.

"You might try the drugstore next door," Grace went on to suggest. "Harold Morgan had a HELP WANTED sign in the front window. I have no idea what the job entails."

"Thanks." A lead was a lead. "By the way, I love the Queen of Hearts outfit on display."

"A special order. It's one of a kind. The queen of Wonderland was a tyrant, but the costume is to die for. It will take a curvy woman to pull it off. You'd be the perfect person. Wear it and write your own story." Grace went on to offer, "Want to try it on? See how it fits? I rent many of my costumes, but I'd prefer to sell the Queen outright. If you're interested, I could save it for you."

Lara sadly shook her head. "No guarantee I could afford it," she replied honestly. "Depends on my job hunt."

A woman approached the counter with a Wonder Woman costume in hand. Lara recognized her as a nurse from the hospital. They exchanged smiles and a short conversation. Lara soon departed.

On her way out of the store she took a moment to flip through the hangers, considering alternate costumes should she not be able to come up with the money for the Queen of Hearts. A red satin fringed flapper dress was an option, as was a white angel gown with a gold halo and sparkling silver wings.

Minutes later she was back out on the sidewalk. An alley separated Charade and Morgan's Apothecary. The drugstore had opened its doors in 1920. Family owned and operated, it hadn't changed much, according to the town's history. Harold Morgan, the third-generation pharmacist, filled prescriptions and catered to all customers, no matter their age.

Business the old-fashioned way worked in present-day Moonbright. The front window showcased a tower of stacked vitamins and supplements, children's games and toys, locally made treats—benne wafers, taffy, and lemon biscuits—as well as specialty bath and body products. The store owner was faithful to his elderly female customers and did his best to keep them happy. He continued to stock their favorite retro perfumes—Emeraude, Tabu, Chantilly, Moon Drops, along with their preferred Mavis talcum powder and Bigelow Rose Wonder facial creams. Items the ladies refused to live without.

The HELP WANTED sign hung in one corner, visible to passersby. Lara entered the drugstore, equally apprehensive and hopeful. Once inside, she was greeted by the original glass cabinets and white and blue ceramic tiles. She was a regular on Wednesdays, taking her lunch hour at the old-fashioned soda fountain. She always ordered the $2.99 midweek special, a white American grilled cheese sandwich and an egg cream soda.

She slowly wandered back toward the raised pharmacy, which was fronted by glass. The two-step elevation allowed the pharmacist a good view of the retail floor. Harold was on the phone. He held up one finger, indicating that he would be with her momentarily. A revolving rack of greeting cards stood adjacent to the counter. She scanned the selection. Those with *Congratulations on Your New Job!* caught her eye. She would buy and send herself such a card if she found employment.

Harold soon wrapped up his call. He came to the pharmacy consultation window. He was a tall man with brown hair, even features, and a compassionate nature. "Hello, Lara," he said with a welcoming smile. "How can I help you?"

She was direct. "The HELP WANTED sign in the window. Have you hired someone?"

He shook his head. "Not yet. Are you asking for yourself or for someone else?" He sounded curious.

She hesitated, suddenly unwilling to fully commit. "Asking in general." She'd get the particulars and then decide if the job was for her or not.

"I'm still interviewing," he told her. He opened a drawer beneath the counter and withdrew a stack of applications. "I've been swamped with candidates. I'm in need of a morning stock and inventory person who can shift to the soda fountain from noon to close. Someone versatile and personable. Someone who likes ice cream but doesn't eat my profits." He quoted a salary that she could live with.

Here was employment she could easily handle. She was about to ask if he would mind adding one more application to the pile when a young man entered the pharmacy. She recognized Nate Harper. He was a recent graduate of Southern Maine Community College. He'd returned to town with a two-year business degree and a fiancée.

Nate approached them, looking anxious and fidgety. He jammed his hands in the pockets of his navy slacks and shifted his weight from foot to foot. "Lara." He side-eyed her, then went on to address the pharmacist. "Sorry to interrupt, but a quick question, please. Mr. Morgan—"

The pharmacist seemed to know what he was about to ask and was quick to answer. "I've not hired anyone, Nate. You're still my front runner unless someone with more experience applies. I'll let you know soon, one way or the other."

"By the end of the week, sir?"

"By the end of the day."

"You've got my contact info, right?" Nate was covering his bases. "Home phone, cell?"

"All noted on your application and on a dozen sticky notes," Harold reassured him.

Nate slapped his palms against his thighs. He dipped his head. "Sorry to be such a pest. The sooner I find work, the sooner Valerie and I can set a wedding date. I refuse to get married without a job. I want to support my wife."

Lara figured Nate was twenty or twenty-one, and already a responsible young adult. He loved Valerie and wanted to take care of her. Admirable.

"That's all I needed." Nate turned on his heel. "Thanks, Mr. Morgan. Bye, Lara."

The pharmacist waved him off. "Have a good day, Nate."

Lara watched Nate leave, noting his slumped

shoulders and heavy footfalls. The younger man had hoped for a thumbs-up on the job and was forced to wait a few more hours. Harold had called him the "front runner." Lara had more work experience than Nate and would have had a good chance of being hired. Nate, however, needed employment to marry.

She decided in that moment not to fill out an application. She would not stand in the way of young love. She hoped to see Nate hard at work the next time she entered the drugstore.

"Lara," the pharmacist apologized, "Nate didn't mean to be pushy, but he's hard-pressed to find a job. What can I do for you now?"

She cut her gaze one aisle over. "I only wanted to say hello on my way to the books and magazines."

"I'm always glad to see you," said Harold. "Browse as long as you like."

An older man next approached the pharmacy. Walter Terrell and Sons built furniture, substantial pieces that withstood the test of time to become family heirlooms. Lara had once splurged and purchased one of Walter's chairs. A white cedar rocking love seat with a scalloped backrest, thick armrests, decorated with tufted, deep eggplant-colored cushions. Sturdy and made for two, it was meant to be shared. She'd never sat side by side and snuggled with her ex-boyfriend. Glen swore the rocking motion made him nauseous.

So she'd sat alone and spent countless hours reading and relaxing in it. The smooth rocking motion often put her to sleep. She wished for the right man to ease down beside her on the love seat, to wrap his arm about her shoulders and to hold her close. Jack Hanson came to mind. Wishful thinking. He'd shown passing interest, but nothing more. Still, the unexpected thought of him warmed her all over. Lingered. He was a big man. They'd fit tight. Romantically snug.

"I have your prescription ready," the pharmacist called to Walter.

Perfect timing, Lara thought, as the older man covered his mouth with a wrinkled handkerchief and coughed. A full-blown throat hacking. His whole body shook.

"Feel better, Mr. Terrell," Lara said.

Walter gave her a weak wave.

She crossed two aisles to the shelved reading material, located against the west wall. New monthly magazines and the latest bestsellers caught her eye. Temptation nudged her to buy a book. Reality negated the purchase. It came down to reading or eating. She was on a tight budget. Pinching pennies. A late lunch won out. She would combine her noon meal and supper. She'd grab an early-bird special at Franklin's Diner on her way home. A turkey sandwich and cup of soup would hit the spot. She could always stop by the library for a favorite title.

She soon left Morgan's Apothecary. Where to next? Once on the sidewalk, she scanned both sides of the street. There was minimal traffic and even fewer pedestrians. Her job hunt was a total bust. She decided to call it a day and start again tomorrow.

Jack had requested she report in after her search. She wished she had something exciting to tell him. Sadly she had nothing to relay. Still, the man had a sympathetic ear and she felt strongly drawn to see him.

She walked around the block and entered the building from Court Street. She climbed the wide cement steps. The clock tower chimed four o'clock. The sound echoed across town. Beneath the tower, six ionic columns stood tall and stately. An enormous eagle with its wings widespread protected the main entryway. Below the national bird, large Roman numerals were carved into the limestone, showing the date of construction.

Double doors provided entrance to an expansive hallway of gray granite tiles, a high ceiling, and circular reception center. Three elevators rose to the second floor. A polished copper-clad central dome capped off the building.

Lifetime resident Stella Abrams manned the front desk. She was a living fixture at the courthouse. Seventy, sharp, and spry, she was the local historian and had yet to retire.

Lara admired the older woman. She wore her gray hair long. It fell becomingly to her shoulders. Her style was vintage, yet fashionable—today she wore her signature tweed skirt suit. Her green gaze was sharp behind square-framed brown glasses. Her smile was genuine.

Stella knew everyone. Generations of families. She also welcomed newcomers to town. "Good afternoon, Lara," she said. "What brings you to the courthouse?"

"I stopped by to see the mayor," she informed Stella.

Stella eyed her over the rim of her glasses. "So has half the town. Is Mayor Hanson expecting you?"

How to answer? "Sort of . . ."

Stella waited patiently for her to elaborate.

"I saw him this morning at Bellaluna's Bakeshop," Lara slowly said. "We talked about my job hunt, and he asked me to let him know how it went today."

"You'd like to see him in person then, instead of leaving a note?"

"If possible."

"Anything's possible," said Stella. "Although you may have a long wait." She pointed to the bank of elevators. "You'll find him in the conference room on the second floor. Him and half the town, that is. It's a bit chaotic. I've never seen people go so crazy over a parade. I'm sure Jack will be glad to see you. You'll be a much-needed break amid all the Halloween groundwork."

The parade. He'd spoken earlier of the trials of organizing and satisfying his constituents. He wanted to keep everyone happy. The mayor was patient, positive, and charming. Lara was certain that he'd work through the situation, no matter how frenzied.

She left the reception desk, composed herself, and stepped into an elevator. It ascended slowly. With a slight shake, it stopped on the second floor. Noise and commotion drew her to the conference room, a glass-walled space designated for governmental meetings. Today the town's parade took precedence. Barely visible, Jack sat at the far end of the long, rectangular table, buried in people arguing over the festivities. Citizens crowded six-deep around him, some seated while others stood nearly atop each other. The group spilled out into the hallway. It seemed everyone was talking at once, each speaking louder than the other to be heard over the next guy.

One of the loudest was her ex-boyfriend, Glen Meyers. He'd elbowed his way forward, one arm draped around Janice Stanley-Stark's shoulders. They were an odd couple, Lara thought, not being critical, merely observant. He wore a plaid Pendleton and work jeans, while she was turned out in a gray cashmere sweater dress. Both his hair and beard needed combing. Janice was flawless with a high ponytail that accented her perfect features. Her gaze was as sharp as her cheekbones.

From what Lara could decipher of Glen's rant, it appeared he wanted the parade route lengthened by five blocks, so it would pass by Meyers' Lumberyard. He had no desire to take part in the parade, yet wanted to advertise his family business. *Selfish man,* Lara thought. He wanted the promotional benefits without making a contribution. Janice supported him, her voice equally shrill and demanding.

To stay or to leave? Lara debated. Glen had yet to notice her. She would prefer to avoid the man. He would only smirk. Janice's smile would be triumphant. Still, something held her in place. A sudden unexplainable need to see Jack. She hoped to catch his eye.

Such a moment opened up for her. The crowd shifted, just enough for her to get a quick look at him. He leaned forward on his chair, his elbows resting on the tabletop. His wide shoulders strained. He shoved his hands into his dark hair, the ends spiked between his fingers. His mouth pulled tight. The scar on his forehead stood out, visibly white within the crease of his brow.

Lara felt for him. He was only one man, yet everyone wanted his attention. He finally raised his hands, palms out, and pushed back his chair, standing. "Fifteen-minute break," she heard him say.

People begrudgingly cleared a path for him. She stepped back along with those flocking around the doorway. Jack stared straight ahead, his gaze narrowed, hard and focused. Ignoring anyone who dared a further comment or question. Lara wasn't certain he'd even see her wedged between the banker and the owner of a snow removal service. Each man topped her by head. And outweighed her by sixty pounds.

Somehow Jack spotted her. Honed in on her, actually. He blinked her into his reality. He seemed surprised, yet relieved to see her. Their gazes held, and the crowd momentarily vanished. It was just the two of them. She inhaled. He exhaled. His expression relaxed. Her heart softened.

He took a step toward her and, without a word, curved his hand over her arm, just above her elbow. He was all warm palm and calloused fingers. Male body heat and woodsy cologne. He turned her toward his office, a short walk down the hallway. He opened the door for her, and she entered ahead of him. The door closed on a click.

She'd never been to his office. Never had a reason to meet with him. Until today. She took in his work space. Masculine, modest, yet comfortable. Positioned front and center, a leather-top walnut desk faced three brown armchairs. An enormous Maine coon cat stretched across one entire corner of the computer table. A tortoiseshell with green eyes and a lion-like ruff.

Jack watched her watch the cat. "That's Warhol," he said. "Named after my favorite pop art artist. He's a courthouse stray. He arrived last winter and stayed. Scrawny and unkempt, he meowed and talked us to death. No one had the heart to shoo him out. He mostly stays in my office, although nearly everyone feeds him or offers treats. He has tons of toys. He often follows me around like a dog. Maintenance and custodial workers keep him company in the evenings. I take him home on weekends."

"Warhol." She tilted her head, studying the cat with the tufted feet and bushy tail. "I might have gone with Van Gogh."

"That would have been a good name, too," Jack agreed. "He's embattled. Only one ear."

Their conversation slowed, and the office grew quiet. She suddenly felt unsure of herself. She was taking up his valuable time. His break was nearly over. "You're busy," she apologized. "I'm so sorry to bother you. I have no news on the job front." She quickly condensed her day, confirming she was still unemployed. "I'll leave now—"

"Please stay," he insisted. "I invited you to stop by." He motioned for her to take a seat. She chose the center chair. He rounded the desk, dropped onto a leather swivel. He rolled his shoulders; ran one hand down his face. Released a tired breath. Refocused.

She allowed him several seconds to himself. While he cleared his head, she admired the black-and-white framed pictures on one wall. Photographs of Moonbright in its infancy. The apothecary, bank, and five-and-dime variety store flanked Pumpkin Lane. History on a dirt street, as yet unpaved. A Ford Model T and a farm truck were parked at the roadside. A lone shaggy dog sat nearby.

"Coffee, tea?" he finally asked her. A Keurig and an assortment of K-Cups atop a short bookcase offered hot beverages.

She shook her head. "I'm good, thanks."

He eyed her thoughtfully, warmly. "My day's been hectic. Parade pandemonium. I'm glad you stopped by. Your timing is perfect. I'm sorry your job hunt didn't prove more fruitful."

She sighed. "It is what it is." *Right place. Right time.* Amelia's words at Rose Cottage ran through her mind. Lara believed a position would open up for her.

"Are you disappointed?" he asked.

She bit down on her bottom lip, admitted, "Very."

He grew contemplative. Leaning back in his chair, he clasped his hands behind his head. He stared up at the ceiling, then down at her. His eyebrows pulled together. His mouth pursed. "I wish I had a position for you."

"So do I." The courthouse would be a great place to work.

"Perhaps a job could be created."

Her heart skipped a beat. Was he serious?

"What do you know about parades?" he asked her.

"Moonbright has a great one each Halloween."

"Tell me about yourself, Lara," he requested. "Are you organized? A team player? A people person?" All seemed important to him.

"I can multitask. I stick to a project until it's completed. I'm a bit shy, but get along well with others."

He nodded his approval. "Punctual to work?"

Their conversation confused her. Casual, yet direct, it felt like an interview. She went with it. "I set three alarms in the morning, and arrive fifteen minutes ahead of time."

"Your greatest strength?" he prompted.

"I finish what I start."

"Weakness?"

She was aware of her shortcomings and admitted, "I tend to take on too much when I should delegate."

"Sometimes you need to let go and let others do for you."

Good advice, but difficult for her. She took

each task seriously. She left her personal stamp on her work.

"Would you jeopardize your private life if you had to work late? Overtime?"

"I'm single, mayor." Glen Meyers had ditched her. There were no date nights on her calendar. "No obligations."

"Challenges and confrontations. Do you have a strong backbone? The ability to say no, if needed?"

"I don't bend under pressure."

He stared at her, his gaze hot and intense. Her body tingled. An unexpected warmth spread from her breasts to her thighs. She shifted on her chair, finding it difficult to sit still.

If he noticed her unease, he made no mention. Instead he was quiet. Deep in thought. She waited on the edge of her seat, her hands clutched on her lap so tightly her knuckles turned white and her thumbs went numb.

Jack slowly nodded, more to himself than to her, as he came to a decision. She listened intently. "Come work with me, Lara," he proposed. "You'd fit nicely into a recently created position. An events coordinator. The courthouse sponsors numerous activities throughout the year. The Halloween Festival. Followed by the Winter Carnival and a Dickens Christmas. The Valentine's Red Heart Fund-raiser and the Easter Egg Hunt, and so on.

"Moonbright is passionate and opinionated on the parade, as you witnessed in the conference room. There has never been one central person in charge. It's been a committee effort. That hasn't worked well, especially this year. People need direction. Someone to organize their endeavors. It won't be easy, but I believe you're capable." He quoted a salary and clarified the benefits. "Might you be interested? Are you up to the task?"

She was. Still she raised an eyebrow, voiced her suspicion, "When did you establish this position, Mayor?"

"A minute ago," he replied honestly. "Give or take a few seconds."

She instantly understood. "The parade. You're offering me a job that you don't want."

"Never wanted it. The parade was handed to me."

Silence settled between them. He appeared hopeful. "You need employment," he pressed. "I have a job available."

Right place. Right time. "I'll take it off your hands."

"Thank you." He exhaled, relieved. "How soon can you start?"

"How soon do you need me?"

"Yesterday."

"I'll talk to my employer at Keepsake Antiques. Business is slow, and I doubt he'll require notice." Pause. "So how about Monday?"

"Excellent. But be aware," he gently forewarned. "Tempers will flare. You'll make decisions and some will disagree. Especially when it comes to selecting the Pumpkin Festival Queen. It's your call. Wear your emotional armor. You'll be called Pumpkin Head. It's not all that endearing. Don't take it personally."

Chapter 2

Monday morning, and Mayor Jack Hanson paced his office. He was on edge and couldn't sit still. His Maine coon Warhol stretched out on the computer table. He flipped his tail lazily, eyeing Jack with a calm cat reserve. Supremely unconcerned and ignoring Jack's unease. Warhol had the gall to purr. Loudly.

It was Lara Shaw's first day of work, and he'd personally met her at the main door. She had arrived fifteen minutes early as promised. He'd directed her to Human Resources so she could fill out the stack of paperwork that came with being newly employed. Attractively attired, she'd looked every inch the professional in a houndstooth jacket and black slacks. A gold suede headband swept back her dark blond hair.

He hadn't wanted to appear anxious, so he'd left Personnel and hovered instead at the reception desk. There, Stella filled him in on her weekend with her great-grandchildren. How the family had gone to the Pumpkin Patch, purchased pumpkins, and then carved them. She'd later

341

baked pumpkin spice cookies and pumpkin bread.

He had politely listened, yet kept one eye out for Lara. She had entered his office the previous Friday, her eyes sad, her shoulders slumped. Her defeat touched him deeply. He'd felt bad for her. Something inside him was triggered, and he'd wanted to help her. *Needed* to help her.

That's when he'd proposed the events coordinator option. Strictly on impulse. It was a much-needed position, but in the rough draft stage. Nothing had been finalized. He'd hurriedly spoken to Human Resources. The head of the department agreed to the hire. He'd worked late on Friday and finalized job guidelines for her. Lara's salary was budgeted into the fiscal year. She was officially a courthouse employee. Jack was exceedingly pleased.

Once Lara had filled out her paperwork, they'd shared an elevator to the second floor. Gratitude curved her hand over his forearm. She'd given a gentle squeeze. Her gaze was bright, her expression animated. They conversed easily. She was excited to start work.

Jack had assigned her a small office at the end of the hallway with easy access to the larger conference room. There she would appoint committee members and hold meetings. He hoped it wouldn't get as wild and crazy as the previous Friday. Which had gotten out of hand. A first for

Jack. He'd valued order and control, and had lost it. Never again.

He'd never have imagined the parade causing such commotion. He'd been totally blindsided. The town had taken on a life of its own. Emotions ran high and opinions were loudly expressed. No one had been more obnoxious than Glen Meyers, the ring leader. He'd started it all. Had egged everyone on. Loud, rude, and intrusive, he'd arrived with a personal agenda that he tried to shove down Jack's throat. The family lumberyard always had a big sale over Halloween weekend. It was a major moneymaker going into winter. The business slashed prices on both commercial construction and household improvement projects. Glen wanted to extend the parade route to draw in customer traffic. Jack had refused him. Despite the denial, Jack expected Glen to return. He would press his point a second time. Possibly even a third. He didn't know when to quit. Jack hoped Lara would take a firm stand against her ex-boyfriend.

To that end, he'd assigned his assistant, Paula, to work with Lara through the planning of the parade. Paula might be young, but she was smart, savvy, and so blunt she made people blink. No one, not even Glen, would bulldoze Lara with Paula in the room. Paula had push-back.

Lara. A friend who held his interest. He liked what he saw in her. A pretty lady with a curvy body. Expressive hazel eyes and full lips that parted in surprise. Years ago her parents had moved to Chicago. So they could be nearer to her married sister, husband, and their grand-children. Lara still loved the small town of Moonbright, as did Jack. She was now employed by the courthouse. He would see her every day. He smiled at the thought. She was easy on the eyes.

It was still early, and Lara would be in her office getting organized for the parade blitz. Jack had planned her introduction. He felt an undefined need to protect her. He would affirm her position to the townspeople and request their respect during the committee meetings. An ambush was not on his agenda. He would not allow a repeat of Friday.

He'd instructed Paula to post a notice on the conference room door, indicating a new events coordinator had been hired, and that she would open discussion on the Halloween festivities at 9 a.m. It was a quarter 'til the hour. Deciding to take a peek into the hall, he cracked his office door.

No sign of either Lara or Paula. His initial look drew him fully into the corridor. He stood off to the side, positioning himself behind a column. People now gathered outside the conference room. The door remained locked against an early onslaught. Lara had a key. That protective urge rose in him again. He wanted her first day to go smoothly.

"Mayor, are you hiding or spying?" Paula asked, coming up behind him. She carried a stack of photocopied pamphlets that weighed her arms down.

Jack took half the pile from her. He noted the headline on the top page: HALLOWEEN PROCEDURES. "I'm here to help."

"If you say so."

"I'm taking a break," he told her. "I was thirsty and headed to the water fountain."

"You have a small refrigerator filled with bottled water in your office."

"I'm stretching my legs."

"Legs that jogged three miles this morning?"

She knew his exercise routine. "Your point being?"

She openly studied him. Observant to the point of being annoying. Her eyes twinkled. Her smile curved. "Haircut, new navy suit, snazzy lavender paisley tie. The courthouse staff knows your basic style, yet you've dressed to impress. Impress *who*, Mayor Hanson?"

Heat crept beneath his pale-blue shirt collar. Then stole up his neck. Blushed his chin. His assistant was far too perceptive. He steadily stared back at her, refusing to blink. Unwilling to admit his attraction to Lara Shaw. He didn't understand it himself. He liked what he knew of her, and hoped to know her better. He declined to share his intention with curiously nosy Paula. He'd never been the center of courthouse gossip, and he wasn't about to start now.

She shifted the papers against her chest, and that's when he noticed her T-shirt. A crisp yellow cotton scripted with a gold Q&A.

> *Mommy, Mommy, are there*
> *such things as mummies?*
> *Yes, dear. Now wrap your bandages*
> *tightly, it's cold outside.*

"New?" he asked.

She nodded. "Looks like we both did some shopping over the weekend."

"Looks like." Enough said. "I like your Halloween spirit."

"More T-shirts to come."

He glanced over her shoulder.

"Looking for Lara?"

He played it cool. "I wanted to be available to introduce her. I'll hang around a while, in case there's something she might need."

"Isn't that why you assigned me to her?"

He pursed his lips. "Fair enough." Paula had his number.

Lara left her office at that moment, which saved him from Paula's scrutiny. He watched her approach. She, too, carried a stack of photocopied papers. She gave him a tentative smile. He smiled back. All three elevator doors opened behind him, and people spilled out. The lifts had been loaded to their weight capacity.

Lara nodded to the arrivals. "I'll be with you shortly."

Eighty-year-old Edna Milner narrowed her gaze. Squinted behind thick, round glasses. "Lara Shaw, that you?"

"Yes, ma'am," Lara replied respectfully.

Her expression pinched. "What are you doing here, girl?"

Jack intervened. "I'm about to explain her presence."

Amid the ascending elevators and the widening crowd, Paula clapped her hands and gained everyone's attention. Jack spoke then, keeping his voice even, firm. "I've hired Lara Shaw as the new events coordinator. She'll now be in charge of the parade and future town activities. Give her a few minutes, and she'll meet with you in the conference room."

The group gave a slight shove forward, and Lara held up one hand, palm out. "Orderly, please. I will honor your thoughts, concerns, and requests by addressing six people at a time. Paula will pass out information pamphlets with my initial overview on the parade. She'll also post a sign-up sheet. First come, first heard. She will usher you in when it's your turn. Discussion will follow." After a pause, surprised buzzing echoed in the hallway, along with a few grumbles. "Are we good? Everyone understand?"

Nods, and an unladylike snort. "Pumpkin Head," came from Edna.

Lara cut the older woman a look, but let it go. She next glanced at Jack and whispered, "If that's the worst I'm called this morning, then it will be a respectable day."

He admired her control. She then withdrew a key from her blazer pocket and opened the conference room door. Only to immediately close it behind her after Paula and Jack entered.

She unloaded the stack of papers onto the table, released a breath, said, "So far so good."

"You're doing great," Paula assured her.

Jack hoped the day would progress as it had begun. Lara seemed on top of the situation. He set down all but one pamphlet, then flipped through it. A very organized three pages. Lara was prepared. She'd outlined procedures and what she hoped to achieve. He returned the pamphlet to the pile.

Paula turned to Lara. "I'm going to pass out the pamphlets now. I'll leave the extras on the hallway table by the vase of fresh flowers. The sign-up sheet will follow." She side-eyed Jack. "You coming, Mayor?"

He had no other choice but to do so. Staying would suggest that he questioned Lara's ability to handle the parade. He had faith in her. He liked being around her, but lingering would raise eyebrows. Paula's in particular.

"My staff takes a coffee break at ten thirty should you wish to join us," he mentioned to Lara on his way out.

"I'll be there," said Paula. "I'll be sure Lara takes a breather, too," she added for his benefit.

Jack left then with Paula on his heels. "Back up, please, no rushing or crushing," the young woman instructed the crowd, as she handed out the pamphlets. She hung a sign-up sheet to the left of the door. "Print your names. I'll call you when we're ready."

She then set the remaining pamphlets on the table and ducked back into the conference room. There, she conversed briefly with Lara. At Lara's nod, Paula returned to the hall and called the first six names listed. They filed in.

Still Jack couldn't bring himself to leave. So he stepped off to the side, near the water cooler. From there he could observe Lara, but she couldn't see him. He leaned a shoulder against the wall, crossed one ankle over the other, and watched the action go down.

Lara had a way with people. She was cordial, and they were civilized. She listened, jotted down their ideas, and most left with a smile. All but a displeased Edna Milner. She marched stiffly from the conference room, her expression sour.

Jack took the older woman's attitude with a grain of salt. He hoped Lara did as well. He assumed Edna was still pushing to be honorary Pumpkin Festival Queen, despite her age. Traditionally the title was awarded to a female involved in community service. Someone devoted to Moonbright. Despite the fact that Edna had never volunteered or sat on a committee, she continuously nominated herself. Year after year. She harangued whoever headed the parade and openly campaigned for the crown. Sadly, her disposition wasn't queenly. She was cranky and showed little kindness or compassion. She tended to insult people, whether on purpose or not. She now elbowed her way to the elevators, descending in a huff.

Jack looked over the packed hallway. People conversed in small groups. There was a calmness to the morning. Almost too composed. Similar to a calm before the storm. He was an intuitive man, good at reading people. He had the gut feeling all hell would break loose— he just didn't know when. That made him very uneasy.

Deep in thought, he missed Paula's approach. She snuck up on him and tapped him on the shoulder. "Are you holding up the wall?" she asked with mock innocence. "Perhaps we should move your desk into the hallway? You could work and watch Lara at the same time."

"Funny, Paula, really funny."

"I wasn't joking, Mayor."

"I'm headed to my office."

"When?"

He frowned at her. "You're not my keeper today. You're assigned to Lara."

"She's holding her own. Doing amazingly well. People seem inspired by her suggestions. Many are agreeable."

Good to hear. Lara was conscientious and capable. And apparently getting far more accomplished than he was. He had a stack of week-old paperwork on his desk that needed his attention. The parade had put him behind. He ran a hand through his hair. He narrowed his gaze on Paula. "Find me if she needs anything."

"She won't need a thing. She's got me to look out for her," Paula emphasized. "Trust me."

She was doing fine without him. Paula's assessment of the situation should've pleased him. It did, to some extent. But a part of him wanted Lara to need him for something, anything. However small. He was the mayor. This was his courthouse. He was the problem-solver.

Paula pressed past him. "Catch you at the coffee break. It's Monday, and the bakery special is German chocolate layer bars. My favorite."

"Each daily special is your favorite."

"I like everything Sofia bakes."

Jack had enjoyed the Italian cookies on Friday,

as had Lara. He wondered if they'd be available again today. Two hours until their coffee break. He'd have to wait and see.

Back in his office, Warhol greeted him at the door with an insistent meow. His food bowl was empty, and he wanted Jack to fill it. Warhol was a snack cat. He grazed on his kibble throughout the day. There was no such thing as an empty dish in his world. Jack obliged, and the big cat purred.

Business awaited. He circled his desk and lowered himself into his chair. His thoughts strayed to Lara one final time before he dug into a proposal for roadway repair and maintenance. She was pretty and soft-spoken. Curvy and feminine. Qualities that attracted him. His life was full and incredibly busy. He hadn't dated for some time. He'd never been seriously involved. He hadn't met *the one*.

Perhaps he'd invite Lara to supper. To celebrate her first day on the job. It was something to contemplate between street potholes, deteriorating cement curbs, and repainting crosswalks.

The early part of the morning passed quickly. In no time Paula popped her head inside the door, calling, "Bellaluna's, five minutes."

Jack looked up from his desk and asked her, "How's it going in the conference room?"

She scrunched her nose. "It's . . . going." Too vague.

"Going *how?*"

"Only one issue, and Lara handled it well."

"Issue?" he pressed.

"Minor dustup. Glen Meyers and Janice Stanley-Stark cut in line, came and went."

That would be Lara's ex-boyfriend and his new girlfriend. Glen and Lara's breakup was recent. Jack had dealt with Glen on Friday, and closed the door on extending the parade route to the lumberyard. Apparently Glen didn't take his no as the final answer. Jack wouldn't tolerate Glen's in-your-face with Lara.

Jack kept his cool. "What happened?" He wanted details.

"Glen refused to take a number and wait in line like everyone else," she informed him. "He was all huff and puff and blow the conference room down. Janice sided with him, and added her own snide comments."

Jack locked his jaw. Refused to lose his temper. He and Glen were the same age. They'd gone to school together but had never run with the same crowd. Jack had let his scholastics and sports speak for him. He'd excelled. And was true to himself. Whereas Glen was self-centered. He talked himself up and put others down. Jack wasn't certain what Lara had ever seen in the man. Then there was Janice. *Beauty is as beauty does,* Jack thought. She could be cutting.

Paula gave him a wave as she closed the door. "See you in a few."

His office phone rang. When he picked it up, the caller was City Councilman Anders. He was a talker. The reason for his call was long in coming. When the point was finally reached, it turned out he wanted to discuss the Five-Year Capital Improvements Plan. Which would take hours and didn't need approval until the end of the year.

Jack cleared his throat and slowly closed the conversation. The city council met once a month. He proposed Anders schedule an interim meeting for next week. His suggestion pleased Anders. The man was recently widowed. His days stretched long and lonely. He sought ways to fill his time. Jack made a note on his desk calendar to invite Anders to lunch on Friday.

He stood, scratched Warhol behind the ear. The cat jumped off the corner of his desk and went straight to his food bowl. He pawed the rim. Jack saw it as half-full. Warhol eyed it as half-empty.

He shook his head. "Really?" An insistent meow, and the cat won him over. Jack took a bag of kibble from the cabinet beneath the coffee-maker and added a small amount to the dish. Warhol circled his ankles, purred. Then chowed down. Jack returned the bag. He tried to monitor the cat's intake of food, but he wasn't always successful. Had he left the bag out, Warhol would have eaten his way into tomorrow.

He was late getting to the hallway. The corridor

was empty. He'd expected his staff to go on ahead. They knew he was often held up by such phone calls. He was standing before the elevator banks, holding the button with his thumb, when he heard the conference room door open, close. Lara came to stand beside him.

He couldn't help but smile. He was pleased to see her. She looked pretty standing in the flood of sunshine through the wide crescent window. Her hair was slightly mussed, several strands spiking over the headband. At least no one had caused her to pull out her hair. Neither Edna Milner nor Glen Meyers.

She went perfectly still when he lifted his hand and patted down the dark blond points. Smoother now. So soft. "Better," he said. His innocent gesture caused her cheeks to turn pink. Silence stretched between them until the elevator arrived. The doors opened and he stepped back, letting her enter. He joined her, pushing the first floor button. He flexed his hands. They felt suddenly heavy and awkward. Sweaty. He pushed them in the pockets of his pants.

The elevator showed its age. A creak, a slight shake, and a drawn-out descent. The public staircase at the back of the building would've been quicker, Jack thought. Courthouse employees took the steps when they were in a hurry. He didn't need fast. He valued these private moments with Lara. Enclosed and quiet.

"How's your job thus far?" he initiated when the elevator bumped to a stop. Their bodies shifted for balance. Brushed. A suggestive touching. Her hip skimmed his thigh and his arm grazed her shoulder. Static sparks. Awareness jarred them both.

She left the elevator all wide-eyed and parted lips.

He followed with a sharply indrawn breath.

Once on the sidewalk, the red stop light on the corner of Pumpkin Lane held them at the curb. "I'm on a learning curve with the position," she said, returning to his question as the light changed and they crossed the street. "Paula's smart and helpful and one step ahead of me."

Jack nodded his agreement. Paula was observant, intuitive, and a damn good personal assistant. She was under the assumption he was attracted to Lara. True or not, he didn't want her speculating with staff. He planned to give her his darkest "don't go there" stare should she raise an eyebrow when he arrived at Bellaluna's. With Lara.

Paula was in line ahead of them in the bakeshop. She glanced over her shoulder, and not only lifted a brow but winked at him. Smug assistant. His glare should've turned her around. It did not. She grinned at him.

"I've already enjoyed a German chocolate layer bar." She held up an empty china plate. "Seconds, and there's the best assortment of Halloween decorated sugar cookies. I'm ordering a vanilla-frosted ghost."

Eating cookies might keep Paula from reflecting on Lara and him. "Get two cookies," he suggested.

"Maybe three," she teased back.

Lara shifted alongside him. Their bodies lightly touched. He liked the momentary feel of her. Womanly curves and appealing warmth. Nice. She craned her neck to check out the display case, all sparkling glass and silver trays of delicacies. They soon reached the front of the line. Sofia Bellaluna was working the counter. She made suggestions to those undecided. Customers always walked away satisfied with their purchases.

Sofia served Paula her ghost-shaped cookies. "On the mayor's tab," he heard Paula say as she crossed to a side table. She'd eaten one entire cookie and licked vanilla frosting from her fingertips by the time she sat down with the others from the courthouse. She smacked her lips. "Tasty ghostie."

Sofia glanced from Jack to Lara. She seemed pleased they were together. "What can I get for you today?" she asked.

Lara didn't hesitate. She knew exactly what she wanted. "A pumpkin scone and a small hot apple cider." She withdrew a ten-dollar bill from the pocket of her blazer. "I'll pay for whatever the mayor orders as well."

Jack blinked. None of his staff had ever bought him coffee or bakery goods. Paula was notorious for putting her sweet on his tab, as she had just done today. She was saving for college. He didn't mind. All in all, an assistant with a sugar fix was a happy assistant.

Lara's gesture of buying him a snack was kind and generous. It also opened up the opportunity for him to suggest she join him for supper. His excuse to pay her back. He'd locate her at the end of the day. Issue the invitation.

"Mayor Hanson?" Sofia caught his attention.

He made a quick decision. "I'll have a Brown Butter Shortbread Cookie, black coffee."

Sofia handed Lara her change, along with one plate, instead of two separate. It was as if the bakeshop owner expected them to sit together. She'd assumed right. The place was packed, with only one available small table. The same table where he'd joined Lara the previous Friday when her world was so dark and dim.

Jack picked up the drinks. They headed for their spot. "Déjà vu," she murmured as they lowered themselves into their seats.

He scooted his chair in, then looked around the bakery. He nodded to those he knew, which was nearly everyone. His gaze met Paula's. No change in her expression, although her blue eyes

358

were bright, knowing. He paid her no attention.

He returned to Lara. "How's your scone?" he asked.

Her answer came with half-closed eyes and an audible sigh. "I love all things pumpkin. Autumn is my favorite season," she said between bites. She dabbed her napkin to her lips, then took a sip of warm cider. "Halloween and Thanksgiving, no better time of the year."

He nodded, agreed. "I'm with you. I like the cooler weather. You can turn off the air conditioner and open the windows. Fresh air."

"The foliage," she went on. "There's a big maple tree outside my apartment building. The leaves are as vibrant as a sunset. I miss them in the winter." She hesitated, went on to softly share, "Before the first snow, I collect fading flowers and petals, leaves, and bark, and make my own potpourri. Once everything is dried, I arrange it in a large glass bowl. I go on to add a few drops of tea tree and cinnamon essential oils. The rich autumn scent carries me through the ice, snow, and below-zero temperatures."

Pretty amazing. She was creative. "Have you been to the Pumpkin Patch?" he asked. "Carved a pumpkin?"

"I'm headed there this weekend," she informed him. "A single, small pumpkin for me, as well as several bigger ones for the courthouse. Paula suggested we place them in the hallways. They'll be fun decorations."

He liked that idea. "I can help you haul the pumpkins if you need some muscle." He was strong. Should there be any he couldn't lift, he'd contact Three Men and a Truck.

She nodded. "I'd like your opinion on the pumpkins."

He'd enjoy spending time with her. "You're on."

"I had also planned to stop at Herbert's Orchard and pick a basket of apples."

He could do apples. There was a small family store on-site that featured homemade fudge, pies, jams, jellies, and maple syrup, plus Maine-made crafts and gifts.

"Do you have a favorite apple?" he asked.

"Two favorites, actually. The Honeycrisp for sweetness and crunch, and the Ginger Gold, sliced with sharp cheddar cheese on salads. How about you?"

"Macintosh, all-around good. The best for pies, in my mom's opinion." He sipped his coffee, was curious. "Do you bake?"

Her gaze shifted to the bakeshop display case, then back to him. "I like sweets and enjoy being in the kitchen, though I don't make anything from scratch like Sofia. My cakes come from a boxed mix. My cookies are slice and bake."

"How much Halloween candy do you have at your apartment?"

"I'm stockpiled. I get a lot of trick-or-treaters."

"Favorite candy?"

"Mini Heath Bars. You?"

"Reese's Peanut Butter Cups."

"From Halloween we head into Thanksgiving."

He rubbed his chin. "No-Shave November."

"Ahh, the Novem-beard. There's a lot of facial hair in Moonbright."

"Men like the scruff."

"Women appreciate rough and rugged, too."

She took a last bite of her scone.

He polished off his shortbread cookie.

They sipped their drinks, while eyeing each other over the rims of their china cups. He set his back on the saucer. She did so more slowly. "Downtime?" What did she enjoy outside of work?

She grew thoughtful. "Afternoon walks as long as the weather permits. I dress warmly. My favorite winter words are *fleece, flannel,* and *fireplace.*"

"My words are *sledding, skiing,* and *snow-shoeing.*"

"I'm more indoors than out," she confessed. "I tend to read more books during the colder months. I curl up on the sofa, cozy under a Pendleton blanket, savoring a mug of hot chocolate."

He could picture her snuggled beneath a thick plaid blanket. "Big or mini-marshmallows?"

She grinned. "Big. They take longer to melt."

"What are you reading now?"

"Alyssa Palombo's *The Spellbook of Katrina Van Tassel: A Story of Sleepy Hollow.* It's quite good. Ichabod Crane arrives in the spooky little village as the new schoolmaster. Katrina is drawn to him. A secret love affair. Ichabod's disappearance . . ." She trailed off.

"And . . . ?" he asked.

"Read the book."

"What? Not even a hint?"

"Not a chance." The end. "How about you? What's on your bedside stand?"

He had the crazy urge to suggest she see for herself. He had a flash of her sitting on the edge of his bed, flipping through the pages of a novel. He'd ease down beside her—

He caught himself. Where had that image come from? It didn't belong in Bellaluna's. He cleared his throat. "I'm reading *It* by Stephen King. Seven adults return to their hometown to confront a nightmare they first stumbled on as teenagers. An evil without a name."

She shivered. "Sounds scary. A book I'd have to read during the day, with all the lights on."

Their friendship came to life, and the conversation flowed easily. No stops or starts or awkward moments. He liked getting to know her on a deeper, more personal level.

He caught Paula approaching their table from

the corner of his eye. "Staff has returned to the courthouse," she reported with a grin. "Our twenty-minute coffee break turned into a social *hour*."

Jack glanced at his leather band Seiko. He couldn't believe the time. Paula was off by ten. Fifty minutes was not quite an hour. He'd been so into Lara that he had forgotten to set the alarm on his watch. He looked up and noticed the bakery box in Paula's hand.

"Two chocolate crème Bundt cakes for the road," she told him.

"Again on my account?"

"You're the only one Sofia allows to run a tab." Her gaze held his. "Want me to wait for you?"

"I think we can find our way back to the courthouse."

"Safely?"

"We'll yield to the traffic light."

"I'll tell those waiting outside the conference room that Lara will be back shortly." She headed for the door.

Lara hopped to her feet, looking worried and anxious. "Shortly is now. I hate being late."

She hurriedly tossed their napkins in a small trash receptacle while he collected the china cups and saucers and returned them to Sofia. The bakeshop owner handed him a small bakery bag filled with two marble brownies for Stella. The town took good care of the courthouse receptionist. She was never left out and received her fair share of treats.

Jack realized in that moment that his staff hadn't said a word when they'd picked up and left. No one had interrupted his and Lara's conversation. He hoped they'd taken into account that this was her first day, and that he was merely monitoring her progress. That's what he told himself, anyway.

He further wondered how much they'd overheard. He and Lara hadn't talked shop. The topics were quite personal. Potpourri, No-Shave November, and their favorite books. What had been said was said. He'd enjoyed his time with her, more than he cared to admit. He anticipated another such chat at supper, should she join him for a meal.

"I'm sorry we're late," she apologized to him on their walk back to the courthouse.

"You were with me," he reminded her as they entered the building. "No one's going to call you out. Besides, I enjoyed our extended coffee break; how about you?"

She gave him a small smile. "Very nice."

Stella acknowledged their return from behind the central desk. She held out her hand, palm up. She knew what was coming. Jack gave her the brownies. She smiled her appreciation. Dug into the bag.

He and Lara crossed the lobby and took an

elevator to the second floor. He touched her lightly on the shoulder as they turned to go their separate ways. "My afternoon is slammed. Back-to-back meetings. I'll see you after work. Stop by my office."

"Five o'clock, then."

The rest of the day flew by. Paula stuck her head in the door between meetings and gave him a thumbs-up. Her way of reporting that all was going well with Lara and the parade. He exhaled his relief. Warhol slept the afternoon away, curled high on a bookshelf between a thick volume on city codes and a thinner one on blizzard management.

Jack wrapped up his day with the chief of police. With a prestigious and sterling forty-year career, Barton Donner had risen through the ranks, from rookie cop to police chief. He was now nearing retirement. Jack valued Barton's opinion on possible replacements. They evaluated and discussed likely candidates but had yet to come to a decision. Ultimately, they tabled their conversation for another time. They shook hands as Donner left.

Moments later, Paula appeared. He glanced up from the financial report. She held up the bakery box. "Me and my mini-Bundt's are out of here."

"Have a good evening."

"You and Lara are the last two on the floor,"

she remarked. "She's wrapping up, and you're a workaholic."

He appreciated knowing that Lara was still here. He'd wanted to speak to her. To invite her to supper.

Paula was way ahead of him. She scrunched her nose. "It would be a shame for you and your new suit to head straight home."

"What suggestion might you have for this man and his suit?"

"A dinner date," she hinted, "Lara skipped lunch. She felt guilty for the long coffee break and made up time."

"I wish she hadn't done that." Although he'd done the same.

"She's very conscientious."

Which didn't surprise him in the least.

"It's been a long afternoon for her," Paula updated. "She went a further round with both Edna Milner and Glen Meyers. Pushy people. Diplomacy burns a lot of calories. Feed the woman. You could buy her a fabulous Greek dinner at Castellanos'."

He'd thought more along the lines of Italian.

"I'll give it some thought."

"Think fast. Lara's coming down the hall." Paula disappeared.

There was a light rap on his door, and he called out, "Come in."

Lara slipped inside. The day had worn on

her, and she appeared tired. Her headband was crooked, her hair mussed, her expression weary. Her shoulders slumped so she was barely standing.

He closed down his computer. Stood and stretched, was sympathetic. "Some days seem longer than others."

She yawned, and her stomach growled.

The lady was hungry. Here was the opportunity for him to ask, "Any plans for supper?"

"A take-out sandwich from Franklin's Diner."

"I'd like to celebrate your first day of work," he slowly said. "I was hoping you'd join me at Enzio's." While most locals and visitors to Moonbright chose lobster rolls, fried haddock, and steamers, Jack liked Italian cuisine.

Enzio's was wedged between a bank and a real-estate office. Small and intimate, the ristorante brought Italy to Maine. Stone columns and pillars supported the entryway. Low lighting muted the Tuscan-style colors, marble floors, and murals of the Italian countryside. Candlesticks flickered in wine bottles.

Lara stood still before him. She'd yet to respond. "Enzio's never disappoints," he attempted to convince her. "I called ahead and checked on the evening specials. The chef recommended four courses: Garden Minestrone soup, Olive Caprese salad, Brown Butter and Sage Ravioli, and Raspberry Gelato. Sounds good to me—how about you?"

She clutched her hands before her. Tiredness creased her brow. "Not tonight, Mayor."

Shut down. He shrugged. Significantly disappointed. "Perhaps some other time, then."

"Actually, tonight is fine, but . . . someplace less fancy?"

Relief had him asking, "Your call. Where would you like to go?"

She crooked her finger. "Follow me."

He could do that. "Be good, Warhol," he called over his shoulder.

"He'll be okay overnight?" she asked, concerned.

"He's the courthouse cat," he reminded her. "The custodial staff lets him walk around while they clean. They spoil him rotten. Treats and toys. Warhol patrols and then finds his way back to my office around midnight. He has a very comfortable cat bed."

He clicked off his office lights, closed and locked the door. "Lead the way. I'm right behind you."

Business kept the courthouse buzzing during the day. The security guard started his evening patrol in the basement, then worked his way to the second floor. Being the last two to leave, they were enveloped by the stillness and hollowness of the building. "Small town, big history," he said as they passed the glassed-in display cases maintained by the historical society. His voice

368

echoed off the hallway and the copper-clad central dome.

Jack walked beside her on the sidewalk as they headed north on Pumpkin Lane. He was unhurried and slowed his stride to match her own. Dusk challenged the last of the daylight. The air cooled. Her steps slowed further, and she stopped before Morgan's Apothecary. "My dinner destination of choice," she told him. "No reservation necessary."

The drugstore? He was surprised, but also gratified to dine with her, wherever she wished. He held the door for her. Followed her inside. He admired the vintage ambiance, as well as Lara's backside as they headed down the center aisle. She was graceful, curvy; her hips hypnotized. The gentle sway distracted him, and he walked into the corner of the soda fountain counter. The edge jabbed his hip. Painfully. Embarrassingly.

Fortunately, Lara hadn't noticed. She'd lowered herself onto a red leather stool and picked up a laminated menu. He rubbed his hip and dropped down beside her. The stools were close together, and Lara and he seemed almost attached in the small space. The slightest shift of their bodies and their thighs brushed. He stretched, reaching for a menu just as she withdrew a napkin from the metal holder. It was a moment neither of them could've expected or predicted. Yet one that would be imprinted in time. Forever. Her shorter legs parted and his knee pushed in. Way in. Connecting with her crotch.

She was jarred forward. Gasping. Her arms flayed. She clutched his thigh with one hand and saved herself from falling off the stool. Her fingertips inched near his zipper. So very close. An innocent reflex pressed her legs together, which only rooted him deeper into her. Her softness held him. Sensually snug.

His thigh muscles flexed, bunched. His stomach knotted. Awareness heated his body, and he stiffened. Her blazer parted, and he saw that her nipples were puckered beneath her white silk blouse. Responsive feminine points. She blushed, dipped her head, unable to look at him. Her leather hair band slipped forward. Strands spiked high. A familiar sight.

Damn. He hated that he'd embarrassed her. She released his leg, and he eased back slowly, calmly, trying not to prolong the awkwardness of the moment. The withdrawal was as disturbingly sexual as when he'd initially pressed deep between her thighs. Once separated, they both swiveled their stools to face the counter. They sat up straight. Spines rigid.

Lara fanned her face with a menu. He was overly warm. So warm that he shrugged off his suit jacket, shook it out, accidentally clipping her elbow. First a knee, now an elbow. He'd touched her twice now in under five minutes. He needed to be far more careful.

"Sorry," he apologized as he placed the jacket on the empty stool beside him.

She let the touch slide. "Not a problem." Glancing his way, she admired, "That's a very nice suit. I especially like your tie."

Her compliment stroked his ego, without her even realizing it. He wore a suit to work most days. All but casual Friday. Suits lent a professional aura to his mayoral position. He had a nice selection in his closet. This particular suit had been a spur-of-the-moment choice. A part of him had wanted to look extra sharp for her. Her approval made the effort all worthwhile. "Thank you." He then gently reached over and straightened her headband. He patted down the blond spikes.

"Appreciated," she said on a sigh. "I love hair bands. They don't always like me. The bands are supposed to smooth back my hair. However the strands go every which way on a good day."

"I don't mind your spikes."

"Yet you patted them down."

"Just the ones that were tall as beanstalks."

"Beanstalks?" Her gaze narrowed.

He sucked air. Had he hurt her feelings? "I was joking."

"So together we're Jackass and the Beanstalk."

Good one. He couldn't help but smile. He

appreciated a woman with a quick comeback. He hadn't meant to offend her. *Jackass* . . . really? He defended his comment, explained, "I read Jack and the Beanstalk to my four-year-old nephew, Drew, over the weekend. Seven separate times. Beanstalk stuck in my mind."

"Four is a cute age."

"Drew likes repetition. He doesn't read himself, but he could pretty much retell the story from memory by the seventh read."

"You were patient with him."

"I like kids."

"So do I." A short, contemplative pause. "Maybe someday I'll have family with the right man."

"Same here. Right woman."

They had a similar focus on their futures. They both wanted marriage and children. He wondered if she and Glen had not broken up, whether she would have gone the distance with the man. The two didn't seem evenly matched. Glen was loud and obnoxious at times. Pushy to a fault. Lara had a soft seriousness and subtle wit. Jack liked her. His growing fondness for her surged. Swift and surprising. He went with it. She had a warm heart. Perpetual smile.

Community college graduate Nate Harper pushed through the swinging door that separated the soda fountain and small kitchen. He wore an apron, welcoming them. "Mayor, Lara, good to see you both."

"I see you got the job," Lara was quick to say.

"I was sweating it," Nate admitted. "Today's my first day."

"My first day at the courthouse, too," Lara told him.

"So I heard." Word spread fast in Moonbright. Nate offered his hand. "Congrats to us both." The two shook hands.

"We're here for supper," Jack told him.

Nate startled. "You are?"

Lara nodded. "I'm in the mood for a toasted ham and cheese on rye and a root beer float."

Jack ordered next. "Patty melt and a chocolate milkshake."

Nate repeated their order, nodded. "Got it. Food will be out in a few." He returned to the kitchen.

Jack and Lara smiled at one another. All normal and natural. Easygoing. As if they were a couple, and silence was acceptable. No words needed to be necessary. Oddly enough, they were soon joined by Edna Milner. The older woman was short, and she rose on tiptoe to slide onto her stool. The toes on her scuffed brown oxfords barely skimmed the floor. Dressed for the cooler weather, she wore a knit cap, thick cable-knit sweater, and a dark wool skirt. A few strands of yarn unraveled at the hem of her sweater.

Nate had seen her arrive through the small window cut into the swinging door. He popped his head out, said, "Be with you in a minute, Ms. Milner."

"That's sixty seconds, boy. I'm counting."

During those seconds, Edna looked down the counter at Jack and Lara. She huffed, commented, "Another courthouse romance, I see."

Jack glanced her way. "Another one?" He didn't understand. How many were there?

Edna swiveled her stool to face him. "Quite a few, actually. There's no rule against staff dating, from what I gather. Mary White and Martin Nix from the Department of Motor Vehicles see each other on a regular basis. Chances are good that Court Bailiff Taft and Carol Linder from Accounting will get engaged at Christmas. Now there's the two of you," she pointedly said.

Lara leaned forward, spoke around him. "We're just friends, Ms. Milner. We're celebrating my first day on the job."

Edna sniffed. "Enjoy yourselves. Quite the party. I love the balloons, box of chocolates, and confetti."

There were none. Sarcasm and Edna walked hand in hand. Jack preferred that he and Lara not be caught in the gossip mill. So he shifted the subject. Backed up a bit. "How do you know who's dating who at the courthouse?" he asked, curious.

"I'm there several times a week. One reason or another. People don't seek me out, but I have eyes and ears. Abigail Warner in Personnel and Larry Krantz, the building inspector, have gone from flirting to a serious relationship. You'd have to be blind not to see the couples."

Jack was at a loss for words. He had his finger on the business pulse of the courthouse. Yet he'd somehow missed the heartbeat of romance. He hadn't a clue who dated whom. Such involvements meant little to him, as long as everyone worked hard while on the clock. Still, it was quite an awakening.

"Nate!" Edna called out. "It's been over a minute."

More like three or four, Jack calculated. Edna was impatient, and in a hurry to order. She must be hungry. Or just plain ornery.

Nate must have heard the older woman. He quickly appeared, knocking open the door with his hip. He carried a small tray with plates of food and their soda fountain drinks. He served them. He'd graciously added potato chips to Lara's sandwich and French fries with Jack's patty melt. "No extra charge for the sides. We appreciate your business."

He then worked his way down the counter. "Your turn, Ms. Edna. Your regular?"

Edna frowned. "You're new to the soda fountain. How do you know about my regular?"

"From Mr. Morgan." The pharmacist.

One corner of her mouth tipped in the faintest

hint of a smile for Nate. This was a first for Jack. He'd never received more than a sneer from her.

"Harold and his father have served me once a week for fifty years," she informed Nate. "I have high expectations for my sundae. Do your best. You have a lot to live up to."

Fifty years caught Jack's attention. She must like ice cream. He elbowed Lara. She got his message. They were both curious about Edna Milner. They bit into their sandwiches, and discreetly watched and listened.

Nate moved down the counter to the dipping station. The freezer case displayed ten flavors of ice cream and two of sherbet. He located a retro rectangular glass dish, then bent over the case and began to scoop. His hand shook slightly. Jack realized the young man was nervous. Nate wanted to make the sundae to her exact requirements. Edna demanded perfection, even with her ice cream. Nate carefully dipped vanilla, butter pecan, strawberry, and rocky road. Each scoop was full and rounded.

Jack and Lara blinked at the same time. Four big scoops for the small lady. Could Edna really eat it all?

Apparently so, and more to boot, as she went on to remind Nate. "The works."

Nate gave her a thumbs-up.

Jack resumed eating. His patty melt was delicious, thick with cheese and perfectly cooked.

Beside him, Lara enjoyed her own sandwich. They silently anticipated *the works.*

Which was soon realized. With dramatic flair, Nate proceeded to drizzle hot fudge topping over the rocky road, add strawberry sauce to the strawberry ice cream, caramel to the butter pecan, and a spoonful of warm melted marshmallow to the vanilla.

Jack's jaw dropped and Lara's eyes went wide. The dish was as big as one meant for a banana split, minus the fruit. Possibly even bigger once topped with whipped cream and four cherries.

"Bottomless leg?" Jack whispered to Lara.

"Her eyes have to be bigger than her stomach," Lara softly responded.

Nate presented the sundae to Edna, along with two spoons. The two spoons puzzled Jack. Nate stepped back, inhaled deeply, awaiting her approval.

Jack realized he and Lara were both holding their breath, too.

Edna turned the dish side to side. She savored its visual appeal. To Jack the sundae was picture-perfect. The ice cream was ideally measured. The toppings in proportion, and didn't run together. One of the cherries sank into the whipped cream. The stem remained visible.

The woman picked up the spoon, scooped deep, devouring an enormous bite of whipped cream, warm marshmallow, and vanilla ice cream. She closed her eyes for a heartbeat. "What do you think, Marvin?" Jack overheard her say.

Marvin? A strange question, to say the least. She sat alone at the counter. Yet there was a second spoon. Left untouched.

Nate, Lara, and Jack simultaneously exhaled when Edna nodded at the younger man. "Not bad. Next time less caramel and more marshmallow."

Nate was so relieved he staggered back to the kitchen.

Their meal progressed. Lara snagged a French fry from Jack's plate, as easily as if they'd dated for years, and she knew he'd share with her. He stole one of her potato chips. "Have two," she offered. And nabbed another fry.

They finished their meals, both pleasantly full. Jack complimented, "Nate makes a mean chocolate milkshake."

Lara sipped the last of her root beer float through the straw. It made a sucking, slurping noise. She set the fluted glass aside. Grinned.

"That good?" asked Jack.

"I like root beer and I love ice cream."

Edna slid off her stool, passed them on her way out. "Lots of calories in both," she said. "Careful, girl, or you'll get fat."

Lara startled. Her lips parted, but she had no words. A response would've been pointless. Reacting to rudeness was equally rude.

Jack shook his head. He'd thought the sundae might have sweetened Edna up, even for a moment. Apparently not. He glanced down the counter, and the ice cream dish caught his eye. It held his attention.

He touched Lara's arm, nodded to the right. "Check it out."

Lara frowned back at him. "Edna didn't finish her sundae."

"She only ate half."

"That's all Edna ever eats," explained Nate, returning from the kitchen. "My boss warned me in advance not to take it personally."

"She wasted two scoops," Jack noted.

"Not wasted in her mind," said Nate. "She was saving them for Marvin."

"Who's Marvin?" asked Lara.

Nate grew uncomfortable. "Not sure I'm supposed to say. I don't want to gossip."

"Whatever you say goes no further than us," Jack assured him.

"Well . . ." Still, Nate hesitated. He cleared away the retro dish and two spoons, setting them in the small sink on the opposite side of the counter to be washed later. He then came back and faced the two of them. He spoke quickly, quietly, "Long before I was born, and you, too"—he indicated Jack and Lara—"Edna Milner was engaged to Marvin Wright. Both grew up in Moonbright. According to Harold's dad, they were inseparable. Best friends as children. Engaged as adults."

Jack took it all in. The story originated with the pharmacist's father. He, Edna, and Marvin would've been about the same age growing up. Coming from a small town, they'd have known each other well.

"Long story short"—Nate kept his voice low—"for countless years of dating, Edna and Marvin enjoyed an ice cream sundae every Monday night. Each would pick two flavors of ice cream and toppings. They ate the sundae fast and messy as kids, then more slowly and romantically as grownups. He always called her 'his queen.'

"Maine winters are wicked. A blizzard was forecast one Monday night. Despite the weather warning, Edna insisted they go for ice cream. She pushed him to drive into town for their date. He did. They ate their sundae, left the apothecary. Edna lived in town with her parents, and Marvin drove her to the rooming house. He and his family lived more rural, on the old Wright Orchard, ten miles out of town. The road wasn't paved. A white-out, drifting snow, and he landed in a ditch." Nate swallowed hard. "Marvin never made it home." Pause. "Edna never forgave herself."

"Oh . . . no." Lara covered her heart with her hand.

Jack's own chest tightened. An unbelievable tragedy.

"Edna was never the same after that. She buried her future and all her happiness with Marvin. She became angry and bitter. The only time Harold has ever seen her relax is when she orders her sundae. She eats half, leaves the rest for Marvin. Who knows? Perhaps that's how she connects with him in the afterlife. No one talks about the two of them anymore. It was a long time ago. Few even remember. I only learned the story because Harold wanted Edna served with dignity."

"You did a great job," Jack assured him.

Lara agreed. "You honored Marvin's memory."

Nate noted the two coins left by the napkin holder. He picked them up. Rubbed them together. "I was told Edna always leaves thirty cents. A quarter for the sundae, which was the price back in her day, and a nickel for a tip. My boss won't ever charge her more."

Two high school boys entered the drug-store and headed toward the soda fountain. They were big and tall and wore lettermen jackets. This time of year, Jack assumed they played football. Nate scribbled their bill on a lined pad and left it with Jack. He then went to wait on the jocks.

Lara leaned lightly against his shoulder. He wasn't sure if she was even aware of the contact. Her expression was incredibly sad.

He lowered his voice, said, "I feel as bad about Edna as you. She lost the love of her life and never recovered. To this day, she's mad at herself."

"She's still hurting, so she hurts others."

"She strikes out often."

Lara sighed. "I might, too, given her circumstance. Edna's alone, and alone can be lonely. I need to be nicer to her."

"Nice will only go so far. She'll still call you Pumpkin Head."

"I also got 'pumpkin guts for brains.' "

Jack rolled his eyes. "Edna has a way with words."

"We may never get along, but I understand her now."

He retrieved his wallet from his pants pocket. He paid their bill, leaving Nate a generous tip. "Supper was decent."

She met his gaze. "But you'd rather have had Italian?"

Her hazel eyes were warm, searching. She needed reassurance. "Enzio's isn't going anywhere. There'll be other nights. At the end of the day, we shared a meal. I wanted to spend time with you."

"I enjoyed it, too."

They turned in opposite directions and slid off their stools. It was safer that way. No more of his knee between her thighs. He slipped on his suit jacket. They strolled down the nearest aisle toward the exit.

Walking ahead of him, Lara suddenly detoured right. He followed. She stopped before the card rack and began flipping through those congratulating someone on a new job. "What's up?" he asked.

Color heightened her cheeks. She hesitated, then said, "I promised myself that if I found work, I'd send myself a card."

"You now have a job."

"You hired me. I should send you a thank-you card."

"No need. I'm appreciative you're onboard." He sorted through the cards alongside her. Found one he liked. He handed it to her, saying, "We'll both sign the card."

She took the card, designed with colorful balloons and confetti. She read the cover aloud, *"Congratulations on Your New Job!"* She opened it. *"Throw confetti! Throw a Party! Throw a Parade!"* She closed the card, located the envelope. "A parade for Moonbright."

"Get ready," from Jack. "Pumpkins, Scarecrows, and Costumes, oh my!"

She blew out a soft breath. "Oh . . . my."

Chapter 3

O *h . . . my,* Lara had said in the drugstore the previous evening, reflecting on the parade. Organizing such an event weighed heavily on her mind. There was so much to do in so little time.

Oh . . . my took on a whole new meaning when Jack Hanson drove her home. He'd walked her to the front door of her apartment. They'd stood incredibly close. The air between them seemed to compress. She wondered in those seconds if he would kiss her.

He had. It was the kiss of her lifetime, and one she'd never forget. He'd leaned in, allowing their bodies to meet. His male heat and muscle pressed against her full curves. He slid his hands into her hair. Her headband slipped. His thumbs traced the surprise and insecurity from her brow. Then the corners of her eyes. He grazed her bottom lip. Desire warmed her. Her eyelids shuttered. She wanted his mouth on hers.

Their kiss was beyond anything she could ever have imagined. Soft and gentle, short and sweet. Testing and discovering. Intensifying. Their kiss took over the moment. His tongue flicked, tasting her. Getting to know her. Time slowed. She was lost to him.

Had he moaned or had she when they finally separated? Perhaps both of them had echoed their need for increasing intimacy. They stared openly and honestly at each other. His gaze was as hot as her body. She desperately wanted to kiss him again. To feel his strength and maleness against her.

She wasn't given that chance. A breath shuddered in his chest. His common sense seemed to kick in and he pushed back. He ran one hand down his face. Shifted his stance. He couldn't hide his heavy breathing or his erection. Inches hard. Highly impressive.

"Tomorrow, Lara," he'd said, as he turned away from her and walked down the sidewalk to his Range Rover. She gave him a small wave when he drove off.

She'd shakily entered her apartment, glanced in the wall mirror. She barely recognized the woman with the slightly tilted headband, starry eyes, and puffy lips. She'd had a one-sided crush on Jack when she was younger. Two consenting adults had kissed tonight. She heaved a breath. The man could kiss. The very thought of him left her light-headed. Her stomach fluttery.

Now at work, she shifted restlessly in her chair.

Highlighted by sensation. Her pulse skipped. Her skin tingled. She crossed her ankles, squeezed her thighs together.

Oh . . . my.

Paula soon made her morning appearance. Her assistant approached the conference room table, flattened her palms on the top. She stared at Lara with one eyebrow raised. "Wow, you and the mayor have the same dazed expression."

"Pardon me?"

Paula blinked. "That's exactly what he said a minute ago when I checked in with him. He has no attention span. I asked him twice if he liked my T-shirt, and he answered, 'Pardon, come again?' "

Lara managed to focus. She checked out Paula's shirt and smiled. Another perfect shirt for Halloween, designed with a smiling ghost gripping a triple-scoop chocolate cone. The caption read:

What do ghosts serve for dessert?
Ice Scream

The ice cream reminded Lara of her dinner with Jack at the soda fountain. She was momentarily lost to the thought. Deeply lost.

"Earth to Lara," Paula called to her.

"I'm with you."

"You sure?"

"I'm certain."

"Another busy day ahead," said Paula. She fisted a handful of messages. "Some news on the parade and festivities."

"Good news, I hope."

"Halloween is coming together. Slow, but steady."

Relief settled bone-deep. Yesterday Lara hadn't been sure whether she could pull everything together. She'd made a dozen lists with a dozen thoughts and ideas per page. The parade alone was an outlandish amount of work. It would start at one o'clock in the afternoon and end several hours later. Once the last float passed, businesses along Pumpkin Lane would throw open their doors and encourage children to trick-or-treat. At twilight, the downtown area shifted to a big street party. Music, singing, shopping, and socializing. A night to remember.

Lara was smart enough to realize she couldn't handle it all herself. Even with Paula's assistance. Not at this late date. Halloween was an event that should've been in development months in advance. Not just two short weeks. She'd do her best, and hope it was good enough.

Throughout the previous day she'd suggested to those with true Halloween spirit that they should volunteer. She'd hoped that someone would step up to handle some of the many tasks that still needed doing. She'd received a few maybes and several we'll sees. No one had fully committed. Maybe today.

"Your news?" she prodded Paula.

Paula grinned. "The mayor and I arrived at the courthouse early this morning. He asked what I planned to accomplish today, and I shared my list. At the top is pulling permits and licenses for the parade. Jack's a facilitator. We stopped by the police chief's office, filled out the necessary forms, and the chief signed off when he arrived."

Lara was amazed. "That was fast."

"We're moving forward," said Paula. "I've also received good news from Caleb Dimitriou."

Lara shook her head. "I don't recognize his name."

"George Castellanos owns the Greek restaurant in town, and Caleb Dimitriou is his nephew," Paula explained. "George and his wife are presently traveling in Greece. Caleb, from Philly, is running the restaurant while they're away. I'm sure you've seen George driving the Pumpkin Queen in the parade every year. She rides on the top of the backseat of his classic convertible Cadillac. This Halloween, Caleb will be behind the wheel."

Lara nodded. "Works for me."

"Have you chosen the queen?"

"I haven't given it much thought."

"The name of the queen is kept secret until Thursday afternoon, before the Saturday parade.

Whoever's running the parade stands on the courthouse steps and makes the big announcement."

"That's quite a responsibility."

"It's a pretty big deal," Paula noted. "In years past, the scarecrow marching high school band has always led the parade. Energetic music sets the mood. The queen in the Cadillac comes next. She's front and center and gets a lot of attention. People cheer her on."

Lara grew thoughtful. She'd have to give the selection of the Pumpkin Festival Queen considerable attention. It was part of her job. A very important part.

"I have even more news," Paula said. "I bumped into sisters Lana and Louise Stratton at Bennett's Grocery Store last night. We had a lengthy convo. Both are great organizers. They've headed numerous courthouse committees over the years. They will be stopping by to see you today."

Lara released a breath she hadn't realized she'd been holding. "It's all taking shape."

"Great shape, actually. You're getting there. What's on your agenda for today?"

"We need to establish the order of the parade. Who will fall in where? We know the marching band comes first, followed by the Pumpkin Queen. I'll go down my list of all those who've signed up to participate. We'll do a tentative lineup, from floats to pets."

"Does that include the big, pumpkin-faced Mickey Mouse balloon?" asked Paula.

"A tough fit, but we'll give it a try."

"You are one fair events coordinator."

"Fair, my ass," Glen Meyers said sharply from the doorway. He stood large and irritated, his expression ornery. "I've asked three times now for you to lengthen the parade."

"Four times, actually." Paula included today.

"That's three times too many."

Glen shot her a death stare. He crossed to the table, leaned over Lara. Intimidatingly close. "How difficult could it be? Five additional blocks is hardly out of your way."

Lara kept her voice even. "It's a long-established parade route that begins and ends on Pumpkin Lane. The progression takes a turn at Moonbright Park, where there's plenty of open space. That's where those involved in the parade disperse."

"Long-established? Bullshit," Glen scoffed. "You're in charge of the parade and could make it happen if you wanted to."

"*Wanted to* is the operative word, dude," Paula injected.

Glen clenched his fists. Silence hit like a punch. Until he hissed, "It's all because of our breakup, isn't it? You're getting even with me by excluding my family business from the parade."

Lara held her ground. "We have a very short time to pull this event together," she told him. "I'm not making unnecessary adjustments. What's worked in the past will work in the present. Sorry."

"You're a bitch."

"You have bat breath." No one had noticed Edna Milner's arrival. Yet there she stood, next to Glen, a small woman overshadowed by a large man. She nudged him aside with her elbow. A brave move. Lady was fearless. She then glanced at Lara. "I have business with Pumpkin Head. So move along."

Pumpkin Head, again? Lara blanched. Better than Pumpkin Butt, she supposed. Still, not a pretty image.

The conference room bristled with the older woman's presence. No one argued with Edna. Ever. Not even Glen. He curled his lip, snarled low in his throat, and then took his leave. He shot Lara an I'll-get-even look, which left her slightly uneasy.

She drew a relieved breath, glad that Glen was gone. "Good morning, Ms. Milner," she initiated. "Can I be of some assistance?"

"No," Edna flatly said. "I was down the hall at the DMV getting my driver's license renewed. I had difficulty with the eye chart. It now says on my new license I have to wear my glasses to drive."

Lara was amazed she was still operating a vehicle at eighty. "New photo, too, then?"

"One wearing my glasses. All bug-eyed."

This was the longest Lara had ever conversed with Edna. It was going fairly smoothly, until the older woman asked, "How was supper with Jack-O'-Lantern?"

Jack-O'-Lantern? The mayor. Was Edna being snarky or silly? Lara was not certain. Edna seemed to have a Halloween name for every-one.

Paula perked up. Her expression was as curious as Edna's own. "A meal, huh?"

Lara gave them little. "Our work carried over to supper."

"I didn't hear much shop talk."

Edna must have eavesdropped at the soda fountain counter. "We were quietly discussing the parade," Lara informed her. On a whim she asked, "There's a great deal left to do. Care to help out?"

Edna sniffed. "I've already done enough. I got rid of Bat Breath for you. The Meyers boy wants his own way, and has never compromised." She tugged her gray wool cape tighter about her thin body. Then inched toward the door. "Get busy, Pumpkin Head and Tricksy Treats." She disappeared like a ghost.

Paula's eyes rounded. "Tricksy Treats? *Really?* What's with Edna?"

Lara shrugged. "Maybe she's trying to be funny."

"I'm not laughing, are you?"

"A little on the inside." Lara grew thoughtful. "Evil eye for evil eye. Edna started the Halloween name-calling. If she can dish it out, she should be able to take it. Paybacks are now part of the festivities. We need a name for her, too, for when we next see her."

"How about Grumpy Mummy?"

"That makes her sound grouchy and old."

"She is both," Paula defended. "Guess that rules out Rattling Bag of Bones."

"Despite the fact she can be testy, we don't want to purposely hurt her feelings. All things considered, Edna was on target today with Glen."

Paula giggled. "You mean Bat Breath?"

"He was in my face, and I can attest to his breath." She rearranged the papers on the table. "We'll come up with the right name for Edna. Give it time."

They returned to work, which lasted all of five minutes for Paula. She tapped her ink pen on the table, got Lara's attention. "So . . . tell me about supper with Jack-O'-Lantern."

Lara gave the easy answer. Truthful, without details. "I was tired, and he was considerate. He took me out to eat."

"Where did this romantic meal take place?"

"The soda fountain at Morgan's Apothecary. I had a sandwich, he had a burger."

Paula's face fell. "That's it?" There was disappointment in her tone.

"What did you expect?"

"I'm not sure, but counter stools fall short of a private table and candlelight."

"It's all about the company."

"The mayor is hot. The best-looking man in Moonbright. In all of Maine."

Lara silently agreed. She went back to work while Paula doodled on her notepad. "So . . . what caused your distracted looks this morning?" she asked. "He was dazed and you were dreamy-eyed."

"Enough said. You've an active imagination."

"When people say enough, there's usually a whole lot more."

"Not between us."

Paula seemed skeptical.

Lara got serious. "The parade's not going to plan itself."

Townspeople slowly trickled in to volunteer for one aspect of the parade or another. Everyone was cooperative and orderly, and Lara was pleased by the turnout. She'd had no idea how the folks of Moonbright would react to her being in charge. They seemed to fall in line just fine. They received their assignments and took off to achieve them.

Midmorning, Paula stood up and stretched. "Coffee break?" she asked Lara once the conference room had cleared out.

Lara was hesitant. She'd yet to see the mayor that morning, and wasn't certain she was ready to face him after their kiss. How should she react? Should she show how glad she was to see him, or should she play it cool? As if their kiss meant nothing . . . when in actuality it meant everything to her.

She waved Paula off. "I'm good. You go ahead."

"Passing on Bellaluna's is a courthouse sin."

"Perhaps you could bring me back a cranberry-orange scone."

"Better yet, get it yourself."

"Whatever, Tricksy Treats."

"Bye, Pumpkin Head."

"Ladies, what's with the name-calling?" The mayor now stood in the doorway. He raised a brow, only to smile seconds later. "I see Edna Milner's made her morning rounds. She's tagged my whole staff with Halloween names."

"Jack-O'-Lantern," Paula called with a grin as she squeezed past him, left them alone.

He turned to Laura. Met her gaze squarely. "Can I buy you a cup of coffee? I heard you mention a scone."

"I was going to work through the break."

"Why?"

"Because . . ." She had nothing.

"Because you're stressed and unsure over our kiss," he said so casually, so easily, so unaffectedly. "Were you avoiding me?"

She peeled a label off a file folder, unintentionally. "You're here. I'm here."

He came to the table, took a chair beside her. He looked so handsome, Lara thought, in his brown suit, cream-colored shirt, and dark blue tie. His hair was brushed back off his face. His features were masculine and strong.

"The second floor is fairly quiet. Let's talk."

"About what?"

"Us."

"I'm not sure what to say."

"I am. I like you, Lara Shaw." His voice was deep, assured. "We've been aware of each other for years, but never acted on it. Am I right?"

She'd side-eyed him hundreds of times, but was surprised he'd noticed her. "You've thought of me?"

He nodded. "Of the shy girl in school who studied in the library and seldom socialized. I started to approach you dozens of times, but you always looked down and buried your nose in a book. You blew me off."

"I wasn't ignoring you," she rushed to say. "You were popular and a hockey jock. I couldn't imagine you speaking to me, for any reason. Ever."

"I had my reasons. I have a soft spot for shyness and sincerity. For blondes with light hazel eyes and tilted hairbands."

Oh . . . my.

"I don't want to go too fast for you or make you feel uncomfortable. You not taking a coffee break at the bakeshop has me believing I've done just that." He laid his hand on hers atop the table, squeezed. "I'm sweet on you. We can make as little or as much of the kiss as we want. Although it meant a lot to me."

"A lot to me, too."

He grinned then, all sexy and pleased. "Good to know."

Yes, it was.

"So shall we go to Bellaluna's?"

"Together?"

"Together will actually cause less talk than you entering and me following five minutes later, as if planned." He winked at her. "I want to spend time with you. People will get used to seeing us in each other's company."

"Pumpkin Head and the Jack-O'-Lantern."

"They match just fine. Edna named us well."

They strolled to Bellaluna's, ordered coffee and bakery treats, and settled at a large table with the rest of his courthouse staff. Paula gave her the eye, but no one else seemed to notice their arrival. The conversation centered on Halloween costumes. Which reminded Lara that she needed to stop at Charade and try on the Queen of Hearts. She would do so after work. Anticipation quickened her heart. Warmed her. If it fit, she would buy it. She was grateful for her job and the money she was earning.

Twenty quick minutes and the mayor's watch alarm beeped. Their coffee break was over. Sofia called to Jack on his way out. She had a bakery bag to take back to Stella the receptionist. Lara stood by the door, overheard their exchange.

"A carrot cupcake with white chocolate frosting for Screaming Scary Claws," said Sofia.

Jack shook his head. "Edna Milner, at it again."

"Stella recently had a manicure. Long, bright red nails. The name does fit."

"Anyone mad at her over the nicknames?"

Sofia shook her head. "Not that I'm aware of. She's dubbed me Spooky O'Sweets. I look upon it as a badge of honor. In my opinion, she's irritable on a good day, but close to Halloween, she picks on those she secretly likes."

Lara agreed with Sofia. She told Jack so as they headed back to the courthouse. "Paula and I plan to come up with a name for Edna. Soon. I want her to feel part of the festivities."

"Good luck with that. She's sarcastic and critical, and she's never taken part in anything."

Back at the courthouse, Stella greeted them. "Pumpkin Head, Jack-O'-Lantern."

Lara couldn't resist. "Screaming Scary Claws."

Jack handed off the bakery bag, and Stella wiggled her fingers. "Not too frightening. I can live with it."

Lara and Jack took the elevator to the second floor. He lightly touched her on the shoulder with a faint hint of affection. Nothing notable, but still her entire body flushed. She fanned her face as she entered the conference room. Paula was already seated at the table. Fortunately for Lara, she didn't look up. Pen in her hand, she was busy checking off a long list of to-dos.

They put their noses to the grindstone, and the day zipped by. Paula split at five sharp for a date. Lara slipped on her Windbreaker. She had her own mission. To try on a costume for Halloween. She debated telling Jack of her destination, but decided to go it alone.

The elevator door was open, making for a quick exit. She wished Stella a good evening. Outside, she ducked her head against the wind, which was sharp and crisp. Winter was giving autumn a hard shove. But autumn would hold out for another month if Moonbright was lucky.

Charade was packed with wall-to-wall people. Lara inched in the door. She squeezed between customers until she located the store owner. She crooked her finger at Catwoman Grace Alden and pointed toward the window display. Grace understood. She went to the window, withdrew the mannequin, and carried it to the back room.

After removing the Queen of Hearts costume, she hung it on a padded hanger and passed it off to Lara.

Grace crossed her fingers. "Good luck; I hope it fits."

So did Lara. A man carrying a pirate costume vacated one of the dressing rooms, and she slipped in behind him. It was a small space with a short black stool and an elongated mirror. She carefully hooked the hanger over a wooden peg. Then stood back and admired the costume fully. She lightly stroked the velvet and lace. It was truly elegant.

A knock on the dressing room door startled her. "Lara, it's Jack," he said just loud enough for her to hear him. "You in there?"

"Yes, trying on a costume." She cracked the door. Peeked out. "How'd you find me?"

He kept his voice low. "My office door was open, and I heard you leave the conference room. You took the elevator before I could catch you. I ran down the back stairs. Still missed you. Stella mentioned you'd turned left on the sidewalk. Outside I caught a glimpse of you. I was close behind and saw you enter Charade."

"I'm costume shopping."

He grinned. "Good idea. I'll do the same. I have a couple ideas in mind. You show me yours, and I'll show you mine."

"Costumes, right?"

"You can show me anything at any time."

She couldn't help but smile. She quietly closed the door. Privacy was minimal. The dressing room walls were thin. She heard Jack leave, then return. She wondered what costumes he'd chosen. He was so handsome, he'd look good in any one.

She swallowed hard and began to undress. She'd worn a forest green wool dress to work. It had a gently fitting bodice with a pleated skirt. With a single tug, it came off easily, up and over her head. She stood in a white cotton bra and bikini panties. Not very glamorous in comparison to the sexy corset.

She slipped off her bra to get the full benefit of the heart-shaped garment. She was a 34C, and the boning lifted her chest dramatically. Her white breasts and shadowed cleavage were a sensual contrast to the red velvet. Once hooked, the corset fit snuggly, but didn't cut off her breath.

She next stepped into the black gauze petticoat. It had an elastic waist, no problem. The short gold brocade skirt with the black lace train followed. She sucked in her tummy and closed the side zipper. She added the faux gem heart pendant choker. Then came the red velvet crown edged in gold. She centered it on her head. It fit better than a hair band.

She took a long moment and stared at herself in the mirror. Wonderland surrounded her. The fantasy made her feel feminine and sexy. Self-assured.

Reality returned with a tap on the dressing room door. "You dressed?" asked Jack.

"Yes . . ."

"I'm coming in, then." A turn of the knob and he bumped the door open with his hip. "Do you feel the need for—" One look at her and *speed* died in his throat. Silence collected. Awareness amplified. The mirror reflected her uncertainty. His self-confidence.

The fluorescent lights cast Jack on the fast track with his *Top Gun* zip-front flight suit. His white T-shirt peeked from beneath. A Maverick name badge and dark aviator glasses were included. He could easily give Tom Cruise a run for his money.

"You look like a movie star," she managed.

He leaned a shoulder against the doorjamb. Crossed his arms over his wide chest. His gaze was a visual touch. "The Queen of Hearts," he admired, his voice husky. He reached out, skimmed his forefinger along her heart-shaped bodice. "I have few words. You're indescribable and desirable as hell. A fantasy, sweetheart."

In spite of the customer traffic in a nearby aisle, he leaned in, his whisper possessive. "I'm looking forward to a night in Wonderland." He kissed her then, full on the mouth. A lingering kiss that sped up her heart and tented his flight suit.

"You do it for me," he murmured. "Time to change." He retreated to his own dressing room. Closed the door.

Lara breathed deeply. Her nipples puckered. Fortunately they weren't visible beneath the velvet corset. She was seconds from removing her costume when Grace walked by and caught her as the Queen.

Catwoman smiled. "That outfit was meant for you," she said, sincere and honest, not trying to make a sale. "Lady, you look amazing."

Lara pressed her hand to her chest, needing assurance the corset wasn't too low-cut. "It's not too much?"

"Never too much with your figure."

"I plan to buy the costume," she told Grace. "I might also rent a cape. In case the temperature dips."

Grace had an idea. "No need to rent. I could lend you the red velvet cape that goes with a Red Riding Hood outfit. Cape and corset would match just right."

Lara nodded. "Sounds perfect." She took her time changing out of the costume. Careful not to crease the velvet or to tear the lace. Her street clothes were far less enchanting than the fairy-tale ensemble.

She met up with Jack at the counter register. There was a never-ending line of paying customers. Grace and an assistant were busy ringing up sales. Jack offered to buy her costume, which she appreciated. It was expensive. Still, she gently declined. It was important to her to pay for it. She'd had her eye on the Queen of Hearts from the moment Grace displayed it in the front window. She'd stood on the sidewalk and envisioned this very moment. Her money. Her purchase.

The noise level in the shop rose, then fell. Lara noticed the sudden change in volume. She turned slightly to see who or what had brought Charade to silence. It was Edna Milner, she realized. The door opened, and she blew in on the night air, all narrowed gaze and sour expression. The older woman took in the crowd. Once locating Grace, she walked straight for the counter. She cut in line, ahead of Jack and Lara. A pushy woman with a purpose.

The shoppers returned to the costumes. Pursuing the perfect one. Lara noticed the conversations had quieted. Gazes flicked to Edna. Just as quickly looked away. There was a heightened curiosity about her visit to Charade.

"Good evening, Ms. Milner," Grace acknowledged.

Edna pulled a face. "What's good about it, Cackling Stripy Socks?"

Lara's eyes rounded. Apparently Edna had a Halloween name for Grace as well. The shop owner explained to those in line, "I was wearing the Wicked Witch costume from *The Wizard of Oz* when Ms. Milner was last here. The outfit included black-and-white striped knee-high socks and red shoes."

Lara thought the nickname quite appropriate. It was one of Edna's nicer names. She nodded to the older woman. Edna eyed her steadily. The shop quieted further. Those nearby listened intently— Edna was known to be rude. Antagonistic. Fortunately, Grace got to her quickly.

The shop owner reached beneath the counter, then brought out a medium-sized brown box. Laura was intrigued. *What costume would appeal to Edna?* she wondered. Would Edna attend the local Halloween parties? Would she be recognized?

"That will be twenty-six dollars," Grace said, quoting the price.

Edna pushed aside a panel on her wool cape, locating a zipper in the lining. She paid in cash. "Thank you, Cackling Stripy Socks."

Lara couldn't remember ever hearing Edna show gratitude. It was startling. Edna stepped out of line, turned to Lara and Jack. She spoke without reservation. "Together again, I see." Her voice carried.

Together caught a lot of attention. People turned their way. Jack didn't blink an eye. "We're shopping for costumes, same as you," he politely informed her.

Edna was on a roll. She outed them. "A peanut butter and jelly set? Paired Popeye and Olive Oyl?" She focused on couples' costumes.

Everyone took note. There were a few smiles. Numerous raised eyebrows. Followed by nods of approval. Jack curved his hand over Lara's shoulder. Squeezed. No words were necessary. He didn't want her to worry about what other people might think. They had connected and weren't trying to hide it. Thanks to Edna, their relationship had come to light and was moving fast forward. So be it.

Edna cut her hand in a wave. Then turned to go. "See you, Pumpkin Head, Jack-O'-Lantern."

Lara spoke without thinking, labeling Edna with an intuitive rather than intentional nick-name. "Have a good evening, *Moonie McBright,*" floated through the store.

She was as stunned as Edna that she'd spoken aloud.

Edna's face creased. Her mouth pinched.

Lara's lips parted in apology. What had she done? The last thing she ever wanted to do was embarrass the older woman in public. There were so many people in the store. All as startled as she. All awaiting Edna's reaction.

"Moonie McBright . . ." Edna tested her nick-name. She looked directly at Lara. Her expression relaxed. "Is that the best you have?"

"It's all I have."

"Not bad for an amateur."

"I'm a rookie compared to you."

"Give some thought to next year. I'm sure you'll do better." The crowd drew back, and Moonie McBright Milner departed the store.

Lara caught the older woman's expression reflected in the window of the door. She was smiling.

Chapter 4

Saturday morning arrived. Jack rubbed his jaw. He hadn't stopped smiling since Charade. That was four days ago. Lara had called Edna Milner Moonie McBright, and the older woman had actually gotten a kick out of it. There'd been no repercussions. Since then the locals had all chimed in. Gently teasing Edna as well. Oddly enough, the older woman had become a part of the community. All due to a nickname.

He and Lara presently strolled through the Pumpkin Patch on the outskirts of town. It was the largest one in Maine. The assortment of offerings was enormous. A collection of sixty thousand pumpkins, gourds, and squash, along with a fifteen-acre corn maze. Scarecrows and witches were freckled throughout the acreage, which showcased an extensive collection of orange, yellow, blue, pink, and even speckled pumpkins. Some pumpkins were smooth, others had slightly ribbed textures.

Hayrides and pedal cars transported customers about the property. Row by row they could view and select the stacked pumpkins surrounding the red barn or ride into the fields and pick the perfect pumpkin right off the vine.

Lara loved Halloween. She embraced every aspect of the holiday. At that very moment she assessed the pumpkins. She wanted one for each office at the courthouse. Along with a circular grouping at the reception desk. She'd tagged the perfect ones with a courthouse sticker. To be retrieved that afternoon.

Eyeing the size of those she'd already chosen, Jack was glad he'd gone ahead and hired Three Men and a Truck. Otherwise he'd break his back lifting. Following her final decisions, the crew would haul the pumpkins to the government building. They would be given a pencil and paper sketch, and would place the decorations as diagrammed.

The sky told of fall. An authentic blue with just enough sunshine, and there was little to no wind. Excitement was as sharp and crisp as the day. Screeches echoed from the corn maze nearby. The Walton triplets nearly ran them over as the boys exited the cornstalks in a flourish of super-hero capes and eye masks. Their mother brought up the rear. Powerwalking, but still losing ground to her eight-year-old sons. She just couldn't keep up.

Jack smiled at Ellen Walton. "Your boys have super energy."

"Today they are the dynamic trio. Stay close," she shouted to her sons. Surprisingly, they stopped, dropped onto the ground. She sighed. "They are recharging. They ran through the maze, got lost, and backtracked, a dozen times. I've promised bags of kettle corn and caramel apples on our way home. Maybe they'll be good for a few minutes and let me catch my breath."

Lara came to join them. Jack curved his arm about her shoulders, and she leaned against him. He liked the feel of her. Familiarity held them close. He felt as if he'd known her forever. "Those are great capes," she noted. "I love the colorful emblems: Superman, Batman, and Captain America."

Ellen dipped her head, said, "Times are tight for us, despite my husband working two jobs. Our three growing boys eat us out of house and home. They've shot up several inches since school started, which means no hand-me-downs, only new clothes."

"Yet you bought them costumes," Lara noted.

"Not me," she slowly admitted. "Moonie McBright."

Lara startled. "Edna Milner?"

"One and the same." Ellen hesitated. "It's a secret, actually. She hates to be recognized for her good deeds. She ordered the capes through Grace at Charade. She's quite generous."

Jack glanced at Lara. They read each other's

minds. They now knew what was in the brown box. Halloween gifts for those boys.

"Edna lives down the block from us," Ellen continued, "and often bakes cookies for the family. She's also known to babysit in an emergency. She'll often go along with my boys when they walk the dog. To keep an eye out and make sure they're safe."

"We're still talking Edna Milner, right?" Jack had to ask. Had to be sure.

Ellen nodded. "Although she's going by Moonie McBright now. I was in Merchants National yesterday, and even the banker greeted her by her nickname. The tellers clapped."

He and Lara were stunned to silence.

"Mom!" the three boys interrupted. "Let's go." They jumped up and sprinted for the barn.

"That's my cue," said Ellen. "Have fun picking out your pumpkins." She followed her sons at a much slower pace.

"Edna . . ." muttered Jack, not sure how to process the benevolent side of the often crotchety older woman.

"Moonie McBright . . ." Lara seemed just as mystified.

"I'm liking Halloween Edna," said Jack.

"I want to buy her a pumpkin," Lara decided.

"She might not accept it."

"Deny a gift from Pumpkin Head and Jack-O'-Lantern? I don't think so."

He chuckled over her logic.

She left him and walked slowly along the edge of the Pumpkin Patch. Stretching, bending, and eyeing countless pumpkins.

He watched her every move. She looked cute and adventurous. Ready for fun in a long-sleeve pale-blue sweater with a navy puffer vest. All quilted and warm over black jeans, wool socks, and loafers. Today her tortoiseshell headband stayed in place.

She slowed near an enormous pumpkin, one nearly as big as Edna herself. It had to weigh one hundred pounds or more. Her back was to him. She bent over, bottom up. *Nice butt,* he thought, as her jeans tightened over her ass and thighs.

"That pumpkin's quite large, Lara. We could deliver it to Edna, but how would she remove it after Halloween? It will eventually rot and decompose on her doorstep. Not pretty."

She straightened, planting one hand on her hip, the other one bunched, as if forming a fist. She looked ready to punch him. But did not.

"Go big or go home." He gave in. "You want that huge pumpkin for Moonie McBright, and it's hers."

She came to him then, held up one hand. She unclenched her fingers. There on her palm was the smallest pumpkin he'd ever seen. Three inches in circumference, pale orange in color, and perfectly formed. "A miniature," he said.

"Just right for Edna. Being so tiny, it might not be easy to carve, but she could design a face with permanent black marker."

"You think she'd go to such lengths?"

"I think there's a lot about the woman we don't know, and might never know."

He agreed. "I'm sure you're right."

"I know I'm right." She rose on tiptoe, kissed him lightly on the lips. "Right about Edna, and right about you."

"I had no idea I was under consideration."

"I came to a decision on you when you hired me."

"What did you decide?" He was curious. He was crazy for her. Suddenly his life had a purpose beyond being mayor. She was constantly on his mind. His heart warmed for her. People embraced them as a couple. There'd been initial speculation, followed by congratulations once they made it official. But while he enjoyed dating her, he desired permanence. A home. Children. He hoped she wanted the same.

He wrapped his arms about her waist, hugged her close, and listened carefully as she said, "I recognized that you were a kind, considerate, and caring man. Respectful and genuine. You created a job for me in my darkest hour. I was grateful. I'd always had a crush on you, Jack, but I never really knew you. I imagined your personality. Your future." She sighed against him.

"My assumptions were lacking. You are so much more than I ever believed. A man larger than life who's—"

"Who's falling in love with you," he finished for her.

"I'm falling in love, too."

"What we're feeling isn't happening too fast for you?" he asked, concerned. He didn't want her to feel rushed. To be the least bit unsure.

"It's a little scary," she admitted.

"But not Halloween scary," he teased her.

"Scary, just how happy I am. I find myself smiling for no reason. Paula thinks the parade has made me crazy."

"Paula delights in repeating herself. She's nudged and asked me to do things, twice."

"I'm enjoying you, Jack Hanson."

"The pleasure is all mine."

He released her, only to take her by the hand and draw her along the pumpkin path. He tugged her inside the cornstalk maze. A bit prickly, but, ten feet in, they were snug among the stalks and well-hidden. Invisible to the public eye. And able to kiss and appreciate each other. She tucked the tiny pumpkin in her vest pocket. Faced him then, with wide-eyed openness and a soft blush of innocence.

His kiss was full of gentleness and promise. Her mouth was soft. Responsive. Her taste was sweet. Addicting. He allowed her to settle into him. To wrap her arms about his waist. To kiss him when she was ready. There was no hesitation on her part. She was there, with him, profoundly into him.

Their closed-mouth kisses were no longer enough. He soon slipped his tongue between her lips, prompting a deeper intimacy and passion. Moist hunger and profound need. She massaged his back above the waistband of his worn jeans. Jeans that dated back to college. She then finger-walked beneath the hem on his thick blue sweatshirt, bearing the logo of the Maine Mariners, the minor league hockey team from Portland. She kneaded upward, then scraped her fingernails down his sides. Her touch turned him on. He widened his stance. Cupped her butt, and fit her flush against him. They were soon so into themselves that seconds, minutes became a timeless embrace. All ragged breathing. Fondling. Carnal and hot.

Up until—*Caw*. They were interrupted by a crow. The big black bird perched on a cornstalk overhead, its beady eyes honed on them. A disruptive chaperone. Jack sucked air, drew back. Lara dipped her head, rested her brow against his chest.

"So much for privacy." He rolled his shoulders, shook out his legs, and attempted to bring his body under control. Not an easy task. This close to Lara, he wanted to take her amid the cornstalks.

She eased back, her eyes dilated, her expression dazed. She grasped his forearms for support. He restored her balance. A moment later, she rubbed her butt, laughed. "Goosed by an ear of corn."

He reached around and massaged the spot, high on her left buttock. "Sorry, sweetheart. I wanted to kiss you, but the cornfield might not have been my best option."

She touched his cheek with her fingertips. "You can kiss me anywhere at any time."

He cut his gaze to the crow. Glared. "Without an audience."

With an angry caw, the bird flew off. Jack took Lara's hand and led her from the corn maze. It seemed pricklier going out than it had going in. Anticipation had dulled their senses to the stab of the stalks. Leaving now, they were jabbed numerous times, and felt each one.

Once out in the open, Lara heaved a sigh. "I've chosen the courthouse pumpkins. Let's move on."

"Herbert's Apple Orchard?" It was an hour down the road.

She nodded. "I can't bake you an apple pie, but I can purchase one for you."

"Caramel apple." He knew exactly the one he wanted. There was no second-guessing.

Jack spoke briefly with the manager of the Pumpkin Patch. A generous man who offered to donate the courthouse pumpkins. Lara refused his kindness when it came to Edna Milner's tiny pumpkin. She wanted to pay for it herself. The man charged her a dollar. She tucked it back into her vest pocket for safekeeping. Then she took Jack's hand as they crossed the immense grounds toward the parking lot and his SUV.

Traffic was heavy, and they soon realized every car ahead of them was traveling to the working farm. Their arrival took longer than expected. Which was immaterial to two people who took every slowdown opportunity and stop sign to kiss. Tender, sensitive, romantic kisses. Extra soft and sweet. With a desire for more. Many more.

They soon spotted the converted red barn off in the distance. A red dot on the horizon. A family store in the barn featured Maine products, including ice cream, maple syrup, maple candy and cream, jams and jellies. Locals produced candles, pottery, and goat soap. New England cookbooks, mulling spices, apple peelers, and whittled wooden toys filled out the shelves.

Jack spotted a parking space. A Hummer backed up, and he pulled in. It was a short walk to the barn. A tall man in overalls met them at the entrance. "Prepicked apples, or do you plan to get hands-on with the fruit and pick it yourself?"

Jack left the decision to Lara.

"We pick."

"Half-bushel or full-bushel boxes?" the man asked.

"Bushel," from Lara.

"There are Red Flyer wagons and wire hand-carts around the side of the building," the man added. "The ground is flat until you reach the hillside. There's no need to carry the heavy containers. Use a transport."

He passed them two bushel boxes. "Just a reminder: when picking, lift and twist the apples, don't yank. Don't break off the fruit spur for next year's crop. Those are the small, thorn-like shoots. There are ladders provided throughout the orchard. Plant the legs securely and don't climb too high." He finished with, "There are signs directing you to the different varieties. They're alphabetical. Pick only ripe fruit." He then welcomed those next in line.

Jack stacked the boxes onto a Red Flyer and towed it toward the orchard. Lara trailed beside him. She swung her arms wide and drew deep breath after deep breath. "The air is so clean and fresh. So invigorating. There's nothing like the scent of apples."

Jack agreed. "I'm thinking apple cider, apple pie, apple crisp, apple butter."

"All can be purchased at the store before we leave."

They walked a ways, soon noticing the Honey-crisp sign. They turned down the lane. The two of them selectively picked the low-hanging fruit. Until Lara saw the perfect Honeycrisp, way up

419

high. She went after an aluminum tripod ladder, lightweight and sturdy. She set the legs, ready to climb.

"I'll get the apple for you," Jack was quick to offer.

"You don't know which one I want."

"Point it out." The tree was loaded with apples. She'd have to be specific.

"Lean left, lean right, stretch higher—by the time you figure out the one I want, I would have it plucked and packed it in the box." She'd made up her mind. His lady was determined. She scooted up the ladder before he could stop her.

Picking apples brought out her daring side. She wasn't afraid of heights. She extended, strained, wiggled on the rungs of the ten-foot ladder. Shaking it slightly. He held tight to the sides. He was only mildly distracted by her sweet butt. Her shapely legs. All the while remaining observant and prepared to catch her should she fall.

There was no falling, only a delighted whoop of success when she snagged her apple of choice. She pumped her arm. Victorious. He reached for her as she descended the ladder. When she'd nearly reached the ground, he lifted her the remainder of the way. Securing her to him. Her backside pressed his front. A sexy slide down. All womanly warmth and crooked headband. Which he straightened for her.

He glanced down the lane. No sign of anyone.

No sound of voices. They were alone. Nice. A little early foreplay would keep her on edge for later in the day. Anticipation was a sex toy. He liked the idea of her wanting him in the hours to come. As much as he desired her. All hot and intense. Rapidly pulsing hearts. Waiting and wanting. A physical craving.

He kissed her slowly, whisper-soft. From behind. Starting at the corner of her eye, then flicking his tongue at the shell of her ear, and biting the lobe. Hard enough to elicit her intake of breath and full-body shiver. Goose bumps captured them both. He nipped the curve of her lower lip, and her mouth parted on a sigh.

His hands made her moan. He parted her puffer vest, went on to trace her breasts and cleavage over the top of her blue angora sweater. Supple woman. Amazing curves. Her full, rounded breasts fit his palms. He stroked his thumbs over her nipples. Then gently squeezed. She rose on tiptoe, her bottom brushing his groin. He'd been out to tease her, but was now turned-on, nearly to the point of no return. His jeans were worn, with laddered tears on his thigh near his zipper. His boxer briefs held his privates in place. Barely. It was stop now or embarrass himself. He eased back. Hastily made an adjustment before she turned around.

She closed her eyes, drew a steadying breath, and slowly faced him. Eyes wide now. Pink blushed her cheeks. Slightly swollen lips. Her expression, sexually awakened. "I've gotten my favorite Honeycrisps, so let's cross the bridge for your Macintoshes."

That suited him just fine. He grasped the handle on the wagon with one hand, took her own with the other. They walked half a mile to Pond Bridge. The small body of water was clear and still. Glassy. Reflecting the bridge, a single white oak tree, and the shoreline rushes.

An entrance plaque offered information on the bridge. Constructed in 1928, it was the only solid masonry bridge in the county. The stone and mortar substructures were surfaced in rough-dressed random laid rubble stone.

Lara peered over the side as they crossed. She caught her reflection, pulled a face, and straightened her headband. "Why didn't you tell me that my hair band was lopsided?" she asked, patting down the spikes.

Jack grinned. "The crooked band is you, Beanstalk. All you. I wouldn't change a thing."

Her smile was sweet, her tone sarcastic. "Jackass."

He couldn't help but laugh. He curved his arm about her shoulders as they traversed the narrow bridge. "We made it across. No battling the Troll, and the grass really is greener on the other side."

"Three Billy Goats Gruff?"

"The latest fairy tale I read to my nephew."

"How often do you see Drew?"

Jack liked that she'd remembered the boy's name. "Twice a week. I may work late, but I always arrive for his bedtime story."

"I love your attention to your nephew."

"He's important to me." He came to a stop, then leaned down and kissed her on the forehead. "So are you, Lara Shaw. Let's pick a box of Macintosh apples and then go back to your place. I'll show you exactly what you mean to me."

She gave him her own special kiss. Soft and sweet. Desiring him. "I'll show you back."

Lara had the best weekend of her life. She and Jack returned to her apartment. He carried in the bushels of apples, making two trips. Inside, they kicked back and relaxed. Sipping warm apple cider, consuming apple cider donuts and big slices of caramel apple pie à la mode. Food and drink became foreplay. They fed each other. Licked fingertips. Kissed ice cream from each other's lips. Along with other sensitive body parts.

They snuggled for hours on the padded love seat. Clothes eventually disappeared, and he initiated her to all the possibilities inherent in a rocker big enough for two. She'd ridden his thighs. She would never look at that piece of furniture the same way again. As the sun buckled to the day, darkness led them to her bedroom. There she lighted evergreen-scented candles. Their hearts raced and their feelings deepened. Naked, aroused, they became one amid the flickering flames and shifting shadows. Afterward he tucked her so tightly against his body she became an imprint on his skin. They were soon overtaken by a deep satisfying sleep.

Sunday morning, and they'd taken their time in bed. Lazy and content. Eventually showering together. Warm water, soapy sponges, and slippery flesh. They'd gone on to make apple fritters together for breakfast. Nourishment that would be spent on a repeat day of long conversations and great sex. She now knew him nearly as well as she knew herself. She liked his mind and his body. Their philosophies on life aligned. They were physically in tune. They matched on so many levels.

It was difficult to return to work on Monday. Jack had left her apartment before sunrise, and she'd strolled into the courthouse at the designated time. Paula met her in the conference room shortly thereafter. Her assistant was high on Halloween. Her latest orange T-shirt with brown script made Lara smile.

What do you get when you drop a pumpkin?
Squash.

Paula took a seat at the table and asked, "How was your weekend?"

"I went to the Pumpkin Patch and Herbert's Apple Orchard."

"I saw the array of pumpkins throughout the courthouse. Very decorative. I heard a lot of good comments on my way upstairs."

"I brought you a Honeycrisp for a snack later."

"Your weekend treks, were they alone or . . ."

"Leave it at 'or.' "

"For now," said Paula. "The parade's five days away. We have a lot of work to wrap up before Saturday."

"We need to finalize the lineup. That's our top priority."

Paula rustled through a stack of file folders. All crammed with parade information. She found the one she was looking for. "We made a tentative list last week."

"Will it still hold up this week?"

"Pretty much so."

"Let me hear your list." Edna Milner entered the conference room, in a swish of eight-year-old authority and attitude. "I'll tell you if it will or if it won't."

Lara eyed the older woman. "What makes you such an authority, Moonie McBright?"

"I've stood on the sidewalk and watched seven decades of parades. It was too cold during my earliest years to stand outside. My parents wouldn't allow it."

"You do have time on your side," said Paula.

"Time that's passing with your gab. Do you want my thoughts or not?"

Why not? Perhaps Edna would notice something that she had overlooked. Lara handed the parade list to Edna. It was written in pencil. Edna took a moment to locate her glasses in an old-fashioned brocade handbag. She settled the wire-rimmed spectacles on her nose. Then ran her finger down the page. "You have the first two spots correct," she said. "The scarecrow marching high school band, followed by the Pumpkin Queen in her Cadillac."

Edna tapped her bony finger on the paper. "Shift the hayride behind the three convertible roadsters with the mayor and city council members. You want the vehicles clustered behind the caddy. The haunted hayride with its swooping and dancing ghosts would otherwise block the view of the upcoming officials. They are more important than the bales of hay."

Lara slowly nodded. The change made sense. "Good point." She erased and revised.

"No need for bumper-to-bumper Halloween-themed floats. It's monotonous. Break them up. A business float, then the costumed pets. Keep a decent distance between the two so the pets don't get spooked."

Lara was fine with that. She again altered the lineup.

Edna was on a roll. "How many pets in the parade?" she asked.

Lara informed her. "Twenty-eight."

"Bow-wow, meow, whinny, and a snort," added Paula.

"A snort." Edna rolled her eyes. "Frazier, the spotted hog."

Lara nodded. "None other."

"The pig's been banned from the parade in past years."

Lara was not aware of that fact. "I had no idea. No one told me."

"You're new and Able Hodgins took advantage of you. Frazier has no manners. He's three hundred pounds of bristly snout and grunt. He also stinks. He once nipped the miniature donkey Daisy. His owner said he was flirting, but Daisy disagreed. She kicked him. Frazier broke free of his harness and plowed through the crowd. Scattering all those on the sidewalk. Not a pretty sight."

Lara ran her hand down her face. "Oh, great. I don't want a repeat performance."

Edna surprised her with, "Don't be discouraged, girl. Don't scratch the hog off your list just yet. It's an easy fix, actually, should you want to include Frazier. A double harness and two walkers could control him. Just keep him away from Daisy."

"Workable . . . I think." Lara would give it

some thought. She didn't want any mishaps.

"Furthermore," Edna said insistently, "tell Able to bathe Frazier and put him in a tux."

The bath was doable; Lara wasn't certain on the tux. She would insist Frazier be in costume. A cape might be a better option.

"The sizes of the other pets?" Edna went on to ask.

Lara glanced at her list. "Biggest is the Great Dane Warrior. He's larger than Magnus the Shetland pony. Smallest range from a caged gerbil to a bowl with a goldfish."

"Goldfish?" Disbelief from Edna.

"Tommy Johnson promised to decorate the bowl with orange crepe paper."

"You're sure taking 'town inclusive' to a whole new level."

"I don't want anyone to feel left out or disappointed."

"The gang's all here." Edna continued down the list. She checked off the pumpkin jugglers, individual adult masqueraders and their children, along with five-piece garage bands. She put her stamp of approval on all the floats. Then drew big question marks beside the decorated machinery: a compact tractor and riding lawn mower.

"It is what it is, Edna," Lara said on a sigh. "Perhaps I'll set new parameters next year. This year's groundwork was laid out before I came onboard."

"Let's blame the mayor, then."

"We could do that."

"Or not." Jack Hanson appeared on the scene.

Lara's face heated and her heart stuttered. He looked handsome and in charge in a black suit, white and gray print shirt, and maroon tie. She tried to separate their weekend together from their working relationship. It was extremely difficult to do. She'd seen him naked. He looked good in his skin.

His gaze locked on her for a heartbeat before he spoke to Paula and Edna. "Ladies. I hope things are going well."

Far better now that he was here, Lara thought. She'd missed the man. They'd only been apart four hours. "Moonie McBright has offered her opinion on the parade. Valuable insight."

Edna gave details. "I'm the smart one here."

"Especially when it comes to hogs gone wild," added Paula.

Jack looked confused. Surprisingly, not one of the women explained. Lara realized they'd drawn together into a tight group. Surprising but true. The three even shared a private joke. Interesting.

"Lastly—" Edna ignored Jack as she wrapped up their meeting. "What about that ridiculous pumpkin-faced Disney balloon? Isn't Mickey Mouse as wide as the street? Even wider?"

"The balloon is enormous, but Parker Price has

guaranteed that it's workable. He wants to bring the big city to our small town."

Edna contemplated the issue. "Should the balloon burst, it will blow those watching the parade right off the sidewalk. Fly them like kites."

Lara cringed. That would be a disaster she hadn't anticipated.

"Won't there be pumpkins lining the curb?" Edna wanted to know. "They would narrow the parade route even further."

Edna was observant. Lara confirmed, "It's open season on arranging pumpkins along both sides of Pumpkin Lane. First to come get the best spots. Some will be carved, others not. Names in indelible marker go on the bottom. People will retrieve their pumpkins after the parade."

Lara suddenly remembered her gift for Edna. She reached for her shoulder bag and removed the mini-pumpkin. She hadn't planned to see Edna at the courthouse, but this was as good a time as any to hand it off. "I have something for you," she said. She set the itty-bitty pumpkin on the table.

Edna stared, scrunched her lined face into deeper wrinkles. "You couldn't find something smaller?"

Lara drew a breath. "I thought of you, and hoped you'd like it."

Edna picked it up. "Thought of me?"

"Small but mighty."

"That's how you see me, girl?"

"Better than orange and round."

A hint of a smile, gone just as quickly. She shoved the pumpkin in her handbag. None too gently. "It's okay, I guess. Pumpkins are purchased by the pound. You certainly didn't spare any expense."

Edna stood slowly. She favored her right knee. Lara guessed it was arthritis. "My work here is done," she said.

"I appreciate your input, Moonie McBright."

"I'll check back with you, Pumpkin Head. In case you need my expert feedback later in the week."

Edna was nearly out the door when an elevator arrived. It opened across the hallway. Janice Stanley-Stark appeared. There was no sign of her boyfriend, Glen. Lara was relieved. She had no idea why Janice was at the government center, but her purpose soon became clear. She noticed the mayor and made her way to him. She looked as if she had just walked off the Fashion Week runway. Her steps were calculated, graceful, purposeful.

She was dressed more for a party than a trip to the courthouse. Her blouse was white silk, sleek and flowing. Pintucks flattered her breasts. Her black leather pants fit ass-tight. Molding to her stomach and long legs. Her stiletto boots brought her eye level with the mayor. She draped a leather coat over her arm.

Janice tapped Jack on the arm with a long, manicured mauve fingernail. "Do you have a few minutes in your busy schedule for me, Mayor?" she asked.

Lara looked at Jack. He didn't appear overly taken by Janice, but neither did he deny her. He was an elected official. Janice a voter. He gave her his time. "I was headed out along with my staff," he told her. "Coffee break at Bellaluna's. Perhaps we could meet afterward."

"Or . . ." She drew out the syllable. "Perhaps they could go ahead and you can follow."

Jack glanced at Lara. She pushed off her chair. Gave him a weak smile. "We'll meet you there."

"Or . . ." from Paula. "We could wait for you."

Janice looked down her nose at Paula. "I don't want to hold you up. Our meeting might take longer than your break."

Lara moved to the door with Paula right behind her. Edna Milner hadn't gotten far. She'd slowed, overseeing the moment. Jack eased back and let them pass. Janice, on the other hand, purposely brushed against Lara. Close enough to lean in and snidely whisper, "I took Glen from you. The mayor is next."

Janice caught Jack's arm with an easy familiarity as they headed toward his office. Lara watched them go. Their steps matched. In truth, she could imagine them a couple. Their looks complemented each other. Handsome and gorgeous. Both dark haired. Well-dressed. They had their own stature in the community.

Standing before the elevator bank, Lara suddenly felt odd woman out. Emotions took her back to when Glen had broken up with her at the bakeshop. She'd been hollow and numb. Her feet were leaden weights.

"Witch's Britches." Edna's Halloween name for Janice pegged her perfectly. The elevator door creeped open, and Edna nudged Lara inside. "Wipe that stricken expression off your face, girl. Have faith in Jack-O'-Lantern. He's a politician. She's a manipulator. Our mayor won't be easily influenced."

Edna had taken her side. Lara was surprised and oddly pleased. The older woman's words soothed her. Despite the present situation, Lara had a parade to plan. That took precedence. She centered herself. "Would you care to join us for something sweet at the bakeshop?" she asked Edna during their descent. "My treat."

The older woman looked uncertain. She was seldom seen with a group of people. More often solo. Usually, she walked into the bakery and walked out with her purchase, engaging in no social interaction whatsoever. Perhaps today would be different.

Paula made up Edna's mind for her. "No

one's paying but the mayor," she said once they reached the first floor. "Snacks go on his tab."

Edna nodded, sarcastic in her agreement. "He owes me after Lara picked my brain most of the morning. I'm tuckered out."

"Sugar will recharge you," said Paula.

The older woman didn't say much during the coffee break. Lara snagged an extra chair, and Edna sat with the courthouse staff at a table meant for six, but now seating seven. Conversation centered on the Halloween festivities.

The fire department planned to sponsor a pumpkin-carving contest Friday night at the firehouse for children twelve and under. Any child who entered would win a prize. The Frightfully Fun 5K run was scheduled for early Saturday morning. Lara was not responsible for the race. Thank goodness. It fell on the shoulders of the high school track coach. One of his runners always took first place.

The exchange between the staff would've included Edna, had she chosen to participate. She did not. Instead she sat quietly with her back as stiff as a broomstick and enjoyed a cup of hot Earl Grey tea and two pieces of caramel apple crunch coffee cake. She picked up the crumbs with her fingertips.

Paula soon noted the time and said, "Sorry,

ladies. Break's over for us, although here comes the mayor." Just as Jack appeared through the front door.

Everyone at the table stood, including Edna. "Maybe I'll see you tomorrow, Pumpkin Head."

Lara nodded, welcoming her help. "You know where to find me, Moonie McBright."

Lara turned to leave behind Edna, but Jack was now beside her, blocking her path. "Got a minute?" he asked.

"I'm on the courthouse clock."

"Let's stop time, then."

She looked up into his strong, familiar face and realized how much she loved him. He embodied everything she wanted in a man. She silently prayed he hadn't lost interest in her.

"Sorry I'm late," he apologized.

She licked her lips, said, "You're here sooner than I thought you might be."

"What, exactly, were you thinking?"

"About you and Janice, in your office."

"Don't read too much into our meeting," he stated. "Yes, she initially put the moves on me. I backed off. I told her that you and I are involved. That we're a couple. She came with an ulterior motive, actually. She mentioned the Pumpkin Queen, believing I would nominate her and that I had the final vote. She thought herself a shoe-in. I corrected her assumption, letting her know the appointment was all up to you. She stomped from my office. Lady has a foul mouth and a wicked temper."

"I'll announce the queen Thursday afternoon," said Lara.

"Do I get a hint as to who it might be?"

"Not a chance. But it won't be Witch's Britches."

"Edna again?"

"She has such a way with nicknames."

He kissed her then and didn't hold back.

They'd officially gone public with their affection.

"Back to work?" she asked when the kiss ended.

"Unless I can convince you to take the afternoon off."

"Saturday will be here before we know it," Lara said with a smile. "The parade has almost come together. Only so many working hours remain."

"We'll catch up tonight, then."

"You know where to find me."

Thursday snuck up on Lara, and anticipation ran high. The Pumpkin Queen would be announced at 6 p.m. It was a big deal for the locals. They would gather on the courthouse steps to cheer on whoever was crowned. Speculation centered on Paula and the local high school homecoming queen. Both were popular and volunteered extensively in the community.

Lara held the name close to her chest. She hadn't even shared her pick with Jack. Though he'd tried to wheedle the name out of her, still her lips remained sealed. In spite of his persuasive kisses and their phenomenal sex. Slipping a sparkling solitaire engagement ring on her finger hadn't entitled him to a hint, either. However lovely and endearing his proposal had been.

"I think we're as prepared for the parade as we'll ever be," she told Paula as they sat together at the table in the conference room. "Barring unforeseen problems."

"Do you think we've seen the last of Glen Meyers?" Paula wondered aloud. "That man needs to realize that yelling and threatening won't change anyone's mind."

"He's not one of the good guys."

"Not like your mayor."

Her mayor. Lara liked the sound of that. Jack belonged to Moonbright during the day. But at night, he was all hers.

Jack appeared whenever she was thinking about him. They seemed to have a special mental link. He stood in the doorway now. "Close to time for your big announcement, Lara. You ready?"

She rose and walked to the arch-shaped window that overlooked Pumpkin Lane. A crowd had gathered, with many more to come. She hoped her decision was a wise one, and that cheers of support and approval would unite everyone for the weekend ahead. She would hate to be the only one clapping her hands. If so, she would do so loudly.

She left the conference room for her office. There she located the velvet burgundy cape and rhinestone tiara that would be worn by the newly crowned queen. She slipped on her own gray microfleece jacket. Zipped it. Then draped the cape over one arm. She settled the tiara in a satin-lined box. And returned to Paula and Jack. They awaited her at the elevator bank.

The second floor emptied out behind them. It was the end of the working day. Staff would find a place on the courthouse steps in support of her big news. It was time.

Lara soon found herself next to the mayor on the top step. Dusk hovered. Streetlights turned on. All those before her were cast in the hues of a fading Thursday. Pale yellow, soft orange, and barely blue. She looked out over all those gathered. She'd grown up in town and recognized nearly everyone. The faces were warmly familiar.

Paula passed her a cordless microphone. Lara's initial "welcome" silenced the crowd. There was no real need to amplify her voice. So she spoke just loudly enough to be easily heard. "Thank you for joining me," she began. "I've had the honor of organizing the Pumpkin Parade. I hope it will do the town justice."

A nice round of applause gave her the courage

to continue. "One of my duties as events coordinator is to appoint a Pumpkin Queen. Someone who best represents Moonbright. It's been a difficult decision. All the women in town, young and old, are deserving. Each one of you brings a unique quality to the festivities. You are so very special."

She looked deeply into the crowd and found the person she sought. Standing in the back, beneath a light pole. Alone. "This Halloween I'm choosing a lady who has lived here a long time. She's helped raise the town. She's known disappointment, and can be a bit . . . mercurial. But beneath her prickly exterior, she has a very kind heart. I've heard stories about her recently that demonstrate great compassion over the years. I've recognized her goodness this past week. And I'm proud and thankful to know her."

Lara paused, let her words sink in. "I hope tonight, and throughout the weekend, she will experience great happiness. I wish that for her." She caught the small figure turning, about to slip through the crowd. So she quickly took hold of the microphone and called out, "Don't you dare leave, Edna Milner. You are our Pumpkin Queen."

The silence spoke for itself. Her name sucked the air from the atmosphere. People were stunned, but no one more than Edna herself. She was an unexpected and unprecedented choice.

Lara would be forever grateful to Jack and Paula, who initiated the applause. Soon it spread, slowly at first, but gathered speed. Echoing down the courthouse steps and into the street. Up onto the sidewalk. Reaching the storefronts.

Jack went into the crowd and escorted Edna up the courthouse stairs. She shakily took his arm. "Me?" the older woman mouthed, unable to speak.

"You, Moonie McBright." Lara hugged her. Careful not to hug her too hard. She was small and thin. Brittle boned.

Edna hugged her back. With the surprising strength of a much younger woman. She accepted the velvet cape and tiara with grace, momentarily transformed. Her eyes brightened, and her face softened. Her wrinkles seemed to fade. She looked thirty years younger. Her smile was weak. But sincere. She raised her hand in a queenly wave to the crowd, then softly said to Lara, "Thank you, Pumpkin Head."

People climbed the steps to congratulate Edna. Jack pulled Lara out of the way. They stood hidden behind an ionic column. That's where he embraced her. Kissed her soundly. "You did a good thing," he whispered. "Folks' astonishment over your choice is already wearing off. Edna may be a small woman, but she has a big role to fill."

"She will fill it well. Wait and see."

Pumpkins, Scarecrows, and Costumes, oh my!

Saturday, one o'clock. The high school marching band tuned up and the scarecrows immediately hit their stride. Lara gripped her iPhone, ready to respond, should there be major problems or minor glitches. Paula was positioned at the corner of Pumpkin and Spice, making sure the masqueraders and floats proceeded smoothly and that no one cut in line. She looked cute in her latest orange T-shirt with black lettering.

What do witches put on their hair?
Scare spray!

Lara was back on the courthouse steps. High enough that she could see each passing participant. Her heart warmed and she felt a lump in her throat when Queen Edna passed, seated on the edge of the rear seat of the vintage Cadillac. Caleb Dimitriou drove slowly, allowing Edna her memories. There would be many. As they passed Bellaluna's, Sofia and her granddaughter, Abriana, came out to wave at the passing queen. Lara caught Bree flashing Caleb a smile that was pure magic.

Edna was the most popular person in town that day. The locals waved and called out to her all along the parade route. She would be remembered.

The city government officials came next. They rode in convertible yellow Volkswagens. The mayor and the city council were cheered and revered. Jack located her on the steps and gave her a thumbs-up. He was proud of her efforts. The parade took on a life of its own and was spectacular. Enthusiasm and jubilance spread throughout the day. Moonbright at its happiest.

Lara crossed her fingers until the pets passed. Paula had put Frazier the hog at the rear of the group. Hog and cape went the distance without incident. Both children and adults were accompanied by their furry companions. She spotted Captain America with his arm around the Wicked Witch, leading a dog and cat dressed as Hansel and Gretel. Only the young boy carrying the goldfish tripped. Water sloshed from the bowl, but the goldfish survived.

The enormous pumpkin-faced Mickey Mouse balloon was soon sighted, towering high above the storefront rooftops. The day was moderately sunny and still. Yet the balloon caught an updraft and shifted amid the low-hanging clouds. Lara held her breath as the handlers rounded the corner near the city park. Safe and sound.

People picked up their individual pumpkins along the sidewalk and began to disperse. There was trick-or-treating, along with individual home and street parties ahead. An exciting end to the parade.

Only Glen Meyers didn't honor the finish. The chug of an engine and backfiring of a tailpipe drew everyone's attention to a back street. Here came Glen on a forklift. *Un-freakin'-believable,* Lara thought, thumping her forehead with her palm.

He drove through the dispersing crowd. People shrieked, dodged out of his way. A sign was attached to the rear of the machine, painted with SALE! FOLLOW ME TO MEYERS' LUMBERYARD. He drove past Moonbright Park, the end of the parade route, and continued down Pumpkin Lane.

Disgusted by his maneuver, no one involved with the parade trailed after him. Although a police car showed interest. Siren blaring, it gave chase and pulled Glen over. Lara figured he'd get a ticket for being disruptive and unlawful participation. Operating machinery on a public access road. Glen was out of her life, long in her past.

Her future now climbed the courthouse steps. Jack Hanson came to her. Stood close. Praised her. "Lady, that was one hell of a parade."

"So you're pleased?"

"I'll show you how much following the Halloween party at Rose Cottage."

"The Queen of Hearts and Maverick from *Top Gun* need to make an appearance."

"We'd be missed, no matter the crowd."

"Then we go."

"For a short time."
"Then back to my apartment.
"For a long night in bed."
"I'm with you, Jack-O'-Lantern."
"With you for life, Pumpkin Head."
They kissed. It was the best Halloween ever.

Pumpkin Spice Sugar Cookies with Pumpkin Buttercream Frosting

COOKIES

3 cups cake flour

3 teaspoons baking powder

1 teaspoon pumpkin pie spice

½ teaspoon cinnamon

½ teaspoon salt

½ cup (1 stick) butter, room temperature

1 cup sugar

2 large eggs

½ teaspoon vanilla extract

1 cup pumpkin puree

In a medium bowl, combine cake flour, baking powder, pumpkin pie spice, cinnamon, and salt. Set aside.

Using an electric mixer, cream butter and sugar. Add in eggs one at a time, stirring after each addition, followed by vanilla extract, then pumpkin purée. Gradually add in flour mixture until combined.

Chill dough for at least one hour in refrigerator. Makes one dozen cookies.

Preheat oven to 350 degrees Fahrenheit. Line baking sheets with parchment paper.

Roll 3 tablespoons of dough into a ball. Use flour on your hands if needed. Place ball on baking sheet and flatten to about ½ inch thick, molding sides to keep round shape if necessary. Continue with remaining dough, placing each 2 inches apart.

Bake in preheated oven for 10 to 12 minutes, just until bottoms begin to lightly brown. Cool for a few minutes on baking sheet, then transfer to a wire rack to cool completely.

PUMPKIN BUTTERCREAM FROSTING
3 to 3½ cups confectioners' sugar
1 teaspoon pumpkin pie spice
¼ teaspoon cinnamon
½ cup (1 stick) unsalted butter, softened
⅓ cup pumpkin purée

In a medium bowl, combine confectioners' sugar, pumpkin pie spice, and cinnamon and set aside.

Using an electric mixer, combine butter and pumpkin until combined. Gradually add in confectioners' sugar mixture.

If frosting is too thick, add more pumpkin purée, milk, or water until desired consistency is reached. If frosting is too thin, add in a little more confectioners' sugar.

Frost cookies and set aside for frosting to dry.

| Books are produced in the United States using U.S.-based materials | Books are printed using a revolutionary new process called THINKtech™ that lowers energy usage by 70% and increases overall quality | Books are durable and flexible because of Smyth-sewing | Paper is sourced using environmentally responsible foresting methods and the paper is acid-free |

Center Point Large Print

600 Brooks Road / PO Box 1
Thorndike, ME 04986-0001 USA

(207) 568-3717

US & Canada:
1 800 929-9108
www.centerpointlargeprint.com